Chapter 1

Shadow Hawk froze when his father laid a firm hand on his shoulder. He stared ahead through the low brush. In a small clearing, a buck grazed uneasily, raising his nose, assuring himself there were no enemies nearby. Shadow Hawk watched the buck, feeling for a small instant, as he always did, sorry for the beautiful animal. He knew it would have no chance. He silently said a prayer for the animal that would soon give them meat. Then he looked at his father. Black Hawk pulled an arrow from his quiver and notched it into his bow. The boy watched as his father slowly pulled the arrow back, sighting it along the smooth ashwood shaft. He paused for only an instant before he released the arrow. The animal stumbled, tried to run, then fell to the ground. Shadow Hawk followed his father as they ran to it. Black Hawk took out the knife and slit the animal's throat. The last spark of life flickered and then died in the buck's eyes.

"Do not let the animal suffer, my son. He sacrifices much for us." Black Hawk pulled the arrow free, cleaned it, and returned it to its quiver.

"Yes, Father," Shadow Hawk replied solemnly. He bent down and his father helped him lift the large animal onto his shoulders. Shadow Hawk stumbled slightly, but he wouldn't give under the weight of the animal. He felt the warmth from the buck's body against his skin as he walked. It was an odd feeling. It was as if the buck's life flowed into his own.

"Shadow."

Shadow Hawk stopped, hearing the slight irritation in his father's voice. "Yes, Father?"

"Where are you going?"

Shadow Hawk looked around, orienting himself. The tall stand of oaks was behind them. He was leading them away from the horses. "I am sorry, Father. My thoughts . . ."

"Yes, I know, your thoughts were elsewhere. Have I not told you before, my son, that you must always be aware of what is around you? You can not be caught dreaming, not ever. For that is the time when the enemy will show its face."

Shadow Hawk stood silently. His father's voice had been gentle. He was a good teacher, one of the best in the tribe. Shadow Hawk wanted more than anything to be a Comanche warrior like Black Hawk. He must stop his wandering thoughts. He must learn well.

Without speaking, he turned and led his father to their horses, refusing to slow his pace, even when the weight of the buck wearied him. His father helped him lift the carcass onto his horse. Blood from the buck covered his shoulders. He tried to imagine the pain of an arrow in his back.

"You lead us back to camp, Shadow."

The boy nodded and swung up behind the carcass. Shadow Hawk eased his horse along the narrow game trail that ran between the tall silver sage and the rough rust-colored chemise. His horse moved heavily under the added burden of the buck, and Shadow Hawk concentrated on the ground before him. A single rabbit hole could cost a warrior his horse, and the loss of a horse could mean death for its rider. Shadow Hawk chose the easiest paths along the steep-sided arroyos, riding around the ones that might shorten their ride but that would also endanger their horses. He heard his father's quiet sounds of approval and straightened his shoulders.

They had been lucky to find the buck; most of the game animals had sought higher ground where there was food and water. The lack of rain had turned the soil into dust and the green brush into a brown, crackling tangle that scratched their legs as they rode.

As they came out of the cover of the brush, Shadow Hawk scanned the horizon. They were close to Kiowa-Apache territory, and they were not the only ones desperate for food. The buck's carcass would make them a target if they were seen. And here they could be seen for miles. Across the sandy flats, Shadow Hawk urged his horse a little faster, eager to be on safer ground—but not so fast that they raised a telltale cloud of dust. Again he heard his father's grunt of approval. Shadow Hawk looked over at him, proud to be his son, proud his father trusted him enough to take him on hunts.

"We will ride to your grandfather's and share some of the meat with him."

Shadow Hawk smiled. He had wanted to go to his grandfather's but had been afraid to ask. His father wasn't always comfortable going to a white man's lodge, even if the white man was his own father. Shadow Hawk loved his grandfather. The old man had survived many dangers, had had a life any warrior would envy. Shadow Hawk had heard the story of his grandfather many times.

Marsh Bradley had been a trapper in the early days, when there were still beaver in the mountains. When all the good streams had been trapped out, he had scouted for wagon trains going west. While he was leading one train along the Santa Fe Trail, they were attacked by Kiowa. Everyone, including Marsh, was left for dead. But some Comanche had come along and found Marsh, taken him back to their camp, and made him well.

Marsh never really knew why the Comanche had bothered with him, but he took it as a sign. He lived with them for a time and, after saving the life of one of the chiefs, was given a wife. He didn't want to be married, but he couldn't resist the comely Sparrow. A year after Marsh and Sparrow were married, Black Hawk was born. He had black hair, dark skin, and blue eyes, like his father. Sparrow bore Marsh two more children, daughters, and she died soon after. Much to his surprise, Marsh was devastated. He missed his wife terribly. So he went away for a time, trying to escape his loss, leaving the children with his wife's family. Marsh built a cabin beside the Rio Grande and spent most of his time there for the next ten years. By the time he took his children there to live with him, they had become strangers, cautious of him and his white man's ways, so he took them back to the Comanche and visited them whenever he could. His daughters came to adore him, but Black Hawk always resented the fact that his father had left them.

When Shadow Hawk was born, Marsh showed the child a kind of affection he hadn't been able to show his own children. There was a special bond between him and Shadow Hawk—he found in his grandson what he missed most in Sparrow. Although Shadow's eyes were a dark blue, it was the look on his face, the smile that came so easily to his lips, that reminded Marsh of Sparrow. Sparrow had been a dreamer, too, a thinker of deep thoughts. Marsh became a devoted grandfather.

In time, even Black Hawk was won over by his father's affection for Shadow Hawk. He allowed the child to spend time with his grandfather at his cabin and even to learn the awkward and ugly English that the white man spoke. Shadow Hawk never fully realized how much of a link he was between his father and grandfather—how they used him as a bridge to carry their uneasy and unspoken love.

Shadow Hawk and Black Hawk rode for most of the day; just before sunset they reached the big river. It ran low in its banks. Like the land, it was hungry for rain. They watered the horses, then cut away from the bank and into a thick stand of cottonwood trees. Shadow Hawk dismounted and led his horse, keeping his head low to avoid the tangled branches.

"You lead us in, boy," Black Hawk said from behind him.

Shadow Hawk nodded. As many times as he'd been to his grandfather's cabin, it always surprised him how well the place was hidden. More than once he had veered too far one way or the other. This time, leading his father, he wanted to come out of the trees right at the cabin site. He peered through the dusk, looking for the tall sycamore that rose behind the cabin. There? Yes, there it was. When he saw the cabin, he smiled. It seemed to appear out of nowhere and it was impossible to find unless you knew where you were going. You couldn't track anyone to the cabin because the tracks were quickly covered by the leaves from the trees, and his grandfather was careful to vary his route, to avoid wearing a path.

Shadow Hawk waited until his father dismounted and together they carried the buck to the wooden porch. Before they could drop the animal, the door to the cabin opened and Marsh stood before them, his long gray hair and beard belying the fact that he was still in his prime.

"I have told you many times, Father, do not open the door until you are sure who is behind it."

"I knew who was behind it, Black Hawk. I heard you two a half mile away. Who ever said Indians were quiet?"

Shadow Hawk looked at his father. He saw the barest hint of a smile on his face. "We have brought some meat for you."

"Nice-sized buck. Heart-shot, too. Yours, Shadow?"

"No, Grandfather. My arrow is not as true as my father's."

"How do you know if you haven't tried it?"

"He will try it when the time is right." Black Hawk lifted the buck onto one of the hooks March had hanging from the porch beams. He took out his knife, deftly gutted the animal, and then cut out a portion of the hindquarter. "Here, Father, we will have this. We will skin it in the morning when there is light."

9

"Thank you, son. I haven't had fresh meat in a while. I've been fishing, mostly. I have some potatoes and corn from the garden, and some fresh berries. Must've known you were coming."

Shadow Hawk followed his father and grandfather into the cabin. The place had always fascinated him. Marsh had built it by himself, log by log. As you stood in the doorway looking in, there were two wide log boxes, topped with cornshuck mattresses built into the left side of the cabin. Above them was a small loft, the ladder leaning against the wall between the two beds. There was a huge stone fireplace in the rear of the cabin and a mantel above it. A coyote's skull graced the mantel, along with the flattened bullet the Comanche had dug from Marsh's leg. Sparrow's necklace lay there too, beside a tiny pair of moccasins Black Hawk had worn as a baby. A metal arm held a bubbling and steaming pot over the fire. A rough-hewn table and chairs sat to the right of the room, and behind them was a small bookcase filled with the books Marsh had read and reread dozens of times. Shadow Hawk's gaze lingered on the books. When his father was not with him, Marsh often took down one of the books and they would read together. Shadow Hawk still found it very strange to look at the paper words that spoke without sound, but he liked the stories. They reminded him of the stories Old Bear had often told the children in camp. Sometimes after Marsh fell asleep he would read on his own, struggling to understand. In the morning, Marsh would explain to him the parts that he could not figure out by himself.

"Reckon I'll just throw the meat in with the vegetables." Marsh took the hunk of meat from Black Hawk and put it in the pot. "Wash your hands in the bucket," he directed his son and grandson. "Over there, next to the fire. Bet I know what you want, Shadow." Marsh walked to the fireplace and reached for the small coffeepot on the hearth. He poured some into a mug and spooned in two helpings of sugar from the bowl on the table. "Here you go, boy."

"Thank you, Grandfather. I have not had this since last I saw you." Shadow sipped at the hot liquid, not sure whether he liked the bitter taste of the coffee or the sweet taste of the sugar.

"How about you, Black Hawk?"

"You know I do not like that drink, Father." He paced around the room.

Marsh watched him in silence for a moment, then he spoke. "You don't have to sleep inside. I know you hate it in here."

Shadow Hawk looked from his father to his grandfather. He knew how difficult it had been for his father to come here. It was still difficult for Black Hawk to accept the fact that his father was white, that he had left him and his sisters to live in the white man's world. Shadow Hawk, as always, tried to ease the tension. "I will sleep outside with you, Father."

"No, you sleep here with your grandfather. It is the only time you'll have to talk to him." Black Hawk walked to the fire. "I see you still take all the taste out of your meat by throwing it in water, Father."

"Well, I figured since I was already boiling the vegetables, I'd throw the meat in with them. We can still roast you some, though."

Black Hawk held up his hand. "It is good."

"How are your sisters and my other grandchildren?"

Black Hawk's two sisters, Little Sparrow and Bright Star, each had two girls. "They are well and send you their regards."

"I'll come to the camp soon to visit. I have presents for the children." Marsh walked to the cupboard next to the fireplace and took down a bottle and two glasses. "Will you drink with me, Black Hawk?"

Shadow Hawk smiled slightly, knowing that this was one white man's habit his father did like. His father never drank more than one glass, but he would hold the drink and sip at it

11

for a long time.

"Yes, Father." Black Hawk walked to the table and picked up a glass. He started to lift it to his mouth, but Marsh stopped him with a gesture.

"Remember this tradition? We toast." Marsh clinked his glass against Black Hawk's. "Let's see, to my son and grandson. May you have long and prosperous lives." Marsh drank part of his glass and laughed as Black Hawk stood, as always, perplexed. He had never understood the toast, nor did he understand why the white man did such a foolish thing before he drank.

Shadow Hawk finished his coffee and set the tin cup down on the table. "Father says that soon we will ride north to hunt for buffalo."

"Is that wise, Black Hawk?" Marsh sat down at the table. "There are many hostile tribes in the north, not to mention soldiers."

"Our people need to eat, Father. We must follow the buffalo."

"But what about the Kiowa and the Apache? I don't think they'll take too kindly to you trespassing on their land."

"Our hunger is stronger than our fear." Black Hawk took a drink of the whiskey. "I will sleep under the stars." He walked out of the cabin, leaving his half-full glass on the table.

Marsh stared at the cabin door. "I think I've angered your father, Shadow. I never did know how to make him happy." Marsh walked to the pot and looked at the meat.

"He means well, Grandfather. It is difficult for him to come here."

"I know that. He'll never forgive me for leaving him and his sisters after their mother died. And I don't suppose he should. It must be hard to have a white man as a father."

Shadow Hawk heard the sadness in his grandfather's voice. "You are his father. He loves you, just as I do. It does not matter that you are white."

Marsh pushed the pot back over the fire and nodded slightly. "I'm sorry for you, Shadow. I'm afraid you're going to get caught between the white world and the Comanche. I hope you won't ever have to choose between the two." He had spoken in English.

Shadow Hawk watched as his grandfather poured himself another drink. He wondered what he meant. As far as Shadow Hawk was concerned, he had the best of both worlds. He couldn't imagine what problems could ever arise from him having one foot in the white world and one in the Comanche world. "I will be all right," he answered in English. "I am fortunate to have you, to have the gifts of both worlds."

When Shadow Hawk and his father returned to their tribe they found that the hunt had been fruitful for many. Shadow Hawk watched the busy camp, enjoying the smiles and laughter of his people.

Broken Moon caught his eye and Shadow Hawk thought, as he often did, how pretty his mother was.

"Shadow, come show me the new toy your grandfather has given you."

Shadow Hawk went to his mother, smiling. He sensed her sadness and loved the strength with which she bore her burden. She was an Apache. She had been stolen during a raid to their camp many summers before. Shadow Hawk never forgot she was Apache. Since the time he was able to talk she had insisted on teaching him her language. When he heard her singing Apache chants, or when he saw the sadness in her eyes, he knew she was missing her people. As much as she loved him and his father, he knew she longed to see her family and people again.

Shadow Hawk looked down into his mother's eyes. Already he towered over her. She was small and delicate, and he felt naturally protective of her. "Grandfather gave me this watch." He pressd a button and the watch opened to reveal the face. He held it up, listening to the sound. "Here." Shadow Hawk held it up to his mother's ear.

She smiled and shook her head. "Your grandfather is a strange one, but he is a good man. And his heart is full of you, Shadow." Broken Moon reached up to touch her son's face. "You are almost a man, my son. Soon you will have a wife of your own."

Shadow Hawk scoffed indignantly. "I will never have a wife, Mother. I will always be free to hunt and go wherever I please."

Broken Moon laughed. "You try to be like your father. But do not mistake false indifference for strength, Shadow."

Again, Shadow Hawk saw the sadness in his mother's eyes. "Are you so unhappy?"

"I am not unhappy, Shadow. You have made my life full."

"What about father?"

Broken Moon narrowed her eyes. "I hated Black Hawk for many years, even after you were born. I begged him to take me back to my people, but he refused to listen. I thought he was the cruelest man on earth. But he came to care for me in his own way." A different look touched her face now, a look of love. "He left little bunches of flowers on my robe. He brought so much meat to me that I was always able to give some to the old people. He even took walks with me in the woods."

"Father?" Shadow Hawk asked, surprised.

"Yes, your father. As you grew, his affection for me deepened."

"And yours for him?"

Broken Moon blushed. "I could not resist his charm, much as I tried. He won me over in many ways, but especially when he offered to take me back to my people."

"Father said he would take you back?"

"Yes, he did."

"I cannot believe it."

"It was his way of showing his love for me. He wanted me to be happy."

A group of children ran past, shouting and laughing, chasing an older boy who was pretending to be a buffalo. As their voices faded, Shadow Hawk spoke.

"But you chose to stay here?"

"This is my home, Shadow, with you and your father."

"But what about your people?"

"There are times when I wish I could see my parents and my brothers, and I wish that they could see that I am happy and have a wonderful son. It is natural to miss those who were a part of your life for so long." She squeezed his hand. "Do not worry about me, my son. Go now."

Shadow Hawk went to get one of his small fishing spears. Before he left the lodge he put the watch into a deerhide pouch, along with the other treasures Marsh and his father had given him, and put the pouch under his sleeping robe. He turned once more to look at his mother. She had a lovely face that hid lies poorly. She was not happy. Most of the women in the Comanche camp didn't treat her well and never let her forget that she was an Apache. But his mother never complained. Her sadness would remain silent, in her eyes.

Shadow Hawk turned down the path that led to the river. He heard a voice call out behind him.

"Have you heard the news, Shadow Hawk?"

Shadow Hawk steeled himself for Red Arrow and his loyal group of followers. For as long as Shadow Hawk could remember, Red Arrow had been his tormentor, always reminding him that he was an outsider, a Comanche with precious little Comanche blood. "What are you talking about, Red Arrow?" Shadow Hawk replied, not slowing his pace.

"I will be going with my father on the buffalo hunt. What about you, Shadow Hawk? Will your father permit you to go?" Red Arrow laughed and nudged one of his friends.

15

Shadow Hawk had suffered this abuse all his life and he was used to it. He passed them without answering, walking toward the river. When he got to the bank he stood there, watching the water wind its way downstream. This was the river that the whites called the Red River. His people had camped here for as long as he could remember. He walked downstream to a shallow spot, ignoring the footsteps he could hear behind him.

"Will you be helping the women again, Shadow Hawk?"

Shadow Hawk kept walking, concentrating on the flow of the water, looking for fish swimming between the rocks. There . . . in the lee of a boulder, three big fish moved slowly, calmly. He squatted down to look at the water, careful not to let his shadow scare them. He heard Red Arrow and the others coming closer but still he ignored them, concentrating only on the fish. He knew Red Arrow was strutting, trying to impress his friends, but he didn't think he would actually start a fight. It startled him when Red Arrow leapt forward and shoved him. Shadow Hawk fell sideways, rolling along the bank, and landed on his feet, his spear held out in front of him.

"What's the matter, the fishing is not good today?" Red Arrow laughed and the others joined in.

"Leave him alone!" A small boy ran along the bank. He pummeled Red Arrow, flailing his arms at the bigger boy's face. It was Little One, a thin, frail boy with bowed legs. He had often suffered the same kind of torment. Many times Shadow Hawk had defended him.

"Get away from me!" Red Arrow said angrily and shoved the undersized boy to the ground. He spun to glare at Shadow Hawk. "Why is it the only person who will defend you is not really a boy but a gnat?" The others laughed.

Shadow Hawk looked at Little One. "I am all right, Little One. I want you to go. Do you understand?"

"But—"

"Do not argue with me. Go now." When the boy was gone,

Shadow Hawk faced Red Arrow. "Why is it, Red Arrow, that you have never approached me alone? Why must you always have your friends with you? Are you so afraid of me?"

The group fell quiet and Red Arrow stepped toward the bank. "It is not possible to be afraid of a coward."

"If that is so, then let us fight like true warriors. This is what you have wanted for a very long time, is it not?"

Red Arrow smiled. "Yes, I have looked forward to this for as long as I can remember. But your father has always been in the way. Can you fight without him here to protect you?"

"Can you fight without the others standing behind you?" Shadow Hawk watched as Red Arrow set himself. He was a summer older and much bigger than Shadow Hawk, but he was guided by his pride, not his intelligence. He had goaded Shadow Hawk since they were children, and Shadow Hawk had known, even as a small boy, that he could defeat Red Arrow. He held up the fishing spear and threw it onto the bank. "I am ready when you are, Red Arrow."

As the bigger boy leapt at him, Shadow Hawk feinted to the right, dodging him completely. Red Arrow slammed into the rocky bank, rolled, and was on his feet again. Shadow Hawk stood still, waiting. Red Arow ran at him once more, but Shadow Hawk moved deftly to one side again. This time Red Arow did not fall. When he turned, he was holding his knife.

"I will end this quickly, Shadow Hawk." He lunged forward, swiping at Shadow Hawk's belly.

Shadow Hawk felt the rip of skin as the knife grazed his belly, but he didn't look down. "No knives, Red Arrow. I am not armed."

"Today we fight like men."

Again he ran at Shadow Hawk, and this time Shadow Hawk stood his ground. He dodged the slashing knife, then hooked Red Arrow's foot with his own and back-heeled him. Red Arrow fell, twisting. Shadow Hawk put his fists together and clubbed Red Arrow on the back of the neck.

Red Arrow groaned and lowered his head. Shadow Hawk kicked him in the side until Red Arrow fell face forward into the water. Shadow Hawk turned him over and pulled the knife from his still clenched fist. He wrapped his hand in Red Arrow's wet hair and yanked his head up. "Who is the Comanche warrior now, Red Arrow?" He threw the knife into the water. "You did not fight honorably today. You shamed yourself and your family." Shadow Hawk retrieved his spear from the ground. He looked at the quiet group which stood watching Red Arrow and he walked away. He walked until his thoughts cleared, until his anger cooled.

"Shadow Hawk."

He stopped when he heard his father's voice. Black Hawk stepped out of the woods and walked up to his son.

"I fought Red Arrow, Father."

"I know."

"You saw the fight and you did not stop it? Why?"

"It is time for you to fight your own fights."

"I hate him, Father."

"Why do you hate him so much, Shadow Hawk?"

"He has always been my enemy. He is like a demon who is always by my side. I am never free of him."

"You are free of him now. Red Arrow will not bother you anymore."

"He will not give up so easily, Father. You do not know him as I do." Shadow Hawk stopped along the bank to watch the fish as they swam in the muddy shallows.

"He will not bother you again, my son."

"How do you know this to be true, Father?"

"Because you have taken his power from him."

"I do not understand."

"He was able to hurt you because he said things that you yourself were afraid of."

Shadow Hawk thought for a moment. "I suppose that is true."

"But why did you allow him to do that to you, Shadow

Hawk? Why did you give him so much power?" Black Hawk gripped his son's shoulder. "Because you were afraid that you were not as good a Comanche as Red Arrow or any of the others."

"It is true. There were many times I thought I was not a true Comanche because I am so different. But now I know that to be false."

"And because you know that, you stripped Red Arrow of his power over you."

"It did feel good to beat him, though, Father." Shadow Hawk looked up to see his father smile.

"Yes, I am sure it did."

"Can I ask you something, Father?"

Black Hawk nodded.

Shadow Hawk hesitated for a moment. His voice was low when he spoke. "Why did you take mother away from her people, and why did you keep her here for so long when you knew that all she wanted was to go home?" Shadow Hawk watched his father's face, certain he was going to be angry, but he wasn't. Instead, Black Hawk sat down on the bank. Shadow Hawk sat next to him.

"It is not an easy question to answer, my son. I was young. I wanted to prove that I was the best Comanche brave, that I did not have any white man's blood in me." He glanced at Shadow Hawk. "I let everyone have power over me. I was ashamed of who I was."

"I cannot believe that of you, Father."

"It is true. We went on a hunt and discovered a small band of Apache traveling west. We attacked them during the night. I found your mother hiding behind a tree, a knife in her hand. I could see the fear in her face."

"But still you took her."

"Yes, I took her. I wanted to prove that I could take captives as well as the other braves."

"Did you ever intend to let her go, Father?"

Black Hawk looked steadily out over the water. "After

one moon I could see how unhappy she was. I thought of letting her go, but I was beginning to grow fond of her. She had a fire in her, she was not afraid of anyone. I liked that. It was not long before I took her for my wife." He looked at Shadow Hawk. "I loved her then and I love her even more now."

"Yes, I know."

"But I did not answer your question, did I? Why did I take her and why did I keep her? Because I felt I had to prove something to the others of this tribe. I was not strong enough to say that I am proud of the white blood that flows through my veins. I did not have the courage that you do, Shadow."

"I do not have courage, Father. You and Mother have taught me not to be ashamed."

"I am proud of you."

"Thank you, Father."

"I want you to promise me something."

"Anything, Father."

"If I should die, I want you to promise me that you will take your mother back to her people. It is still her truest wish, as much as she might deny it."

"Nothing will happen to you, Father."

"Promise me."

"I promise you."

"Have you been practicing with the bow I made you?"

Shadow Hawk looked up quickly. His father's face was serious, but a smile played at the corner of his mouth. "Yes, I practice every day."

"Good. I would not want you to shame me during the hunt."

Shadow Hawk and his father stood up. "I want to do well in the hunt."

"You will, my son. Remember what I have told you about the buffalo. They are big, heavy, and strong, but they are slow-witted. Do not underestimate the danger of the hunt or the power of the animal. Once the herd starts running, it is impossible to stop or turn. A rider who is careless can be thrown and crushed."

Shadow Hawk nodded. He remembered everything his father had ever told him about the buffalo: it had multiplied because it had no natural enemy; not even a wolf could bring down a full grown bull. In the days before horses, his father had told him, his people had run the animals off cliffs. It was the only way for men on foot to kill them in great numbers. But in the dust-choked stampedes, too many were killed. Hundreds of carcasses were sometimes left to rot because the men had no means to transport the meat. Marsh had told Shadow Hawk about seeing the weathered piles of bones. But now the Comanche had horses. They killed only as many buffalo as they needed, and they used every part of the animal. After the hunt, there would be an exhausted and happy journey home, the travois loaded with meat and hides.

Shadow Hawk had been waiting for this moment all his life. He wanted to make both of his parents proud.

Chapter 2

They had ridden northward for many days before they saw the first signs of buffalo. Once the herd was spotted, the women immediately set up camp, preparing themselves for the enormous task of butchering the buffalo, curing the hides, drying the meat, and making from the bones rough tools that would be refined and polished later. The men readied their weapons.

It was a small herd, about a hundred animals; enough to sustain the band for many months. It was late summer and the animals were already growing their thick brown coats and had put on most of their winter fat.

Shadow Hawk had been with his parents on many hunts but had always been left to help his mother butcher animals and carry the meat back to camp. This time, in his fourteenth summer, he would actually be allowed to carry a bow and ride in the hunt.

He sat tall on his horse, his arrows in a quiver on his back, his bow over one shoulder. He was excited but he was also scared. He had heard the stories over the years, the stories of men who had fallen from their horses and been trampled to death. One careless move and a horse could be gored by the much larger buffalo. A man on foot would be killed almost instantly. Shadow Hawk knew that was why his father had made him observe for so many years. And he had given him a swift horse to ride, fleetfooted and experienced.

Shadow Hawk waited for his father and the other braves. He watched the herd graze on the prairie as he sat nervously twisting a strand of his horse's mane. It had always intrigued him that the buffalo didn't seem frightened of them. It was as if they knew they were there to help the Indian survive. As soon as they rode into the herd, the animals would start to run, but until then they were content to graze.

"Shadow."

Shadow Hawk looked over at his father, mounted on his tall paint stallion. "Yes, Father?"

"Are you ready?"

"Yes."

"You will ride on the outside of the herd. Do not let yourself be boxed in by the animals or your horse might panic and throw you. Always stay to the outside. Only fools eager to prove themselves or to die ride within the herd. Shoot from behind the animal and aim for the neck. Remember that the buffalo has many layers of skin and fat, so pull your bow hard. Aim for the place I have shown you, the area behind the short rib. Prepare to use more than one arrow."

Shadow Hawk smiled, unable to contain his eagerness. "Yes, Father."

"This is not a game, Shadow. One mistake, and your life will be over. I could not imagine this life without you, my son."

Shadow Hawk was surprised by his father's expression of love for him. "Nothing will happen to me, Father. Do not worry. You have taught me well."

Black Hawk nodded his head. "Let us join the others, then."

They rode to meet the other men and boys of the band,

about fifty in all. Shadow Hawk could see the herd milling about. They smelled the scent of humans all around them. Shadow Hawk took the bow from his shoulder and pulled an arrow from his quiver. He notched it firmly and settled himself on his horse's back. As soon as he heard his father's shout, he kneed his horse into a gallop. Immediately the thunderous sound of the buffalo's hooves rose as the herd began to run. Shadow Hawk felt a surge of excitement. The wind whipped at his hair. He could feel his mount's muscles straining as the horse drove itself toward the herd. Shadow Hawk leaned forward, urging him faster, and a shrill cry burst from his lips.

He rode alongside the herd, his bow steady in his right hand, his left hand tight on the reins. Shadow Hawk had ridden since he had been able to walk. His first bow had been made for a baby's hands. Thousands of hours of his boyhood had been spent in practice games. Like all Comanche, he was a masterful horseman, a good hunter. And today, for the first time, he felt himself to be a man.

Shadow Hawk spotted a large bull. He pulled his mount in and dropped behind the bull, marveling at its size. Foam flecked its woolly jaws. Shadow Hawk raised his bow and took aim. The thunder of hooves and the sharp cries of the hunters around him faded as he concentrated. He pulled his bow to its limit, aimed carefully, and let the arrow fly.

The huge animal stumbled, crashing to its knees, slewing sideways in death. Shadow Hawk screamed his pride. A single arrow. A kill worthy of a man. The ashwood shafts of his arrows and the broad flint points were more powerful than he had imagined.

Shadow Hawk heard the sounds of the hunt around him again, and his triumphant joy quieted. He urged his horse back into a full gallop, scanning the herd. He chose another animal, a cow with a big hump and a thick, dark brown coat that would make a fine robe. Again he drew his bow with all his strength and shot. The cow fell hard, rolling from the force of her own momentum. Shadow Hawk lifted his head and let the sunlit sky receive his cry of victory.

By the end of the hunt, he had killed two more buffalo, and all but one had fallen with his first arrow. He rode back slowly to help his mother, his horse blowing hard, its shoulders streaked with sweat. There were many carcasses, so many that it amazed him. The tribe would have meat for a long time to come.

"Shadow? Shadow, come here."

He looked up to see his mother, her hands bloodied as she worked. He saw the feathers of his own arrow sticking out of the animal's neck. It was his first kill. The bull.

His mother smiled. "I can tell by the marking on this shaft that you killed this animal, this one and others. You have done well, my son. Come, eat."

Shadow Hawk took the still-warm liver from his mother's hands. It was salty and he delighted in the taste. All around him, men, women and children were eating livers and gall bladders, and brains taken from the cracked skulls of the animals. They also drank the warm blood. Gorging themselves after months of hunger, they feasted.

Shadow Hawk knelt down next to his mother.

She looked up at him sharply. "What are you doing?"

"I am helping you, what do you think?"

"You are a hunter now. You have done your work. Now it is my turn."

"I know that the work is only now beginning, Mother."

"But your friends will make fun of you."

"It does not matter. Harsh words are like rain and run off my back."

"You are getting wise now that you are in your fourteenth summer. I will not refuse your help."

They set to work. Shadow Hawk helped his mother butcher the animals and carry the meat back to the camp.

The meat was cooked on pointed sticks over open fires and would come out charred on the outside and red on the inside. They ate as they worked. It was not possible to know when they would have this much meat again.

Women had already started the laborious task of tanning the hides. Flat rocks gripped firmly in their strong hands, they were scraping the flesh from the hides, which had been stretched out and staked to the ground. While other women butchered the meat, the rhythm of their scraping went on and on. Next, they used a flesher, a sharp-edged tool, to clean the hides perfectly, removing every bit of meat before the sun could dry it and mar the leather. Shadow Hawk saw the women turning some of the hides to scrape away the thick hair. The leather that came from these would be used for moccasins, lodge covers, and clothing. In their baskets, the women had carried the tanning mixture of soapweed, to which they would now add brains, liver, and grease, rubbing it into the skins to condition and tan the leather. As each skin was finished, it was folded and set aside, and the process was begun again. It was killing labor, yet the women worked without complaint.

Shadow Hawk could see a woman he knew, Laughing Waters, instructing her daughter. They were cutting meat into long, thin strips, packing it into bloody bundles. Back in the camp, fires would burn for days while the meat smoked and dried, hung on racks that would keep it from the dogs.

Shadow Hawk took his knife from its sheath and set to work, cutting the strips of meat carefully, so the drying would be even and the meat would not rot. He breathed deeply as he worked, content. This meat would keep them alive in the leaner days of winter.

Almost no part of the buffalo was left behind. The bones and horns were used to make tools and weapons, the paunch used as a pot for boiling. Cups and buckets were made from the lining of the paunch, stiffened by a circular wooden ring sewn to the membrane with sinew.

Broken Moon looked up from her work. "I have had enough help, Shadow; go now."

"I do not mind, Mother."

"If you want to help, bring the rest of the meat in. When you are here, you are doing woman's work."

Shadow Hawk smiled. "Does that bother you, Mother?"

Broken Moon shook her head. "This is your first hunt. You should not be here with your mother; you should be out with the other hunters, celebrating your good fortune. Take the gelding. I will care for your horse."

"All right, but I will be back." Shadow Hawk tightened the gelding's belly band and checked the travois, then rode slowly back out to where the carcasses lay. Quickly and deftly he butchered an animal and dragged the huge slabs of meat onto the travois. He saw Little One standing, watching, and he yelled at him to come closer. When the boy stood next to him, he handed him the liver.

"Here, Little One, eat this, it will help you to grow."

The boy took a tentative step forward but stopped. "I cannot, Shadow Hawk. Those parts are only for the hunters."

Shadow Hawk sat back on his haunches and regarded Little One. He was ten summers old, yet he looked half that age. His family treated him badly. They were convinced that a bad spirit inhabited his body. But Shadow Hawk knew better. His grandfather said the boy simply had not grown because he was starving. It was true. He was the youngest of many children, and his mother had not had enough milk. Even once he could eat, the family usually left him only scraps. Shadow Hawk had taken it upon himself in the last winter to give Little One food to help him grow.

"I am much bigger than you, am I not, Little One?"

"Yes, Shadow Hawk, it is easy to see that you are."

"Do you suppose I am also stronger?"

"Yes."

"Well, then, if you do not wish for me to hurt you, I want you to come here and eat this liver." He smiled to soften his words.

Little One hesitated for a moment but knelt next to Shadow Hawk. He took the liver from his hands. "Thank you, Shadow Hawk."

"Do not thank me. Eat."

Little One quickly devoured the bloody organ and wiped his hand across his mouth when he was through. "It was very salty."

"Yes, the salts from the gall bladder. Have you never tasted the liver before?"

"Never."

"Come closer." Shadow Hawk was intoxicated with his own manhood. He had killed this buffalo. With a grave expression, he stuck his hands into the bloodied flesh of the buffalo and smeared it on Little One's face. "Do not wash it off until later."

"But I was not part of the hunt, Shadow Hawk."

"I was in the hunt and I give you the blood. It will bring you good luck." Shadow Hawk thought for a moment. "I think it is also time to change your name."

"This is not good, Shadow Hawk. My family—"

"What of your family? They do not care for you, they treat you as if you are some kind of demon sent to destroy them. I know what happens to the food I have been giving to you. They have been stealing most of it. It will happen no more. You are my friend, my brother, and I will care for you."

Little One's fear showed on his face. It somehow made Shadow Hawk stronger, sure of what he was doing. "I am frightened of them, Shadow Hawk."

"I understand fear, Little One, but I will help you. I will speak to my father about you. Would you come and be my brother, Little One?"

28

"I would be honored, Shadow Hawk." Little One's eyes were flooded with tears of pride.

Shadow Hawk stood straight. "Now, you need a name."

Little One shook his head. "I have done nothing to deserve a new name. I have had no vision."

"That is not true. When I was fighting with Red Arrow, you were the only one who was willing to help me. From now on I will call you Brave Heart."

"Brave Heart," the boy repeated, his eyes dancing. "I like it much better than Little One."

"Good, it will be your new name."

Brave Heart took pieces of the butchered animal and placed them on the travois. "I will work hard, Shadow Hawk. You will not be ashamed of me."

"I know I will not be ashamed of you, Brave Heart." Shadow Hawk smiled as he looked at the boy. He *was* a brave heart, a boy who had gone through life unloved and uncomplaining. Yet he would still fight to defend a friend.

Shadow Hawk and Brave Heart loaded the travois many times, taking the meat back to camp, unloading it, going back and getting more. When Shadow Hawk had butchered all of his animals, he helped others, women without husbands, warriors who were older and past their prime. He felt every inch a warrior and, like his father, he made sure everyone had meat.

When he was finished, he stood at his mother's fire. His father handed him a piece of roasted meat.

"Your mother tells me you did well today. Four animals."

Shadow Hawk nodded solemnly at his father's words. He did not want to seem too proud of his accomplishments.

"Were you ever afraid during the hunt?"

"At first I was very afraid, but then I did not think about it. I did what you told me, Father. I hunted the buffalo but I also respected them."

"Did you thank them?"

Shadow Hawk hesitated. How could he have forgotten? "No, I did not."

"You are always to thank the animal that gives himself to you for food. Do not forget that."

"Yes, Father."

"And did you give food to the ones who cannot hunt for themselves?"

Shadow Hawk lifted his head. "Yes, I made sure everyone had meat."

"Good."

Shadow Hawk took a deep breath. He had been so excited, so sure of himself earlier. Now he was almost afraid to ask. But he had to. "Father, can we take Little One into our family?"

"Little One?"

"The small boy. He is not treated well by his family and barely gets enough to eat." Shadow Hawk watched his father's face. It remained stern, unreadable.

"And why should this concern you?"

"I do not like to see him treated so. I would like to adopt him, make him my brother, and make sure that he is fed well and treated with kindness."

"Why is this so important to you, Shadow?"

"You have said I should speak up if I do not believe something is right. Brave Heart deserves more than he is getting from his family."

"So, you have already given him a name?"

"Yes," he responded, embarrassed. He knew it was not his place to name the boy. That was traditionally done by the boy's relatives. "He deserves a better name than the one he has."

"Are you sure you do not seek to help Little One because he is on the outside of the circle, just as you have always been, my son?"

Shadow Hawk thought for a moment. "Perhaps, father,

but I also want to help him because he is my friend. If I do not, I think he will be dead before he sees his eleventh summer."

Black Hawk looked across the fire to Broken Moon. She sat working a hide between her hands. "What do you think of this, Broken Moon? Our son wishes to adopt Little One into our family. He wants to make him a brother."

Broken Moon stood without speaking and hung more strips of meat on the drying rack. She regarded her son for a moment and smiled. "I think it is good. The boy has never been treated well by his people."

Shadow Hawk could barely contain his smile. If his mother agreed with him, he knew his father wouldn't say no.

Black Hawk nodded. "After I am done eating, we will go to Little One's family. We will take them much meat. We should even take them some horses."

"One horse," Shadow Hawk said decisively. "If we offer them more than one, they will think he is valuable and they might not let Little One go."

Black Hawk nodded in agreement. "Yes, you are right. One horse and a large amount of meat. I do not think they will say no."

Shadow Hawk nodded and smiled. He felt good inside. Soon he would have a brother.

Shadow Hawk pulled his robe close around his shoulders. He recalled the day in late summer when he had gone on his first buffalo hunt. His mouth watered as he remembered the taste of the fresh roasted buffalo meat. He had eaten so much that day his stomach ached. Now his stomach ached from hunger. The band had been subsisting on pemmican and dried berries for weeks, now his stomach cried out for something more. It had been a long winter and a cold one. Now he sat with his father, waiting for any kind of fresh

31

game. They had been in this spot for a long while and they had not seen even a snowshoe rabbit.

"Have we angered the Great Spirit, Father?"

"I do not know, my son. Perhaps he saves the meat for others who need it more."

"But we need the meat, Father."

"We are not yet starving, Shadow. Do not be selfish."

Shadow Hawk grew impatient. They had been sitting in the snow concealed by branches for most of the day. It was not a preferred way to hunt, but sometimes when it was so cold it was best to wait and hope that an animal would pass by. Still, Shadow Hawk couldn't understand how his father could accept things so easily. It angered him to know that if his father believed the Great Spirit didn't want them to have meat, he wouldn't hunt for it.

"Listen, Shadow," Black Hawk whispered.

Shadow Hawk listened but could hear nothing. But he knew his father. Something was there. Before long he saw it. It was a deer. It bounded into the clearing in front of them and stopped. It raised its nose to the wind. When it felt safe, it began pawing at the snow, trying to uncover some roots or grass. Shadow Hawk lifted his bow and arrow. The arrow had been notched for hours, his fingers felt as if they were frozen in place.

"Thank you, brother deer," he murmured softly as he let go of the arrow. The deer stumbled, its head thrown back, then fell. Shadow Hawk stood up, his stomach already aching for the fresh meat.

"Well done, Shadow," Black Hawk said as he rose from his place in the snow.

As Shadow Hawk bent down next to the animal, he looked at Black Hawk. "It seems the Great Spirit took pity on us after all, Father."

"Yes, he probably grew tired of listening to you bawl like a buffalo calf."

32

Shadow Hawk was offended, but only for a moment, and then he smiled. Quickly he and his father slit open the animal and ate the vital organs. They would butcher the rest of the meat when they got back to camp. In this cold there were many animals that were hungry, and they would fight for the meat. Shadow Hawk recalled a story his father had once told him. As a boy, Black Hawk had gone hunting with his own father in the winter. Much like this, they had waited until they had finally seen a deer. They had butchered the animal, taken what they needed, and ridden toward camp. But they had been followed by a pack of hungry wolves. Many of the animals had stayed to fight over the carcass of the deer, but the others had followed Black Hawk and his father, smelling the fresh meat. Black Hawk and Marsh had had to throw pieces of the meat to the animals to keep them away from the frightened horses. By the time they had reached their camp, they had had almost nothing left.

Shadow Hawk threw the deer across the front of his horse. He and his father mounted and rode toward camp. Black Hawk took the lead. Shadow Hawk rode behind him, thinking. He had become an able hunter, but there was something more—his father finally trusted him as an equal. Shadow Hawk imagined his mother's face as they brought the much-needed meat into camp. He was lost in his reverie when he saw his father pull up, his hand held in the air. Shadow Hawk immediately pulled back on his horse. Something was wrong.

"Go, into the trees," Black Hawk said quietly, following behind his son.

If it was an enemy, there was no hope of hiding their tracks or of running. The best they could do was quiet the horses, wait, and be ready. Shadow Hawk shoved the robe from his shoulders. He pulled an arrow from his quiver and quickly notched it in his bow. He sat motionless, hoping he wouldn't have to use it. He looked over at his father. Black Hawk looked grand. He sat tall on his painted horse, his long black hair halfway down his chest. He commanded respect.

Shadow Hawk saw his father raise his hand again. In seconds, four Indians rode into the clearing. They were Kiowa, sometimes allies, mostly enemies. With aching stomachs, today they would be enemies. It wouldn't be long before they saw the blood from the deer and their horses' tracks leading into the trees. Shadow Hawk looked at his father again. Black Hawk's eyes were strong and reassuring, they told him not to be afraid. Shadow Hawk nodded slightly. He would not shame his father, no matter what happened.

The Kiowa rode to the spot where the deer had been killed. One of them dismounted and tasted the bloodied snow. He gestured to the others, then got back on his horse. They followed the bloody trail and stopped when they saw that it led into the trees.

Again Shadow Hawk looked over at his father. Would they just sit here? Why didn't they shoot the Kiowa while they had the chance? Perhaps all they wanted was the meat. Two of the Kiowa rode off in opposite directions, circling the trees. They were going to approach from the rear or the side, then the two in front would attack.

Black Hawk raised his bow and turned to meet Shadow Hawk's eyes. Shadow Hawk tried hard not to betray his fear. He wanted his father to know he rode with a warrior, not a boy. His father smiled at him, then turned back to take aim. Simultaneously, they released their arrows.

The Kiowa screamed and their horses reared. One man fell, motionless. The other, Shadow Hawk's man, took longer to die. Finally, his horse skittering uneasily, he fell and did not move again. Shadow Hawk pulled another arrow from the quiver and notched it, his eyes searching the trees. Where were the others? He waited for his father's signal or for him to turn, but his father only sat his horse quietly, facing the clearing.

Suddenly, there was a strange strangled whinnying sound and Shadow Hawk jerked his horse around. A Kiowa, his war club raised and ready, was riding at him. Before Shadow Hawk could loosen his arrow, the Kiowa threw his war club and it smashed heavily into Shadow Hawk's side, knocking him from his horse. Shadow Hawk scrambled to his feet, his bow lost in the snow, his quiver a useless tangle on his arm. He tried desperately to get out of his heavy, clumsy robe, but the Kiowa was on him, driving him backward. The snow stung Shadow Hawk's face and arms as the two men struggled on the ground. Shadow Hawk felt the warrior reaching, and a second later the war club was in his hand again. Shadow Hawk wrenched to the side, ignoring the pain in his bruised ribs. The blow landed on his shoulder, sending fire down his arm. The Kiowa, momentarily off balance, staggered back a step. Shadow Hawk shrugged off his robe and reached for his knife, pulling it free from the thongs tying it to his leg. The Kiowa was a big, heavy man, and he slipped a little in the snow, giving Shadow Hawk the split second he needed.

Lunging forward, Shadow Hawk stabbed wildly at the Kiowa's stomach and chest. He stumbled backward, blood staining the snow at his feet, his eyes widening. Shadow Hawk realized that the warrior had not expected much of a fight from him, had not thought that a boy could hurt him. Shadow Hawk swung the knife out again, slashing at the Kiowa's upper arm. Screaming in rage and pain, he swung his war club and Shadow Hawk stepped aside. The Kiowa was bigger and stronger, but Shadow Hawk was quicker, stabbing at the warrior's back before he could turn. Shadow Hawk heard the warrior moan and saw him fight to keep his feet. He stabbed once more and the Kiowa reeled and fell.

Shadow Hawk stood still, his hands shaking, the bitter cold of the snow seeping into his skin. His side ached sharply, as he turned in a slow circle, scanning the trees. One more, he heard himself thinking. There is one more. His father might have . . . Shadow Hawk spun to look for his father, but he was alone in the trees.

Shivering, Shadow Hawk found and followed the tracks of his father's horse, his knife ready. The animal had run out of the trees into the clearing. Shadow Hawk broke into an unsteady run, calling his father. There was no answer. As he ran into the clearing, Shadow Hawk saw three bodies crumpled on the ground. As he got closer, he realized they were all Kiowa. So his father had killed again. "Father!" Shadow Hawk shouted, then he saw him. Black Hawk was lying on his back, an arrow protruding from his chest. Shadow Hawk rushed to him. If the arrow was barbed, it would be better to push it through than to pull it out. Then Shadow Hawk realized that would be impossible. Blood covered his father's chest. If he pushed the arrowhead through, he would drive it through his father's lung.

Black Hawk opened his eyes. "Are they dead, Shadow?"

"Yes, Father."

"You did well, my son."

"Father, I need to get you back to camp. We need to—"

"There is not time to get me back to camp, Shadow. I want you to listen to me."

"Father, you must rest. I will get your robe and the horses and—"

Black Hawk grabbed his son's arm with a vise-like grip. "You must promise me you will take your mother back to her people. If you do not, the husband of my sister will seek to take her for his wife. I would never rest if this were to happen. Promise me, Shadow."

Shadow Hawk felt his throat tighten and burn. "I promise you, Father."

"You must be strong for her, Shadow. You are the man now. You must take care of her and Brave Heart. Make sure your mother gets to her people. I owe her this much."

"I will take her back to her people. Do not worry. But please, let me get you back to camp."

"No, it is already too late. Do not feel sad for me, Shadow. I have had a good life."

Shadow Hawk felt tears roll down his cheeks. "What will I do without you? How will I learn the ways of the world?"

"You have already learned much from me. You are wise, my son, and you have a good heart."

"I am afraid, Father." Shadow Hawk felt his father's hand tighten on his arm.

"You are well prepared for this life, Shadow. And do not forget your grandfather. He loves you very much. He is also wise. You can learn much from him." Black Hawk closed his eyes.

Shadow Hawk felt the final darkness of death coming closer. "Father! Father, do not leave me yet!"

Black Hawk opened his eyes once more. "Tell your mother that I love her, tell her she gave me a good life. Tell my father that I did love him. And always remember how full my heart is of you, Shadow. A father could not be more proud of his son."

Shadow Hawk felt his father's grip loosen on his arm and he knew that he was dead. He pulled him close, holding him in his arms. He rocked back and forth for a few moments, trying to compose himself. He was a man now, and he had to act like a man. He looked up at the sky as he cradled his father's body. "Oh, Great Father, please accept this man called Black Hawk into your world. There was never a more honorable man to walk this earth. He was a good husband and a good father. He was generous with his knowledge and his love. Let him hunt many buffalo and let him know no more pain." He held his father to him. "Good-bye, Black Hawk, warrior and chief. Good-bye, Father." Shadow Hawk never knew how long he sat in the snow holding his father's body. He never felt the cold or the snow falling on his bare shoulders. Nothing could permeate the sadness he now felt. Part of his heart had been cut away, never again to be replaced.

"This is the story of the *Nermernuh*, the People. We are the True Human beings. We have no written history like the white man. We have no books. We have brought our history with us in the spoken word. Long ago, we had no horses and we hunted on foot. Our travois were pulled by dogs, and we did not travel as far for the hunt. But we stole the horse from the brown man and we tamed and bred it. We became the finest horseman on these plains.

"We sprang from the magical mating of animals and we can see the animal in ourselves. We honor the wolf and his cousin, the coyote, and we will not eat the coyote's relative, the dog. Some of our enemies say we look like wolves, that we are wild creatures that travel in packs, that we are cunning like the coyote, and wild when we smell blood. But like the wolf, we are loyal and loving to our families. We are nothing without our families."

Shadow Hawk sat upright. His mother was to his right, Marsh and Brave Heart were to his left. Old Bear was speaking. He was the oldest living member of the band. Some said he was sixty summers old, some said seventy. However old he was, he was full of wisdom and knowledge and his voice was still resonant, powerful.

"I knew Black Hawk all of his life. He was a brave warrior." Old Bear moved to stand in front of the family. "I remember when he realized that his father was different from everyone else's. He fought many battles to prove the strength of his father's blood. I remember when he brought an Apache woman into camp and he made her his wife. He loved her as if there were no other woman on this earth. And

38

when Broken Moon gave him a son, Black Hawk could see no end to his happiness. He taught the boy to be proud of his differences.

"There was a great love between Black Hawk and his son, a strong bond. Shadow Hawk will have a heavy burden to bear as he walks through life without his father. But he will have his father's teachings to guide him, and I do not think he will wander far from the path that was laid out for him.

"Let us not feel sorrow for Black Hawk, for he had a full life. Let us face our brother toward the rising sun, where he can be carried into the shadow land beyond, to the valley where the buffalo graze unendingly and the grass is green. There will be pounded corn and cool water and many animals to hunt. There Black Hawk will know no sorrow or pain, nor will he feel cold or hunger."

Shadow Hawk stood up and helped his mother to her feet. He put his arm around her. "Do you wish to say good-bye, Mother?"

Broken Moon looked at her husband, already placed on the scaffolding, and she shook her head. "No, I have already said my good-byes. He would not want me to wail."

Shadow Hawk smiled sadly. "You are strong, Mother." He went to Marsh. "Do you wish to say good-bye, Grandfather?"

Marsh stood still, staring at the scaffolding. "I wonder if he knew that I was proud of him. We were as different as night and day but I loved him. He was my son."

"He knew that you loved him, Grandfather."

"I think he always hated the fact that I was white. That was hard on him."

"I do not think it was so hard. He always told me to be proud of my white blood."

Marsh nodded, trying to control himself. "I'll walk with your mother."

39

As Marsh walked away, Brave Heart came to stand by Shadow Hawk. "I will let you say good-bye to Black Hawk, Shadow."

"You do not have to leave, Brave Heart. He was your father also."

"He was not my blood father." He reached into his robe and handed Shadow Hawk something. "Put this on his scaffolding. Let him take it to the hunting ground with him. Perhaps when he is tired of hunting, he can play music."

Shadow Hawk looked at the ornate flute that Brave Heart had carved, and smiled. "I know he will like it. Thank you." Shadow Hawk saw Old Bear standing off to the side, waiting until he was finished saying good-bye to his father. Shadow Hawk climbed the scaffolding, hung the flute on one of the poles, and looked down at his father's robed body. "I did as you asked, Father. I did not kill your favorite horse. I know you think it is a waste to kill all your horses and I know you want me to have your paint. And as you always said, if it truly is a happy hunting ground, there will be horses there as well as buffalo, elk, and deer." Shadow Hawk looked around and whispered. "But in case there are no horses, I have given you mine. Do not be angry with me. He is a good horse and will serve you well."

Shadow Hawk leaned against the scaffolding, his head down. "I love you, Father. I will try to make you proud. I will do as you ask and take Mother to her people. But someday I will return."

Old Bear came up to Shadow Hawk when he had climbed down.

"Thank you for speaking so eloquently today about my father, Old Bear." They walked away from the scaffolding toward the village. "I have many things to do," Shadow Hawk said, speaking his thoughts.

"You are not planning vengeance, I hope."

Shadow Hawk shook his head. "I must prepare to take my

mother back to her people. I promised my father that I would."

"What about you, Shadow?"

"I cannot worry about myself now, Old Bear." Shadow Hawk stopped. "Sometimes I feel as if I belong in no one place. Will I ever find my true home?"

Old Bear smiled slightly, his long gray hair framing his stately face. He placed his hand on Shadow Hawk's chest. "This is your home, Shadow, someday you will learn that. When you are at peace here, you will be home."

Shadow Hawk watched Old Bear as he walked away. He turned once more and looked at his father's scaffolding. Black Hawk was gone now. He had no more worries. Shadow Hawk sighed deeply. He was no longer a boy. He felt as if the weight of the world had suddenly come to rest on his shoulders.

Chapter 3

Shadow Hawk watched his mother ride. She sat her horse proudly but she looked empty, hollow. She missed his father and her life had been forever altered. Brave Heart rode behind Broken Moon, the sadness written on his face. They all missed Black Hawk.

They had waited until the heaviest of the snows were over and then they had set out on their journey. Shadow Hawk had insisted that they visit Marsh, and Broken Moon had not objected. She had always liked the strange white man. They had spent two days with Marsh. Shadow Hawk never before realized how much he depended on his grandfather. It had been very difficult saying good-bye to him. As always, Marsh gave him a present. Shadow Hawk smiled as he took the silver comb from his pouch. "It will be a good gift for your bride," his grandfather said. But Shadow Hawk was sure he would never marry. He would stay to see his mother settled with her people and then he would take Brave Heart and he would roam the prairie. He would find his own home, make a home as his grandfather had.

They were riding southwest into New Mexico territory. He knew it would be difficult to find his mother's people—it had been many years since his mother had been there, and the Mescalero Apache were always on the move. But he would do his best.

Shadow Hawk had never traveled for so long or ventured so far before. Twice they had seen white men from a distance but had made sure that the white men had not seen them. Sometimes he wondered—if he cut his hair and dressed in white man's clothes, could he walk in their world unnoticed? He knew his English was probably good enough but his knowledge of their customs was incomplete. He knew only what Marsh had taught him.

The brush-dotted land stretched away from them in every direction, the mountains rising smoky blue-gray in the distance.

"It grows cool, Shadow Hawk," Broken Moon said gently, riding up beside her son, "perhaps we should find shelter."

"Are you all right, Mother? Perhaps we have been riding too far each day."

"I am fine, Shadow, but I think we could all use a rest. Brave Heart is still only a boy."

Shadow Hawk looked back at his little brother. Brave Heart hadn't uttered a sound, but he looked tired. Ever since Brave Heart's parents had so easily given him up to Shadow Hawk's family, Brave Heart had gone out of his way to show his gratitude. If he were dying, he would not complain.

Shadow Hawk looked around him. Here, in the foothills, it would be easy to find a good camp. The flatlands had been more dangerous; and water there had been much harder to find.

They had established a routine as they traveled. Shadow Hawk led them until he found a good camp. Broken Moon and Brave Heart rested as he rode the area, making sure the campsite was safe. Then they all went to work.

Broken Moon took the dried roots and berries from her pack and cleared a place to prepare food, sweeping away the pebbles and twigs from her chosen fire spot. Brave Heart tended the horses, watering them, then hobbling them so that they could graze without wandering too far. Then he found firewood while Shadow Hawk arranged their sleeping mats.

Once the fire was started, they all sat near it, Broken Moon cooking whatever game they had killed that day. When there was none, she made a meal from the food that they had brought—or from the roots and plants she had gathered as they rode. Many times they ate fish, speared by Shadow Hawk in the rivers they crossed. Then, with their stomachs appeased, their weary muscles resting, they began their language lessons.

Broken Moon insisted, no matter how tired they were, or how hungry, or how thirsty. Each evening, before they could sleep, they had to practice speaking Apache. Shadow Hawk had spoken Apache since he was a child—or so he had thought. Now he realized he had spoken a child's Apache, that he knew only the names of common objects and how to ask for simple things. His mother spoke to him in rapid Apache now, using new words for complex thoughts. He replied as best he could, adding new words everyday.

Brave Heart was just beginning. Broken Moon pointed at the fire. He named it for her in Apache, and she smiled. She pointed at their horses, their sleeping mats, and the trees around them, smiling when he answered correctly. Then she would point to something new and say the name slowly several times. Broken Heart repeated it until the strange sounds became familiar.

They slept lightly, always alert for danger. Shadow Hawk was grateful each night that no one was hurt, that the horses were sound, and that his belly was full or at least quieted. But the dried foods in Broken's Moon's pouches were diminishing. They had been fortunate so far, finding game and easily gathering food plants. But it would not remain so forever, Shadow Hawk knew. It never did. Food would become scarce. Enemies would come, or sickness, or a rabbit hole to

44

break the leg of one of the horses. Shadow Hawk was not pessimistic—these were the realities of his young life. He was young, and the burden of protecting his mother and brother weighed heavily on his shoulders.

They had traveled for one moon when Broken Moon recognized a river where her people had camped many times. "I know this place, Shadow," she said, reining in her horse. There were open meadows leading to the mountains in the distance, scattered with oak and cedar. Rabbit trails ran through the grass. Shadow Hawk had seen deer tracks three times that morning. It was apparent that this area provided much game for people who lived here.

Shadow Hawk looked at his mother. He could see a change in her face as she looked around. She looked like a young girl. "Do you recognize it, Mother?"

"Yes, my father used to bring me here when he and my brothers went hunting. See that bank over the deep channel? I used to dive into the water there with my youngest brother. It gave me great joy to beat him up," she laughed.

Shadow Hawk smiled. "I thought you were gentle, Mother."

"I was never gentle with my brothers, for they were not gentle with me." Broken Moon urged her horse into the shallows.

Shadow Hawk and Brave Heart followed her.

"See?" She called back to them. "We can cross safely just up there."

The horses swam easily across and Broken Moon was still smiling as they climbed the far bank, water streaming from the horses' manes and tails. They rode well into the day as Broken Moon led them toward the mountains. The land became drier, more like a desert, yet it had an abundance of small, hard-barked trees. Shadow Hawk saw the gnawed bark and the bruised green shoots that meant deer often browsed in the area. Sinuous, curving marks in the sand told him that there were rattlesnakes. Bobcats, coyotes, and mountain lions had also left their sign.

"This is a strange place, is it not, Brother?" Brave Heart asked, riding next to Shadow Hawk.

"It is unlike any I have ever seen." The shadows from the trees and the hills seemed to shift and change. "This is a strange place, Brave Heart. It plays tricks on the eyes."

"I feel we are being watched, Shadow," Brave Heart said softly.

Shadow Hawk looked around him. Brave Heart had had feelings like this before, and Shadow Hawk had begun to trust him. He slid the bow from his shoulder, notched an arrow, then laid the bow across his legs.

"The shadows are moving, Brother," Brave Heart said, trying to keep the fear from his voice.

"Mother," Shadow Hawk said calmly. "I think we are being followed. These are your people. What is the wise thing to do?"

Broken Moon pulled up on her horse. She looked around at the trees and cupped her hands to her mouth. She spoke in her native tongue. "I am Broken Moon of the Mescalero Apache. I was taken captive by the Comanche fifteen summers ago. Now my son has brought me back to find my people. Will you help me?"

The three of them sat on their horses, alert, watching. Shadow Hawk's large paint, his father's horse, was nervous. He snorted loudly and shifted, pawing the ground. Shadow Hawk reined him in tightly, the bow and arrow ready in his right hand.

"Who is your family, Broken Moon?" A voice came out of the trees.

Shadow Hawk realized he had understood the Apache perfectly and was grateful for his mother's lessons.

"I am daughter of Gray Fox, war chief, and his wife, Ocha," Broken Moon called back. "I have two brothers—Sotso and Ataza."

"Why do you wish to return to your people after all this

time? How do we know that you are not Comanche and our enemy?"

Broken Moon shook her head. "Do such great warriors as the Mescalero Apache fear a woman and two boys?" she asked disdainfully.

Shadow Hawk glared at his mother. He didn't consider himself a boy. But before he had time to be angry, the shadows came to life and men appeared, walking out of the trees, holding short rifles in their hands. One man came forward. His hair was long and he wore a red cloth band around his forehead. He wore buckskins and a cloth shirt, much the color of the sky, and a leather belt studded with cartridges was around his waist. He didn't look young, yet he didn't look old. He looked powerful. His arms and torso were thick and muscled. His eyes were steady, fearless. Shadow Hawk could see immediately that he was a man to be careful of.

"So, woman, tell me about your brother Ataza." He stood in front of Broken Moon, looking up at her. Shadow Hawk tightened his right hand. The Apache glanced at him. "Leave the bow, boy, or you will be dead before you can lift it."

Shadow Hawk relaxed the grip on his bow, feeling foolish. He realized for the first time that the man was speaking slowly and distinctly. Why? Did he know that Shadow Hawk and Brave Heart were not yet fluent in Apache? Why would he care? Shadow Hawk looked at his mother.

Broken Moon was smiling mischieviously. "Ataza? He was my eldest brother and far too serious. He did not like to joke. Even as a boy, he talked of becoming a chief. I pushed him into that river once."

"And what did he do?"

"He got angry and then he laughed. My father said I was the only person who could make Ataza laugh."

The brave nodded his head, a serious expression on his face. "Have you heard news of your brother?"

"I have not heard of any of my family since I was taken

captive. I do not even know if they are alive."

"It matters to you, woman, that they are alive?"

"They are my family. I lived with the Comanche. I had a good husband and I bore him a son. But now my husband is dead and my son has brought me back to my people. I want to be with my family."

"And if we force you to go?"

"I will not go. This is my home."

"You are stubborn, woman."

"Just like you, Ataza," Broken Moon said softly, smiling at her brother.

Ataza walked to the horse and reached up, pulling his sister down. "I did not think I would ever look upon your sweet face again, Sister. Yusn, the Creator, smiles on us this day."

Shadow Hawk watched in fascination as the hard-looking man held Broken Moon gently, touching her with disbelief and joy. She leaned against him, trusting and happy. Shadow Hawk had never seen his mother act that way with anyone but his father. Shadow Hawk caught the man looking at him over his mother's shoulder. His eyes were direct, piercing. So this was Ataza, his uncle. This man would either be a friend to die beside or an enemy who would try to kill him. Shadow Hawk dismounted.

"I greet you, Uncle."

Ataza held Shadow Hawk's eyes with a steady gaze. He pulled away from his sister. "And this one with the protective look in his eyes and the quick hand on the bow, he is my nephew?"

Shadow Hawk wasn't sure he liked being talked about as if he weren't there, but he stood, silent and respectful.

"Yes, this is Shadow Hawk, son of Black Hawk of the Comanche tribe. Shadow, come meet your uncle."

Shadow Hawk stepped forward. He was a full head taller than his uncle, but he felt like a child next to the man. Ataza radiated an incredible power without moving or saying a word.

"Shadow Hawk," Ataza repeated. "How did you come by the name, boy?"

Shadow Hawk held his uncle's gaze and spoke slowly, carefully, willing himself to pronounce the words perfectly. "My father held me in the sunlight after I was born. He was proud and he wanted all to see his new son. As he held me up, the shadow of a hawk passed over my body and his screech was heard in the sky above."

Ataza nodded. "It is a good sign and a good name. I like it."

"I did not realize my name needed your approval, Uncle," Shadow Hawk responded dryly.

"Shadow!" Broken Moon rebuked him.

"Your son has a sharp tongue, Sister." Ataza stepped forward. He stood very close to Shadow Hawk. "How do you feel about coming to the Apache, boy?"

"Am I to answer honestly, Uncle, or am I to say what will be pleasing to your ears?" He stumbled on a word or two but he was proud of how easily he could frame his thoughts in Apache.

Ataza nodded and then laughed. "I like you, Shadow Hawk. You remind me of my sister at your age. Even when your father stole her from us, it was your father I felt sorry for, not my sister."

Shadow Hawk couldn't resist a slight smile.

"Ah, I see I have made you smile. Good. So, answer my question, Nephew, how do you feel about joining the Apache?"

"I did not say I was going to join the Apache, Uncle. I promised my father I would bring my mother here when he died. I have fulfilled that promise."

"And what are your plans now? Do you go back to the Comanche, or do you go to live with the white man?"

Shadow Hawk lowered his eyes for the first time, embarrassed. If only he had had dark eyes. His white blood was so obvious.

"Where is that sharp tongue of yours now, Shadow Hawk?" Ataza urged.

Shadow Hawk raised his deep blue eyes and glared at his uncle. "I will go where I please, Uncle. I am bound by no person and no tribe."

"Not even your mother?"

Shadow Hawk looked at Broken Moon. He could already see the change in her face. She looked softer somehow, happy. "My mother no longer needs me. She has her family now."

"You are her family, Shadow Hawk. Do not ever forget that." Ataza looked past Shadow Hawk. "Who is the boy? Is he also your son, Broken Moon?"

"He is my adopted brother," Shadow Hawk responded defensively, stepping in front of Brave Heart's horse. "I will take care of him."

"You have much anger, Shadow Hawk." Ataza's voice softened. "Perhaps it is time to put some of it away."

"Please, Shadow," his mother implored, "stay here for a while. If after a time you wish to go back to the Comanche, then you can go. You are not bound to stay with me. You are a man now."

Shadow Hawk couldn't resist the joy in his mother's voice. "I will stay, Mother, if only for a short while."

Ataza nodded brusquely. "It is done. Follow me and my men to our camp."

Shadow Hawk watched Ataza walk away, his arm around Broken Moon.

"He is a frightening man, Shadow Hawk," Brave Heart said in whispered Comanche from astride his horse.

"He is only a man," Shadow Hawk replied, shrugging his shoulders. He mounted up. "Speak only Apache now. You must practice."

Brave Heart switched languages, pronouncing the simple words with effort. "He likes you, Shadow."

"I do not care if he hates me. It means nothing to me."

"Your uncle is right, Shadow, you carry much anger in your heart."

"Still your tongue, Brave Heart, or I will cut it out!"

Brave Heart laughed and lapsed into Comanche again. "That is a false threat, Shadow. You would never hurt me."

"I should never have taken you into this family. You are nothing but a burden," Shadow Hawk hissed. Instantly he regretted it. "I am sorry, Brave Heart. You have done nothing to deserve my anger. My anger is for the heavens and for the earth and for no place in particular."

"Your anger is strong because you miss Black Hawk."

"I miss him more than I thought possible. I wonder that my mother can forget him so easily."

"You wrong Broken Moon by saying such a thing, Shadow. Your father would be glad for her happiness. You only wish it were your own."

Shadow Hawk looked at the boy who rode next to him. That was one of the things he truly loved about Brave Heart—his ability to see the truth beyond all else. Old Bear had said that someday Brave Heart would make a good shaman. Shadow Hawk thought that he would. "Perhaps I do envy her."

"You have not given these people a chance, Shadow. Already your uncle has taken to you."

"I will try for my mother's sake, but if I do not feel welcome, I will leave."

"Where will you go?"

"I do not know. Perhaps I will stay with my grandfather for a time." Shadow Hawk realized how selfish he was being. "We will try it, Brave Heart. Perhaps you will like it here. These people do not know you."

"Nor do they know you. Perhaps it can be a new beginning for all of us, Brother."

"Perhaps," Shadow Hawk replied, the uneasiness still in his heart. How could he ever feel at home in a place where his father and grandfather did not live?

They rode through cactus and rock-covered land, heading toward the rocky foothills. It was forbidding land, not the kind where children ran and played. Shadow Hawk already missed the flowing water of the big river where the Comanche camped and the tall, sparkling cottonwood trees that dotted the land where he had played as a child. Here the plants were thorny, hostile. The sun glared on the hard, sandy soil. Shadow Hawk tried to learn the country they rode through, but all the signs looked the same—cactus, rocks, low, gnarled shrubs—nothing stood out. He leaned down to look at the ground. Even the hoofprints that the horses left wouldn't be there for long. The dirt was so hard and thin that only faint tracks were made. The first wind would erase them. Shadow Hawk didn't like it here.

When they reached the rocky foothills, Ataza slowed their pace. Following paths that were almost invisible to Shadow Hawk, Ataza led them upward. Stands of cedar and pine grew, wind-bent and strong. Thickets of chokecherries bloomed. The shadows lengthened as they rode. Brave Heart looked tired, but still he did not complain. At a place that looked no different from the country they had just ridden through, Ataza suddenly stopped.

"The short path?" Ataza asked Broken Moon.

She nodded.

They dismounted and Ataza gestured for them to carry their belongings and leave their horses with the other warriors. Shadow Hawk was reluctant to leave his father's paint, but Broken Moon smiled reassuringly at him and he relinquished the reins.

They followed Ataza upward. If there was a path, Shadow Hawk couldn't see it. He struggled to keep up, watching his mother. She climbed the rocks easily, and her laughter rang out along with her brother's. Shadow Hawk slowed his pace to wait for Brave Heart. It was hard going for the younger boy. Shadow Hawk looked back across the desert, trying to get his bearings, but he felt completely unsure of himself. He had always been proud of his tracking ability but how was it possible to track in a place like this?

"You do not have to wait for me, Brother," Brave Heart said as he came up behind Shadow Hawk. He leaned against a rock. "I must catch my breath. I am not used to climbing hills like these."

"I do not think this is a hill, Brave Heart, I think this is a mountain." Shadow Hawk looked up the rocky slope. Above them a dark green pine forest began.

"How can anyone live here?"

"My mother says that the Apache can disappear into rocks and hills never to be found again. She remembers her father and some of the braves walking fifty miles a day, as much as we would cover on a horse! And did you see them? They are not big men or long-legged! How is this possible?"

"No one is taller than you, Brother. All human beings are made for different things. The Apache is made so that he can climb and walk well."

"We do not even know if they are human beings, Brave Heart. There is something about them," Shadow Hawk murmured, still looking around.

"What is it about us, Nephew?"

Shadow Hawk and Brave Heart both jumped involuntarily when Ataza appeared on a rock above them. He laughed loudly.

"Are you in the habit of scaring people?" Shadow Hawk asked angrily, his pride obviously injured.

"Did you hear nothing, Shadow Hawk?" Ataza looked at Brave Heart. "What about you, boy? You heard nothing?"

"I heard nothing," Brave Heart replied evenly in Apache, staring at Ataza.

"I heard the sound of pebbles rolling," Shadow Hawk said. "I thought it was the wind."

"Good," Ataza replied, nodding his head. "Pay attention to the sound next time. It could be your enemy sneaking up behind you." He regarded Brave Heart. "What is it that ails you, boy?"

"I am tired, Ataza, and I do not climb well. Do not wait for me. I will catch up later."

"I will wait with him," Shadow Hawk said, frowning.

"You are protective of this boy, Nephew. Do you not think that he can care for himself?"

"He is weak, Uncle."

"Why did you decide to take care of him?"

Shadow Hawk was irritated by the question. "What do you mean, 'Why'? Why do you eat and drink every day? Why do you protect your people?"

Ataza ignored Shadow Hawk's angry outburst. He took a pouch from his belt and handed it to Brave Heart. "Eat these berries, boy, they are fresh. But don't eat too many or you will get cramps. And be sure to drink water. Come with me, Nephew," Ataza ordered.

Shadow Hawk followed Ataza, glancing back at Brave Heart. Ataza led him to a high point, then turned and gestured, sweeping his arm to indicate the rugged country that surrounded them. "This is our land, boy. Our land," he said emphatically, thumping his fist against his chest. "We call ourselves *Tin-eh-ah*. Our lands runs from the river the whites call the Rio Grande, south into Mexico. Our brothers, the Lipan Apache, live to the east, the Jicarilla Apache to the southeast. The Chiricahua live to our west, and further west live the White Mountain Apache. We have so many brothers I am not able to name them all. Our land is so vast that we live in our own bands and seldom mix with the others. But we help each other if the need arises."

"I do not mean to sound disrespectful, Uncle, but why do you tell me this?"

Ataza stood, surveying the land below. "If you are to stay here for a time, it is good that you know some things about your mother's people. Your people."

"My people are in the Comancheria," Shadow Hawk said stubbornly.

"And your people are also in the Apacheria," Ataza replied just as resolutely. "You cannot make your Apache blood disappear. Just as you cannot make your white blood disappear."

"Does it please you to mock me, Uncle?"

"I only say what is true, Nephew. You judge us and you do not even know us. Your mother looks pleased to be here, does she not?"

Shadow Hawk had to admit that he had never seen his mother so happy. "You are her family. Of course she is pleased to see you."

"I am sorry about your father, Shadow Hawk. Your mother told me of his leaving. I am sorry he is gone. He was a true warrior."

Shadow Hawk didn't know what to say. Why had this man started talking about his father? "My father was a true warrior in everything that he did." Shadow Hawk was surprised at the emotion in his voice.

"I hated your father for taking my sister away from us," Ataza said simply. "But I can see by the loyalty that he instilled in you and by the way that my sister speaks of him, that he must have been a good man."

"I do not wish to speak about my father with you," Shadow Hawk said suddenly, turning away from Ataza.

"Shadow Hawk," Ataza commanded his nephew.

Shadow Hawk stopped. It was a tone he had heard many times from his father. He looked at Ataza. "What is it, Uncle?"

"I know that it is not your wish to be here. I understand that. But remember that it was your father's wish that you bring your mother here. Be careful with your anger. You wear it like a shield in front of you." Ataza started back down, light-footed, agile. "Hurry, boy, your mother is waiting."

Shadow Hawk followed him back to Brave Heart. He felt ashamed. He did not wish to embarrass his mother in this

55

way. Brave Heart handed the pouch back to Ataza.

"Thank you for the berries, Ataza. They were sweet."

"Keep them," Ataza replied. "Are you well enough for the rest of the walk?"

"Yes. I am better."

"Let us go then." He glanced sharply at Shadow Hawk and led them upward.

Shadow Hawk followed behind Brave Heart, making sure to catch him when he slipped. As they neared the camp, they passed lookouts sitting as still as the stones, hard to see in the sharp-edged shadows. The men nodded to Ataza as he walked by. Shadow Hawk stopped to let Brave Heart rest a moment. He could see the desert below. The lookouts could see people coming from as far away as twenty or thirty miles. These Apache had chosen a good camp.

Shadow Hawk could hear the sound of his mother's laughter and he walked on, with a silent Brave Heart following behind him. The land leveled out and for the first time Shadow Hawk could see the camp. There were a hundred hide lodges in a rough semicircle. There were smaller structures, too, unfamiliar to Shadow Hawk. Just beyond them the pines grew tall and dark as the land rose again. A group of women stood around his mother and an older woman grasped her hand. They talked excitedly. Ataza looked at the group and smiled.

"It is your grandmother. She has never given up hope that Broken Moon was alive."

Shadow Hawk looked at the old woman. She was very small, like his mother. She wore her hair long and straight with just a headband. She wore silver around her neck and around both wrists. She didn't wear a buckskin dress but a shirt and blouse of bright rose-colored material, belted with a blue sash. All the women, he noted, were dressed this way. They looked like flowers, like spring birds.

"What of my grandfather?" Shadow Hawk asked Ataza.

"He left us two summers ago. Like you, my heart was

heavy for a very long time. But his teachings have stayed with me, just as your father's will stay with you."

Shadow Hawk looked at Ataza. He was a formidable man, but he was also a kind man. "Have you sons of your own, Uncle?"

"Two sons and a daughter. You will meet them soon."

"Perhaps they will not want to meet me."

"This is not easy for you, is it, Shadow Hawk?"

Shadow Hawk hesitated. "I feel as strange here as I would in the white world. It is all so different to me."

"It will not be easy. We are different people than the Comanche, but we are your family. You are welcome here. Remember that."

"Thank you, Uncle."

"Come, meet your grandmother."

Shadow Hawk let himself be led into the group of women, most of whom stared and pointed at him. He knew he was an object of curiosity, not only because of his mixed blood, but because he was Broken Moon's son.

Ataza approached the small woman and gently took her arm. The group quieted. Broken Moon stood to one side. "Mother, meet your grandson, Shadow Hawk. Shadow Hawk, this is your grandmother, Ocha."

Ocha stepped forward and looked at Shadow Hawk. Abruptly, she reached up and ran her fingers over his face. "You are tall."

Shadow Hawk glanced at his mother and saw by the look on her face that he should be respectful. "Yes, Grandmother."

"And your eyes, is it true they are the color of the sky on a cloudy day?"

Shadow Hawk was puzzled. "Yes, Grandmother."

"And you are no doubt handsome."

Shadow Hawk smiled. "Some might say so, others would not." He saw his mother laugh. His grandmother's hands ran across his bare shoulders and arms. It felt strange, as if she were getting to know him through her touch. He looked into

57

her eyes. He had seen blind people before and usually their eyes betrayed them, but Ocha's eyes looked perfect.

"You are wondering if I can see?"

"Yes, Grandmother."

"I cannot see with my eyes, but I see almost as well with my ears and my hands. Where is the boy Brave Heart? I want to meet him."

Shadow Hawk turned around. Brave Heart was standing on the periphery of the circle, silent and patient. Shadow Hawk waved Brave Heart forward and pushed him toward his grandmother. "This is Ocha, our grandmother."

"I am pleased to meet you, Grandmother."

Ocha ran her fingers over Brave Heart's face and upper body, just as she had done with Shadow Hawk. "How old are you, boy?"

"I am almost eleven summers old, Grandmother."

"You are small for your age, boy. We must see that you eat better. I have teas that you will drink to help make you grow. You will drink them everyday."

"Yes, Grandmother."

"I will visit with my daughter now. You boys meet your cousins." The old woman turned then hesitated, looking back. "You speak Apache well, boy, as if you were born here."

Shadow Hawk winced at his grandmother's words. As much as he liked her brusque kindness, he knew he would never be an Apache. His place was not with these people.

The sound of Ataza's voice scattered his thoughts. "Shadow Hawk, Brave Heart. Come meet your cousins."

Shadow Hawk and Brave Heart followed Ataza to the edge of camp. He gestured toward one of the lodges.

"You will stay here with us until we build a lodge for you and your mother." Standing beside the lodge were a pretty woman and an even prettier young girl. "This is your aunt, Little Fox, and your cousin, Singing Bird."

Shadow Hawk greeted his aunt and cousin. They were

friendly to him, but it was Brave Heart who held their attention. They took Brave Heart inside the lodge with them. He bade Shadow Hawk good-bye, smiling, obviously enjoying the woman's offers of food and rest. Shadow Hawk followed his uncle out of the camp. Ataza was determined to find his sons, who were off hunting in the hills.

Shadow Hawk was young and strong, but he wasn't used to climbing rocks in the mountains. His thighs ached and his breath came quicker. He was amazed at the strength and agility of his uncle—Ataza seemed to glide over the rocks with little or no effort. His footing was so sure that he seldom looked down as he climbed, while Shadow Hawk, unsure of the terrain, constantly watched where he was going.

The rocky path was faint and hard to see, then disappeared altogether. Ataza bore southwest, descending the mountainside. Cedars dotted the rocky slope. Abruptly, Ataza halted and Shadow Hawk looked down into a steep-sided valley. Sunflowers were scattered across the valley floor and the sun sparkled off a beautiful creek. Farther down the valley Shadow Hawk could see a corral. His uncle's band had many horses. They grazed peacefully in the rich green grass. Above the corral, beaver dams had widened the creek into deep ponds. Shadow Hawk tried to still his deep breaths, embarrassed that his uncle was so much stronger than he.

"They do this often," Ataza said, annoyed, looking down into the valley.

"Do what, uncle?"

"My sons—they take off to hunt and they do not return until the sun has passed across the sky. They think they are safe here, that no harm can come to them."

"Are they not safe here, Uncle?"

"No place is secure from the enemy, Nephew."

Ataza put his hands up to his mouth and made a yipping sound like a coyote. He did it three times. He nodded his head. "My sons, they think they are playing with me." He looked around. "Do you wish to join in the game, Nephew?"

"What game is this, Uncle?"

"Follow me. When I tell you, you will circle above me. I know where they hunt. They think they are too old to listen to me, but they will learn a different lesson today. When they see a Comanche warrior prepared to attack them, perhaps they will heed my warnings." He glared at Shadow Hawk. "Can you look fierce?"

"Fierce?" Shadow Hawk couldn't resist a smile.

"I don't want you to scare them into killing you, but I do want you to look fierce."

"I will do as you say, Uncle." Shadow Hawk was amused. He followed his uncle along the rim of the valley, walking in a crouch, trying to stay as low as Ataza. As they approached a thicket of scrub oak, Ataza motioned Shadow Hawk to stop.

"I hear them. Circle around," he whispered, "notch your arrow, and—"

"Look fierce?"

Ataza nodded solemnly but Shadow Hawk was sure he saw his uncle smile. "Be careful, Nephew, I will be close behind."

Shadow Hawk went slowly, carefully. He moved as his father had taught him, shifting his weight smoothly, keeping his stride short, his balance strong. He heard his cousins before he saw them. They were laughing. Shadow Hawk notched an arrow and crept through the scrub oak until he was directly behind the two boys.

"Father will be angry, Miho."

"Father is always angry. We are men. It is time we are treated like men, Gitano."

"But he has told us not to come here alone. We will pay dearly for this." Gitano looked around. "You heard his call. Where do you suppose he is?"

"He went back to the camp. He does not know we come here." Miho gestured. "Father will be proud when he sees the bear we have killed."

"Why do you make him so angry, Miho? Does it give you pleasure?"

Miho shrugged his shoulders. "Yes, I suppose it does."

Shadow Hawk listened to the two brothers talk for a while longer, waiting until they were both sitting with their backs to him. They had leaned their rifles against a rock, four or five paces away from where they sat. He crept closer, the fiercest look he could muster on his face, and bow drawn tight and ready. "Do not move."

Both Miho and Gitano turned, starting for their rifles, but Shadow Hawk stepped forward, letting his arrow go by Miho, barely missing his hand. Quickly he pulled and notched another. "If you move again I will have to kill you."

Miho glanced at his rifle and back at Shadow Hawk. "What is a Comanche doing on our land?"

"I will ask the questions."

"You are Comanche. You are far from your territory." Miho took one step closer to his rifle.

"I go where I please."

"Then leave this place. This is not Comancheria."

"Miho," Gitano shot his brother a warning look. "We were just hunting." He pointed to the bear. "Please, take as much as you like."

"I will take it all."

"No!" Miho shouted. "We will not share our meat with you. We hunted it. It is ours."

"You do not have a say in the matter." Shadow Hawk lifted his bow.

"No, please!" Gitano pleaded, stepping in front of his brother. "Take the meat. We do not need it."

Shadow Hawk did not want to play the game any longer. He lowered the bow. "I do not want your meat."

"And lucky for you he does not," Ataza said sternly, appearing from behind a boulder. He walked to his sons. "So, again you have defied me, Miho."

Miho's eyes never wavered as he looked at his father. "You treat us like children, Father. We come here to hunt like men."

"But you are not men, you are boys. I protect you because I want you to live a long life."

Miho started to speak but stopped, looking at Shadow Hawk. "Father, the Comanche—"

"Ah, the Comanche. Allow me to introduce Shadow Hawk, your cousin. Nephew, these are my sons, Miho and Gitano."

Miho stepped closer, critically appraising Shadow Hawk. "I could not possibly have a Comanche cousin. Besides, he looks as if he is more mongrel than Comanche. His blood has been mixed too many times."

Shadow Hawk had heard the taunt so often before that he remained calm. "Perhaps it is my mixed blood that has allowed me the keen sense to know when I am going to be ambushed instead of listening to myself talk," he said in precise Apache.

Miho reached out to shove Shadow Hawk, but Ataza pushed him back. "Enough, Miho! Gitano, return to camp with your cousin. Your brother and I must have a talk."

"It was not all Miho's fault, Father. I was as much to blame."

"I will speak to you later, Gitano. Go!"

Shadow Hawk watched Gitano as he picked up his rifle, glanced at his brother, and headed toward the camp. He followed silently. Gitano was about his age, Miho a little older. They both looked like their father—muscular and compact. Gitano's strides were short and quick, and although Shadow Hawk was much taller, he had to work hard to keep up with him. When they reached the top of the trail, Gitano sat down on a fallen cedar, taking a drink from his hide bag. He offered some to Shadow Hawk.

"So, you are our cousin. How is this possible?"

"My mother is Broken Moon, sister to Ataza."

"I know that story. Your mother was taken captive many summers ago. Why are you here now?"

"My father was killed. He wanted me to bring my mother back."

"Will you be staying here?"

"No." Shadow Hawk took a drink from the bag and returned it to Gitano.

"My brother is not always so mean. He was embarrassed by your game with my father."

"I know."

"Miho is seventeen summers and has already ridden on raids with my father. He is a skillful hunter and a brave warrior, but he forgets that he still has things to learn."

Shadow Hawk recalled the many times he had grown impatient with his father. "Only once was I able to fight in battle with my father. It was the day he was killed."

"I am truly sorry, Cousin."

Shadow Hawk liked Gitano. It was impossible not to like his boyish face and eager smile. "I am sorry I played a trick on you."

"I was afraid I would be dead before the sun set this day."

When they reached camp, Gitano led Shadow Hawk to his lodge. Beside the lodge was a hut made of brush and sticks. Gitano saw Shadow Hawk staring at it.

"You do not have wickiups?" Shadow Hawk shook his head. "We use this one to store our food, but we sometimes live in them when the buffalo are scarce and we cannot get hides." The wickiup was a dome-shaped brush hut. The frame was a circle of poles bent over and tied together in the center. The spaces between the poles were thatched with yucca leaves and scrub brush. A smoke hole was left open at the top and a blanket served as the door. It looked quite small to Shadow Hawk. He knew he would not want to live in a wickiup.

His mother, his aunt, his cousin, and several women were sitting behind the wickiup, talking. His aunt was speaking in rapid Apache to Gitano, explaining Broken Moon's arrival. Gitano went to Broken Moon and greeted her politely. Broken Moon smiled and told him he reminded her of Ataza as a boy. Gitano escaped the women, gesturing for Shadow Hawk to follow him. As they passed a drying rack, he grabbed some strips of meat and handed a piece to Shadow Hawk.

"It is good to have your mother here. My father and uncle have spoken of her often."

They walked behind the camp and climbed up a series of boulders; a giant, natural stairway. Shadow Hawk could see the mountains and the valley, then, turning, the distant white glare of the desert below.

Gitano pulled off a piece of the dried meat with his teeth. "I like this place. We have been here for only one moon but we will probably stay through the summer." He pointed. "See, there are my brother and father. Miho is carrying the bear."

Shadow Hawk hadn't seen them coming. Shadow Hawk felt strange. Was he becoming careless? Or was it the shadowy hillsides, the huge rocks? Shadow Hawk felt an ache of longing for the Plains, for his people. Could he learn to think like a mountain Indian, like an Apache? And who would teach him? "Is my other uncle here?"

"He is with a hunting party. He will return sometime soon."

"What is he like?"

"Be careful with Sotso. He is not like my father."

"Do I have more cousins?"

"There is Teroz. You would do well to stay away from him."

Shadow Hawk looked at Gitano and saw an odd expression on his face. "What is it?"

"Teroz is our cousin; he has our blood running through his veins, but sometimes he frightens me. He is the same age as Miho. They have always been rivals. They hate each other."

"How do you feel about him?"

"Truly?" Gitano chewed on another piece of meat and considered the question. "If I had the courage to fight him, I would."

Shadow Hawk didn't know what to say. Until he met Teroz, he didn't want to judge him.

"I have seen him angry three or four times in my life. It is as though he is ruled by a beast inside him. I have seen him shout at Ocha."

"He is permitted to do this? In our tribe, a young man could be punished for treating an elder with disrespect."

"Sotso cannot control him, but my father would not permit it."

Shadow Hawk nodded. He could fully imagine Ataza taking anyone to task for any transgression. "Do your father and Sotso get along?"

"Not well. At every council meeting they argue."

"What of Sotso's wife?"

"Lota is not Teroz's mother. His mother died when he was very small. Lota has a daughter, a quiet, gentle girl named Paloma. I feel sorry for her." He put his hand on Shadow Hawk's shoulder, patting him gently. "I feel sorry for you, too, Cousin. Teroz will hate you simply because you are not full-blooded Apache."

"I am not afraid of Teroz, Cousin."

Gitano shrugged. "Perhaps you are braver than I."

"Gitano!"

Gitano and Shadow Hawk stood up at the sound of Ataza's voice. He was standing behind them. Miho was standing next to him, not masking the anger that he obviously felt. Shadow Hawk clenched his fists. Did all Apaches appear and disappear without making a sound?

Ataza looked grim. "You will come with me, Gitano. Miho, you will stay here and get acquainted with your cousin." Miho scowled and let the bear carcass slide to the ground.

Shadow Hawk didn't blame Miho for being angry with him. Gitano followed his father, carrying the bear carcass. Miho walked past Shadow Hawk and stood on the edge of the rocks, looking out into the desert below. He waited until his father and brother were out of earshot.

"I am sorry for the death of your father," he said slowly, "but I do not welcome you here." He turned to face Shadow Hawk.

"I do not expect you to welcome me. We are nothing to each other."

"Our parents will expect us to be like brothers."

"Do not worry, Miho, I am going to leave soon."

"You are going back to your people?"

"I do not know." Shadow Hawk walked to the edge and stood next to Miho. He smiled wryly. "I have many people."

"How is it you have white blood when your father was a Comanche?"

"My father's father is a white man. He is still living and I am fond of him. I have been thinking that perhaps I will live with him."

"You would live in a white man's lodge?" Miho shook his head. "I have seen them. They are dark, like a dirty cave."

"They are not all so dirty. I have spent many moons with my grandfather in his cabin. It is peaceful there."

"What is it like out there?" Miho asked, pointing out toward the desert. "Past the sands."

"The land takes on many shapes as you travel east. There is your desert, there are the mountains, and beyond them, the Plains. Where I grew up the land is flat and there are many trees and rivers. I used to swim in the river everyday and I would fish." Shadow Hawk grew silent. "It was beautiful there."

"It is said the Comanche are the best horsemen on the Plains. Is this true?"

"It is true. I have seen warriors riding at a full gallop shoot an arrow at an enemy under their horse's neck."

"Can you do this trick?"

"I now how it is done. I have practiced it many times but I have been in only one fight with the enemy, Miho."

"And were you victorious?"

Shadow Hawk hesitated. "We killed the enemy, but I lost my father. No, I was not victorious."

They were both silent. Miho spoke first.

"I will give you a warning, since you are my cousin. Stay away from Teroz."

"Gitano already told me about him."

"You would be no match for Teroz if he were truly angry."

"Perhaps you are frightened of him, Cousin, but I am not."

"I have warned you." Miho glared at Shadow Hawk and descended the giant rock stairway that led back to the camp.

Shadow Hawk wouldn't have to worry about Teroz or the rest of them. There was no use trying to make friends with anyone. He wouldn't be here that long. Soon he would be on his own and he would answer to no one.

Chapter 4

Shadow Hawk had been in the Apache camp for three days and had not yet slept in his uncle's lodge. The doorway was too low and it wasn't large enough inside, not like the lodge he used to live in. He slept on a blanket outside, looking up at the stars in the clear spring sky, impatient to leave this place. This Apache camp is strange, he thought. True, his mother's people were Indians like the Comanche, but they were as different from him as the white man was. Broken Moon had told him that most Apache bands lived in wickiups rather than hide lodges and the camps were always in well-disguised places like this one. Secrecy was prized by the Apache. Miho had boasted that no one had ever found this camp or any of the others they used.

When they left a camp, they made sure it looked as though no one had ever lived there. Fire pits were smoothed over and the brush bed frames were placed in a central pile and burned. Shrubs were dragged through the camp to erase all footprints and light paths.

Shadow Hawk had ridden with his uncle and cousin and found, to his surprise, that they were extremely good horsemen, but their skill at horsemanship was nothing compared to their skill afoot. He never ceased to be amazed at the way all the Apache, men, women, and children, climbed up and down the rocky paths as if they were on perfectly flat land. The young boys played war and hunting games among the rocks and trees, the girls picked berries and dug roots that clung to steep mountainsides. One thing was very obvious to Shadow Hawk—these Apache had adapted well to their surroundings. A Comanche without a horse was a crippled man, but an Apache saw the horse as a luxury, not a necessity. He could travel farther and faster on foot in this forbidding country he called home.

Shadow Hawk had been worried about Brave Heart but was glad to see that his cousin, Singing Bird, had already taken a liking to his brother. In a short time they had become good friends. Shadow Hawk liked his uncle, aunt, and cousins, but he had yet to meet Sotso and Teroz.

Broken Moon was already helping in the daily work of the camp as if she had never been gone. As always, Shadow Hawk still felt like an outsider. Often he sat on the rough boulder "stairway" that overlooked the valley. He liked the view from there and he liked the solitude.

This day he sat on the boulders, squinting into the morning sun. He saw something moving in the foothills below camp. He shielded his eyes. There were two men on horses riding at an easy lope. Behind them were three or four heavily loaded pack animals.

He was distracted by the nearly inaudible sound of Gitano's approach, and turned to face him. Shadow Hawk grinned. "You cannot sneak up on me anymore, Cousin."

Gitano jumped up on the rock next to Shadow Hawk. "I was trying to make noise like a Comanche."

Shadow Hawk turned to hide his smile. "I see riders coming toward camp."

"My uncle and cousin return from the hunt. I am sure there will be twenty deer and Teroz will have killed them all himself."

Shadow Hawk laughed. "You really do not like him."

Gitano shrugged his shoulders. "I used to like Teroz when

69

we were younger, but now he breaks many of our rules. He never abides by them when he hunts. The Child of the Water laid down the rules on this earth hundreds of summers ago, and to violate them could spoil our future hunts and bring harm to our people." Gitano shook his head. "Sometimes I do not believe the tales that the old ones tell, but I have seen things happen when people do not listen. That is one of the reasons my father was so angry at Miho. He broke one of the hunting rules."

"What did he do?"

"He was too boastful. Instead of thanking Mother Earth for the gift of food, he boasted of his skill. He rarely offers to share meat with our family and friends. So my father took the bear and gave it away. There are always rules to be followed, Cousin."

Shadow Hawk understood. That was one of the first things his father had taught him and he remembered how proud he had been on the buffalo hunt. He also remembered that his father had gotten angry at him because he had not thanked the buffalo. Now he never hunted without thanking the animal. "My father was much like your father."

"Will you stay with us, Cousin?"

"I do not know, Gitano." Shadow Hawk was able to see the men and horses clearly now, In spite of himself, he was feeling somewhat apprehensive. Miho and Gitano both disliked Sotso and Teroz.

Gitano stood up. "Come, let us greet the victorious hunter."

They climbed off the rocks and walked to the other side of the camp. Many of the women had run down the path and were coming back already, helping to bring the fresh meat into camp. They giggled and laughed, their colorful skirts flashing in the sunlight.

Gitano shook his head in dismay. "The women are blinded by Teroz's boastful acts. Fresh meat will make anyone look like an honorable person."

"You are not jealous of Teroz, are you, Cousin?"

"Jealous? I do not covet anything that Teroz has except perhaps his strength."

"You can make your own strength."

"Not his kind of strength." Gitano shoved Shadow Hawk. "Look, there he is."

Shadow Hawk watched a young man about Miho's age walking up the path, a deer slung over his shoulders. The animal was bleeding down Teroz's chest and legs. Teroz's face was streaked with sweat. When he got into the camp, he dropped the animal as if it weighed nothing. He gestured casually to the travois that some of the women were pulling up that path.

"I have killed many deer today. Help me butcher them and I will give each of you some meat."

Gitano turned away in disgust. "You see what he does? He tempts the spirits! He boasts of his kills and does not freely offer the food to the others. He makes them admire him first."

Shadow Hawk was surprised Gitano showed his disapproval so openly, but Teroz seemed not to hear. Shadow Hawk studied Teroz. His face was young, but his body was that of a grown man. He was not tall, but he was one of the most muscular men Shadow Hawk had ever seen. His chest was broad, and unlike most of the other men, he wore no shirt. It was obvious he wanted everyone to admire his strength. He was sure that Teroz was a formidable fighter.

"What do you think? Is he as I said, or have I exaggerated?" This time Gitano whispered.

"He appears to be physically strong, but he is being generous enough."

"That is because he has all eyes on him now."

Shadow Hawk watched Teroz with great interest. As he returned with more meat, Shadow Hawk noticed a young girl behind him. She struggled up the path with a load that was obviously too heavy for her. She tried to maintain her

71

footing on the rocky ground but fell, dropping the fresh meat in the dirt. Teroz spun and glared at her.

"You stupid girl!" he yelled. He slapped her. "Do you not realize how hard I hunted for this meat?"

The girl began to cry. "I am sorry, Teroz."

Teroz showed no emotion. "Do not make excuses to me, Paloma."

"Now do you believe me?" Shadow Hawk heard Gitano's voice behind him. "That is Paloma, his sister."

Shadow Hawk turned. "This is how he treats his own sister?"

"She is not his blood sister, and Teroz hates the girl's mother. So Paloma suffers for it."

"I do not understand you people, Gitano. I thought the Apache were fearless. Why do the men not stand up for the women?" Shadow Hawk moved forward and positioned himself between Paloma and Teroz. He offered his hand to the girl. "Come," he said gently, "I will help you carry the meat."

Paloma looked at Shadow Hawk with guarded eyes. Then, without speaking, she ran off.

"What is this?" Teroz asked, stepping forward and appraising Shadow Hawk. "Why is this Comanche in our camp?"

"I am Shadow Hawk, son of Black Hawk and Broken Moon, nephew to Ataza and Sotso. I am also your cousin."

Teroz glared at Shadow Hawk for a moment then threw his head back and laughed loudly. "You? You are no cousin of mine. I would not have a Comanche as my dog, much less my relative."

Shadow Hawk kept his temper in check. All those years of taunting by Red Arrow had taught him to be patient. "And I would not have someone who hits women as a relative of mine."

Teroz stepped even closer, his teeth clenched. "I could break you with my bare hands."

"I am sure you could, Cousin. But I do not think you will, unless you want to see your insides spill onto the ground." Shadow Hawk had drawn his knife and he touched the point against Teroz's bare belly, forcing him to back up a step.

"Enough!" Ataza's voice could be heard above everything else in the camp as he rushed to his two nephews. "Put your knife away, Shadow Hawk."

"How can you have this dog in our midst, Uncle? It is not right."

Shadow Hawk put his knife away and watched his uncle. Ataza had the kind of strength that Teroz would never have and even Teroz seemed to know it. The younger man appeared to shrink, his bravado fading into silent respect.

"Did you decide to become chief while you were hunting, Teroz? Did you have a vision?"

"He is Comanche!" Teroz spat the name.

"He is also Apache, and he is my sister's son. He is welcome here."

"I do not welcome him."

"You would do well to hold your tongue, Teroz."

"My father will not be pleased that you have allowed an outsider into our camp. Listen, Uncle, I think—"

Ataza put a firm hand on Teroz's shoulder. "You broke a sacred rule today, Nephew. You came into this camp and boasted of your ability as a hunter. You offered to give people meat only if they helped you. That is not our way."

Teroz shrugged free of Ataza's hand. "It is my way. Do you think I am frightened of the spirits? I laugh in their faces!"

Ataza struck Teroz across the face. Everyone was shocked into silence. Ataza was known as a gentle man. "You mock everything we hold sacred."

Teroz did not flinch from the slap. "And you mock our people by allowing this Comanche into our camp."

"This Comanche is also my nephew, and he will be treated with respect."

"Just as you treat me with respect, Uncle?" Teroz asked, rubbing his face.

"What is this, Ataza? Why have you hit Teroz?" Another man, built almost as powerfully as Teroz, appeared at the top of the path.

"Why do you permit your son to act as he does, Sotso?"

"My son is the best hunter in the camp and a brave fighter." He looked past Ataza and saw Shadow Hawk. "Who is this?"

Teroz stepped forward to stand next to his father. "This is your nephew, Father. Did you know you have a Comanche for a nephew?"

Sotso looked at Shadow Hawk. "What is your name?"

"My name is Shadow Hawk."

"Why are you here?"

"My father was killed and I promised him I would bring my mother back to her people." Shadow Hawk watched Sotso's eyes widen.

"Broken Moon is here?" Sotso turned to Ataza. "This is true?"

"Yes, it is true, Sotso. She is well."

"Can this be possible?" Sotso's features softened.

"Father, what are you going to do about this Comanche?" Teroz glanced at Shadow Hawk. "Not even a full Comanche. Look at his eyes."

Sotso ignored Teroz, still speaking to Ataza. "Where is Broken Moon?"

"She is at my lodge."

Sotso nodded and walked away without looking back.

Teroz faced Shadow Hawk. "This is not over between us."

"Enough, Teroz," Ataza said, obviously trying to control his anger. "Shadow Hawk is welcome in this camp. I have spoken."

Teroz reached down and rubbed the place where Shadow Hawk's knife had pricked his skin. His eyes, dark with hatred, raked Shadow Hawk's face. Then he walked away, angrily shoving his way through the throng of people that had gathered.

"I am sorry, Uncle," Shadow Hawk said quietly.

"I am not. He deserved it." Gitano was smiling.

"Leave us!" Ataza commanded his eyes fierce. Gitano's smile faded and he walked away. Ataza pulled Shadow Hawk aside. "You did nothing wrong. I saw what you did to help Paloma."

"I have seen the way some Comanche men treat their women. My father hated it. How can a man truly feel like a man if he hurts a woman or a child?"

Ataza nodded his head and grasped his nephew's shoulder. "I am pleased to have you here. I wish I had known your father. I am glad to know that he treated my sister in such a way." Ataza smiled suddenly. "Of course, knowing my sister, he had no choice."

Shadow Hawk nodded. "There was a time about two summers ago when I thought I no longer had to listen to my mother. So one day I openly defied her in front of many people in the tribe. I knew it was wrong because I saw the hurt in her eyes. But I could not stop myself and I said cruel things to her." Shadow Hawk was silent for a moment. "I had never seen my mother cry. When I saw her tears I felt ashamed. By the time my father returned from the hunt, I had forgotten what I had done to my mother." Shadow Hawk smiled weakly. "My father said nothing to me, but I could tell by his eyes that he knew what I had done. One day we rode together and he told me what pride he had in me. Then he spoke of the way he respected me because I was unafraid to show my affection for my mother. I told him what I had done and I admitted to him that there had been an odd sense of power in my cruelty, even though I knew it was wrong. He told me to go alone into the mountains to discover my true power, my medicine."

"That is how children learn, Nephew."

"I went to the mountains. I stayed there for many days. At

first I hunted, but then I decided to fast to cleanse myself."

"Did you find your medicine, Nephew?"

He nodded, remembering. "I saw the shadow of the hawk pass over me and when I looked up, I could see into his yellow eyes." Shadow Hawk paused. "I returned to camp and I apologized to my mother. I told her how much I respected her and how thankful I was for the life she had given me." Shadow Hawk turned away from Ataza, suddenly overcome with emotion. "My mother said that no woman could love a son more than she loved me." He looked at Ataza, his head held high. "I often speak of my father and what he has taught me, but I have learned much from my mother. She is wise in ways that no man knows."

Ataza nodded. "Yes, I know. Even as a child Broken Moon understood things that Sotso and I did not." Ataza's voice was gentle as he spoke. "I am honored that you shared this story with me, Shadow Hawk."

Shadow Hawk watched as Ataza walked away, his blue shirt reflecting the sky above. He had never told anyone about his vision except Black Hawk, but he was glad he had told Ataza.

Shadow Hawk stood awkwardly as some girls walked by him, staring and giggling. Suddenly he wanted nothing more than to be with people he knew, and people who knew him. He started toward the lodge to find his mother and Brave Heart. He straightened his shoulders and began to walk. Halfway across the camp he saw Gitano and Miho coming toward him. Shadow Hawk sighed deeply. He was not ready for another fight with another cousin.

"Shadow Hawk, come walk with us."

Shadow Hawk shook his head. "I must see if my mother needs help."

"Your mother is with her own people now, Shadow Hawk," Miho said harsly.

Before Shadow Hawk could respond, Gitano interrupted. "Do not mind him, Cousin. He is angry because our father spoke of your good deed."

"It was a foolish thing to do." Miho could not hide the irritation in his voice.

"Perhaps," Shadow Hawk replied, "but I saw no need for the girl to be hit simply because she dropped Teroz's meat."

"There are some things you cannot change, cousin," Miho replied tersely.

"Would you stand by if Teroz hit Singing Bird or Gitano?"

"That is different."

"Why?" Shadow Hawk stood straight, willing to confront Miho.

"Because they are my family."

"It does not matter that Paloma is no relation to me, Miho. It matters that she is an innocent girl who was hurt by a man twice her size. It is not right."

"He is right, Brother. How many times have we seen Teroz bully people just for the fun of it?"

"We cannot watch Teroz all the time."

"I am proud of Shadow Hawk for standing up to Teroz." Gitano stood next to Shadow Hawk, slapping him on the back. "What did it feel like to press your knife into his belly, Cousin?"

Shadow Hawk shook his head. "Do you never stop talking, Gitano?"

"No, he never stops," Miho replied, reaching down to pick up a rock from the ground. "He is not a brother to me but to the crow. Is that not right, Gitano?" Miho laughed as Gitano shoved him. "He can even jabber in the white man's tongue."

"You will be sorry someday, Brother. If we are ever captured by the whites, I will be able to talk my way out. But you, you will be hung!" Gitano put both hands around his throat and made a choking sound.

Shadow Hawk shook his head. "I believe you could talk your way out of anything, Gitano."

"Unlike you two, I prefer to use my wit rather than my knife."

Shadow Hawk exchanged an amused glance with Miho and clapped Gitano on the shoulder. "I must go now." Shadow Hawk walked toward his uncle's lodge. He ignored the continued stares of the girls and women as he passed them. He didn't know if they talked about him because he was Comanche or because he had almost fought with Teroz.

When he approached Ataza's lodge, he saw Brave Heart sitting out in front with Singing Bird. They were both laughing.

"Hello, Brother," Brave Heart said. He was helping Singing Bird scrape a deer skin.

"Hello, Singing Bird. How is it you got my brother to help you?"

Singing Bird blushed. "Miho and Gitano never help me. But your brother is different." She smiled at Brave Heart.

"Yes, he is," Shadow Hawk mused, looking at Brave Heart. The boy was smart. What better way to get a girl's attention than to help her?

"You have a visitor, cousin," Singing Bird said. "Inside the lodge."

Shadow Hawk went inside. He still didn't feel comfortable here. He was used to a much taller lodge. In this one, he couldn't stand up straight. He saw someone sitting on the floor of the lodge. "Is that you, Mother?" He realized after he said it, his mother wouldn't be sitting alone in the lodge.

"I am Paloma. I wanted to thank you for helping me." The girl stood up. "You were brave to face up to my brother like that."

The light in the lodge was dim, but even the shadows couldn't hide how lovely Paloma was. "You do not need to thank me."

"But I do."

"I do not understand why. He is not yet a man."

"He fights like a man."

"He is your brother, Paloma. Your brother is supposed to protect you."

"He is not my brother. My mother married his father. That is all."

"And your mother? She will say nothing to Sotso?"

"Sotso is just the same when he is angry."

"I am sorry, Paloma."

"You are a strange boy. From what tribe do you come?"

"The Comanche to the east."

"But Broken Moon is your mother?"

"My father took my mother captive many summers ago. I grew up in the Comanche camp. I have known no other home."

"Will you return to the Comanche?"

Shadow Hawk shrugged. "It is my only home." He looked at Paloma. "Will you be punished for coming to talk to me?"

"It does not matter. I wanted to thank you." Paloma walked to the door of the lodge. "I talked to your mother today. It is easy to see why you are so kind."

Shadow Hawk followed Paloma out the door. She flashed him a tentative smile, then quickly hurried across camp, her full skirt swinging with her stride.

Shadow Hawk squatted next to Singing Bird. "Is Paloma Apache?"

"Jicarilla Apache. Sotso took her mother, Lota, for his wife many summers ago. She had lost her husband and she and Paloma were alone. Sotso's wife had died and he needed a wife, so he married Lota. He does not love her." She lowered her voice. "It is said he beats her."

"I cannot believe he is blood brother to Ataza," Shadow Hawk said.

Singing Bird looked up from her work. "Sotso is cruel."

"And what do you think of Teroz, Cousin?"

"I think you ask too many questions, Brother," Brave Heart interrupted, staring at Shadow Hawk.

"It is all right," Singing Bird said quickly, smiling at Brave Heart. "I do not think that Teroz is as bad as everyone says. He knows no other way. Look at Sotso."

"You do not hate him?" Shadow Hawk asked, surprised.

"No, I do not hate Teroz. He has never hurt me. I do not even fear him."

"Why is that, Singing Bird?" Shadow Hawk was intrigued.

Singing Bird laid down the skin, rubbing her hands together. "Teroz has helped me many times."

"What do you mean?"

"Miho and Gitano left me in a tree once and I could not climb down. Teroz climbed up and carried me down on his back."

"Teroz?"

"Yes, Teroz. He also carried me back to our camp when I was bitten by a scorpion."

"This is the same Teroz that your brothers hate?"

"It is different with boys, is it not?" Singing Bird looked up at Shadow Hawk with large brown eyes. "Miho also tries to act like an angry bear, but he has a soft heart."

"So, Brother, do you plan to do woman's work all day or do you wish to walk with me?" Shadow Hawk smiled at Singing Bird when he spoke.

"I will help Singing Bird a while longer. Perhaps I will walk with you later. Perhaps if all men did women's work, Cousin, they would not have so much idle time on their hands." Singing Bird smiled again. Her teeth were even and white.

"I cannot argue with a girl as smart as you, Singing Bird." Shadow Hawk walked away, marveling at the change in Brave Heart. He seemed happy and he looked healthier already. It appeared that living here would be good for him.

Shadow Hawk spent as much time as he could with Gitano. Together they rode to the valley floor and followed the river down into the canyon. Gitano had promised him that soon they would follow the canyon all the way to the desert.

Sotso and Teroz had left camp again and Shadow Hawk was glad. He had managed to avoid them both but he knew it bothered his mother.

This morning he rose early and walked alone to watch the sun rise from the great natural stairway of tumbled boulders above the camp. On his way back down, he saw his mother. Standing with her was Sotso.

"Shadow."

Shadow Hawk stopped when he saw his mother. Broken Moon stepped away from her brother and placed her hand lightly on Shadow Hawk's forearm.

"Shadow Hawk, it is time for you to greet your uncle."

Shadow Hawk nodded. There was no look of welcome in Sotso's eyes. "I am pleased to meet you," Shadow Hawk said with careful politeness. "I have heard stories of you and Ataza for many years."

"And in these stories, was Ataza always the hero?"

Shadow Hawk hesitated. Sotso's face was impossible to read. Was he making a joke? Or was he trying to provoke an argument? "There was no hero in the story, Sotso. My mother only spoke of you two with love."

Sotso eyed Shadow Hawk suspiciously. "What is it you want here, boy?"

Shadow Hawk felt the pressure of his mother's hand on his arm increase. "I want only for my mother to be happy."

"My sister is happy now. You can go back to your people."

"Sotso!" Broken Moon said sharply. "Shadow Hawk is my son. If he is not welcome here, then I am not welcome."

"He is a Comanche," Sotso said angrily.

"And I was the wife of a Comanche."

"Against your will."

"But it became my choice as the years passed. Many times Black Hawk offered to take me home."

Sotso made a sound of disbelief and Shadow Hawk saw

his mother's face darken with anger. "At least," Sotso said deliberately, "you remember our ways and do not interfere in the affairs of others."

"No girl deserves to be hit," Shadow Hawk replied evenly. "Tell me, Sotso, would you have hit your own sister if she dropped meat on the ground?"

Sotso tensed. "You are an insolent boy."

"I merely asked you a question."

Sotso glanced at his sister. "I never hit her. I loved her. Tell him, Broken Moon."

"It is true. Sotso and Ataza were my protectors."

"Then why do you not teach your son to behave the same way toward his own sister? I do not understand."

"It is not for you to understand. You are only a boy. I do not have to answer to you." Sotso looked at Broken Moon. "I am pleased that you are back with us, little sister. My heart is full. But do not expect me to welcome your son." Sotso walked away.

"Sotso!" Broken Moon cried.

"Do not, Mother," Shadow Hawk held her back. "It does not matter."

"It matters to me, Shadow. You are my son. I love you." She reached up and gently stroked his cheek.

"I am sorry, Mother. It seems no one will accept a Comanche here."

"Should we go back home? Perhaps it was a mistake to come here," Broken Moon said sadly.

Shadow Hawk put his hands on his mother's shoulders. "You are happy here, Mother. We will stay."

"Shadow—"

"Do not argue with me, Mother. Father prepared me for this. I am strong. My only wish is for you to be happy."

Broken Moon hugged her son. "You have much of your father in you. Thank you, Shadow."

*   *   *

The weeks passed quickly for Shadow Hawk. He thought less often about going back to the Comanche. His mother's life was here now, and he would not leave her. He avoided Sotso and Teroz as well as he could. Sometimes he saw Paloma and her mother, Lota. Lota rarely smiled, and when she spoke to Paloma or Teroz, her voice was sharp, bitter. She went about her work in silence, graceless, as though she resented everything she had to do.

Shadow Hawk found solace in Gitano's company. Even Miho, though he remained somewhat distant, seemed to accept him. They hunted together, and Shadow Hawk began to learn the skills of his Apache cousins. In return, he began to teach them Comanche horsemanship. Shadow Hawk took secret delight in Miho's astonishment of his skill.

Ocha, his grandmother, quickly became one of his favorites, and he made it a point to visit with her each day. At first he often sought out Brave Heart, but his brother had already made new friends and it was easy to see that his friendship with Singing Bird had grown to be something special. Brave Heart seemed like a different boy. He was still small but he had gained weight, and his eyes reflected his newfound contentment.

Then there was Ataza. He was strong and he was wise. He made a point of showing Shadow Hawk their way of life and asking him questions about the Comanche way of life. Ataza had made Shadow Hawk feel like he was one of his own sons, like he was truly one of the family.

Shadow Hawk's life had settled into a peaceful routine that ended abruptly when whites attacked a hunting party. Ataza and his council decided to retaliate. Ataza did not wish to start a war with the whites, but he wanted to give them a warning. Around the smoky council fire, the plan was laid. They would ride to several ranches, steal horses, and return to camp.

Against Sotso's wishes, Ataza convinced the other warriors that his nephew should be allowed to go along on the raid. Who else, he maintained, could handle the stolen horses better than a Comanche?

Shadow Hawk was eager to go. He wanted to prove himself, and even more, he wanted to learn how the Apache raided. He knew that his uncle had risked much by convicing the others to allow him to go. He vowed that he would make his uncle proud.

As they rode, Ataza asked Shadow Hawk to show Sotso and Teroz the new trick he and his sons were learning. Shadow Hawk understood that Ataza was giving him a chance to prove himself to Sotso and Teroz.

Shadow Hawk cinched a rawhide strip around his horse's belly, then secured another loop around its neck. Kneeing the paint into a gallop, he rode away from the group. As he turned to come back toward them, he slipped his left elbow into the neck loop and his right foot beneath the belly band. He pounded past them, lying hidden along the far side of his galloping horse. He heard Gitano shout in admiration, and remembered the first time his father had shown him the trick. It was impressive. An apparently riderless horse hid a warrior who could shoot beneath his horse's neck without exposing himself as a target. Shadow Hawk circled the others twice to show that the position could be held for a long time. Then he slid back astride his horse and pulled the paint back into a trot next to his cousins.

"He makes it look easy, does he not, Brother?" Gitano was looking at Miho, but his voice was pitched to carry. "I do not think any of us is strong enough to match him."

Shadow Hawk saw Teroz glance sharply at Gitano. If Ataza had meant for Shadow Hawk to impress Sotso and Teroz, the plan had failed. They were both scowling.

"The Comanche," Teroz said slowly, without looking at Shadow Hawk, "has much need to hide from his enemies. We do not."

Shadow Hawk could not ignore the remark. "Everyone knows the Apache often ends a fight by disappearing into the shadows." Shadow Hawk urged his paint into a lope and rode slightly ahead. After a few moments, Gitano joined him and the two of them rode apart from the group.

They had left early in the morning and had ridden down the mountain and into the foothills. Bearing west, they descended into the long river valley, where Shadow Hawk had first seen Teroz and Sotso returning from the hunt. They followed the valley out of the mountains. The sides of the valley became steeper as they went, and rockier. The soil beneath their horses' hooves became sandier and drier as they rode. The cedar and pine trees gave way to sumac and chemise. Scrub oak grew along the rim of what was now a canyon. The trail narrowed and Shadow Hawk was forced to ride closer to the others, but Gitano stayed beside him and they spoke only to each other.

At the mouth of the canyon, Ataza led them south across the sun-scalded desert. Within a few hours they came upon a fence line. Ataza pulled up to survey the area. Shadow Hawk dismounted and touched the wire. "What is this, Uncle?"

"The whites build these thinking they will keep us out and their cattle and horses in."

"For the animals, yes. But for us, what good does it do?"

"They seek to deter us, but if they keep attacking our hunters, they must know that nothing will keep us out."

"How long do we sit here, Uncle?" Teroz interrupted. "If the Comanche does not understand what to do on a raid, leave him here."

"He understands well enough, Teroz. It is you I worry about." Ataza glanced at Sotso, silently bidding him to stay quiet. "I want no bloodshed. If you must shoot, shoot only to defend yourself."

"You ask too much, Uncle."

"Then perhaps you should stay here. I want no one here who will not follow me."

"He will do as you say, Brother," Sotso interjected.

Ataza nodded. "Good. Remember, they will not be

expecting us to ride onto their land while it is still light. Take as many horses as you can. Let the cattle run loose. Scatter them. They will want to get the cattle back before they chase us."

Ataza found a slack place in the wire and bent it back and forth with his hands. When it snapped, he pulled it back, opening a big section of the fence. He broke the top wire the same way. They weighted the bottom strand with rocks, pinning it to the ground. Ataza directed half of the men to ride east, while he directed Sotso, his sons, and his nephew to keep riding south.

Shadow Hawk had never been on a raid, but he had heard many stories from his father. The Comanche were known for stealing horses from whites and from other tribes, and many times they, too, chose not to fight. That was the point of a raid—to steal without getting caught.

Shadow Hawk looked around. He wondered where the men were who worked on the ranch. Ataza told him that many times he had seen men riding the land, moving the cattle, but here there were none. There were cattle grazing in the hills, lazily moving from spot to spot, occasionally lifting their heads to look at the riders. In the distance, there was a ranchhouse. As they approached it, he could see a woman's clothing hanging from a line to dry in the breeze. The ranchhouse was small and not what he had expected. There were no people here, no crazy white men with guns and rifles. How could this place pose a threat to them? No one was even here to protect the horses.

Shadow Hawk and Gitano dismounted and went to the barn, while the others rode around to the corral and the horses. Shadow Hawk opened the big double doors. He pulled the large hunting knife from the sheath on his thigh. Tense and ready, he looked into the shadowy interior but nothing moved. He went inside. Gitano followed.

"Do you see anything of value, Cousin?" Gitano whispered.

Shadow Hawk looked around and pointed to the tack hanging on the back wall. His eyes rested on a gleaming silver saddle. "That saddle is of value."

"I do not covet it, Shadow, but I will get it for you."

Shadow Hawk walked around the barn. The stalls were empty and he saw nothing of value, except a rifle that was leaning against a wall. He had never used one. Some of his people used them, but his father insisted the he learn to fight in the traditional way. But he had seen how much the Apache prized the rifle, so he tucked it under his arm.

Gitano headed outside with the saddle. Shadow Hawk was about to follow when he heard a noise from the loft above. Quietly, he moved to the ladder and inched his way up toward the loft, his knife held in front of him, the rifle still under his arm. When he reached the top he saw nothing but bales of hay and loose-piled straw. He waited, unmoving, on the ladder.

The sound came again, a rustling in the stacked bales. So, this is what whites did when they saw warriors coming? He started to call Gitano but thought better of it. Perhaps it was just some small animal. He held the rifle in front of him as if he knew how to use it, and moved into the loft. When the sound did not come again, he grew impatient. Careful and ready to fight, he climbed onto the stack, peering into the crevices between the heavy bales. He had prepared himself to fight, but what he saw caused him to lower the rifle. A girl about his age had wedged herself down into the hay. She looked up at him, her face contorted with fear. She had luminous blond hair that hung almost to her waist, and her eyes were a pale blue. Shadow had not seen many white people in his life. This girl and the lightness of her skin astonished him.

She looked at him, her eyes pleading, but she uttered not a word. It was obvious that she was trying very hard to be brave. Shadow Hawk couldn't stop staring at her—here was a white girl with hair the color of cornsilk and eyes the color of a clear spring day. He wondered what Teroz would say if he brought her back as a captive. There was no doubt in his mind, this girl was a prize. But as he thought about taking her captive, he just as quickly remembered his mother. She had often told him of the fear she had endured when his father had first taken her.

"Are you going to kill me?" the girl asked in a small, tremulous voice, her large eyes unable to hide her fear. She had spoken in English and he had understood her clearly.

He was about to reply when he heard voices below. He recognized Teroz's belligerent tone. Shadow Hawk pushed the girl back down into the hay and jumped down from the bales. He went to the ladder and began climbing down. He heard a clicking sound.

"You are lucky, Comanche, I almost shot you." Teroz slowly lowered his rifle.

Shadow Hawk dropped to the ground and looked at Teroz. "Gitano and I have already searched the barn. There is nothing in here, except this." He held up the rifle. "And a silver saddle."

"Forgive me if I do not trust you, Comanche. I will search for myself." Teroz pushed past Shadow Hawk, looking into each of the empty stalls. Shadow Hawk wanted to stop Teroz, but he knew if he tried, Teroz would suspect something. Shadow Hawk worried about the girl—he could well imagine what she would suffer at the hands of someone like Teroz. He forced himself to leave the barn, hoping that the girl would keep herself well hidden.

Shadow Hawk mounted his horse, looking around him. Still there were no white people, only the girl. Had her family left her here alone? Miho and the others had released the horses from the corrals and were running them past the house, while still other Apache rummaged through the house, carrying clothing, pots, sugar, and liquor.

They rode out, driving the stolen horses. Shadow Hawk looked for Teroz in the confusion but could not spot him.

Gitano whooped exuberantly, slapping Shadow Hawk as he galloped past. Shadow Hawk's paint lunged into a gallop, trying to keep up with Gitano's horse.

They pushed the horses hard, until they reached the fence line, then eased the pace. Crossing the desert, Shadow Hawk squinted against the dust raised by the running horses. He still hadn't seen Teroz. Where was he, and had he found the girl?

At the mouth of the canyon, they watered the horses and waited for the rest of the men to catch up. Shadow Hawk rode through the herd, pushing them back from the stream, making sure none of them drank enough to founder. There were hoofbeats, and the rest of the Apache rode up, coming from different directions, driving horses before them. He heard Sotso call Teroz's name and jerked around to look. Teroz had the white girl in front of him on his horse, a muscular arm locked around her waist. Her face was dirty and her long, honey-colored hair was tangled. All Shadow Hawk could do was watch.

"Comanche dog, look at what you were too stupid to find!"

Shadow Hawk forced himself to ignore Teroz's taunts, but he could not ignore the look in the girl's eyes. He wanted to help her, but for now, at least, it was impossible.

Ataza led the raiding party through the canyon and up into the mountain stronghold. Several warriors came after the raiding party, dragging brush behind their horses, obscuring all of their tracks. Shadow Hawk, Miho and Gitano guided the horses into the upper pasture, then dismounted and started up the path to the camp.

"Did you see Teroz's captive?" Gitano asked.

"What will he do with her?" Shadow Hawk tried to sound disinterested.

"Come, Cousin, you are not that young. You know what Teroz will do with her." Miho's tone was impatient.

"But she is only a girl. It is not right, Miho."

"She is old enough to bear children."

Shadow Hawk shook his head. "It is not right."

"It does not matter. It is not our concern," Miho responded, looking at the rifle Shadow Hawk had given him earlier. "This is a fine gift, Cousin. Thank you."

"What of the girl, Miho?"

Miho stopped in his tracks, his face a mask of anger. "The girl is white. She is a captive. If I were to be captured by the whites, do you think that one of them would care what happened to me?"

"What about Singing Bird? What if she were captured by the whites? Would you not hope that one of them would be kind to her?"

Again Miho stopped. "Why does this matter so much to you, Cousin? She is only a white girl. Soon she will be traded."

"You speak as if she were a horse, Miho."

"And you speak like a white man." Miho shook his head. "I do not know what to think of you, Cousin."

"I do not care what you think of me, Miho. The girl does not belong here. She belongs with her people."

"Teroz will kill you if you try to take the girl from him. She is valuable to him now. He can probably trade her for many horses. You must understand that, Shadow Hawk."

Shadow Hawk was silent as he walked with his cousins. He did understand what Miho was saying. Many times his people had taken captives, many times they had been traded. Why was this girl so different?

"You have not even asked about your saddle, Shadow Hawk. Perhaps I have decided to keep it for myself."

Shadow Hawk glanced at Gitano. "Keep it, I do not care."

"I was only joking. The saddle is yours."

"Where is the girl?" Shadow Hawk asked, distracted.

Gitano shrugged his shoulders. "Teroz dragged her up the path before us."

"He has probably taken her to Sotso's lodge. He will want

to show her off. The women will want to look at her," Miho said.

Shadow Hawk walked faster, passing through the camp without a nod to anyone. He could see the girl before he reached Sotso's lodge. Teroz was holding the girl by her long hair so that she couldn't move. A group of men and women stood around them, looking at the girl, appraising her strengths and weaknesses. The girl never uttered a sound, but the look on her face betrayed her fear. Shadow Hawk started forward, but he felt a hand on his arm.

"This is not your fight, Shadow," Broken Moon said softly. "I have seen that look on your face too many times before."

Shadow Hawk had not even seen his mother. "Look at her, Mother."

"I do not have to look at her to know the kind of fear she is feeling, Shadow." She tugged his arm until they were back, away from the crowd of people. "What are you going to do?"

"I am going to help her."

"You think Teroz will let you take the girl from this camp? He and Sotso would shoot you and her before they would let that happen."

"Mother—"

"Listen to me."

"She is so young, Mother."

Broken Moon spoke in a hushed voice. "If you are determined to help her, wait until night comes. Show no interest in this girl. Do not let Teroz think you even care about her. He will leave her tied up outside the lodge for many days to break her spirit. You must wait for the cover of darkness if you are to have any chance at all."

Shadow Hawk looked at the girl and the crowd that so obviously enjoyed her humiliation, then he looked at Broken Moon. "These are your people, Mother."

"Right now I feel more kinship to that girl. Help her if

91

you must, Shadow, but be careful. If anything happens to you . . ."

"Nothing will happen to me, Mother."

Broken Moon sighed deeply. "Sometimes you are a troublesome child."

Shadow Hawk smiled, putting an arm around his mother's shoulders and leading her away. "It is good, then, that you have Brave Heart. He, at least, will give you no cause for worry."

"Yes, Brave Heart does not go in search of danger." Broken Moon shook her head slightly. "You risk your life for a white girl, a girl you do not even know. I wonder what your father would say."

"I think he would be proud. But even if he would not be proud, this is something I must do."

Chapter 5

Aissa Gerard had never been so frightened in her life. Here she lay on the ground in front of an Apache lodge, a rope around her neck, her hands tied behind her. Her body ached from the punishing ride, and already her wrists and neck felt raw from the rope. She was young, but she was not ignorant. She knew what was going to happen to her. She had heard stories of women who had been taken captive by Indians. Even if they were rescued later, they were never the same. Some of them even went crazy.

She was only fourteen years old, but she knew that her age wouldn't matter to the Apache who had taken her. All day he had held her possessively, and twice he had touched her breasts. It wouldn't be long before he'd be back. Aissa jerked at her ropes frantically. The pain of her already raw wrists stopped her hysteria.

She lay still, trying to calm herself. She thought about the Apache who had first found her in the loft. He hadn't come, as the rest of them had, to poke at her and pull at her hair and clothing. He had looked very different from the others. He was tall, his skin was not so dark, and his eyes were blue. He hadn't harmed her and had actually covered her with hay when he had heard the others. If only the ugly man hadn't found her, she might be home now with her father.

She closed her eyes and tried to escape into sleep. But her exhausted body refused to relax. Her father would be frantic with worry, but she knew he wouldn't find her. Apache captives were seldom found. She couldn't even remember which way they had come. The trail through the foothills had been long and unfamiliar to her. She wondered if she would ever see her father again and her eyes filled with tears. She just wanted to stay alive. Finally, in spite of her fear, she slept.

Aissa woke to feel a hand go over her mouth. Her body tensed and she tried to pull away. He was back. The Apache had come back for her. How could she live through this? She felt the ropes being cut from her wrists and taken from around her neck. The hands that touched her were gentle, reassuring. When she forced herself to open her eyes, she could see in the moonlight that it was the good one, the one who had tried to help her before. Her throat ached and tears of relief flooded her eyes. He kept his hand over her mouth, but when she didn't struggle, he took it away. Aissa nodded, trying to make him understand that she knew he was helping her.

He took her hand and helped her stand up. Following without question, Aissa let the Apache lead her into the night. They skirted the circle of lodges. Twice he gripped her shoulder and she froze. She couldn't hear anything, but she didn't move until he nudged her forward. She almost slipped as they hurried down the rocky path, but he steadied her.

Aissa heard voices and the Apache pulled her down behind a clump of piñon pines. He pointed through the branches. There were two lookouts sitting on a rock above them. She heard them laughing, and eventually both of them turned their backs to the path, absorbed in their conversation. The Apache pulled her into a stumbling run. They ran until her legs burned and her lungs ached.

Somehow, suddenly, there were horses. The Apache helped her mount, keeping her reins in his hand as he swung onto his own horse. Aissa wrapped her hands in the animal's mane as the Apache urged both horses into a gallop. For a long time he led her horse, riding hard.

Further on, when they neared the canyon floor, the Apache threw her her reins. He kneed his horse back into a gallop. Aissa rode after him, but as hard as she tried, she couldn't keep up. But she could see his silhouette in the moonlight, and she let it guide her.

She didn't know how long they rode, but finally he slowed down and then stopped. She pulled up on her horse. She could barely see the Apache's face in the darkness but she would never forget what he looked like. He had a strong, handsome face, and his eyes were kind. She wished she could see him once more in the daylight. He pointed south, and she knew he was showing her the way home. He wheeled his horse around and Aissa knew that in a second he would be gone.

"Wait," she cried. The Apache reined in and looked at her. She took a deep breath, struggling to think of a way to thank him. She touched the bruises on her neck and felt the chain of her locket. Impulsively, she slipped it over head.

"This was my mother's. I want you to have it." When he hesitated, she reached out for his hand, barely able to see it in the dark. She dropped the locket into his palm and closed his roughened fingers around it. She held onto his hand a moment, then turned her horse and rode south, toward home.

Ben Gerard stared at the whiskey bottle, wishing he was the kind of man who could drown his fear and sorrow in liquor. Every muscle in his body ached. He and the search party had ridden the hills until dark. After the moon had come up, he and Joe had continued searching, more because they couldn't stop than because they expected to find anything.

Aissa. For all fourteen years of her life, she had been the reason he had gotten up in the morning. Now she was gone. For the twentieth time he smashed his fist against the scarred wooden tabletop. First Celou to the fever, and now Aissa to the damned Apache! He should have taken them both away from this godforsaken land a long time ago. The image he had been fighting all night came into his mind again—Aissa terrified and struggling, helpless against her captors.

He stood up and paced to the window and looked out. The sky had paled and the sun would be up before long. He could ride into town and organize a bigger search party, but he knew it wouldn't do any good. He'd been sheriff for over ten years and had searched for Apache captives before. The ugly truth was that nobody found an Apache unless that Apache wanted to be found. He remembered the time he'd been tracking some Apache horse thieves. Five times he'd gotten close enough to see them, and five times they had disappeared as if they'd never been there.

He rubbed his hands over his face. In the breaking light of dawn, he could see Aissa's garden. The primrose was about to bloom. All Aissa had ever wanted was for him to fix up the ranch and help her with her garden. And he had never done any of it. Instead of spending money on repairs, he had squirreled it away. Ben laughed bitterly. He had even put the money down a damn hole like a squirrel. And there it sat, in that strongbox, beneath the trapdoor in his room. What good was it now? He could never send Aissa to Paris to meet Celou's family, he could never buy her those beautiful clothes she had dreamed about. He could never give her the life she should have had.

The sound of hoofbeats scattered his thoughts. Instinctively, Ben reached for his shotgun. His back pressed against the wall as he leaned to look out the window, tense and ready, prepared to fight if he had to.

A moment later the shotgun clattered to the floor and Ben

flung open the door. Numb with relief, he called his daughter's name as she rushed into his arms.

Shadow Hawk released his horse, letting it mingle with the herd. He made his way past the guard, climbing the rocks back up to camp. It was easy to get back into camp without anyone seeing him. Everyone slept well, full of the satisfaction after a good raid. He silently made his way behind the tall stand of piñon pines where he had arranged to meet Gitano. His cousin was asleep on a blanket. Gitano had brought another blanket for him and Shadow Hawk laid it out. He lay down, folding his arms beneath his head. It was a foolish thing he had just done, a very foolish thing. Had he helped the girl simply because his mother had once been a captive, or had he helped her because she was so young? He had seen other captives, but none of them had touched his heart as this girl had.

"It is done?" Gitano whispered in the dark.

"Yes. What did Teroz do when he found out she was missing?"

"I have heard nothing. Perhaps the great warrior had too much to drink celebrating the raid even to notice that she was gone. But I am sure we will all hear about it in the morning."

"Yes, I am sure we will."

"I do not envy you, Cousin. You cannot fight Teroz and win."

"I do not plan to fight Teroz. He can accuse me, but he cannot prove that I helped the girl."

"Why did you do it, Cousin?" Gitano asked.

"I do not know, Gitano. Perhaps because my mother was once a captive. When I saw the girl up in the loft, she was shaking like a frightened animal. I could not bring myself to hurt her in any way."

"That is the only reason?"

"I did not want Teroz to touch her. She is only a girl, Gitano. You saw her."

"In our band there are many girls her age who are already mothers. She is not so young."

"Her ways may not be like yours or mine."

"But you went against one of your own, Shadow Hawk."

"I am not an Apache, Gitano."

"And that is what Teroz will say when he forces my father to make you leave." Gitano sighed. "You may have done the right thing for the girl, but not for yourself. I will tell Teroz that you were with me the entire night."

"Thank you, Cousin. I hope I do not get you into trouble with your father."

"My father is a fair man. I do not think he will be so angry."

Shadow Hawk watched the stars glittering through the piñon branches. He reached into the pouch that hung on his belt and he felt the cold metal of the locket. It was a strange thing for the girl to do, to give him something that was of such value to her. He regretted that he had said nothing to her, but perhaps it was best.

He put the locket back into the pouch with the silver comb and watch his grandfather had given him. As he held the pouch in his hand, he realized for the first time that most of the medicine he carried was white man's medicine.

Through the hazy cloud of sleep, Shadow Hawk heard a voice, a voice that kept repeating his name. He opened his eyes and saw Teroz standing over him.

"Get up," Teroz snarled, nudging Shadow Hawk in the ribs with his foot.

"What are you doing, Teroz?" Gitano sat up and glared at his cousin.

"This Comanche dog set my captive free. I want to know where she is."

Shadow Hawk looked up at Teroz—he looked angry enough to kill. "Good morning to you too, Cousin," he said, stumbling to his feet.

"Where is the girl?" Teroz demanded angrily, his face inches from Shadow Hawk's.

Shadow Hawk bent down and picked up the blanket, pulling it around his shoulders. "I thought she was your captive, Teroz. Have you lost her already?" Shadow Hawk tried to appear confident, but he steadied himself. He knew he was provoking Teroz and he knew he might lose a fight if Teroz attacked him.

"I want you to swear on your father's soul that you did not help the girl escape," Teroz said smugly.

Shadow Hawk didn't like this. If he lied and swore something that wasn't true, evil spirits could follow him all of his days on earth. But if he didn't swear, Teroz would know the truth. "I swear nothing on my father's soul," Shadow Hawk said, measuring his words. "My father is at peace now and I will not disturb him."

"So, you admit that you are lying." Teroz moved forward.

"I admit nothing." Shadow Hawk held Teroz's angry eyes.

"I know that you helped her to escape."

"You can prove nothing." Shadow Hawk pushed by Teroz, bumping his shoulder as he walked past.

"I will make you pay. You had no right. She was my captive."

Shadow Hawk stopped abruptly and turned. He pushed the blanket from his shoulders and stood to confront Teroz. "You did not own her, Teroz. She did not belong to you." He stepped forward, for the first time ready to fight.

Teroz drew his knife and widened his stance. Shadow Hawk motioned for Gitano to get back. "I will fight you, Teroz, but there is no need for one of us to die."

"Thieves deserve to die."

"Draw your knife, Shadow," Gitano shouted, an instant before Teroz lunged forward. Shadow Hawk leapt to one side, rolling on the ground. When he regained his feet, his knife was in his hand. He felt fear but his hand was steady. Teroz was a formidable enemy, but Shadow Hawk had grown confident in his own skills and strength.

Teroz moved forward and Shadow Hawk watched for the small signs, the shifting of Teroz's weight that would help him anticipate what he was going to do, the direction Teroz would be looking. Teroz's lips were bloodless and his face was a cold mask of fury. Teroz's face held Shadow Hawk transfixed—the expression in his eyes reminded Shadow Hawk of a mountain cat he and his father had once cornered. The cat had seemed to feel no pain and fought on long after its wounds should have killed it.

Teroz lept at Shadow Hawk, slashing downward with his knife. Shadow Hawk managed to spin away, but Teroz's speed astonished him.

"Will you fight, Comanche? Your words sounded brave enough."

Shadow Hawk feinted to his right, then rushed Teroz, swiping at his face. Teroz staggered backward. Shadow Hawk took advantage of Teroz's momentary loss of balance and drove his fist into Teroz's jaw. He heard Teroz grunt in pain and surprise as he fell backward. As Teroz fell, he flung his arms wide, instinctively trying to break his fall. Shadow Hawk dropped to the ground, pinning Teroz's knife hand with his knee. He smashed the butt of his knife into Teroz's wrist over and over until Teroz loosened his grip. Shadow Hawk threw Teroz's knife as far as he could into the trees. He held his own knife over Teroz's face and spoke.

"It is more difficult to fight a man than it is a little girl, is it not, Teroz?" He lowered the knife until the point touched Teroz's throat. Then he stood quickly, anticipating Teroz's next move.

Slowly, Teroz stood up, rubbing his jaw. He looked at Shadow Hawk, his eyes unreadable. "So, the Comanche can fight after all."

Shadow Hawk waited for Teroz to make a move, but he did not. Instead, he walked slowly away. Shadow Hawk replaced the knife in its sheath.

He saw Miho and Gitano coming toward him. He hadn't even heard Gitano leave.

"Are you all right, Cousin?" Miho walked up to Shadow Hawk.

"Yes," Shadow Hawk replied, looking after Teroz, still wondering why he had quit so easily.

Gitano touched Shadow Hawk. "You are still alive. I cannot believe it."

"You do not give me much credit, Cousin."

"I have seen Teroz fight before."

"It is obvious that our cousin is a good fighter, Gitano. He was well prepared by his Comanche father."

Shadow Hawk grinned suddenly, startled by his own realization. "My father taught me much about fighting, but this time it was the white man's medicine that helped me." Shadow Hawk looked at Gitano. "Why did you bring Miho here?"

Gitano looked sheepish. "I thought you would need help and I did not want to go to our father." Gitano avoided Shadow Hawk's eyes. "I told Miho about the girl. I am sorry, cousin, but I feared for your life."

"My father will be angry when he finds out what both of you did."

"It was not Gitano's fault. I took the girl back. I asked him to help me."

Miho scowled. "Why would you do something so foolish? She was Teroz's property."

"No, Miho, she is no one's property. Teroz kidnapped her."

"It is the way with us. It is also the way with your people. What about your own mother? She was taken captive by

101

your father."

"It was my mother I was thinking about when I saw the girl."

"Still, it was not your place to interfere. Teroz will never forget this, Cousin."

"I am not afraid of Teroz."

Miho looked at Shadow Hawk and shook his head. "You came into this tribe unwelcome, and now you make things even worse for yourself by making an enemy of Teroz. You must be careful of him, Cousin."

"I could have cut his throat but I did not. Teroz should be careful of me." Shadow Hawk watched Miho. He seemed angry, but his mouth betrayed the signs of a smile. Miho threw a pebble into the dirt. "I have grown tired of you both," he said, looking from Shadow Hawk to Gitano. He turned and walked away.

Gitano watched his brother until he was out of sight and then he turned to Shadow Hawk. "I think Miho likes you, Cousin."

Shadow Hawk had watched the sun rise from the boulder stairway. Now he was walking north, across the ridge that overlooked the camp. He could hear laughter and the squeals of children as he started down the hill. This stream, which ran southward, emptied into the river which had carved the valley below the camp. The river was often muddy and was fouled by the grazing horses. But this stream flowed cold and clean all year long. The women washed their families' clothing in the swift water and upstream they filled water jugs. The steep sides of the little valley sheltered the herbs and roots that went into the making of many of the medicines used by the women. A flock of crows jabbered overhead. Shadow Hawk bent to pick up a rock and sailed it upward to scatter the pesky birds.

Shadow Hawk sat down to watch Brave Heart and

Singing Bird as they played in the stream. Brave Heart had grown and he seemed like a different boy, laughing and confident. His Apache was nearly perfect now. Soon, Shadow Hawk thought, he would have to teach him about fighting. He wouldn't be a child much longer.

The move to the Apache camp had been good for Brave Heart and for his mother but Shadow Hawk was unsure of his own place here. Teroz and Sotso aside, he felt a part of his mother's family. Still, there were certain things he missed about his people. But more than anything, he missed his grandfather. He wondered if he would ever see him again.

"Shadow Hawk." Shadow Hawk looked up to see Paloma leading Ocha along the embankment. He stood up and went to meet them. "Greetings, Grandmother. Paloma."

"Grandmother wanted to visit with you, Shadow Hawk. So I brought her here."

"Good," Shadow Hawk replied, leading Ocha to the embankment and gently sitting her down.

"May I talk to you for a moment, Shadow Hawk?" Paloma politely inquired.

"Do you mind, Grandmother?"

"Take your time. I will watch the children play," Ocha replied, a smile on her face as Singing Bird and Brave Heart yelled to her from the water.

Shadow Hawk stared at Ocha. He believed she could "watch" them because her senses were so attuned to everything around her. He walked to Paloma. "Are you all right, Paloma?"

Paloma was shy. She stared at the ground as she spoke, twisting her hands together in front of her. "I know you helped the white girl escape. I saw you cut her loose."

"You said nothing. Why?"

"You know why. I try to get along with Teroz, but he does not like me. He blames me for everything." She raised her eyes and looked at Shadow Hawk. "I am glad that you helped the girl."

"Why do you stay in Sotso's lodge? Why do you not live with Ataza?"

"He is not my blood uncle. I cannot come between him and his brother."

Shadow Hawk nodded. She was not related to Teroz or Sotso but was destined to suffer their abuse simply because her mother had replaced Teroz's mother. "How old are you?"

"I am old enough," she replied stubbornly.

"Old enough to be married?"

"No man would have me."

"Miho would gladly have you."

"Shadow Hawk, please. Do not say such things." A charming blush spread over Paloma's face.

"It is true. I have seen the way he looks at you. I have also seen the way you look at him."

Paloma shook her head. "Miho would never have me because of Teroz and Sotso. I am destined to remain with them the rest of my life."

"That is not so, Paloma. Someday you and Miho will be together if you wish it to be so."

Paloma's large, dark eyes filled with tears, and tentatively she reached out for Shadow Hawk's hand and squeezed it. "Thank you for being my friend."

Shadow Hawk held onto her hand, feeling a rush of pity for this shy, unhappy girl. "You will always be my friend, Paloma. Nothing will change that."

Paloma nodded her head. "Go now, Grandmother is waiting."

She pulled her hand free and turned so quickly that her bright skirt swirled around her legs. She called a farewell to Ocha, then ran up the path.

"Come here, boy. Sit by me," Ocha commanded.

Shadow Hawk sat down next to his grandmother.

"You think Paloma is pretty?" Ocha asked.

"She is very pretty."

"She is already spoken for, Shadow Hawk. I have heard stories of you wild Comanche."

Shadow Hawk laughed. "I am only fifteen summers old, Grandmother. I do not intend to marry for a long time."

"Good."

"Who has spoken for Paloma?"

"Miho, of course. In fact, he is probably jealous that you have become her friend."

"That is all it is, Grandmother. We are friends."

"Good," she nodded approvingly. "It is good for Paloma to have a friend like you." Ocha fixed her sightless eyes on the water. "So, tell me why you helped the white girl escape."

Shadow Hawk shook his head. He should have just taken the girl in daylight—it seemed that everyone knew what he had done anyway. "As I told Miho and Gitano, I did not want her suffering at the hands of Teroz."

"That is all?"

"I thought of my mother and how difficult it had been for her. It did not seem right."

"What did she look like, this white girl? They are such strange-looking creatures. I remember this clearly from the days when my eyes were not darkened."

"This one was beautiful," Shadow Hawk replied, his voice low as he recalled the girl. "Her skin was pale and soft-looking, her hair was the color of new cornsilk, and her eyes were like the sky on a cloudless day."

"You have made an enemy of Teroz, Grandson."

Shadow Hawk looked at his grandmother. "It is over, grandmother. I did what I thought was right."

"It is not over. You will have many battles with Teroz." Ocha spoke with authority.

"So be it," Shadow Hawk replied stubbornly. "I am not afraid of Teroz."

"You are angry with me."

"You say strange things, Grandmother. How is it possible

for you to know about Teroz and me?"

"I have lost the sight of my eyes. I no longer see the trees or the sky, or the children playing in the river, but I see other things more clearly. The white girl gave you something."

Shadow Hawk stared at Ocha, stunned. He reached into his pouch and took out the locket. He placed it in her hand. "She gave this to me for helping her."

Ocha ran her calloused fingers over the gold. "What is this, this round metal thing?"

"It is what the whites call a locket. They keep things inside it."

"What things?"

"Pieces of hair, pictures—"

"Pictures?"

Shadow Hawk realized for the first time how much he had learned from his white grandfather. How could he explain the strange white man's ways to his grandmother? He remembered his own astonishment the first time Marsh had shown him a picture of the white man's town, St. Louis. He had stared at the tiny square lodges and the people standing below, the size of insects. His grandfather had explained that the picture was small but that the people were as tall or taller than any Comanche. The lodges, he had said, were so big that a man falling from the top of one would die.

Shadow Hawk struggled to think of a way to explain this to Ocha. "Do you remember, Grandmother, when you were a little girl, you used to draw pictures in the dirt with your finger or with a stick?"

Ocha nodded, smiling. "Yes, I drew many pictures."

"And you remember the drawings that your people put on their blankets and clothing?"

"Yes, what has this to do with the metal object?"

"The whites draw pictures of people they love on small pieces of paper—" He used the English word.

"Paper, what is paper?" Ocha imitated the sound of the word.

Shadow Hawk sighed in frustration, searching for another word. "They draw a small picture on special cloth. See?" He opened the locket so that Ocha could feel the hollow place within it. "Then they put the cloth in here and close it up. They wear it around their necks. They believe it keeps them close to their loved ones."

Ocha considered what Shadow Hawk said. "Are you not sure an Apache thought of this idea? It sounds much too clever for a white man to have thought of it."

Shadow Hawk smiled and took the locket from Ocha. "I do not know who thought of it, Grandmother. I only know that my grandfather said it is a custom of many white women to wear them."

"And the girl gave you this?"

"Yes."

"Why did you not speak to her in the white man's tongue?"

Shadow Hawk sat silently. How did Ocha know these things? Many people in the band avoided her and said she spoke to spirits. Ocha did not frighten him, but her ability to "see" things that no one could possibly know unsettled him. "I thought it best to say nothing."

"The girl wanted to thank you so she gave you part of her medicine. This is a girl of great heart."

"Yes, Grandmother."

"Where is your heart, Shadow Hawk?"

Shadow Hawk stared at his grandmother. It was as if she could read his thoughts. He shifted nervously. "What do you mean?"

"Will you stay with the Apache, or will you go back to the Comanche? Or will you go to live with your white grandfather?"

"Please, Grandmother, do not speak that way about my grandfather." Shadow Hawk couldn't disguise the anger in his voice.

"I have said nothing bad about him."

"It was there, I heard it in your voice."

Ocha nodded. "You make me uneasy, boy. There are not many who hear beyond my words."

"I love my grandfather, Ocha. And so would you if you could know him."

Ocha shook her head. "The whites are so strange to me, Shadow Hawk, I do not know if I could love any white man. But I was sincere with my question, Shadow. Where does your heart lie?"

Shadow Hawk stared out at the water, smiling slightly as he watched Singing Bird and Brave Heart swim and play. "I do not know. I do not think I have ever known." Shadow Hawk felt Ocha's hand on his. He looked down at her small hand, worn by work and time, and he felt enormous affection for this old woman.

"One day you will know, Shadow. There will come a time when you will see very clearly where you belong and where your heart lies."

Shadow Hawk threw the colorful blanket over his father's horse and smiled. He was a beautiful animal, larger than most. He had carried Shadow Hawk's father into many battles without fear. He was magnificent paint, purest white, with splotches of black. Three of his socks were black, as well as most of his face. People seeing him for the first time always turned to watch.

Shadow Hawk was proud of the paint and took good care of him. He rode everyday, sometimes up the mountain, and sometimes down into the canyon. When he had first come here, the paint had been in good condition and a swift runner. Now he was superbly muscled, and like his rider, surer of foot and confident of the rocky terrain. He rubbed the silky-smooth skin of the horse's nose and fed him a peeled cactus apple. The herd was large now, and many of the mares taken on the raid were in foal. Shadow Hawk hoped that the paint had sired some of the colts. He wanted to give Brave Heart a good horse. The paint's sire had belonged to Old Bear, a prize from a raid in the old man's youth. Old Bear had given the first colt to Black Hawk.

Ataza walked up to Shadow Hawk. "You should be concentrating on your skills as a runner, not as a rider, nephew." Ataza patted the paint admiringly on the neck. "He is a beautiful animal. Your mother tells me that your father gave him to you when he went away."

"Yes," Shadow Hawk replied solemnly, not in the mood to talk about the horse or his father with Ataza. He'd been trying to think less often of his father, but the pain was still there.

"It was a generous thing to do."

"Yes."

"I have angered you," Ataza said, stepping around to the front of the horse and rubbing its nose.

"Yes, Uncle, you have angered me."

"Even so, I will ask you again. Why do you ride everyday, Shadow Hawk, when you should be building your strength as a runner? There will be times when you will not be able to ride your horse."

Shadow Hawk patted the animal on the neck and looked at his uncle. "Why do you assume that I will stay here, Uncle?"

"You seem content here. You have made friends with your cousins, many people like you. I thought you had decided."

"I have decided nothing." Shadow Hawk took the reins and started to lead his horse away.

"Wait, Shadow Hawk."

Shadow Hawk stopped, turning to look at his uncle.

"What has happened, Nephew?"

"Nothing has happened, Uncle. The problem is within me."

"Can I help you?"

"I do not think so."

"Perhaps what you need is to go away. Seek the answers

that you are looking for. There is a place over there," Ataza pointed across the valley to the mountains beyond. "It is more than a day's ride. You follow the ridge southward. There is an outcropping of rocks. A man who stands there can see all the way to the big river. It is a peaceful place, a place where you can think clearly."

"This is not a vision quest, Uncle."

"I did not say you would see visions, I said perhaps you would find answers."

Shadow Hawk smiled, apologetic. "Thank you, Uncle. I am sorry to be so much trouble to you."

"You are no trouble to me, Shadow Hawk. You are my sister's son, my blood. I want to help you if I can."

"You have already helped me."

Ataza fixed his eyes on the mountain above them. "When Broken Moon was kidnapped, I thought I would go mad from grief. She was my little sister and I loved her very much." Ataza looked sharply at Shadow Hawk. "I tried to kill your father, Shadow." He reached out and touched the paint. "Everytime I see this horse I am reminded of the day Broken Moon was taken from us. Your father rode a stallion that looked very much like this one."

Shadow Hawk stared at the stern, kind face of his uncle, a man he had come to respect, trying to absorb what Ataza had told him.

"It is strange to think, is it not, if I had killed your father, you would not be here."

"I did not know you saw my father, Uncle."

Ataza narrowed his eyes, remembering. "When I was unable to kill him, I quickly mounted and followed him. But I realized all too soon that my horse was not as swift as his and I could not match his skill as a rider. Still, I searched for Broken Moon for many moons but I could find no tracks, nothing to lead me to her. I blamed myself. If only I had stopped your father . . ." Ataza nodded toward the distant mountain. "When I returned, I packed my things and I rode to that mountain. I stayed there for five days. I walked, I sat, I slept, and I thought. By the night of the fifth day, I knew that Broken Moon was alive and that someday I would see her again."

"How did you know that, Uncle? Is it possible to see such a thing?"

"I saw Broken Moon. She was smiling and she was well. I knew in my heart I would see her again."

"Are you sure it is not something you wanted to see, Uncle?"

"I wanted to see it and I did see it, Shadow Hawk. It freed me from the guilt and sadness and allowed me to live knowing that Broken Moon was alive. Go there, to the mountain. Perhaps you will see what is important to you."

Shadow Hawk looked out into the distance. "Perhaps," he replied.

"Do what you must, Nephew." Ataza started to leave the pasture.

"Uncle," Shadow Hawk called to him. Ataza stopped and faced him. "Thank you. You have been very patient with me."

Ataza placed a strong hand on Shadow Hawk's shoulder. "If I could take away your pain and confusion, I would do that for you, Nephew. But that is not possible. This is something you must do for yourself."

Shadow Hawk sat atop the flat rock, his legs crossed, his hands folded loosely in his lap. Below him, the land stretched away, at first densely wooded, then dotted with brush. Along the horizon, a narrow band of shining silver marked the path that ran southward toward Mexico. He had been alone on this mountain for four days. It had been hot during the days and cold at night. He had eaten little and drunk only sips of water, moving from the high rocks only to care for his horse. He had tried to open his heart, but still he had seen nothing that would free him.

So now he sat unmoving, his eyes seeing but not seeing. Many things went through his mind. He remembered his father leaning down to swing him up off the ground and onto the back of the painted stallion. He had been frightened but excited. He remembered feeling like he was bigger than everyone. He could picture his father's hands, strong and warm, holding him so that he would not fall.

"I need your guidance, Father," Shadow Hawk whispered. "I wish I could speak to you one more time."

He felt the sun burning into his bare skin, yet he would not move into the shade. He heard the sound of a bird in the distance, and the nicker of his horse as it grazed by the creek below. He heard the treetops below him sigh in the breeze, but he could not feel it on his skin. A shrill cry sounded above him. He opened his eyes to look upward. A black hawk circled above him. Shadow Hawk's eyes watered and he lowered them. He stared in disbelief as the shadow of the hawk glided across the treetops below him, then passed onto the rock itself. The shadow was so distinct, so detailed, that he could see the splinters of sunlight between the flaring feathers of its wings and tail. He watched as the hawk's shadow came closer. How was this possible, he asked himself. He had wanted so badly to speak to his father. Black Hawk and Shadow Hawk—father and son.

Shadow Hawk closed his eyes. "I am afraid, Father. I am unsure where my path in life lies. It troubles me greatly."

The hawk screeched loudly again, but when Shadow Hawk opened his eyes to look, the majestic bird was gone. "I do not understand," he said softly. His mouth was dry, but he would not drink. He would give himself no comfort until he found the answers that he sought. He sat on the rock, unmoving, for the entire day. His body burned from the heat of the sun and his tongue felt thick for want of water. Sweat dripped down his face. Time became like the wind, endless, washing over him without passing. It must be like this for those who have gone, Shadow Hawk thought. But for those still alive, there would always be questions.

"The answers are not always so clear, my son."

Shadow Hawk jerked his head up and opened his eyes. "Father?"

"Close your eyes, Shadow. You will see me."

Shadow Hawk closed his eyes. He felt his heart beating hurriedly as he waited for the sound of his father's voice.

"I am here, my son. Let your body rest."

"I seek answers, Father."

"I cannot give you those answers, Shadow."

"But I need your guidance, Father. I do not know where to go."

"Where do you want to be?"

Shadow Hawk shook his head. "I want to be where I belong."

"And where is that place, Shadow?"

"I do not know, Father."

"Did you live in that place when you were with me and your mother?"

"Yes," Shadow Hawk replied quickly. "I was not so troubled there."

"What of the times you went to stay with your grandfather? Did you not go to him because you felt troubled?"

"Yes," Shadow Hawk replied slowly.

"And how do you feel in this place, with your mother's people?"

"I am not one of them."

"Why do you resist so much, Shadow?"

"I resist because . . ." Shadow hesitated.

"Tell me, Shadow."

His father's voice was deep, drowning out all other sounds around him. "I do not know why, Father."

"Look into your heart, my son."

Shadow Hawk was silent, his body still. He had no

answer. "Your time on this earth is short, my son. You cannot live it without making choices."

"Is it really that simple, Father?"

"Yes, Shadow, it is that simple."

Shadow Hawk waited to hear his father's voice again but there was only silence. He opened his eyes. He looked around him. "Father?" He said quietly, then raised his voice. "Father?" There was no response. He had heard his father's voice, he knew he had. Or had it all been a vision? Had he been so hot and thirsty that he saw his father only because he had wanted to?

He moved out of the sunlight and into the shade. He sat for a time, trying to reason with himself. Of course it had only been his mind playing tricks with him. He had not heard his father. He had only imagined his father's voice. There was no magic up on this mountain. Ataza was wrong. There had been no answers here.

He climbed down to his small camp. He would have to feed and water his horse, but first he had to drink. He walked to his blanket and leaned down to pick up the drinking bag, but as he reached for it, his hand began to shake. He stared for a moment, then reached out again. It was a black feather, the tail feather from a hawk. His father had had a habit of leaving a black feather for Shadow Hawk whenever he went away. He had told Shadow Hawk that it meant he was always nearby, that the feather would bring him strength and good luck.

Shadow Hawk ran his fingers along the quill of the feather. It was an unusually long feather. He took a piece of the leather thong that held his pouch to his leggings and tied it around the end of the feather. He knotted the thong to his belt. His hands were steady now.

Many warriors had trophies hanging from their belts, many spoils of battles fought. This was not a trophy but a piece of good medicine. Shadow Hawk touched it again and looked up at the sky.

"Thank you, Father. You have helped me today. I will try to honor you." He would start back in the morning. It would be good to see Gitano. Perhaps it was time to accept his mother's people as his own.

A hawk screeched overhead and Shadow Hawk smiled. He was not surprised. His father would always be with him.

Chapter 6

"Aissa, Ray has come to visit you!"

Aissa Gerard looked up from her garden. Her father and Ray Grimes were standing on the porch of the house.

"I'll be up in a minute, Father," she replied, trying to control her irritation. She bent back down and grabbed a handful of choke-grass that was trying to strangle her primrose. She yanked it hard until it came out of the ground, roots and all. "Damned weeds," she said to herself, attacking yet another with a vengeance.

"Aissa, haven't I taught you better than to keep a guest waiting?" Ben stood on the edge of the garden, hands on his hips.

Slowly, Aissa stood up, wiping her hands on her apron. "You may be the sheriff in town, but out here you're just my father."

"You're an insolent child."

"It was your idea to invite Ray over here, Father, not mine."

"Still, it's rude to keep him waiting. He's anxious to see you."

"He's always eager to see me," Aissa responded wryly.

"You're acquiring a tart tongue, missy. You're still not so old that I can't take you over my knee, and—"

"I'm nineteen years old and you wouldn't dare." She stared at her father, her arms folded determinedly across her chest.

"What am I going to do with you? Ray's rich, he lives on a beautiful ranch, and I know he's interested in you."

"If I ever marry, it will be for love."

"You can't afford such romantic notions in this day and age, Aissa. I raised you to be more practical than that."

"Yes, but Mother was French and she was extremely romantic and idealistic. She encouraged me to dream." Aissa saw the change in her father's face. It had been eight years since her mother's death but her father still didn't like to talk about it. She put her arm through her father's. "I don't mean to hurt you, Father. I'm just not ready for love and marriage."

"If something should happen to me, what would you do, where would you go?"

"I wouldn't go anywhere. I like it here."

"If you're so determined to stay around this place, I at least want you to have a good life. Ray can give you that."

Aissa pulled off her gardening gloves, slapped the dirt from them, and tossed them by her rake. "I already have a good life," Aissa replied, her voice softening. "I love it here with you and I like being a teacher. I'm a good teacher, you know."

"But that's no life for a beautiful young woman."

"It's my life, Father. When are you going to realize that?" Aissa turned away from Ben and looked out at the mountains. She wondered if he was still up there, the Apache boy who had rescued her five years ago. She would never forget his handsome young face, or the storm-gray eyes that looked at her with such kindness.

"Why do you keep staring up at those blasted mountains? Do you think he's going to come riding out of them someday and take you away on his horse?" Ben gripped Aissa's shoulders. "Aissa, listen to me. This is not one of those medieval tales where the knight rides in to save the princess. This is hostile land filled with savages."

"And I wouldn't be standing here today if one of those savages hadn't saved my life."

"God, you are an exasperating child," Ben said angrily. "All right, I will grant you that he did a good thing. But it's been five years, five more years of training by his people to hate the whites. If he saw you again, I'm not so sure he'd save you this time."

Aissa refused to look away from the mountains. "I think he would."

"Everything all right here?"

Aissa turned around, barely able to disguise the look of annoyance on her face as Ray approached them. She had been seeing Ray for several months and it hadn't taken her long to discover that they didn't have much in common. She was hoping that he would realize it too, but he didn't seem to notice her long silences, or her lack of attraction to him—and there was something else. Aissa was uncomfortable when he snapped orders at his cowhands, or arrogantly demanded the best table in the hotel restaurant. Still, he was the most powerful man in the territory, and his attention flattered her.

"Why don't you come up to the porch and join us for a lemonade, Aissa?" Ben practically pleaded. "You can tend to the garden later."

Aissa considered her father's request. He wasn't asking much of her, after all. She wiped her hands on her apron. "All right, Father." She walked with the men to the porch and sat down on the swing. After her father had poured them some lemonade he made up some excuse, as he always did, and she was left alone with Ray on the swing, with nothing to say to him.

"How have you been, Aissa?"

"I've been well, Ray. You?" She sipped at her lemonade, trying to sound interested in what he had to say.

"Very well. In fact, last month we made more money than ever from the store. We're going to be selling lots of new items. We received a new shipment from St. Louis and—"

Aissa nodded, feigning interest, as again she looked out at the mountains. Where are you, she thought. I wonder, have you changed? If I could just see you one more time.

"Aissa."

"What?" Aissa looked at Ray. "I'm sorry, I didn't hear what you said."

"I asked you what you thought of this." Ray held a small box which contained a large diamond ring.

"It's nice, Ray," she managed.

"Nice? It came all the way from New York," he replied indignantly. Visibly calming himself, he held the box in front of Aissa. "I want you to have it."

"I couldn't possibly accept the ring, Ray." Aissa got up from the swing and leaned against the railing.

"But I want you to have it, Aissa," Ray argued, standing next to her. "You can't be walking around without an engagement ring on. What will people say?"

Aissa dug her fingernails into the wooden railing, trying to control her anger. So, Ray had already decided that they would get married. "I don't care what people say, I don't want to be engaged."

"You aren't seeing anyone else and I know there isn't anyone who can offer you more. I can give you lots of things, Aissa."

"I don't want lots of things, Ray." Aissa stomped down the stairs of the porch to the yard. She heard Ray's footsteps behind her and deliberately walked as fast as she could.

"Aissa, wait!"

Aissa stopped and turned so suddenly, Ray almost ran into her. "How dare you decide what's good for me." She put a finger to her head. "You see this, Ray? This is called a brain. With this brain I have learned to think for myself. I

119

don't need you or my father making decisions for me, do you understand?"

"I thought it was understood that we'd get married."

"Who understood it? I never understood it, because no one ever said anything to me. You and I don't even know each other that well."

"We know each other well enough."

"No, we don't. We don't know anything about each other."

"I don't see that you have many other prospects, Aissa."

There was no mistaking the sudden coldness in Ray's voice. Aissa looked at him. The coldness was also in his eyes. "Any other prospect would be better than this one." She turned and Ray gripped her arm.

"You're making a mistake. I'd make you a good husband. If your father dies and you're left out here all alone, how are you going to manage?"

Now she knew who had been putting worrisome thoughts into her father's mind. Aissa shrugged his hand away. "I'll find a way."

"I own all the land around your ranch."

"So?"

"If you couldn't keep up this place, I might just have to buy it back."

"Do you plan on taking the rest of our land, Ray, is that it? Wasn't it enough that your father stole everything else from my family?" Aissa whirled and ran to the corral where her father was working. His back was to her and he didn't hear her coming. She gripped the top rail of the fence and struggled to compose herself. "Father."

"Aissa?" Ben walked over to the fence, a puzzled expression on his face. "Where's Ray?"

"Make him go, Father, or so help me, I'll go inside and get the shotgun."

"What's wrong? What happened?"

"Make him go, Father."

Ben hesitated then nodded. "Wait here." Aissa watched her father as he walked to Ray. They talked for a few minutes and Ray seemed to be arguing, then he shrugged and went to his horse. After Ray rode away, Ben motioned for Aissa to join him on the porch. "What happened?"

"Why didn't you tell me he was going to give me an engagement ring?"

"I didn't know he was going to ask you today."

"But you did know he was thinking about it, didn't you? How could you do that to me?"

Ben walked to the swing and sat down, wearily wiping the back of his hand across his face. "I blame myself for your mother's death. If we'd lived in a big city, someplace with a real doctor, she probably would've survived that fever. But she never had a chance."

"It wasn't your fault."

"Your mother was beautiful, Aissa—the most beautiful woman I've ever known. Why she fell in love with me, I'll never know."

"I know," Aissa said gently, sitting down next to her father and taking his hand in hers. "She loved you because you are gentle and kind and you could always make her laugh."

"That's not enough, don't you see. We loved each other but I couldn't help her when she needed me. If I made more money, I could've sent her back to Paris to live."

"She never wanted to go back to Paris, Father."

"She spoke of it all the time."

"She only spoke of taking me there to meet her family. That's all. She loved it here. This land belonged to her family. Even if you had tried to force her, you couldn't have made her leave."

"This isn't a good place to raise a daughter. I should've taken you away from here after your mother died. We could've started over someplace new."

"Stop it, Father. I love it here just as much as Mother did."

"This is an unforgiving place, Aissa."

"This is my home. I belong here."

Ben shook his head. "I don't mean to force Ray on you. It's just that he could give you everything you deserve. He had so many men working on his ranch, he could even protect you."

"I don't need Ray to take care of me. You made sure I was educated so I could take care of myself. You even put some money away for me if something should happen. Why are you treating me as if I'm so helpless?"

Ben looked past the corrals and the barn into the wild country beyond. "This land scares me, Aissa. I can't always protect you."

"A husband couldn't always protect me, either, Father."

"But if something happened to me, at least you wouldn't be alone." Ben shook his head. "I keep thinking of the day you were taken by the Apache. I thought I would go crazy. I'd heard stories about what they do to their women captives. When you came back, I promised myself I wouldn't ever leave you alone again. I just want you safe, Aissa."

Aissa kissed her father on the cheek. "I want you to quit talking about leaving me alone."

"You know what Doc says about my heart. Could be anytime."

"He isn't even a real doctor. Besides, he's been saying that for over ten years and you're still as strong as a horse. Of course, if you gave up being sheriff and just worked on the ranch, your heart might be a little stronger."

"In a little two-bit town like this, it's not all that dangerous. Last week I had to put Dode Fisk in jail until he stopped crying and sobered up. The week before that, I didn't even have a drunk to lock up. I could never give up being sheriff, Aissa. It makes me feel like I matter to this town."

"All right, I'll make you a deal, then."

Ben ran his hand through his gray hair. "I don't like your deals."

"This one is fair enough. I won't ask you to give up being sheriff if you won't ask me to see Ray anymore."

Ben shook his head. "It's just not right. A girl your age should be thinking about marriage and children."

"I'm only nineteen, Father, I'm not thirty. When the right man comes along I will think about those things."

"You promise me?"

"Yes, I promise you."

"All right, it's a deal, then."

Aissa squeezed her father's hand and laid her head on his shoulder. She couldn't imagine spending the rest of her life with a man, having his children, and growing old with him. And her chances of meeting any man out here in the desert weren't good.

"What're you thinking about?"

"I was just wondering if I'll ever be as much in love as you and mother were." Aissa felt her father's arm go around her shoulders.

"It'll happen, missy."

"It will never happen if it's forced, Father. Do you understand that?"

"I think I'm beginning to. I'm sorry, Aissa. I was only doing what I thought was best for you."

"I know that, Father. But please, let me make my own decisions from now on."

"All right, I will. Just as long as you dispense with those romantic notions of that damned Indian boy. He'll never be back, Aissa."

Aissa gazed out onto the distant mountains. "I suppose."

"Why do you persist in thinking about him? I know you do. I see you staring out at those mountains all the time like a damned fool. And I'll tell you something else, I wish to hell you'd never given him your mother's locket. I'll never understand why you did that."

"I can't explain it to you. He was so kind to me. Sometimes I think of what my life would've been like if he hadn't saved me or maybe I wouldn't even be alive."

Ben stood up abruptly. "Why do you have to talk about this, Aissa? It's over and done with."

"I'll never forget his face, Father. He looked at me as if he understood, as if he'd been through it himself." She shook her head, embarrassed by the dreamy sound in her own voice. "You're right, it was a long time ago."

Shadow Hawk's chest burned and his legs felt heavier with each step. This was the most difficult race he had ever run. He glanced over his shoulder. There were many runners behind him.

He'd been running every day, up and down the steep and winding paths. He had gained more endurance and could run long distances without tiring. Still, he had never beaten either Miho or Teroz in a race.

Again, he glanced back. None of the of the runners had gained on him. In fact, he had pulled away from most of them. The only runners in front of him were Miho and Teroz. Teroz was strong and seldom tired, but Miho was the truly good runner. He ran as if he were being carried along on a cloud—barefoot, his head thrown back, his long, dark hair flaring out behind him. Miho never seemed to tire and seldom did he breathe hard. He was the kind of Apache the people would talk about, the kind who could run fifty miles in a day if he had to. Shadow Hawk had raced against him more times than he could count and still he had never beaten him. He seldom even came close. But one thing at a time. Today his goal was to beat Teroz.

He tried to clear his mind, a trick that Miho had taught him. He thought about things that he enjoyed doing— riding, swimming in the river, walking with the pretty girls in camp. He smiled. He also couldn't help but think of the white girl he'd rescued those many summers ago. He couldn't get her face out of his mind. He wondered if he ever would.

He breathed easily, forcing himself to relax as he approached a steep path. He ran hard, pumping his arms back and forth. It wasn't until he reached the top of the path that he saw Teroz and realized for the first time that he had a chance to beat him. He dropped his arms to his sides as he ran down the path, shaking them out, keeping himself relaxed. He saw Teroz glance over his shoulder, and Shadow Hawk could see the look of surprise on his face. As the path widened slightly, Shadow Hawk dug in, forcing himself to run even harder, to ignore the pain in his chest and legs. He forced himself to breathe easily, not to gasp for air, and he pushed himself to go faster, even harder. He was so close to Teroz he could hear his cousin's labored breathing, and he knew that Teroz was tiring. It was then that he knew he would beat Teroz. He brushed by him, not looking back, not knowing how far Teroz had dropped back.

He could see the camp in the distance and hear the sounds of the people yelling as they approached the end of the race. More important, he could see Miho. Miho didn't seem to be that far ahead of him, but try as he could, he couldn't bridge the gap between them. Miho never turned back to see who was behind him and it was obvious he didn't care. He just kept running, as only Miho could run, until he won the race. Shadow Hawk finished close behind him.

Shadow Hawk heard the shouts and yells as he followed Miho to the finish. He saw the woman, Lareda, standing apart from the others. He smiled slightly and felt his cheeks burn at the thought of her. A few nights before, she had shown him what it meant to make love to a woman. He had had brief encounters with girls his own age before, but they seemed like childish adventures compared to his night with Lareda. Shadow Hawk forced his thoughts away from her. Now was not the time to be thinking of women. He saw his mother approaching him and he smiled at her.

Broken Moon handed him a water bag, and while he drank, he watched the other runners who came in. Teroz was next, then Gitano, then all the other runners. But where was Brave Heart? He had never run the race before and had never been quite strong enough, never had the endurance. But this summer not even Shadow Hawk could talk him out of running it.

Shadow Hawk spotted Singing Bird in the crowd. She was standing slightly apart, her eyes fixed on the top of the hill. Shadow Hawk walked to stand beside her.

"Where is he, Shadow Hawk"

Shadow Hawk put his arm around her protectively. Singing Bird had grown into a lovely young woman and it was obvious that she and Brave Heart were very much in love. Shadow Hawk thought Ataza might oppose their union. Brave Heart was not a mighty warrior, nor was he the best hunter in the band, but he had learned to hunt well and even to fire a rifle with great accuracy. Shadow Hawk had taken his little brother hunting often, and gradually Brave Heart became skilled. He had always been a good horseman, but now he needed to prove that he had the stamina of an Apache warrior. And this summer he decided to prove it.

"He will be here, Singing Bird."

"What if he is hurt? What if he is lying somewhere out there?"

"He will be all right."

"You need to go look for him, Shadow Hawk. Please."

"I cannot, Singing Bird. If I did that, Brave Heart would never forgive me. This is something he needs to do for himself."

"If you do not look for him, I will go myself." Singing Bird started toward the path, but Shadow Hawk gently pulled her back.

"He will make it, Singing Bird. You must have faith in him."

"How can I have faith when I am so worried?"

Shadow Hawk took his cousin's hand. "You know how much I love my brother. I would do anything to help him, but I will not interfere in something he wants so badly."

"I will only wait a while longer."

Shadow Hawk tried to hide the concern he was now beginning to feel. He knew that his brother was not that strong; he wasn't even sure he could complete the run. But he had to respect Brave Heart's wishes and let him try.

"You ran well today, Cousin." Miho walked up to Shadow Hawk and Singing Bird.

"I have yet to beat you, Cousin," Shadow Hawk replied, smiling.

"You will never beat me. I will always be faster than you on foot."

Shadow Hawk shrugged in resignation. "Perhaps that is true, but I will always be faster than you on horse."

Miho grinned. "I cannot argue with that. Where is Teroz? I thought he would congratulate you on beating him."

"I thought I might receive an arrow in the back."

"The day is young." Miho's eyes flickered over the crowd. Men and women touched him lightly in passing. "Look, here come Gitano and Paloma. It seems to me that they have been spending much time together of late."

Shadow Hawk nudged him. "Why should that matter to you, Cousin? You have told me many times that you would never have a wife."

"That is true, but it does not mean I cannot visit women. It is natural to relieve my desires."

Singing Bird made a small sound of disgust and walked away from them and stood where she could see farther down the steep path.

"So why is it you do not do this with Paloma?"

"Paloma is different from the others. The others have been married, have lost their husbands. I bring them meat and small trinkets and they give me what I desire."

"Why is Paloma different?"

"Paloma is pure."

"You are not as smart as I thought you were, Cousin, if

you wait to take Paloma as your wife. She is one of the most beautiful women in this camp, and she is desired by many men. She will not wait a lifetime for you."

"I never said I wanted to take Paloma as my wife." Miho dropped his voice as Paloma and Gitano got closer.

"So, once again you won the race, Brother," Gitano said. "It seems you can never lose." Gitano whispered something in Paloma's ear and she giggled.

"What is it that you find so amusing, Paloma?" Miho asked, unable to mask the irritation in his voice.

"Gitano makes me laugh."

"That is all?"

"What else could it be?" Paloma stared at Miho, her small foot tapping the ground.

"You look foolish running all over camp, laughing like two children." Miho raised his chin and looked past her, over her head.

"What should we be doing, honoring you because you have won another race?" Paloma hooked her arm through Gitano's. "Come, Gitano, let us go where the air is fresh and there are not so many pests."

Shadow Hawk laughed at Miho's expression as Gitano looked back at them, shrugged, then walked away with Paloma, enjoying his brother's anger. "Have I told you lately, Cousin, what a way you have with the women?"

Miho glowered and muttered something under his breath before striding off in the opposite direction from Paloma and Gitano. Shadow Hawk still saw Singing Bird near the top of the path. He walked to her, "He will be here soon, Singing Bird. If he is not, I will look for him."

"All the runners have finished, Shadow Hawk. It has been too long a time. You must look for him now."

Shadow Hawk hesitated. He was worried too, but he wanted to give Brave Heart a chance to prove himself. Still, if Brave Heart were hurt, it made no sense to wait. "All right, Singing Bird, I will look for him. Wait for me here."

"No, I want to go with you. If he is hurt, I can tend to him."

"Come, then, I will not argue with you anymore." Shadow Hawk took Singing Bird's hand and started to lead her down the steep path that he had run. Then he tightened his grip on her hand and pointed. Brave Heart was below them. As they watched, he stumbled, struggling to keep his feet. Singing Bird started to run to him but Shadow Hawk pulled her back. "No, let him do it by himself."

"He is barely lifting his feet, Shadow Hawk. He is going to fall."

"He will make it." Shadow Hawk pulled Singing Bird away from the path and they watched as Brave Heart staggered past them. They followed him into camp and Shadow Hawk fought the urge to put his arms around him. Brave Heart did not need help. Breathing hard, he pushed past Shadow Hawk and walked to the shade of a nearby tree.

Singing Bird ran forward, wrapping her arms around him.

Shadow Hawk called to his mother and Broken Moon ran to Brave Heart with a water skin.

"Thank you, Mother." Brave Heart drank greedily.

"You were very brave to race, my son. I am proud of you."

"Thank you, Mother."

Shadow Hawk squatted next to Brave Heart. "You are well?"

After drinking as much water as he needed, Brave Heart poured some of it over his head. "I have felt better, Brother. I do not know what to think of these Apache. To run a race such as this on steep trails in the sun . . ." He drank more water, then fell silent, still breathing hard. He suddenly sat straighter, and Shadow Hawk looked up to see Ataza approaching.

"You did well, Nephew," Ataza said, coming up to Brave Heart. "You are a true Apache this day."

Brave Heart looked up, smiling and shaking his head. "I needed to know that I could do it, Uncle, but I was so much slower than the others."

"You finished the race, did you not? That is all we ask a warrior to do."

"Thank you, Uncle."

"I was very proud of you, Brave Heart," Singing Bird said softly.

Broken Moon guided Shadow Hawk and Ataza away from the two young people. "They need time alone."

Ataza looked over his shoulder. "That is what they do not need. Brave Heart is almost sixteen summers old, the same as Singing Bird. They are grown up."

"They will probably marry, my brother. Does that bother you?"

"Singing Bird is but a girl."

"You just said she was grown up." Broken Moon glanced at Shadow Hawk, sharing the joke. "I know many girls her age who are already mothers. Do not stand in their way, Brother. Their love for each other is strong."

Ataza nodded. "I know." He looked at Shadow Hawk. "You know your brother better than anyone. He would not do anything to hurt Singing Bird, would he?"

"He would not," Shadow Hawk answered without hesitation. "He is a man of honor. He will ask your permission when he feels the time is right."

"Good," Ataza said. "Come, Shadow. I must talk to you."

"You want me to go?" Broken Moon asked, sounding annoyed. "It is just like when we were children. You and Sotso would run off to play war and leave me to do the woman's work." Broken Moon narrowed her eyes. "But tell Shadow Hawk who was the best hunter of the three of us."

"Your memory does not waver, does it, Sister?" Ataza looked at Shadow Hawk. "My little sister was the best hunter. She always brought in more game than either of us."

"You never told me this, Mother," Shadow Hawk replied, a smile on his face. "All the times that Father and I would go out to hunt and you never offered to come with us."

Broken Moon laughed. "Did you ever notice the times

130

there was already meat in the stew when you and your father came home from the hunt?" She shrugged her shoulders. "It was easier to do it myself and say nothing to your father."

"But he must have known. Did he ever question you about the meat?"

"Once," she said slyly, "and I told him that my son would never go hungry. He never said anything after that."

Shadow Hawk nodded his head. "Now I understand why Father was always hunting. He wanted to make sure that you did not have to." He smiled. "I did not realize my mother was such a great hunter."

Ataza shook his head. "Your mother's skill with a bow and arrow was better than that of most men. She would have made a great warrior."

Broken Moon looked at her brother, a look of appreciation in her eyes. She waved her hands. "Enough of this. I have work to do."

Shadow Hawk watched his mother as she walked away. "Did my mother fight my father, Ataza?" Shadow Hawk's voice was suddenly grave.

"Yes, she fought him. She fought so hard that she slipped from his grasp and fell to the ground running. I tried to get to her, but your father quicky snatched her again and knocked me aside as he rode away. She fought him until I could no longer see them."

"It seems wrong to me, Uncle, this taking of captives."

"It is the way of your people, Shadow Hawk, just as it is the way of ours."

"I have never seen you take a captive, Uncle. Why is that?"

"Because I never want to hurt someone in the way that my sister was hurt."

"That is why it disturbs me."

"And that is why you helped the white girl to escape those many summers ago."

Shadow Hawk looked up sharply. "Yes."

Ataza patted Shadow Hawk's shoulder. "I understand

131

why you did it, Nephew, but you must understand that you cannot change our people. You are lucky that Teroz did not kill you for what you did. Not everyone feels as we do, Shadow Hawk. When a brave takes a woman captive, he can trade her back to the whites or to another tribe. One captive can be very valuable. You must never do such a thing again."

"I will think about what you have said, Uncle."

Ataza took Shadow Hawk's arm and they began to walk. When they were away from the women he spoke. "There will be another raid soon, Shadow Hawk. We are in need of many things."

"We will go to Mexico?"

"Yes, it is safer for us to go there. I will not go on this raid. Miho will lead. Teroz and Gitano and many of the young braves will go. It is time to see if you young ones can do this on your own. I expect you to respect what Miho says, Shadow."

"I will follow him, Uncle."

"And I want no fighting between you and Teroz. On this raid, you must depend on each other."

"There will be no fighting, Uncle," Shadow Hawk said, and he meant it.

Shadow Hawk sat on his paint, looking across the river at the low adobe buildings and corrals of the ranch. They had never raided this ranch because it was well guarded, even though it had some of the finest horses in Mexico. Ataza had given his young braves a difficult task. But Miho had come up with a plan.

Now Shadow sat waiting for Miho's sign. Earlier, some of the men had created a diversion in the pasture, pretending to steal cattle. They were hoping that the rancher would double the guard on his cattle, leaving the corrals less protected. It had worked. Shadow Hawk could see no cowhands at all near the horses.

As soon as Miho raised his hand, they rode into the river, pushing their horses into the shallows. There were two large corrals filled with horses, and the Apaches quickly unlocked the gates to each, following the frightened animals out. They drove the horses through the yard, knocking over anything in their way, the horses' hooves sounding like rumbling thunder. Shadow Hawk looked back once to see if anyone was following them, but he saw no one. He let the paint have his head, galloping alongside the herd. Miho and the others were fanned out and two braves followed the herd to keep them bunched tightly as they drove them into the river.

When they had crossed the river, they drove the herd hard, unwilling to let them rest until they had put a great distance between them and the ranch. After a few miles they turned eastward, slowing the pace, forcing the horses across an expanse of rock that would hide their tracks. It was tedious and dangerous forcing the animals across sliding shale, but Shadow Hawk smiled to himself. No one, not even the best tracker around, could follow them across this. Miho led them as fast as he dared, looking out for his men and the precious herd.

Shadow Hawk hadn't seen Teroz. He and his group of men had created the diversion. They were to meet in a box canyon on the other side of the rocky expanse. They watered the horses at a spring, then drove the horses into the canyon to wait for the others.

They camped high, outside the mouth of the canyon, taking turns to guard the horses. From this vantage point, they could see riders approaching. Shadow Hawk was unable to eat, knowing that at any moment they might have to ride. It had seemed almost too easy. All of them were pleased with the many horses they had stolen, but they knew they couldn't relax until they had reached the safety of the mountains.

"There are horses," Gitano said, climbing up the rocks. "It is too dark to see but it sounds like only a few and they are not shod. I think it is Teroz and the others."

Miho stood, taking command. "Good. As soon as they eat and drink, we will travel."

"We are lucky that Teroz was not with us. I am glad Miho divided us," Gitano whispered to Shadow Hawk.

"He has done nothing to make us think he is untrustworthy on this raid. Do not make him angry needlessly, Cousin. It will not be long now. We are almost home."

The hoofbeats came closer and slowed. Shadow Hawk heard Teroz's voice in the darkness. Teroz and the others climbed the rocks, talking and laughing. They had had to kill three or four of the cowhands, but none of them had been hurt. Teroz drank from his water bag, then faced Miho. "So, Cousin, did we do well? Did you get enough horses?"

Miho nodded. "You did well, Teroz."

Teroz turned to look at Shadow Hawk, his eyes unreadable. "And you, how did you do?"

"I did what Miho told me to do," Shadow Hawk answered simply.

"Do you always do what Miho tells you to do?"

"Miho is wise for his age. I will listen if I think I can learn from him."

Teroz stepped close to Shadow Hawk. "Was it Miho who planned the white girl's escape, or was it you?"

"That happened a long time ago, Teroz," Gitano said, moving forward. "Can you not forget about it?"

"No," Teroz said, shoving Gitano backward, "I cannot forget about it. The white girl would have brought me many things if I had been able to trade her." His voice was harsh as he looked at Shadow Hawk in the faint light of the moon. "But you took her away from me."

"She never belonged to you, Teroz," Shadow Hawk replied, barely able to control his anger. Patience, he told himself. One day, somehow, Teroz would be killed. Perhaps he would be the one who held the knife.

"Enough!" Miho said. "We do not have time for this.

They will be after us. Do you wish to stand here and argue about past differences, or do you want to get safely back to our camp?"

"I say let Teroz fight the Comanche. He deserves justice." It was Coyote, Teroz's most loyal friend.

"We have no time for fights," Miho admonished. "My father trusted us enough to bring back these horses. If we cannot do this simple thing, then we do not deserve to call ourselves Apache."

Shadow Hawk looked at his cousin. He would make a fine leader someday. He was like Ataza—wise and fair. "I will do as you say, Miho."

"Of course you will do as he says, you always do," Teroz taunted.

Shadow Hawk stood tall in front of Teroz. He was now a good seven or eight inches taller than his cousin. "If you want to fight me, Teroz, you can do it when we get back to camp."

"When your uncle will look out for you?" He shook his head. "I do not think so. This is the only place I will fight you. We are on our own. Let the others take the horses back. You and I can settle matters now."

Shadow Hawk knew that Teroz would not let it rest. He would have to settle this now. "All right, it will be as you say."

"No!" Miho interrupted.

"You must go, Miho. Waste no more time here."

"I will not allow you two to fight."

"You cannot stop us," Teroz said angrily.

"I am the leader of this raiding party. You are to do as I say."

"You are nothing!" Teroz spat on the ground next to Miho. "I listen to no one."

Miho lunged forward, but Shadow Hawk stood in his way. "This is my fight, Miho. I can no longer be patient. Go."

Miho looked from Shadow Hawk to Teroz. "Come with

us, Shadow Hawk. Let this be settled later."

Shadow Hawk shook his head. "No, it must be done now. He will not let it rest."

Miho pulled Shadow Hawk aside. "Do not trust him to fight honorably, Cousin."

"I will be careful. Go now."

"I will make sure you get some of the best horses, Cousin," Gitano said as he walked past Shadow Hawk.

Shadow Hawk nodded to Gitano and waited patiently while his cousins and the others climbed down the rocks to the canyon. When their cries and the thudding hoofbeats had faded, he faced Teroz. "So, why is it you hate me so much, eh?"

Teroz walked around Shadow Hawk as if he were stalking him. "I hate you for many reasons. You came into our camp as if you were one of us, but you were not one of us. You are Comanche."

"Comanche and Apache have ridden together before. They have not always been enemies."

"They have always been my enemy." Teroz stepped closer. "Comanche kidnapped my mother and killed her. I am surprised they did not kill your mother."

Shadow Hawk was stunned into silence. No one had ever told him about Teroz's mother. If this were true, he could understand why Teroz would hate him. "I did not know about your mother, Teroz. I am sorry."

"You are sorry?" Teroz laughed, a bitter, angry laugh. "Can you bring my mother back?"

"You know I cannot. I can only tell you that I am sorry for what my people did to your family."

"The only thing that will heal my wound is to spill Comanche blood."

Shadow Hawk had been taken off guard and had not seen it coming in the dim moonlight. Teroz had drawn his knife and he slashed at Shadow Hawk's belly, cutting him deeply. Shadow Hawk staggered backward, his hand on his bleeding belly. He reached for his own knife but before he could pull it out of the sheath Teroz was on him again, knocking him down. Shadow Hawk fell, rolling to one side, but he felt the searing pain of Teroz's knife as it grazed his arm. Shadow Hawk rolled once more and managed to pull out his knife, but he knew it was too late. Unlike the first time he had fought Teroz, this time he had not been prepared for Teroz's speed and skill.

Shadow Hawk crouched, backing up as Teroz advanced on him. He couldn't see Teroz's eyes but he could imagine the look of hatred that was there. Slowly, Shadow Hawk straightened, never taking his eyes from Teroz. As Teroz lunged at him again, Shadow Hawk dodged to one side and turned, waiting for Teroz to strike again. The wound in Shadow Hawk's belly ached fiercely and he could feel the warm blood seeping into his shirt, but he forced the pain from his mind.

"Do you feel your life dripping away, Comanche? Are you afraid?"

"I have no fear of you, Teroz," Shadow Hawk said, trying to keep up his courage. "You forget, I have beaten you before."

"That was when we were boys."

"And now we are men," he staggered, pretending to be much weaker than he was. He saw Teroz lower his knife. Suddenly, he sprang forward, knocking Teroz to the ground.

Teroz had been right about one thing—they were different now. Teroz was heavier and stronger, more agile, and while Shadow Hawk was tall and strong, he found that Teroz had a different kind of strength. He straddled Teroz, holding Teroz's knife away from him as he tried to gain the advantage. But Teroz quicky twisted his hips and Shadow Hawk fell to one side. The pain in his belly seared like fire and he dropped his knife. He reached out for it but was unable to find it in the darkness.

"You have no knife, Comanche," Teroz said, standing up. Shadow Hawk heard the ringing of the knife blade against the rocks below. "It seems you are beaten."

Shadow Hawk looked up at Teroz. He would have to fight to get away, or he would have to die. Shadow Hawk moved slowly backward, tripping slightly on a rock. He reached down without taking his eyes from Teroz. Perhaps he had a chance after all. He gripped the rock and straightened. He started to lift it, to throw it at Teroz, but something made him stop. "I hear horses, Teroz."

He saw Teroz hesitate for a moment, then continue moving forward. "You will not trick me again, Comanche."

"Listen, Teroz." Shadow Hawk turned, in spite of himself. "There are riders. Can you not hear the iron of their horses' shoes on the rocks?"

Teroz moved next to Shadow Hawk. "I hear them now. Mexicanos."

"We need to get to the horses."

"Yes," Teroz agreed, putting away his knife. "This is not over, Comanche.

Shadow Hawk followed Teroz down the rocks, holding his belly with his hand. He had lost a lot of blood and he was beginning to feel weak. He was lagging behind Teroz as they went to the horses.

"Hurry, they are close," Teroz said, handing the reins of Shadow Hawk's horse to him. "Can you ride?"

"Yes." Shadow Hawk held onto the reins as he tried to swing himself up, but he couldn't hold on and slid off, barely managing to keep his feet.

"Hurry, Comanche. It is time to show me your true riding skill."

"I cannot, Teroz," Shadow Hawk replied, feeling himself weaken. He tried again to swing up onto the horse.

"I will help you."

"No, you must go. The horses are close now. You still have a chance."

"I will not leave you." Teroz started to dismount, but Shadow Hawk cried out.

"Leave now. Ride."

"I did not mean for this to happen, Comanche. I did not mean for you to die this way."

"It does not matter, Teroz. Go now." Shadow Hawk heard the sound of Teroz's horse as he galloped into the darkness. Once more Shadow Hawk attempted to swing up onto his horse, but he could not. He held onto the reins and walked the paint back into the canyon. He stumbled as he walked, and finally his legs gave out completely. He fell to the ground, still holding onto the reins of the paint. Instinctively, he tried to hide himself, tried to crawl into the rocks, but his body would not obey him. He closed his eyes and gave in to the darkness. He was not afraid. All he wanted to do was sleep.

Chapter 7

Aissa waved good-bye to the last of her students and walked back into the schoolhouse. She cleaned the chalk boards, tidied her desk, straightened the rows of desks, and piled the stack of papers to be graded later. She put on her jacket and picked up her purse. She locked the door and walked up the street toward her father's office. She was tired and hoping she could talk him into taking her to dinner at Mabel's Restaurant.

"Miss Gerard." Aissa stopped when she heard the nasal twang of Bessie Runacker. Bessie was in her mid-thirties, she was widowed, and she was quite rotund, always wearing her dress a size too small. She owned the millinery shop and she made it a point to know everyone's business.

Aissa stopped at the millinery shop when she heard Bessie's voice. "Hello, Bessie. Do you have a new hat to show me?"

"Oh, I have lots of new hats, but that isn't what I wanted to ask you about." Bessie tilted her head toward Aissa's in a conspiratorial way. "Have you seen the savage your father captured?"

Aissa's mouth curled into a frown. This had been the talk of the town for two days, ever since her father had brought in

140

a wounded Apache. Aissa refused to become a part of it. She felt sorry for the man. "No, Bessie, I haven't seen him."

"You haven't, but why? Don't you want to see what he looks like? I've heard he's stark naked."

Aissa could barely contain a laugh. "Well, why don't you go see for yourself, Bessie?"

"I've tried, but your father won't let anyone in to see him."

"I'm sure my father has his reasons."

"I think we should be allowed to see the savages who are attacking our homes and stealing our children," Bessie said indignantly. "I should think you, more than anyone else, would want to see this man punished."

"Why should he be punished? What has he done?"

Bessie squirmed as she tugged at the jacket of her tight black dress. "I don't know exactly but it must've been something or your father wouldn't have put him in jail."

"My father puts Dode Fisk in jail every week, Bessie, and I don't consider him to be real dangerous. He found the man lying half-dead in a canyon. He didn't want to leave him to die, so he brought him in so Doc could take a look at him."

"Well, I think he should have let him die. It's nonsense to endanger all of our lives by bringing that savage into our town."

"I think it's wonderful," Aissa replied coldly, standing up to her full five foot eight inches. "My father is a caring person and he wouldn't let any man suffer, no matter who he is."

"I didn't mean to sound like I was insulting your father, Aissa, I'd never do that. It's just that . . ."

Aissa fixed a hard gaze on Bessie. "It's just what, Bessie?"

"You were how old when you were taken by those savages?"

"I was fourteen."

"Well, I know you probably don't want to talk about it and I don't blame you. But how could you be so forgiving when they did such horrible things to you?"

Aissa lowered her head to Bessie's. "What things, Bessie?"

Bessie looked around her. "Well, we all heard what terrible things those savages did to you. It must have been hell for you, poor thing. I commend a man like Raymond Grimes for wanting to marry you after what happened."

Aissa felt her cheeks burn and she had to control her desire to shove Bessie back on her fat bustle. But there was also a devilish side to Aissa, and as her anger faded, she smiled. "Yes, it's true, Bessie, they did do things to me," Aissa said in a soft voice, walking a little farther down the plank sidewalk. Bessie followed as quickly as she could, her boots tapping hurriedly to keep up with Aissa's long strides.

"I knew it," Bessie said, shaking her head. "Those savages."

Aissa stopped suddenly. "Yes, they pulled me into a lodge that very first night, there must have been at least ten of them."

"No!" Bessie replied, her hand over her mouth.

Aissa nodded. "They were all big and strong and naked," Aissa said, trying to hide her smile as she turned away from Bessie. This was good fun, she thought, and if her father ever found out she'd said these things, he'd jail her for life.

"Yes?" Bessie asked breathlessly, her eyes glittering with interest. "Go on."

Aissa looked dreamy. "But there was one in particular," Aissa said slowly. "He was different from the others. He was handsome and he had kind eyes. He held out his hand to me and he pulled me up to him."

"What then?"

"I was enchanted by him. I did anything he asked me to do."

"Anything?"

"Anything," Aissa replied somberly.

"Oh, my," Bessie said in a squeaky little voice, waving her hand frantically in front of her face.

"He stood me in front of the others and he took off all of my clothes."

"No!"

"Yes, and then he danced around me as if he were weaving a spell. I couldn't take my eyes from him." The children would love this story, Aissa thought to herself, and their parents would lynch me.

"What happened next?"

Aissa stopped in front of the shoestore and bent over to look in the window. "Look at these little slippers. I declare, they are the cutest things."

"What happened next, Aissa?" Flushed and breathing noisily, Bessie looked back at her shop and smiled at a woman who walked by.

"Well, he . . ." Aissa lowered her eyes, as if embarrassed. "I couldn't possibly tell you the rest."

"Oh, yes you could. I promise I won't say a word to anyone."

Aissa laughed inside. She knew that what she had already said would be around the town before the sun went down. Bessie was not known for her discretion or for her truthfulness. Most of the people Bessie talked to would think she had made it up. Aissa was tempted to say something really shocking, but as angry as people like Bessie Runacker made her, Aissa had to remember that there were other people who counted on her. Her students and their parents would be terribly embarrassed if Bessie spread some awful rumor, even if they didn't believe it.

"Tell me, Aissa. What happened next?" Bessie was so flushed she looked as if she might pass out.

"He took me to the side and he put a buckskin dress on me. He gave me moccasins for my feet. Then he led me outside and put me up on a horse and he swung up behind me. He put his arms around me and took me home. He never hurt me in any way. I will never forget him."

143

"That's it?" Bessie asked, unable to hide her disappointment.

"Yes, Bessie, that's it. Now if you'll excuse me, I'm going to go visit my father, Good-bye." Aissa knew that Bessie would never repeat the last part—the only part that was true. She crossed the street and stepped up onto the wooden plank sidewalk. She passed some shops, a saloon, the newspaper, and the stable, and then walked up the wooden stairs to her father's office. He had been sheriff all her life and she'd been visiting this office for as long as she could remember. When she opened the door her father's deputy stood in the doorway, blocking her entrance. Joe was in his mid-twenties. He'd come to work for Ben when his parents had died. He was loyal to a fault and Aissa knew he would do anything for Ben.

"Hello, Aissa."

"Hello, Joe. I'd like to see my father."

"He's not here, and he gave me instructions not to let anyone in."

Aissa smiled slightly. If her father gave instructions, Joe followed them to the letter, never varying. "It's all right, Joe, I'm sure he didn't mean me." Aissa tried to step past Joe, but he wouldn't move.

"No, ma'am, he specifically said he didn't want you coming in here and getting anywheres near that Apache."

"He said that?" Aissa said, wondering why her father would try to keep her from seeing the captive Apache. "I have no interest in seeing him, Joe. I just want to sit down at my father's desk, rest my feet, and read until he comes back. He's supposed to take me to dinner."

Joe grinned. "He didn't say nothing about dinner."

"Well, I'm starved. I hope he hurries back soon." Aissa put on the sorriest face she could. "I just want to sit down, Joe. I've been with those children all day and they were a rowdy bunch."

"I bet they were," Joe agreed, smiling. "I'd just a' soon deal with these savages as teach that bunch you got."

"So, you understand. I'm tired and I don't want to stand on my feet anymore today." Aissa took a half step forward.

Joe hesitated. "Well, I guess it'd be all right."

"I promise I'll stay right at my father's desk. In fact, if you don't mind, I might even take a little nap."

"I think that would be all right, Aissa." Joe moved out of the way.

"Thank you, Joe." Aissa pulled off her gloves and jacket and put them on the desk with her purse. She turned to find Joe staring at her. "Did you want something, Joe?"

He blushed. "No, ma'am. I'll just shut the door and wait outside here."

"Thank you." Aissa smiled. Joe was handsome in his own way and she knew he was infatuated with her. She looked around the small office. Her father's large desk dominated the room. It was covered with papers, Wanted posters, and unfinished correspondence to government officials. Those letters, she assumed, were being left for her to pen.

She leaned on the edge of the desk. She loved it here. This was like her other home. After her mother died, her father would have her spend the night with him here, and if there were no prisoners she was allowed to spend the night in one of the cells. Besides the wooden desk, there was a pot-bellied stove in the corner on top of which was always a hot pot of coffee. A wooden railing with a swinging door separated this part of the room from the door to the cells. Aissa looked toward that door. She didn't want to be like everyone else in this town and stare at the "savage" in the next room. But there was a part of her that was curious. What did he look like? Was he completely wild, like the man who had captured her?

She went to the front door and listened. It was silent. Joe wasn't talking to anyone. She moved slowly toward the railing and gently pushed the swinging door open. There was a small window that allowed the sheriff or deputy to look at the three small cells inside. Aissa looked through it. There was a dim light from the lantern that hung on the wall. The indian was in the middle cell, the other two were empty. He was lying on the floor on his side. He looked tall, too tall for an Apache. He wore buckskins, moccasins, and no shirt. His torso was wrapped in white cloth. She had heard that he'd been knifed a number of times and Doc Randall had had a tough time stopping the bleeding. He lay completely immobile, almost as if he were dead.

She put her hand on the door handle and realized that it would be locked. She looked up on the wall for the keys. They weren't there. Her father wasn't taking any chances. She heard voices outside and she hurried back out through the railing, stopping the swinging of the door as she passed through. She dropped into her father's chair, straightened her skirt, and pretended to be looking through his correspondence. The door opened and she smiled.

"I wondered when you'd get here. I'm starving."

Ben looked from Aissa to the jail door. "I told Joe not to let anyone in. That meant you in particular."

"Well, it's nice to know I'm so welcome in the eyes of my own father."

Ben walked to his desk and put down his rifle. He'd been carrying it around town with him ever since he'd taken the Apache into his jail. "I'm keeping you out for your own protection."

Aissa reached up and pushed a hairpin back into place. "How is he going to get out of his locked cell and through another locked door and get to me?"

"I don't know, but I don't want to take any chances." Ben walked to the stove and poured himself a cup of coffee. "So, what do you think of him?"

"Of who?" Aissa asked innocently.

146

"I knew you'd take a look at him, Aissa. Why do you think I kept the keys?"

"You don't trust me very much, do you, Father?"

"It has nothing to do with trust. I know you. Any Apache who's been killed or caught in the last five years, you've had to take a look at. You keep hoping you'll see him."

"What's wrong with that, anyway?" She stood up and walked to the stove, pouring herself a cup of coffee. She sipped at it, making a face. "You still make the worst coffee in the world." She reached for the tin cup on the back of the stove and spooned some sugar into her cup. "I just want to see if it's him."

"So you could help him escape like he helped you escape?"

"He can't hurt me. Please, Father, let me see him."

Ben shrugged. "It's been five years. That boy who saved you is now a man. You wouldn't even recognize him."

"That's right," Aissa agreed eagerly, not telling her father that she'd never forget the boy's eyes, even if they now belonged to a man.

"All right," Ben replied, putting his cup down on the desk. "But you keep it quiet. He's still in pretty bad shape."

Aissa set her cup on the desk next to Ben's. "What do you plan to do with him, Father? He isn't guilty of anything."

"According to the people of this town, he's guilty of everything that any Apache ever did."

"But that's not fair. He didn't do anything. He was almost dead when you found him."

"Maybe he was wounded by a rancher or a Mexican that he stole from. I don't know what he was doing out there, Aissa. He must've done something wrong to be all cut up like that." Ben took the keys from his belt and unlocked the door.

Aissa followed her father into the other room. She could smell the man before they even got close to the cell. It wasn't a bad or dirty smell, but it was wild—like the smell of sage or sumac in the hills. She stepped close to the cell. He *was* tall.

His long legs barely fit in the cramped cell floor. He was lean and muscular, and his skin was lighter than that of most Apaches she'd seen. His hair was black and grew straight and thick to his shoulders. She couldn't see his face.

"That's enough," Ben whispered. "Let's let the man be."

"I just want to see his face," Aissa whispered back.

"No," Ben said, taking Aissa's arm. "He's asleep. Every couple of hours he wakes up and moans, then he sleeps again."

"Then I'll wait," she replied stubbornly, shrugging free of her father's hold. She sat down against the wall opposite the Apache's cell.

Ben squatted down next to his daughter. "You aren't allowing the man any dignity," Ben whispered in a controlled but angry tone.

"Please, Father, I won't do anything to disturb him." Aissa grabbed her father's forearm. "I need to see his face."

Ben hesitated. "All right, but I'm keeping the door open. If you need me, you yell." He looked at his daughter sitting on the dirt floor. "You know, you remind me of your mother when you do fool things like this."

"Is that good?" Aissa smiled broadly.

"That's very good," Ben replied gently, walking out to the other room.

Aissa's eyes filled with tears as she watched her father walk away. It seemed they spent so much time arguing, they didn't have time to tell each other how much they cared. She loved him.

Aissa stared at the Apache's back, squinting her eyes in the dim light. It was hard to see if he was even breathing. She felt sorry for him. It would be terrible for him when he woke up and found himself in a cell like a caged animal. She wondered what her father was going to do with him. She knew what the people of Agua Prieta would like to do with him and she understood why. Over the last several years, the

Apache had raided their ranches. They had stolen horses, ransacked homes, and taken captives.

Aissa crossed her hands over her chest and laid her head back on the cool adobe wall. She closed her eyes. She was hungry and she was also tired. It felt good to sit here in the silence. There was always so much to do—papers to grade, the animals to feed, letters to write for her father, a food basket to take to Old Mrs. Richdale—sometimes it seemed as if she lived her life for everyone but herself.

"Here."

Aissa jumped when she heard her father's voice. She'd been so lost in her reverie she hadn't even heard him come in. He was holding a steaming cup of coffee. She took it from him. "Thank you."

"I even put sugar in it for you." Ben sat next to her on the floor. "Since you're determined to be so damned stubborn, I sent Joe over to the restaurant to get us some dinner. I heard that Mabel made some fresh peach pies today. I even told him to bring cream for your coffee."

Aissa kissed her father on the cheek. "How you do spoil me," she said softly. She sipped at the bittersweet coffee. "Are you going to let him go, Father?"

"I don't know, Aissa. You know how the people around here feel. Hell, I feel the same damned way. If it weren't for that one Apache boy who brought you back, I'd probably shoot every Apache on sight."

"Will you at least let me talk to him? Maybe I can find out what he was doing."

"Since when have you learned Apache?"

"You know my Spanish is better than yours, and a lot of the Apache speak it. Let me try, Father."

"He might not even wake up, honey. Like I said, he opens his eyes, moans, then he's gone again. He hasn't moved for two days. Doc says that maybe he just wants to die."

"Will you let me try to talk to him if he wakes up?"

"Yes, you can talk to him. I don't expect he'll be too friendly." Ben was suddenly silent, staring at the cell in front of him. "Why do you stay here, Aissa?"

"What?" Aissa put her cup on the floor.

"Why do you stay here? You're a beautiful young woman. You should be experiencing the world, not taking care of your father."

"I want to be here, Father. I have you and my students—"

"And what else?" Ben shook his head. "It's not right. You should be married and raising a family of your own. You shouldn't be fretting over me."

"I'm not fretting over you. Besides, I have seen some of the world. I went to school in St. Louis."

"And you hated to come home."

"That's not true."

Ben ran a hand through his hair. "I remember the look on your face when I put you on that train for St. Louis. Your eyes were filled with tears. You begged me not to send you away. But after the Apache had taken you once, I wasn't going to let them do it again. Then, every time I got one of your letters, I could see a change in you. You liked it there. You liked the city and all the hustle and bustle. You were sad when you had to come back here."

"I didn't have to come back here. I could've stayed in St. Louis. I could've gone to Paris. I have my grandparents there, and my aunts and uncles."

"Then why didn't you go?"

"Do you want me to go, Father?"

"Agua Prieta is not a safe place. We should've never stayed here after Celou died."

Aissa took her father's hand. "But the people here need you. You've done a lot for this town. You wouldn't be happy anyplace else."

"Why don't you at least take a trip to Paris? Your grandparents would love to see you. I have money saved up—"

"No, I'm perfectly content here."

"I wish you'd think about it, Aissa. It would make me feel a lot better if you were someplace else. Things are getting worse around here. We're caught between the Mexicans and the Apache. They hate each other and they hate us."

"Maybe I'll take a trip to Paris someday, but not right now. I'm surprised at you. I thought you wanted me to marry Ray." She smiled devilishly.

Ben shook his head. "You're never going to let me forget that, are you? I'm sorry. I know now he wasn't the man for you." Ben stood up. "I'll bring your dinner in when it gets here."

"No, I'll eat out there with you." She watched him walk out. Maybe her father was right, maybe she should go to Paris. She could buy some new clothes and maybe even meet a handsome young man. She smiled and closed her eyes, resting her head against the wall. She'd always been a dreamer, why stop now? But the truth be told, she'd probably wind up here in twenty years, the old schoolmarm, living on the ranch by herself, never having known what it was like to truly love a man. Her dreams, it seemed, would be her only way out of Agua Prieta.

Shadow Hawk moved. He felt a sharp pain in his stomach and then, like an echo, a pain in his arm. He touched the cloth that was wrapped around his stomach. He opened his eyes. Someone had bandaged his wounds. Then he saw the bars. Slowly, he pulled himself to a sitting position, the pain almost intolerable. His thoughts were slow, difficult. He leaned against the bunk, his arm across his stomach. He took in the barred window, the tiny cubicle of the room. One of his grandfather's stories came back to him. This was a white man's jail. The light was dim, but he could see that the other cells were empty. No Teroz. So, he had gotten away.

He wiped the sweat from his face. It was hot and there was no moving air. He was sure he would suffocate. The thought of being locked in this enclosed place made him feel panic, but he fought it down. He would have to wait—wait until his pain lessened, wait until he saw a chance to escape. He started to close his eyes when he looked through the bars and saw something. In the dim light he could see someone sitting on the floor against the wall. He squinted. It was a woman, a young woman with light hair. He struggled to stand up and walked to the bars. He held on, swaying, trying to get a better look at her. Why would there be a woman here?

He leaned his head against the bars and closed his eyes, feeling faint. His wounds throbbed unmercifully and the pain swept through his body. Teroz had cut well. He had underestimated him.

He opened his eyes again. He wished that he could see better. What was the woman doing here? Was she supposed to be guarding him? If so, why was she sitting there asleep? It made no sense to him.

He turned and again saw the small barred window high on the wall over his bunk. He wanted to put his face against it, to breathe in the fresh night air, to see the stars. But he knew he couldn't climb, he could barely walk. Sweat dripped down his face and slowly he eased himself down onto the floor again. It was hot here, hotter than any desert sun he'd been in. He leaned against the bunk and closed his eyes. He needed to call upon all his strength to get well. He had to find a way out of this white man's jail. If he did not, he knew he would die; whether they killed him or not, his spirit would die.

Aissa opened her eyes. She had been sleeping for some time. She remembered eating dinner with her father. They had played a few games of cards, and then she had come back here. It was probably late. She didn't even hear the piano from the saloon. She rubbed her eyes.

She stood up and stretched. She dusted the fine dirt from the skirt of her dress and she walked to the door, looking out. Joe was asleep, his head resting on the desk. Her father must be out in front, sitting on the stairs, making sure that no one tried to get into the jail.

She turned back to the cell. The Apache had moved. He was sitting up now, his back against the bunk, his long legs bent. Blood had seeped through the bandages on his stomach and his hand was resting on it. She still couldn't see his face.

"Wake up," she whispered, and was startled when he moved. He stretched out his legs and lifted his head. She knew she should move, but she couldn't pull herself away. She watched transfixed as he opened his eyes and looked at her. Her fingers gripped the cold iron bars. His face was handsome, and even in the dim light she could see the eyes that were the color of a stormy sky. He hadn't changed much, only grown taller and more handsome. He was the one, the one she had been waiting to see all this time.

"Habla usted Espanol?" He looked at her, his face blank. "You don't speak Spanish," she muttered to herself, "and I know you don't speak English." She put her hand on her chest. "I am Aissa. Do you understand? My name is Aissa." When he showed no sign of understanding her, she leaned closer, peering through the bars. He continued to stare at her, a guarded expression on his face. "I know you're tired and you're in pain, but I'm going to get you to understand me. You saved my life once, and I promise you that I will do the same for you. Rest now."

She walked back to the wall and sat down. He was still watching her, but it didn't make her uneasy. She hoped he would remember who she was. She had found him at last.

*   *   *

When Shadow Hawk woke up, the white woman was standing at the bars. She was beautiful, like a dream. He couldn't take his eyes from her. She was tall, taller than any Indian woman he had ever seen. And her hair hung down her shoulders like new cornsilk. And although he couldn't see them, he knew her eyes were pale blue.

"My name is Aissa," she said softly.

Her voice had a strange quality to it, a certain softness. She spoke to him in Spanish and English. She told him she was the one he had rescued. She also said that she would help him. Maybe he wouldn't have to fight his way out of this white man's jail. As he watched her, she sat down on the floor, peaceful, not at all afraid of him. She had changed. Her face had lost the roundness of girlhood and she had grown tall for a woman. She sat silently for a long time and he watched her eyes close and her body relax in sleep.

Shadow Hawk looked up to the small barred window. Soon it would be daylight. The thought of spending all of his days and nights in this cell frightened him beyond anything else. He could feel the fear rise up in him and threaten to overcome him, but just as quickly he would fight it, calming himself. He would find a way out, even if he had to use the young woman to do it.

Shadow Hawk looked up when he heard the door open. He looked at the man who held the keys—he was older but lean and strong. He carried a rifle in his arms. Shadow Hawk would have no chance of overcoming him, especially in his weak condition. While the man held open the cell door, the woman came from the other room, holding a tray of food.

"Be careful, Aissa."

"Would you stop, Father?" she replied impatiently.

154

"Wait a minute." The man checked the tray of food. "I said no utensils." He took the spoon from the tray.

"What is he going to do with that, beat someone to death?" The girl grabbed it from her father and put it back on the tray. "You go on, I'll be fine."

"I'm not leaving you alone in here. If you stay, I stay."

"All right, bring me a chair and I'll sit outside the cell."

Shadow Hawk watched as the woman put the tray of food on the bunk. Then she sat on the chair her father had brought her. The older man locked the cell.

"I don't like this, you know." The man stood next to Aissa, the rifle held firmly in his hands.

"I know you don't, Father."

Shadow Hawk understood everything they were saying. Still, they were so different. They both seemed perfectly comfortable in this small space with its dead air. The woman's clothes looked so constricting, it was hard to believe she could move around as gracefully as she did. Her hair hung as straight and long as any Apache's, but everytime he looked at her, the color of it startled him anew.

"Eat," the woman ordered. Then her voice became uncertain, girlish. "I brought you some bread, beans, and meat."

Shadow Hawk regarded the woman. Her eyes were so blue and so light, it almost seemed possible to look through them. They were also friendly eyes. This girl was eager to help him. Perhaps it was time for him to become her friend. It would be easy enough. If she could just get her father's keys and a rifle, he would be free.

"Doc will be over in a little while to look at you. You're still bleeding."

This woman was like no other woman he had ever seen. Her eyes met his steadily, easily. She was not frightened of him, did not cower at the sight of him, and did not lower her eyes in deference to him when she spoke. The frightened young girl he had helped had grown into a strong woman.

"Please, eat something." She gestured with her hands.

Shadow Hawk reached up and grabbed the tray from the bunk. The smell of the food immediately assaulted him. He was hungry. He tore off a chunk of bread and dipped it in some gravy, quickly consuming it. His instinct was to eat the entire tray of food, but he pushed it away. Better to let the woman think he had lost his spirit. She watched him as a mother watched a sick child.

"Please, eat something," she pleaded softly, her eyes never leaving his face. "You must build your strength."

Shadow Hawk continued to watch her, but still he said nothing. It was better to let her think he could not understand her. Perhaps he could learn something that would help him escape.

"I wish you could remember," she said, pulling her chair close. She wrapped her fingers around the bars and leaned toward him. "You helped me." She shook her head. "You did more than that. You saved my life. If you hadn't taken me from your camp, I know that I would have died. I don't know why you decided to save me, but I want to thank you."

She looked like a girl again. Tears formed in her eyes and rolled slowly down her cheeks. Her mouth trembled slightly. It was as if she was recalling the fear she had felt that night in the Apache camp.

Shadow Hawk couldn't bear her sadness and was ashamed that he had thought to use her. He fumbled with a hand to open the pouch that hung on his belt. He reached inside and felt for the locket. The metal felt cold against his hand. He wrapped his fingers around it and pulled it out.

"I wish you could understand me," she was saying, leaning her cheek against the bars. She looked so young.

Shadow Hawk struggled to move to the bars. He sat in front of the young woman and held his hand open to show her the locket.

"My locket," she breathed, a smile on her face. "You do understand me."

"Yes," he responded.

"You speak English?" Her face betrayed her astonishment.

Shadow Hawk nodded.

"You've understood everything I've said?"

Shadow Hawk nodded again. He held out his hand to Aissa. "It is yours. Take it."

Aissa reached through the bars and took the locket from Shadow Hawk's hand. She ran a finger over the smooth metal and looked inside. She held it in her hand a minute, then snapped it shut and put it back in Shadow Hawk's hand. "No, I gave it to you and I want you to keep it."

Shadow Hawk extended his hand, but she closed his fingers around the locket. He dropped it back into his pouch and pulled the thongs tight.

"Why did you do it? Why did you take me from the Apache camp?"

Shadow Hawk took a moment to shape his thoughts. It had been a long while since he had spoken the white man's tongue. "The man who took you, his name is Teroz. He is the one who did this to me. He might have hurt you."

"You risked your life by saving me. I know that."

"My life was never in danger."

"I have thought of you all of these years." Aissa reached through the bars and grasped Shadow Hawk's hand.

Shadow Hawk pulled away, startled by the woman's gesture. He wasn't sure what to do. He had thought of her as well but had never imagined that she would remember him. He looked at the door that connected the two rooms. "Is it dangerous for you to be seen talking to me?"

"No, it's not dangerous. My father is the one who brought you here. He is the sheriff. He's a fair man."

"If that is so, why am I in this place?"

"He felt this was the safest place for you."

"What are his plans for me?"

"I don't know, but I do know he'll be fair."

Shadow Hawk steadied himself against the bars. "I did nothing to your people."

"I will talk to my father. He will listen to me."

Shadow Hawk stared at the young woman. Were all white women like this, he wondered? She seemed to have no fear, not even of her father. "Your father will do what he must do. Your pleading will do no good." He moved back to his place by the bunk, every move a painful one. He didn't want to talk anymore. How did he really know he could trust her? His grandfather, who was a white man, had told him of white people who helped Indians and then tried to change them. They tried to dress them as whites, make them talk like whites, and make them take on the white religion. He would not let this woman do that to him.

She kept talking, trying to get him to respond, but he would not. He closed his eyes and purposefully put her from his mind. Nothing mattered to him now but his freedom.

Ben watched the Apache while the doctor changed his bandages. He was cut pretty bad, but he had never uttered a sound. It was hard to tell anything from his expression. His face never changed.

"That'll do it," Doc Randall said, standing up and putting some things into his cracked, worn black medical bag.

"Thanks, Doc."

"He could stand to eat some more. If I didn't know better, I'd say he's trying to starve himself. Heard of that, you know. Indians can't stand to be locked up."

Ben glanced at the Apache. There was still no sign that he understood anything. "I'll see what I can do, Doc. Thanks."

Ben didn't move. The Apache was still sitting on the

floor, staring at the bars in front of him. Ben sat down on the bunk. "Is that true, are you trying to starve yourself?"

The Apache said nothing. He continued to stare ahead.

Ben leaned forward, his elbows on his knees. "My daughter tells me you can speak English, so there's no use pretending you can't."

The Apache looked up at him then. "Why do you keep me here?"

"Right now, it's for your own protection."

"I do not need your protection. I only want to be set free so I can return to my people."

Ben looked at the fresh bandages, then back into the Apache's eyes. "You wouldn't last one hour in the desert, as badly hurt as you are."

"I will make it back."

Ben shook his head. "Nope, I figured to save your life when I brought you here, and I'm going to do it."

"So you will keep me locked up here even though I have done nothing wrong?"

"I don't know that for sure, do I? Had some Mexicans come into town complaining that some Apache had ridden south and raided their ranch. Took some valuable horses. Now, you wouldn't happen to know anything about that, would you?"

The Apache looked at him, his eyes unreadable. "I was hunting and I was attacked by someone while I slept. That is all I know."

"You trying to protect someone?"

"I know nothing of stolen horses."

"All right, then," Ben responded, rubbing his hands along his thighs. "I've got another question. Why did you bring my daughter back here when she was taken captive by your people? Why'd you do it?" Ben watched the Apache's eyes and for a moment, they softened.

"My mother was a Comanche captive."

"So you're not Apache?"

"I am half Apache, half Comanche."

"You have some white blood in you, too." Ben watched the Apache straighten.

"I am not ashamed of my white blood."

Ben stood up. "I want to thank you for saving my daughter's life. I've seen some of the women captives who've come back from the Apache. You saved my daughter from that, and I owe you."

"You owe me nothing."

"I owe you the same chance you gave my daughter." Ben left the cell, locking it behind him. He walked out to the front room, knowing what he had to do. The Apache would need a place to recover, to rest. And a jail cell wasn't the place to do it.

Chapter 8

Shadow Hawk walked out of the house and onto the porch, sitting down in one of the hard chairs. He'd been at the Gerard ranch for over two weeks now and he was finally beginning to regain his strength.

Shadow Hawk was still uncertain of these people. They were kind and good-hearted, and to his surprise, they seemed to trust him. He could have easily killed them both, but they didn't seem to worry about that. These people trusted him with their lives and in so doing, cut through his suspicion faster than he would've believed possible.

Shadow Hawk found that he liked Ben Gerard very much. He reminded him of his grandfather. Ben was open, honest, and very forthright—he never minced words. He also had a good sense of humor and enjoyed playing jokes on his daughter. He never talked down to Shadow Hawk. When he spoke to him, it was always as an equal.

And then there was Aissa. He never ceased to be overwhelmed by her beauty. No woman had ever affected him this way. His feelings for her had confused him at first, and he had made every effort he could to ignore her.

The first night he had stayed at the ranch he had begun bleeding again. Aissa had changed the bandages and she had been very concerned. "I'll make sure the doctor takes a look at you tomorrow," she had said.

Shadow Hawk had looked at her suspiciously. Her voice had been sweet, but still he didn't know if he could trust her. "I do not need you to do things for me," he had replied.

"But I want to help you."

"I do not want your help," he had replied, angry in his confusion. He did not want to feel anything for this woman or her father. His only desire should be to be free of this place and the white people.

Shadow Hawk sighed. He wanted to be back with his people. His people. He had never called the Apache that before, not even to himself. But they were more his people than the whites could ever be. He closed his eyes and let his mind wander. He imagined riding his horse along the river and stopping to swim. He could feel the cool water on his skin. He could taste the freshly roasted deer he had just cooked. And he could imagine the feel of the woman, Lareda, as she lay by him, her naked body touching his.

Lareda was a widow. Shadow Hawk had brought food to her and it wasn't long before she initiated him in the ways of men and women. He liked being with her. She had shown him many ways to please a woman. He missed her physically, not because he wanted to be with her and talk to her. She would have found someone else by now to bring her meat. It was different with Aissa.

Shadow Hawk could see Aissa from the porch. He watched her as she worked diligently in the garden. Aissa told him stories about her students in the white man's school, making him laugh at their tricks and fights. Were all children the same? Aissa was a kind and gentle person, yet she had fire in her. She argued with her father when she didn't agree with him, and she took care of the animals and the ranch as if she were a man twice her own size. He was fascinated by her and more than that, he wondered what it would be like to lie with her. Her skin would glow almost like moonlight.

"You want some coffee, boy?" Ben came onto the porch

holding two tins of coffee. He handed one to Shadow Hawk.

"Thank you." He sipped at the bittersweet coffee that reminded him so much of his grandfather.

Ben sat down in the chair next to him. "Aissa in the garden?"

"Yes."

"She loves that garden of hers. It was her mother's, actually. When her mother died, she took to working in it all the time."

"Her mother, she was fair, like Aissa?"

"Yes," Ben said, his voice low. "She's too fair to be working outside all the time."

"As soon as I am healed, I will help."

"There's no need for that. You can leave whenever you're ready." Ben sipped from his tin. "I thought you'd be out of here as soon as you could."

Shadow Hawk shrugged, never taking his eyes from Aissa. "There are things I must do first."

"What things?"

Shadow Hawk leaned forward and grabbed the porch railing. He shook it and the loose boards rattled. "This needs to be fixed and so does the corral. Aissa tells me that there are many things around here that need to be repaired."

Ben laughed. "And you think you're going to fix them."

"Yes," Shadow Hawk replied seriously.

"I appreciate the offer, Shadow Hawk, but I don't think you'd know what to do."

"You forget, Gerard, that I have a white grandfather and I spent every summer with him as a boy."

"That doesn't make you good with a hammer."

"I have looked around, Gerard, and I think that I am better than you with a hammer."

"I can see Aissa's been talking to you." Ben shrugged. "I may not be the best man with repairs, but I try."

"Aissa says you do not try often enough." Shadow Hawk

saw Ben grinning. "I will help. I helped my grandfather build his cabin."

"Well, if you really want to help, I won't stop you. Truth be told, I hate to work around this place. I just like to sit out here on the porch and look out at the mountains."

"It is a good place to live, Gerard."

"My wife loved it and so does Aissa. After you brought her home, I made her go back east to school. I thought I could get her to stay there, but she wouldn't. She came back here just as soon as she could."

"Perhaps it is not the place she loves so much as it is you, Gerard."

Ben narrowed his eyes over the rim of the coffee tin. "Did she tell you that?"

"It is easy to see how she feels about you. There is no shame in that."

"I wanted more for her. She shouldn't be in a place like Agua Prieta, looking after her father."

"Perhaps this is what Aissa wants, Gerard. She is a woman with a strong will. If she did not want to be here, she would not be."

"You've noticed her will, have you?" Ben asked, laughing. He pointed past the corrals. "Is that dust out there? Is someone coming?" He stood up, his hand immediately on his gun.

Shadow Hawk stood up next to Ben, holding his stomach. He squinted and looked out into the distance. "It is all right. There are three men. They are not Apache."

"How can you tell from here?"

"Apache would not create so much dust to be seen for miles."

Ben nodded in agreement. "Maybe you should go inside. If it's one of the neighbors and they see you, it'll only cause an argument."

"I will do as you say," Shadow Hawk replied, glancing back at Aissa as he went inside. He drew the curtains enough so that he could look out without being seen. If the neighbors were angry, he didn't want Aissa or Gerard getting hurt because of him.

This room reminded him of his grandfather's cabin except that everywhere he looked he could see the touch of a woman's hand. There was a vase of flowers on the table and there were pictures on the wall. Shadow Hawk had looked at them closely. They were not made by painting but by some fine stitchery with colored thread. What had surprised him even more was that the house had two separate rooms for sleeping and a large area in the front room devoted entirely to cooking. Aissa had pots and pans of so many different sizes and shapes that Shadow Hawk could not imagine how she would use them all. Aissa stored her food in tin canisters as Marsh always had, but hers had patterns hammered into the metal and she also used glass jars. White people lived so differently. Ben never seemed eager to hunt. Instead, when they wanted meat, they would kill one of the cattle.

Shadow Hawk heard a shout from outside and recognized the voice. He walked to the rifle rack and quicky loaded one of Ben's rifles, grateful that Miho had made him learn how to use one. He walked back to the window and sat down, looking through the gap in the curtains. Ben sat in the chair on the porch, his feet on the rickety porch railing. Shadow Hawk looked at the men—he had been right. The man called Grimes was there. Shadow Hawk had seen Grimes in town the day that Gerard took Shadow Hawk from the jail. Grimes had a group of people around him as he shouted that Gerard should hang the Apache. Gerard had had to raise his rifle against Grimes in order to get the crowd to break up.

Grimes dismounted, walking up onto the porch. He stomped the dirt from his boots and brushed the dust from his pants.

"Where's the Apache, Ben?"

"What's it to you, Ray?" Ben asked casually, sipping his coffee.

"I have a right to your protection."

"That's right, you do."

"And I feel my life is in danger as long as that Apache is still around here."

"That Apache has been living in my house for two weeks and I don't feel he's the least bit dangerous."

"The people of this town won't stand for it, Ben. We can always elect a new sheriff, you know."

"I don't care what you do, Ray. Frankly, I'm a little old for this job anyway. Been thinking about retiring. It's the heart, you know. Been bad for a long time."

Shadow Hawk smiled. Aissa had told him that Ben always complained of his heart but that he was in better health than most people she knew. It was obvious that Ray had expected Ben to get angry. When he hadn't, he shuffled uncomfortably.

"You know I've always thought you were a good sheriff, Ben. It's just that I don't agree with you keeping an Apache out here."

"He's on my land, Ray, why should it bother you?"

"What if he gets loose and starts raiding our ranches?" one of the other men on horseback said.

Ben looked up at him. "Do you really think one Apache is going to do that much damage, Zeb? Besides, he's already been 'loose' for over two weeks. He doesn't seem interested in much except getting well and getting back to his people."

"That's another thing, Ben," the other man said. "What if he goes back to his people and tells them all about us? They could come here and destroy us."

Ben's boots dropped from the railing to the floor, making a loud thump. "Are you men that stupid?" He clanked the cup onto the porch railing and stood up. "Don't you think the Apache have known about all of us for years? Hell, they rode in here five years ago and took my daughter, or have you forgotten that? They could ride in to any of these ranches anytime they please, but they don't. We're just lucky they hate the Mexicans so much. As long as the Apache and the Mexicans hate each other, the Apache will steer clear of us." Ben pushed by Ray and walked down the porch steps. "Now, if you don't mind, I have to look at a cow that's about to calve."

"Ben."

Ben turned to face Ray. "What do you want, Ray?"

"I'm sorry I came at you like this on your own land. I guess we're all just a little scared. We've all heard things, that's all."

Ben nodded, looking at each of the men in turn before he spoke. "I understand your fear if anybody does. My daughter was taken from me and I thought I'd never see her again. But the man you seem to think I should hang had more courage and decency when he was fifteen than most white boys. He took my daughter from his own people and brought her back here safely." Ben looked at each man again, enjoying their discomfort. "He didn't have to do that, so now I figure I owe him. He's hurt and I intend to make sure he gets well. He can stay here as long as he likes, as long as he doesn't do anything to hurt anyone. I'd never put any of you people in danger, least of all my own daughter."

"All right, Ben," Zeb nodded. "It's just like Ray said, we're all a little jumpy. I won't bother you again."

"Me neither, Ben," the other man said. "But I'll sure feel better when that brave heals up and gets gone."

"There go decent men," Ben said as Zeb and the other man rode away. Then he turned to Ray. "Can I help you with something else?"

"I was just wondering if I could talk to Aissa, Ben."

Ben thought for a moment. "I suppose it'd be all right."

"Thanks, Ben," Ray responded, walking toward the garden while Ben headed toward the barn.

Shadow Hawk watched Grimes. He didn't like the man and he didn't trust him. Already he could tell what Grimes was after. It showed in his ugly eyes. He wanted Aissa.

Aissa had seen Ray and the men ride up. She wiped her

hands on her apron and stood up, stretching. She looked up on the porch. Shadow Hawk was gone.

She liked looking at him. She had never seen a man like him. Two days earlier she had come out from the barn and seen him washing by the pump, wearing only his breechcloth. His body was lean, brown, and muscular, and when he bent over to put his head under the pump, she could see his firm buttocks and the tops of his muscular thighs. She had stared at him for a long while until he had looked up. Her eyes swept his body once more and then, quickly, she had turned away, blushing. Aissa felt her cheeks burn again at the memory and she lowered her head, trying to push the image from her mind. She wiped her face. The sun felt hotter than normal today.

"How are you today, Aissa?"

Aissa's daydream was rudely interrupted by Ray's voice. She turned to look at him, pushing her hair back. "What are you doing here, Ray?"

"Just wanted to talk to your father."

Aissa put a hand up to shield her face from the sun. "What did you want to talk to him about?"

"Oh, just some business. No concern of yours."

"Anything that has to do with my father is my concern."

Ray stepped forward. "Aissa, listen—"

Aissa moved back. "No, you listen, I won't have you coming out here harassing my father."

"You talk a tough fight, but I wonder just how tough you really are." Ray's voice was cold and his eyes betrayed no emotion save bitterness when he spoke. He took another step forward.

Aissa's dislike of Ray was quickly turning into something else—he was beginning to scare her. "I don't want to fight with you, Ray. My father is a good sheriff, the best this place has ever had. I just want you to let him do his job."

"Just what is his job, Aissa? Is it Ben's job to let savages free to roam the countryside? But now that I think of it, that

Apache hasn't done much roaming lately. Maybe you've made him feel so at home, he's content to stay right here."

Aissa lifted her hand to slap Ray but he grabbed her wrist, twisting it back behind her. "Let me go, Ray. I swear, I'll scream if you don't."

"If you scream, I'll have to hurt you."

"You're acting crazy. My father's close."

"Then don't you let on that I'm hurting you. I'd hate for a terrible accident to happen. I wouldn't want to see your father get hurt trying to defend you."

Aissa couldn't believe what she was hearing. "All right, I won't say anything."

"You'll do more than that. You'll consider my marriage proposal."

"Are you out of your mind? I'd rather—"

Ray's hand went over Aissa's mouth. "You better think before you answer, Aissa. I have a lot of power in this territory. I could have your father out of office tomorrow. Or he could have a terrible accident at any time." Ray wrapped his arm around Aissa, pushing the hair from her face with his other hand. "I can also make sure that nothing happens to him."

Aissa shook her head. "You're crazy."

"Maybe. I just know that I always get what I want and I want you, Aissa. I always have. You marry me, you'll never have to want for anything. Neither will your father."

"No!" Aissa tried to pull away, but Ray pinned her arms to her sides, holding her against him.

"I'm not playing games, Aissa. Consider what I just said. And don't tell your father about it; it'll just cause him more worry."

Ray lowered his mouth to Aissa's, but she jerked her face away. He grabbed her jaw with a hand and held it, pressing his mouth on hers. Aissa struggled to pull away, but Ray held her to him.

"Let the woman go."

Aissa heard Shadow Hawk's deep voice and relief flooded through her. She felt Ray's hold loosen and she backed away. Shadow Hawk stood behind Ray, tall, brown, and imposing. His face betrayed no emotion but Aissa detected an anger she hadn't yet seen.

Ray turned around, his hand on his holster. "Well, well, so the savage speaks English." He appraised Shadow Hawk, looking him up and down as if he were a prize steer. "So you're the hero she's been pining over all these years."

"Ray, I think you should go."

Ray turned around, grabbing Aissa's arm. "And I think you should remember what I said, Aissa."

Shadow Hawk moved forward and in one quick motion knocked Ray's hand from Aissa's arm and kicked him behind a knee. Ray fell to the ground, reaching for the gun in his holster. By the time he'd drawn it, Shadow Hawk stood over him, his knife in his hand, poised to throw.

"Do you wish to die today, white eyes?" Shadow Hawk's voice still held no emotion.

Aissa watched Ray's face. He looked scared, but she knew it wouldn't last. When he got back to his ranch and was surrounded by his men, he wouldn't be scared. He'd be angry. "Please go, Ray. We don't want any trouble." She put her hand on Shadow Hawk's arm to still it, and she could feel his tense muscles.

Ray took his hand from the holster and slowly stood up. "You haven't heard the last of me, Aissa." Ray walked heavily toward his horse.

Aissa took her hand from Shadow Hawk's arm. "Thank you," she said softly and turned away. She felt as if Ray had violated her. She was trembling.

"You are all right?"

Aissa nodded without turning. "He didn't hurt me."

"But he intends to hurt you, does he not?"

Aissa turned to look at Shadow Hawk. "He won't hurt me, he's just upset."

"I have seen that look before. You cannot trust him."

"I'll be fine." Aissa tried to sound nonchalant, but she was scared. Ray was powerful enough to back up all of his threats. She felt weak suddenly, as if she were going to faint. She wiped beads of sweat from her forehead. She would rather die than marry Ray Grimes. She felt Shadow Hawk's arm go around her as he led her to a shaded area of the garden. He sat Aissa down on the wooden bench that was against the trunk of a large oak tree.

"What did this man say to you?"

"It doesn't matter." She wiped her face with her apron. She was still sweating. She closed her eyes. Her head throbbed and she felt sick to her stomach.

"Aissa."

She looked up at him. Her name had never sounded so sweet. "Yes."

"Tell me what this man said to you."

Shadow Hawk stood in front of her and all she could see was his bare chest and the sweat that glistened on his brown skin. His body was as beautiful as some of the marble sculptures she had once seen in a museum. She closed her eyes. She felt his hand on her cheek. It felt cool.

"You are hot. I will get you water."

"No, wait," she said, opening her eyes and looking up at him. "Do you have a wife?" As soon as the words left her mouth, she was embarrassed. She couldn't believe she had asked him that.

"I have no wife. I will get you water. Do not move."

Aissa shook her head. How could she have asked something so ridiculous? Even if he didn't have a wife, it wasn't possible for her to consider a relationship with an Apache. Just because he spoke English didn't make him white. She closed her eyes again and leaned her head back against the tree trunk. What was the matter with her? She couldn't concentrate these days. She was like one of her schoolgirls when they had a crush on a boy and couldn't pay

171

attention in class. But she wasn't a schoolgirl, for heaven's sake, she was a nineteen-year-old woman. Why couldn't she get him out of her mind?

"Here is the water."

She opened her eyes at the sound of his voice. "I didn't hear you," she said, sipping from the tin cup that he held to her lips. When she pulled away, he forced the cup to her lips again.

"Finish."

She drank some more and then wiped her hand across her mouth. "Thank you."

"Why do you work here in the middle of the day when the sun is its hottest? Your body is not used to it. You are used to being inside. You can die from the sun if you are not careful."

"Your people work in the sun and don't die."

"My people are used to the sun. They are stronger."

"I'm strong," she said defensively.

He shook his head and poured the rest of the water on his hand. He gently slapped it on her cheeks. "You are not strong enough."

"You make me feel guilty for not being an Apache."

Shadow Hawk squatted down in front of her. "Apache women have a hard life. They die young. This life is better for you."

She looked into his gray-blue eyes. They were a stuning contrast to his dark hair and skin. She wanted to touch him. "I feel as if I have always known you," she said quietly, her voice trembling with emotion. He said nothing, but his hand went to her face, stroking it softly. She closed her eyes, resting her cheek against his hand.

"You are still so young." Abruptly he took his hand away.

She opened her eyes. "What's wrong?"

"You think of me as something I am not. You have built me up in your mind to be a hero."

"You are a hero to me."

"I am no hero, Aissa. You must listen to me." His voice was harsh. "I have white blood in me and I speak English, but I am no white man. I am Apache. I live the Apache way. Apache beliefs are far different from those of the whites."

"But it doesn't matter. You saved me and you didn't have to."

"I saved you because my mother was once kidnapped. That is the only reason."

"No, that isn't the only reason. You helped me because—"

"I helped you because I wanted to right a wrong that was done to my mother. There was no other reason."

"No," she replied, shaking her head.

"I have stolen things and I have killed people, Aissa. I am not the man you think I am. I am not the man you want me to be."

"Then why did you keep my locket all these years?"

"I kept it because it was a good trinket to have." Shadow Hawk stood. "I thought I would one day give it to my wife."

Aissa stood up, pushing past Shadow Hawk. "I don't believe you," she cried, tears rolling down her face. She started to run, but her legs betrayed her and she fell. The pain in her head was getting worse, and when she opened her eyes she saw floating colors. She started to get up but nausea rose and she sank back down to the ground. She thought of her mother and a panic overwhelmed her. Her mother had been overcome by fever and died within days. Was that the fate that awaited her?

"You are a stubborn woman."

She could barely see Shadow Hawk as she felt his arms go around her. "I can walk," she protested halfheartedly, but she laid her head against his bare shoulder when he picked her up in his arms.

"Why do you work like this? Do you try to make yourself sick?"

She liked the sound of his voice. She nuzzled her face into his shoulder. "Why are you angry with me?"

"I am angry because you are a smart woman, yet you do not use your brain." He stepped onto the porch and pushed open the door, carrying Aissa back to her room. Gently he placed her on the bed. She watched him as he poured water from the pitcher into the basin and put a cloth into it. He wrung out the wet cloth and walked back to the bed. He placed the cloth on her head.

"It's hot." She sat up, struggling to take off her apron, but she could barely lift her pounding head. She watched in fascination as Shadow Hawk slipped the apron off and deftly unbuttoned the blouse, pulling it from her skirt. He unlaced her boots and yanked them off, rolling down her stockings and taking them off as well. When he began to unbutton her skirt, she put her hand on his. "No," she pleaded, but he wouldn't listen. Quickly he undid the skirt and slipped it off. Now she lay before him in nothing more than a chemise. But she didn't care. She closed her eyes. The room spun and she felt as if she would be sick. The pain in her head hammered at her, increasing her fear. She reached for his hand, squeezing it tightly. "Am I going to die?"

Shadow Hawk took the cloth from her head and brushed her cheek. "You are not dying, Aisssa. You have a fever. That is all. We must cool your body down."

Shadow Hawk put the basin on the floor by the bed. He put the cloth in it and barely wrung it out, laying it across Aissa's forehead.

Aissa felt the cool cloth as he ran it over her face and neck and the insides of her arms. She opened her eyes. "Please tell me why you saved me. Please." Her eyes silently pleaded with his. He sat down on the edge of the bed, again running the cloth over her face and neck.

"I saved you because I did not want you to be hurt."

"Thank you," she said softly, closing her eyes. She heard his footfall across the room but she didn't open her eyes. Her body ached but didn't seek release from the pain. She only sought to sleep.

"Aissa, open your eyes," Shadow Hawk ordered in a firm voice.

Aissa felt tired. She wanted to sleep, but Shadow Hawk's voice kept intruding on her. She felt him push a cup to her mouth.

"Drink," he ordered.

She sipped at the water, but when it hit her stomach she felt as if she would vomit. She turned her head away. "No more."

Shadow Hawk poured the water on her face and neck, spreading it over her skin and soaking her chemise.

"My head," Aissa moaned. The pain was unbearable.

Shadow Hawk took her face in his hands and rubbed gently at her temples.

"Shadow Hawk!" Ben Gerard's voice boomed as he entered the room and walked to the bed.

Shadow Hawk didn't look up. "She is sick with fever, Gerard. I thought it was only the sun, but now I know it is more. I have seen this before. I have removed some of her clothes, made her drink water, and rubbed her with water. We must cool her body down."

"Here, I'll take that." Ben took the cloth from Shadow Hawk and gently ran it along Aissa's face and neck. He looked up at Shadow Hawk. "What happened? She was fine a couple of hours ago."

"After the white man left, she was upset. We talked and she complained that it was hot. I got her water to drink and she began to walk to the house and she collapsed. I carried her here."

Ben put his hand on Aissa's forehead. "God, she's burning up. I don't understand. She's always been so healthy."

"She works hard, Gerard. She works with her students and she runs this ranch. She does more than most men. Why do you let her work in the garden in the middle of the day? Do you not know how dangerous the sun is?"

"I don't need you to tell me about my daughter, damn it."

Shadow Hawk touched Ben's shoulder. "I am sorry. I worry for her, too."

"I know," Ben nodded, pushing back the stray strands of blond hair that fell on Aissa's face. "She cares deeply for you, Shadow Hawk."

"I hear the worry in your voice, Gerard. You do not think it is wise for your daughter to care for an Apache."

"Do you?"

Shadow Hawk walked to the other side of the bed and looked at Ben. "No, I do not think it is wise. I told Aissa this today."

"It's not you, Shadow Hawk. You understand that, don't you?"

"I understand, Gerard."

Ben shook his head in disgust. "You're bleeding again. You shouldn't have carried her to the house. You're still not completely healed."

"I am fine," Shadow Hawk said, glancing down at the bloodstained bandage around his stomach.

"I think I should ride for the doctor."

"What will he do for her?"

Ben shrugged. "I don't know."

"Let me help her, Gerard. I have seen this fever many times. It begins with a pain here." He touched his eyelids. "I have also seen the fever sweated out of people."

"I'm not going to cover her with blankets, if that's what you mean. I don't believe in that."

"I have medicine with me. Let me make a tea for Aissa. She will shake and sweat, but the fever will be gone quickly."

"I don't know . . ."

"Did this doctor help your wife, Gerard?"

Ben held Aissa's hand. "No."

"Then I will make the tea."

"What if it doesn't work?"

"It will work, Gerard. I would do nothing to hurt your daughter."

Ben nodded. "All right, go brew your tea, Shadow Hawk. Make my daughter well."

Shadow Hawk sat in a chair next to Aissa's bed. Ben had been there until Shadow Hawk had forced him to go to bed. Aissa rested fitfully, waking up but not knowing where she was. She muttered constantly in her sleep and occasionally thrashed around. Her skin glistened in the pale lamplight; she was sweating profusely. As he watched her fight the fever, Shadow Hawk realized just how much he had grown to care for Aissa. Or maybe he always had. Perhaps there had always been a connection between them, one that could never be broken.

As Shadow Hawk looked at Aissa, he contemplated his white heritage. It was something he didn't normally do, something he didn't usually like to think about. He had long ago accepted his grandfather, but he had not accepted the fact that he himself had white blood. He had always considered himself a Comanche, and when faced with a decision he had adapted to the Apache way of life. But never had he seriously considered what it would be like to live as a white man. Even after all the summers he had spent with his grandfather in the cabin, he had never thought of himself as anything but an Indian. Now he found himself in a situation where he owed his life to two white people. And to further complicate matters, he found himself caring for them both.

"Father?"

Aissa's voice sounded small and young in the dim light of the room. Shadow Hawk leaned forward, taking one of her hands. "No, it is Shadow Hawk."

"May I have some water?"

Shadow Hawk took a glass from the table next to the bed and supported her head with his arm as she sipped from it.

"Thank you." Aissa closed her eyes and slowly opened them again. "I thought you had gone back to your people."

177

"Why did you think that?"

"I don't know." She shivered. "Where is my father?"

"He is resting." Shadow Hawk reached for the bedspread and pulled it up to Aissa's waist.

"Have I been sleeping long?"

"For two days."

"Two days? That's not possible . . . I was just out in the garden."

"You fainted. I carried you to the house. You were burning with fever."

"I can't believe I've been asleep for two days. Is my father all right? He must be crazy with worry."

"He will be fine when he sees that you are well."

"You've been staying with me?"

"Yes."

"You don't have to do that anymore." Aissa pulled the bedspread up to cover herself.

"I will stay this night."

"That's not necessary, Shadow Hawk. I'm fine."

"I will decide for myself whether or not you are well."

"You're not my doctor," she said brusquely.

"I can see that you are feeling better. Your tongue has regained its sharpness."

"I don't want you to watch me sleep. It makes me nervous."

"I have watched you sleep for two nights now. I will not leave until your father wakes up." Shadow Hawk leaned back in his chair, propping his feet up on the bed. "If you are not going to sleep, I will." He closed his eyes.

"I never asked for your help."

"But your father did." Shadow Hawk didn't open his eyes.

"I think you should leave. I remember what you said in the garden before I got sick." Her voice sounded angry and hurt.

Shadow Hawk opened his eyes. "I will leave when I am sure that you are well."

"I think you should go now." Aissa could barely get the

178

words out. She turned her head away.

Shadow Hawk sat on the edge of the bed and gently turned Aissa's face toward him. Tears streamed down her cheeks. Her face was still hot. "It is important for you to sleep. We can talk later."

Her lips trembled as she spoke. "There is nothing for us to talk about. Soon you will go back to your people."

"Is that what you want?"

"Yes."

"You are a young woman. Do you not think of a husband and children?"

"No." She replied adamantly, trying to turn away from his grasp. "Please, let me go."

"Listen to my words, Aissa." His voice was deep and strong. She couldn't ignore it. When Aissa finally looked at him, he continued. "I have thought of you many times over the past years. I have thought of your hair that is the color of cornsilk, and your eyes that are the color of the sky on a cloudless day. I have wondered many times if you were happy and if your life was good. At first I wanted to help you because of what had happened to my mother, but then I wanted to help you because you were so innocent, so young. I knew you did not deserve to be hurt in any way." He brushed the tears from her cheeks. "I still do not wish for you to be hurt."

"You're going to leave soon, aren't you?" Aissa couldn't stop crying.

"It is for the best."

"No, it's not for the best." Aissa sat up, throwing her arms around Shadow Hawk's neck and hugging him tightly.

Shadow Hawk froze. He hadn't expected this. He felt Aissa's body as she pressed against his chest. He knew he should push her away, but he couldn't. He wrapped his arms around her, pulling her even closer, knowing all the while that nothing could come of it. He put his hands on her face and pushed her hair back. "You must rest, Aissa. The fever

179

has not yet passed."

"I have never known what it's like to love a man."

"Now is not the time for that," he said, his voice sounding more controlled than he actually felt.

"Just hold me. Please."

Shadow Hawk tightened his hold and pulled her into his lap. He cradled her, continuously stroking her hair. When she lifted her head from his shoulder and looked at him again, her eyes looked different. Slowly, he ran his fingertips over her face, tracing the curve of her cheekbone. When he came to her mouth, he barely touched her trembling lips before running his fingertips down her jaw to the hollow in her neck. "You are so beautiful," he muttered. Softly he pressed his mouth to hers, feeling the sweet fullness of her lips. He knew that in her mind she had already given herself to him. Suddenly he became aware of everything—her firm breasts pressing against his bare chest, her mouth yielding to his, the fact that her body was within his grasp. This woman was his.

He ran his hands down her bare arms and up again until he cupped her face in his hands. He kissed her deeply, never before realizing how gratifying it was to kiss a woman, but overwhelmed by the sheer pleasure of it. His hand found her bare leg and he pushed her chemise up. She moaned slightly as he rubbed her inner thigh. He looked at her face—her cheeks were still flushed from the fever, her lips full, her eyes closed. He wanted more than anything to have this woman, but he knew he could not. She was not yet well, but that was not the only reason. Her fever made her unable to think clearly. What he had said in the garden was true. He would not take her this way. He couldn't do that to Aissa and he couldn't do it to Ben.

He put his hands on her shoulders and gently shoved her back down on the bed. "You still need to rest." He stood up.

Aissa grabbed his hand. "Don't leave."

"I will stay here with you."

"Don't leave the ranch, not yet."

"I will be leaving soon, Aissa. I must."

"Then I will go back with you."

"No!" His reply was so strong he surprised even himself. "You would never survive with my people."

"Then don't leave yet. Give us some time."

"Your father is anxious for me to leave."

"My father does not live my life for me."

"I respect your father for what he has done for me and I know how much you love him." He stroked her hand before letting it go. "We can have no future together, Aissa. You must see that. As soon as I know that you are well, I will leave. You will live your life and I will live mine." Aissa looked away and he could hear that she was crying. But he did nothing to comfort her because he was afraid to touch her again. If he touched her he might not be able to control his desire for her. There was nothing he could do or say. What he had said to her was the truth—an Apache and a white woman could not be together. The only good thing he could do for her was to leave as soon as she was well.

Chapter 9

Ray Grimes was accustomed to getting what he wanted. He looked out his bedroom window to the hills beyond. This land had belonged to his family for over forty years. He smiled when he thought of the land.

His father had not been the most scrupulous of men, but he had been smart enough to switch the names on the deed to Francois Renard's thousands of acres when the old man had returned to France. All it had taken was a few thousand dollars and it was done. Because Renard lived in France, there was no way he could fight Ray's father.

When Renard's daughter, Celou, came to see the land for herself, she had been surprised to find out that her father owned only a small portion of the land, not the thousands of acres he had spoken of. Renard had lost all the money he had invested. Celou hired a lawyer and tried to get the land back, but there was no way to prove that the deeds had been altered, so Celou went to see Ray's father.

Ray thought back to the first time he had seen Celou—she was the most beautiful creature he had ever seen and his father had felt the same way. Even after Celou had married Ben and returned to live on her ranch, Ray's father had tried to get Celou to run away with him. She had always refused and she had made it perfectly clear that she wanted nothing to do with him.

Ray picked up the glass of brandy from the desk and swirled it around, sniffing it. Ray had inherited, or perhaps learned, his father's sense of business. He had improved the mercantile and established business connections in the east so that he could get almost anything any customer wanted. Of course, that wasn't so difficult for him because he was part owner of the railroad and could assure deliveries to his own store—and occasionally prevent deliveries to the three or four stores in the neighboring towns. He owned a saloon that catered to the ranch hands and travelers, providing them with liquor, women, and gambling. But he also owned the restaurant in the hotel that catered to families who wanted to eat good food in a nice place. Not that Ray cared about people; he was just a smart businessman and gave people what they wanted. He also enjoyed the air of respectability that the hotel restaurant gave him.

Ray was used to getting what he wanted, and what he wanted now was to get rid of the Apache. The Apache had posed more of a problem than he had thought, but he would soon be eliminated. What Ray hadn't counted on was the way Aissa cared for the Indian. It complicated matters. But nothing was impossible; Ray had learned that a long time ago.

Ray wanted Aissa Gerard, but he was also a pragmatist. He knew that Aissa didn't love or want him. In truth, he didn't really love her, but he wanted her and what she could give him. She and her father were well-respected in the town and she was the kind of woman people admired. It didn't hurt that she was also French. A lot of people were impressed by that. Also, Aissa was so stunningly beautiful that when she walked down the center of town, men stopped to look at her. Ray knew she could provide him with the kind of respect he had always wanted from the people of Agua Prieta and beyond. He could imagine walking into the Chicago railyards with her on his arm. Those ·big-city bandits would notice, all right. They would never treat him like a backwater baron again.

Now the only question was how to get rid of the Apache. It wouldn't be easy, he knew, but a man of his talents would come up with something. If he was lucky, maybe he could get rid of Ben Gerard and the Apache at the same time. Aissa would have no choice but to turn to him. Then she would be all his.

Aissa smacked her hoe into the soil of the garden, deliberately ignoring Shadow Hawk's warning not to work in the sun. She wore a broad-brimmed hat that kept the sun from her head, but she still worked at a furious pace. When she was finished loosening the soil around the primrose, she walked to the barn and got a hammer, dropping some nails into the pocket of her apron. There were so many things that needed to be mended around the ranch she couldn't count them all. Maybe it was time to hire someone to help out. Or maybe it was time that she worked here full time and gave up teaching. As much as she loved her students, the ranch would fall apart if she didn't do the needed repairs soon.

Aissa left the barn and walked to the corral. The gate was falling apart, and several of the rails needed to be supported. She unlatched the gate and dragged it open. She smiled as she recalled the times when she was a little girl and had stood on the bottom rail of the gate and ridden it all the way to the fence. But that was a long time ago, before her mother died, when things still worked around the ranch, when her father was still happy, and before she had had to grow up much too soon.

She took a piece of wood and steadied it on the rail, holding it in place with her foot as she hammered in the first nail. Then she switched sides and drove in another nail. She held onto the wood, pulling it back and forth. It didn't shake quite as much, but soon she would have to replace most of the fencing. She worked around the corral, fixing weakened railings with supports until the corral was reinforced. She pulled the gate closed and latched it, and walked to the other corral.

She pulled another nail out of her pocket and was about to drive it when she stopped. She stood on the bottom rail, leaning on the top, looking at Shadow Hawk's magnificent paint. As much as she tried not to think about Shadow Hawk, she found it impossible not to. He was always on her mind. A week had passed since they had last spoken, since she had poured out her heart to him, had practically begged him to love her. She grimaced at the thought, embarrassed that she could be so naive, that she could humiliate herself so. Ever since that night, she and Shadow Hawk had made certain to avoid each other. She wasn't even sure why he stayed. He was well enough to ride now. She almost wished he would leave. It would be easier for her if he was gone.

The previous night she had read to her father, as she always did at night, and while turning a page she looked up to find Shadow Hawk staring at her. She met his eyes for a moment, then continued to read. She wasn't sure what she had seen there—she didn't even want to guess. All she knew for sure was that he was an uncomfortable around her as she was around him.

He had been right about one thing, however. As well as he spoke English, he didn't think like a white man, he thought like an Apache. She had misjudged him. She thought that he understood her feelings, but he had not. And as embarrassed as she had been, she couldn't really be angry with him. He had been honest with her.

She pounded nails furiously, wondering what she had been thinking when she said she could live with his people. She had never embarrassed herself like that with any man before.

"Do you need help?"

She closed her eyes for a moment. She hadn't heard

Shadow Hawk come up behind her. She never heard him. She wondered if he did that on purpose. "No, thank you," she replied curtly, pounding so hard the railing shook.

"It would be easier if I held the wood. The nails are not going in straight."

Aissa slammed the hammer down on the wood. "When did you become an expert at this?"

"I spent summers with my grandfather in his cabin. I helped him build many things."

"I don't need your help." Aissa continued pounding nails, trying to ignore Shadow Hawk's looming presence. "Do you mind?" she asked, stopping abruptly. "There's work that has to be done around here."

"I want to help."

"And I told you, I don't need your help. This isn't your ranch. Isn't it about time you went back to your people?" She turned back to the corral, but she felt Shadow Hawk's hand on hers, pulling her around.

"Listen to me, Aissa. Please."

Aissa turned around, resting the hammer in her hand. "What?"

"I am sorry for what happened. I did not mean to hurt you."

"I had a fever, I was delirious. I didn't know what I was saying. You didn't hurt me," Aissa replied coldly, trying to ignore Shadow Hawk. She pounded another nail into the railing. When she turned around, Shadow Hawk was still standing there, watching her. "What do you want from me?"

"I only want to know that you are all right."

"Of course I'm all right, why wouldn't I be?" She marched past him toward the barn, throwing the nails in an old bucket and hanging up the hammer. When she turned around, Shadow Hawk was standing behind her, blocking her way out of the barn. "Would you please move?"

"Not until you look at me."

"I am looking at you."

Shadow Hawk brushed her cheek lightly. "When I look at you, when I am around you, I wish that I had more white blood in me. I wish that I were more like a white man."

Aissa shuffled her feet, lowering her eyes to the ground. She hadn't expected this. "It's all right, really." She attempted to push past him, but he gripped her shoulders.

"If I could take you with me, I would. But the Apache life is not for a woman like you. It is hard and it is unforgiving."

"Please—" Aissa shook her head, unable to look at Shadow Hawk.

"You want to hear the words from me." He lifted her chin, forcing her to look at him. "I will say the words." His eyes pierced hers. "If I could stay here and not cause you and your father harm, I would do that. But we both know that is impossible." He put his fingers on Aissa's mouth, slowly moving them across her full lips.

Aissa felt her mouth tremble and she closed her eyes. She wanted to pull away from him, but she could not. She stepped closer until her head rested on his bare chest. "Why did you have to do this?"

"I could not go away without saying the words."

She wrapped her arms around him. "I don't want you to say anymore." She looked up at him. "I don't want you to say things and then go away."

"I should have taken you away from Teroz that day in camp and kept you for my own. By now you would have been my wife."

"Why are you saying these things now?" Aissa pulled away. "Why?"

"Because I could not leave you with such sadness on your face. You are beautiful and strong, and you have a kind heart. But we are not destined to be together. You cannot live in my world and I cannot live in yours. All we can do is remember how we touched each other."

Aissa tried to pull away, but Shadow Hawk held onto her. "I don't want to hear anymore. Please."

"I want you to hear, Aissa, and I want you to remember." Shadow Hawk tenderly touched her cheek. "I cannot stop thinking of you. I wonder what it would be like to be with you all the time." He held her close. "And I wish I could know you as a man knows a woman."

Aissa shoved him away, shaking her head. "No! I don't want to hear anymore." She pushed by him and ran out of the barn. She kept running until she tired. Then she walked. She stopped when she reached the lake that had always been her favorite place on the ranch. In the middle of this barren land, there was an area that was lush and green. The trees and plants were fed by an underground spring, and even in the hottest of summers, the lake stayed full.

She knelt by the edge and splashed water on her face, trying to cool off, then she cupped her hands and drank. She fell back against the cool, moist bank. She could hear the breeze as it rustled the leaves of the oaks and cottonwoods and she closed her eyes. Her heart was pounding. She felt as if it would explode. She didn't want to think anymore. But Shadow Hawk intruded into her thoughts, not willing to leave her alone. She remembered the feel of his skin as she laid her cheek against it, and the way he had touched her lips. How could she ever explain the way she felt about him to anyone, especially her father? This was a time when people feared Indians, especially Apache, and she was growing to care more deeply for one with each passing day.

She wondered what her mother would have thought. Her mother, Celou, had been educated and opinionated and quite secure in her beauty. She had liked men and they had loved her. She had charmed them with her wit and her French accent, but she had always made it clear that her only love was Ben Gerard. She had met him in New Orleans while she was visiting relatives and Ben was traveling. She could have married any number of men, but she had fallen wildly in love with the maverick American who had dreams of going west. Eventually, Celou and Ben had moved to Agua

Prieta to live on the land Celou's family owned.

Aissa remembered her mother's twinkling eyes as she had told the story of her marriage to Ben and how her parents had disapproved. They had pleaded with her to leave Ben and offered to pay him off, but Celou had convinced her parents that she had found her true love. Aissa wished her mother were here now. She knew she would understand how she felt about Shadow Hawk.

"Aissa."

Shadow Hawk had done it again. He had sneaked up on her and she hadn't heard a sound. Aissa threw an arm over her eyes. She didn't want to see him. She didn't want him to see the weakness in her eyes. "Go away."

"I will be going away. Soon."

Reluctantly, Aissa uncovered her eyes and sat up. "I suppose I'll never see you again after you leave."

"I do not think so."

Aissa nodded. She started to get up, but Shadow Hawk took her hand and sat down next to her.

"Wait."

"I have to get back to the ranch. I still have repairs to do."

"Not yet." Shadow Hawk's voice was insistent.

Aissa shook her head. "I don't have time for this."

"You are a stubborn woman."

"Let me go." Aissa tried to pull her hand from his grasp.

"Listen to my words, Aissa, for I will not say them again."

Aissa stopped, Shadow Hawk's eyes compelling her to stay. Her eyes searched his. "I will listen, Shadow Hawk."

Shadow Hawk again rubbed his fingers along Aissa's cheek. "Do you feel these hands, Aissa? These are not the hands of a man who is used to touching a woman. They are rough and calloused. These hands do not know tenderness." He looked into her eyes. "I have been with women, but I have not known love. I have known only pleasure." He stroked her hair. "When I was with my father, I thought like a Comanche. When I lived with my grandfather, I thought like he did. And now that I am living with my mother's people, I think like an Apache. But when I am with you, I do not think like any people, I think like a man. You make me want that which is not possible, Aissa." He leaned his head forward until it touched hers.

Aissa sighed deeply, moved by Shadow Hawk's words. "Why isn't it possible, Shadow Hawk? You have not been unhappy here. Maybe we could find a place where we could live away from my people and your people."

Shadow Hawk shook his head. "And that would make you happy?"

"It would make me happy to be with you."

"How do you know this? My life has been so different from yours. You do not really know me."

"But I do." She reached up and touched his face. "You are the same person who saved me five years ago. I see the way you are with my father; you care for him deeply. And I see the way you look at me."

"How do I look at you, Aissa?"

"With tenderness."

"Is that all you see in my eyes?"

Aissa felt herself blush. "No."

"What else do you see, Aissa?"

Aissa lowered her eyes for a moment, trying to gather the courage to say what she wanted to say. "I see that you want me."

Shadow Hawk gathered Aissa's thick hair in one hand and lifted it, then let it spill through his fingers. He pressed his lips to her forehead.

Aissa closed her eyes, refusing to let herself feel ashamed or embarrassed. When Shadow Hawk touched his lips to hers, she sighed. She reveled in the warmth of his mouth on hers. She rested her hands on his chest and he pulled her close. She wasn't afraid. She had wanted him for a very long time.

She wrapped her arms around his neck as their kiss

deepened and their bodies pressed against each other. "I don't want you to go," she breathed softly, kissing him passionately.

"Aissa."

"I will go with you."

"No." He moved his mouth down her neck.

"Yes," she sighed, throwing her head back as he moved his mouth lower down her neck. She felt his fingers fumble on the buttons of her bodice, and she was about to help him when she felt his hand on her bare breast, gently pressing it. His mouth sought hers again and her blouse fell from her shoulders. She stroked his hair when his mouth moved to her breasts and she leaned back, arching toward him. Her breath came in quick bursts, as if she'd been running, and she felt as if the world had shrunk around them. There was only this, only the two of them.

"You are so beautiful, Aissa."

Aissa opened her eyes and looked at Shadow Hawk. His face was so handsome, and for once his eyes hid nothing. "I love you, Shadow Hawk," she said, surprised by her own words. His body pressed her gently backward until she lay on the ground. He kissed her again, his body against hers. She had never been kissed like this before, and she yearned for more. Just as she felt they would never stop exploring each other, reveling in each other, Shadow Hawk sat up, yanking on her arm.

"Stand up." He ordered.

"Why?" Aissa looked up at him, puzzled.

"Quickly!" Shadow Hawk pulled Aissa to her feet. "Riders are approaching."

Instinctively, she knew it was trouble. She pulled on her blouse and began to button it, but her fingers trembled nervously. Instead, she tucked it into her skirt, overlapping the edges. It wasn't long before Aissa saw Ray on his black gelding, followed by several of his men. The riders formed a circle around Aissa and Shadow Hawk.

"Stay behind me," Shadow Hawk said quietly. He pulled out his knife and held it flat against his leg.

"Well, well, look what we found," Ray said, smiling broadly as he rode up. "You did a good job, Aissa. I couldn't have planned it better myself."

"What're you talking about?" Aissa demanded, jolted out of her nervousness.

Ray sat calmly atop his horse, one leg hooked over the horn. "What's the matter, Apache, didn't Aissa tell you we had this planned?"

Shadow Hawk looked at Aissa, his eyes questioning.

"I don't know what he's talking about. Honestly, I don't." Aissa pleaded with Shadow Hawk to listen to her. "Can't you see that he's lying."

"Why don't you tell your Apache boyfriend how I knew you were going to be here at this place at this particular time of day? Why don't you ask her, Injun?"

Aissa moved to stand between Ray's horse and Shadow Hawk, trying to get Shadow Hawk to look at her. "I didn't plan anything. He's just doing this to separate us. Can't you see that?"

"I bet she even asked you to take her with you. Hell, she's been trying to get out of here for as long as I've known her. She always makes me out to be the bad guy, but I'm always the one she turns to when she's finished with one of her new men friends." Ray shrugged his shoulders. "Hell, I almost feel sorry for you, Injun. She had you believing real hard, didn't she?"

"Is this true?" Shadow Hawk's voice was hard and his eyes cold.

"No, it's not true." Aissa lowered her voice. "I've never even been with a man before. Ever."

"Course there were all those years you spent in St. Louis. The way your father tells it, you didn't want to come back here. You were having yourself a wild time."

"He's lying!"

"Tell the Apache about the man who visited you from St. Louis."

Aissa shook her head. "He was just a friend."

"And the one from Paris?"

"A friend."

"How about—"

"Stop it!" Aissa yelled. "He's lying, Shadow Hawk. You have to believe me." She put her hands on his chest.

Shadow Hawk looked at her and then up at Ray. "What is your interest in this woman?"

Ray shrugged. "I guess it's no surprise that she took me in once, too. I guess I keep hoping that eventually she'd get tired of chasing every man who comes into town and want to settle down."

"You liar!" Aissa ran to Ray, pounding on his leg with her fists. "I hate you! Why are you doing this to me?"

"Doing what, Aissa? You're the one who told me you'd be out here. You said you'd had enough of this Apache and you wanted him gone. So here I am. But it looks to me like he's ready to leave on his own."

Aissa turned and saw the look of disgust on Shadow Hawk's face. She ran to him. "You don't believe him, do you?"

Shadow Hawk looked at Ray. "Do not worry, white man. I will not be back." He turned and headed toward the ranch.

Aissa grabbed his arm. "You can't go. Please, Shadow Hawk. He's lying. Listen to me."

Shadow Hawk pulled her away from the others. "What about the men he has spoken of?"

"They were only friends, that's all."

"Like me."

"No, you're more than that. Didn't I prove that today?"

"You proved nothing today except that you were willing to give yourself to me. And you were willing to do it quite easily."

"God, no." Aissa lowered her head, not knowing what to

193

say. When Shadow Hawk started walking, she tugged at his arm. "Please, Shadow Hawk, if you don't believe me, talk to my father. You trust him. He knows how I feel about you, and he knows what kind of a man Ray is."

"How did he know we were here?" Shadow Hawk's voice was cold, unfeeling.

"Maybe he followed us, I don't know. He hates you and he wants to force you away from me."

Shadow Hawk shook his head. "It makes sense to me now. White people cannot be trusted, especially white women." Shadow Hawk nodded toward Ray. "Go to this man, be with him if you must." He started toward the ranch.

Aissa grabbed his arm again. "What about my father? What do I tell him?"

"Thank him for his kindness. Tell him my people will not raid his ranch."

"Shadow Hawk, please come back with me. Talk to my father. Don't leave like this."

Again, Shadow Hawk looked at Ray. "No, this is best. Now you can live in your world and I will return to mine." He started running. Aissa started to call his name, then pressed the back of her hand against her mouth. In a moment he was gone, swallowed up by the trees. It seemed as if he had never existed.

Aissa stood stunned. She couldn't believe that Shadow Hawk would take Ray's word over hers. How was it possible that minutes before they had almost been making love, and now he would be leaving her forever? Slowly, without thinking, Aissa started toward the ranch.

"No you don't, not yet." Ray leaned down from his horse, grabbed Aissa's arm, and jerked her around. "I'm not finished yet."

"Let me go!" Aissa screamed, struggling to get away.

Ray dismounted, still holding onto Aissa's arm. He turned to his men. "You ride out of earshot. I'm going to have a talk with Miss Gerard." He tightened his grasp on her arm. "I'm going to give you a choice here, little lady. Either you marry me within the week, or I'll make sure that every Apache from here to those mountains is slaughtered and their scalps hung up for everyone to see."

"Why, Ray? Why would you do something like that?"

"Because it makes me sick to think of you willingly giving yourself to filth like that. And if he ever does come back, I'll skin him alive, you hear me?"

Aissa stared at Ray. He meant it. She shivered and forced herself to speak. "I'll never see him again. He won't be back."

"That's not good enough. I want you as my wife."

"Why? You know I don't love you."

"I don't love you, either. But we're a good match for each other."

"I'll never marry you."

"I think you will. And you'd better convince your father that you want to marry me."

"He'll never believe me."

"You'd better *make* him believe you or I'll make sure he meets with an accident of some kind. I threatened to do it before, and this time I will. It'd be real easy in his line of work."

Aissa turned away from Ray, unable to absorb everything that had just happened. Should she tell her father? He could arrest Ray and then he could help her find Shadow Hawk. But she knew that neither would happen. Her father couldn't arrest Ray because Ray was too powerful. She also knew that Ray was ruthless enough to carry out his threats.

She would never forget the look of disgust on Shadow Hawk's face. He had felt betrayed. The faint sound of hoofbeats in the distance made her raise her eyes. Even from here, there was no mistaking the paint stallion. Now Shadow Hawk was truly gone.

"Didn't take him long to get out of here." Ray laughed. "Well, what's your answer, Aissa?"

Aissa knew she was trapped. Her thought spun, and she

fought an impulse to run. But where would she go? And even if she managed to get away, Ray would be so angry he would hurt her father. There was no way out. Hating herself, she looked up at Ray and nodded. "All right, Ray, I'll marry you." He started to speak but she cut him off. "If anything ever happens to my father, I swear, I'll kill you."

"Do you really expect me to be afraid of anything you say?"

"I expect you to remember how much I love my father. If he dies, nothing will matter to me. Nothing."

Ray held up his hands. "All right, all right. As long as we're married, I'll make sure nothing happens to your father. Hell, I'll even send men over to fix up that ranch for him." Ray narrowed his eyes. "Just as long as you keep your end of the deal."

"I said I'd marry you. I will."

"And convince your father you're marrying me because you want to. No slip-ups. Tell him whatever you want about the Apache, I don't care, but make it sound believable."

Aissa nodded, suddenly weary. "I'd like to go home now."

"Today is Tuesday. I'll give you three days to get ready for the wedding. We'll get married on Saturday."

Aissa nodded, too numb even to respond. Shadow Hawk was gone. She would never see him again, would never feel his arms around her, would never feel his lips touch hers again. Worst of all, he had left believing that she had betrayed him.

Tears welled up in Aissa's eyes and she began to sob as she walked back to the ranchhouse. She wanted to be angry with Shadow Hawk for not believing her, but she could understand why he would not. Ray had sounded convincing. And the truth was that Shadow Hawk didn't really believe they belonged together. Maybe this was the excuse he had been looking for to leave her and return to his people.

Aissa turned her head and looked out at the distant mountains. "Good-bye," she sobbed loudly, running to the house, trying to forget that she had ever known Shadow Hawk and been so close to loving him.

Aissa wandered through her wedding day in a daze. She barely remembered the ceremony, and when Ray kissed her she cringed. But she put on a good enough act for just about everyone to believe that she really wanted to marry Ray. Everyone, that is, except Ben.

Aissa was accepting congratulations from neighbors when Ben took her by the elbow and led her away from the guests in the parlor to the porch outside. There were a few ranchhands standing on the porch, drinking whiskey from a bottle, so Ben led Aissa down the stairs.

"Let's walk," he said, holding his daughter's hand.

"I really should be inside, Father. I have guests to talk to and Ray will wonder where I am."

"Is this what you really want, Aissa?" Ben stopped, taking his daughter's hands in his. His expression was gentle.

Aissa wanted to tell her father everything at that moment, but she couldn't take a chance. She couldn't risk his life for any reason. Her father was a good man, an honest man, but he was no match for Ray Grimes. She smiled wanly. "Yes, Father, this is what I want."

"I don't believe you."

"I told you before, I changed my mind."

"Aissa Marie, this is me, your father. You can't lie to me. You never could."

"I'm not lying to you, Father."

"Then tell me what happened to Shadow Hawk."

"I already told you, he just left. I was working on the corral, we talked, and the next thing I knew, he was on his horse and gone."

"You're lying."

Aissa fiddled with the lace on her cuff. "I am not."

"Shadow Hawk wouldn't leave without saying good-bye

to me."

"He's an Apache, Father. No matter how well he speaks English, he will always be an Apache. I think you and I forgot that."

Ben seemed to consider what Aissa said. "Maybe. What about your change of heart concerning Ray?" Ben shook his head. "You don't love him, Aissa. Hell, I don't think you even like him."

"That's not true. Ray and I have a lot in common."

"Like what?"

Aissa tried to think of something, but she couldn't. She and Ray didn't agree on one thing. She turned away from her father. "I really should be getting back. My guests will be wondering where I am."

Ben grabbed Aissa's arm. "He forced you into this, didn't he? I swear, I'll kill the bastard if he's threatened you in any way."

Aissa saw the look on her father's face and she knew she had to convince him that she was all right. She touched his cheek. "I'm just fine, father. I admit that I grew to care for Shadow Hawk while he was here, but I never loved him. I lied to you about something else—Ray and I have been seeing each other almost every day for a long time. We'd meet out by the lake. I can talk to him. I may not love him, but I'll have a good life with him."

Ben's eyes held Aissa's. "You're sure? You wouldn't lie to me, would you?"

"No, Father, I wouldn't lie to you. This is what I want." Aissa kissed Ben on the cheek. "Let's go back now."

"Aissa."

"Yes, Father?"

"If you ever need to talk to me about anything, you can come to me. You know that, don't you?"

"Yes, I know that." Aissa took her father's hand.

"If you ever get lonely or you just want to visit, you come by. All right?"

Aissa almost started to cry. She hugged him and kissed him on the cheek. "I'll be over almost every day. It'll be like I never left. Besides, Ray says that I can use some of his men to help fix up the ranch."

"I don't need his help. I'll do just fine on my own."

"Father, please, I want to help you. Let me."

Ben softened. "We'll see."

Aissa put her arm through her father's as they walked back to Ray's enormous house. This wasn't how she had pictured her wedding day. She had always imagined her wedding day to be one of overwhelming joy and happiness. Instead, she felt nothing but dread for what was to come.

"Did Shadow Hawk say anything before he left?"

Aissa realized then how fond her father had grown of Shadow Hawk. She nodded. "Yes, he wanted me to thank you for your kindness to him. He said to tell you he would make sure your ranch is never raided by his people."

Ben nodded, seemingly satisfied. "I wish I'd been able to say good-bye."

"I don't think he wanted it that way, Father. I think it was easier for him to just go."

Ben nodded his head and shrugged his shoulders. "Guess so."

They reached the porch steps and Ben stopped. Aissa turned to him. "Aren't you coming inside?"

"No, I think I'll head on home. I'm kind of tired today."

"Please don't go yet, Father." Aissa hugged her father again, burying her face in his shoulder.

"Aissa!" Ray's voice commanded her from the door. "Our guests are waiting."

Aissa looked at her father. "Please stay."

"No, you go on to your husband. This is your day. I'll be dropping by in the next day or two." He kissed her on each cheek. "I love you, Aissa. Be happy."

"Thank you, Father." Aissa watched her father walk toward his horse and she was certain he was walking a step slower. He knew. He knew the marriage wasn't right.

"So, is he convinced?" Ray stood on the step behind Aissa, his arms around her waist.

Aissa forced herself to remain calm. "Yes, I think so."

"Then why is he leaving already?"

"He's not feeling well." Aissa unwrapped Ray's arms from around her waist.

"Are you sure?"

"Yes, Ray, I'm sure," she replied brusquely, brushing by him and up the stairs. She went back inside the parlor and played the dutiful bride and hostess. She talked with neighbors, gossiped with some of the ladies, talked to parents about their children, and even talked horses with some of the ranchers. All the while she forced herself not to think of her father or Shadow Hawk.

By the end of the day, Aissa was exhausted and Ray had had too much to drink. She was hoping that he would pass out before they went to bed. By the time the last guests had left, Aissa began to clear platters of food but Ray stopped her, taking her wrist and leading her to the stairs.

"Leave it. The servants will get it."

"But all the food—"

"I said leave it. It's our wedding night." Ray kissed her. "Why don't you go on up to your room while I grab another bottle of champagne? There's something on your bed. I want you to put it on."

Aissa didn't respond. Slowly she walked up the stairs until she reached her room. Once inside, she shut the door and leaned against it, closing her eyes, willing the world away. Finally she walked to the bed and saw what Ray wanted her to wear. It was nightgown, sheer and red, the kind prostitutes wore for their customers. She snatched it up and began ripping the flimsy material. When she was finished, she threw the pieces on the floor. When she heard Ray's boots, she hurried to the door and locked it, backing slowly away. She went to her nightstand and poured the water into

200

the bowl, holding the pitcher in front of her. It wasn't much of a weapon, but if she had to use it, she would. Ray tried the door handle and began banging on the door.

"Open the God-damned door, Aissa. It's a little late for you to be playing the blushing bride. You forget, I saw you with that Apache."

Aissa felt her face burn but it wasn't from shame, it was from fury. "I'm not going to."

"Well, that's just too bad. You're a married woman now and you have duties to fulfill. I'll just have to break it down."

"I said I'd marry you, I never said I'd do anything else." Aissa gripped the pitcher.

"You little bitch!" Ray yelled. He began kicking the door. "Open the door, Aissa!"

"No." Aissa backed up against the wall as Ray's furious pounding became louder and louder until at last, the door broke open. Ray stood before her, his chest heaving, the champagne spilling out of the bottle. "We had a deal, little lady. You break your end of it, your daddy could wind up dead."

"Sharing your bed was not part of the deal, Ray."

Ray walked forward, swigging from the champagne bottle. "It goes unsaid that a man's wife is supposed to share his bed." He stopped when he saw the nightgown on the floor. He bent over and picked it up. He looked at Aissa, his eyes cold and empty. He walked to her, backing her up against the wall. She held the pitcher in front of her but Ray knocked it out of her hand. He shoved the red material in her face. "So this is what you think of my present."

Aissa turned her head away. "Red's not my color." Her voice was hard but she was frightened. Still, she wouldn't back down from Ray.

"You really are a little bitch, aren't you?" He wrapped a piece of the nightgown around Aissa's neck and pulled it tightly. When she reached up to loosen it, he knocked her hand away. "Not so funny now, is it?" He twisted the ends of the nightgown until Aissa could barely breathe. "If I were you, I wouldn't move. I wouldn't want you to choke to death on our wedding night." Ray grabbed the bodice of Aissa's wedding dress and jerked downward, ripping it and the chemise that was underneath. Her breasts were exposed and when she reached up to cover them, he tightened the material around her throat. "I wouldn't," he warned.

"Ray, please," Aissa gasped, "I can't breathe."

"Then you better do as I ask." He turned her around and stripped her naked to the waist, then shoved her toward the bed. "Take hold of one of those bedposts."

Aissa tried to move away but Ray grabbed her hair, forcing her toward the bed. He took the nightgown from around her neck and tied her wrists around the bedpost so she couldn't pull away. "Ray, please—" Aissa struggled to free her hands.

Ray walked to the door and kicked it closed. "You'd better shut your mouth. You've said too much already."

Aissa had never been this afraid, not even in the Apache camp. "Ray, I'm sorry. I didn't mean to make you angry." Aissa said desperately.

"It's a little late for that, Frenchy," he whispered in her ear as he stood behind her. "You've always thought you were so much better than everyone else around here, haven't you? Just because your mother was some French whore. Well, that's all you are, Aissa, is another French whore, only you don't even know how to please a man." Ray reached from behind and grabbed Aissa's breasts, squeezing them.

Aissa froze. She felt Ray's body press against her from behind. His hands were rough and he didn't care how much he hurt her. She bit her lip to keep from saying anything, to keep from crying out.

"What's the matter, don't you like that? Answer me, damn it!"

Aissa remained silent as Ray ran his hand down her belly. She steeled herself for whatever was to come. Her fear excited him, she knew, so she stood motionless.

"All right, you want to play that way, I can do that."

Aissa looked over her shoulder. She saw Ray take his belt from his pants and wrap it around his hand.

"Before this night is out, you're going to beg my forgiveness."

"Never," Aissa gasped as the belt slapped across her back and cut into her flesh. "My father will kill you for this."

"I'm too smart to leave any scars, Aissa. Your father will never know." The belt hit her again, and the force of it knocked her forward. She hit her head on the post, but she managed to stand, grasping the polished wood as tightly as she could. When the belt came again, it seemed worse than the first time. She felt as if her back had been sliced into pieces. As the pain started to subside, Ray hit her again and again until her legs buckled. She half-leaned, half-hung against the post. She didn't even hear him leave. She only heard the sound of her pain.

When Aissa opened her eyes, moonlight was pouring through the window, pale and cold. She could barely move but she willed herself to stand up as she used her teeth to untie the knots that bound her hands. Her arms shook, but she finally loosened the material and got her hands free. She sat on the edge of the bed, her head in her hands. She wanted to cry but she wouldn't allow herself to. Somehow she had to remain strong.

Slowly she got up from the bed and walked to her trunk, pulling out one of her nightgowns. She started to push the rest of her dress off but stopped suddenly, shocked by what she saw. The skirt of her wedding dress was spattered with blood, her blood. Her hands shaking, she shoved the skirt off, along with her stockings, shoes, and pantaloons. Then she walked to her nightstand, holding her gown in front of her. She half-turned so she could see her back. Just as quickly, she turned away and braced herself on the stand, taking deep breaths. She splashed water from the bowl onto her face and again she turned to look at her back. She was covered with blood and thick welts.

She pulled the nightgown over her head, crying out as the material stuck to her bloody back. There was nothing she could do. She couldn't clean the wounds herself and she had nothing to put on them. All she could do now was try to rest.

She walked to the bed and turned down the lamp. She sat on the edge of the bed and looked through the lace curtains to the yard outside her window. People were still singing and dancing. They were enjoying her wedding day. Her shoulders shook as she began to cry, and she put a pillow to her mouth to stifle the sobs. As gently as she could, she eased herself onto her stomach and buried her face in the pillow. She would do anything to save her father's life, but she wouldn't endure this kind of agony day after day. And somehow she knew it would never end with Ray. He would always find some excuse to beat her.

Crying had helped her to relax and Aissa closed her eyes, shutting out the noise and the horrible memories of this brutal night. She comforted herself with thoughts of her mother and father, and, without wanting to, with thoughts of Shadow Hawk. She wished he were here to help her, to take her away. But that would never happen now. She couldn't rely on Shadow Hawk to help her again, and she couldn't rely on her father. The only person she could really count on was herself.

Aissa took a deep breath, willing the pain away. She began to relax. Before she fell asleep she made a vow to herself—she would never endure such treatment from any man again. It was then that she began to plan a way to kill Ray.

Shadow Hawk walked from the circle of men, talking to no one, his silence a warning to everyone to keep their distance. It had been one full moon since he had returned from the white people and he had tried, without success, to keep Aissa from his mind.

"Nephew," Ataza called from behind him.

Shadow Hawk stopped, waiting for Ataza to catch up to him. He had known that it was only a matter of time before Ataza came to him. Up until now he had not questioned him, had left him alone, but now he wanted answers.

"Yes, Uncle?"

"Let us talk."

Shadow Hawk followed Ataza as he led the way. They climbed to the boulder stairway and sat. They looked out on the valley and the mountains beyond.

"Do you like it here, Shadow Hawk?"

"It is my home," Shadow Hawk answered cryptically, staring in front of him.

"That is not what I asked you. I asked you if you like it here."

Shadow Hawk turned, his eyes clouded with bitterness and anger. "Is this a time for honesty, Uncle?"

"If it were not, I would not have asked you the question."

Shadow Hawk nodded slightly, considering his uncle's reply. "I do not know that I like any place well enough. Do you remember many summers ago when I went there," Shadow Hawk pointed, "to that far-off mountain and saw the shadow of the hawk? I told you that I did not belong anywhere, that I did not have a people of my own. That has not changed, uncle. I feel as if I am wandering in the desert looking for water but there is none. I still feel as if I have no people."

"This is a good answer," Ataza nodded his approval. "But are you being honest, Nephew?"

"I am being more honest with you than I have been with anyone, Uncle."

"Not completely, Shadow."

Shadow Hawk looked at his uncle. "I do not lie to you, Uncle."

"Not intentionally."

"What do you mean?"

"You say that you do not belong to any people, that you are searching for where you belong. I do not believe it is a place you are looking for, Nephew. I believe it is a person." Ataza pressed Shadow Hawk's shoulder. "I believe that you found this person in the white world and this confuses you even more."

Shadow Hawk squinted his eyes as he looked out at the mountains. "I do not understand women, Uncle."

Ataza laughed loudly, slapping his thigh. "If that is what you are confused about, Nephew, that will never change. Man was not put on this earth to understand women. I have lived many summers more than you and I still do not understand them."

"They lie, Uncle. I found this to be true."

"Not all women lie, Shadow."

"I was fooled by one. I thought I was smarter than that."

"Aye, men have thought that for hundreds of summers. Wars have been fought over women, Shadow, do you know this? Look around you in our camp. The women do all of the work and we men sit around and make weapons, and hunt, and make war. It seems like we are mighty warriors, but we are nothing without the women. They make our lives possible. If we had to do all that they do, we could not." Ataza shook his head. "Think of it. They cook the food, tan the hides, make the clothes, build the lodges, give birth to and raise the children. Think, nephew, of the power they possess."

"I already know of the power they possess, Uncle."

"You saw the white girl, did you not?"

Shadow Hawk looked at his uncle, a puzzled expression on his face.

Ataza continued. "I am speaking of the white girl that you took from Teroz those summers ago. You saw her again."

Shadow Hawk glanced at his uncle and nodded. "Yes, Uncle, I saw her. It was she and her father who saved my life.

I stayed with them."

"You did not come back to us for much time, Shadow. Did you begin to feel comfortable in the white world with this girl?"

"She is a woman now, Uncle, and she is beautiful. Her eyes are like the sky on a cloudless day, and her hair—" Shadow Hawk stopped, feeling embarrassed.

"It is all right, Shadow. We are taught to be manly and to fight for our women and children. But there is no shame in saying how you feel about those you love."

"I do not love her, Uncle."

"Well, then, there is no shame in saying that you cared for her."

Shadow Hawk nodded slightly. "I did care for her."

"But you came back here."

"I was deceived by her."

"You are sure of this?"

"I am sure."

"I am sorry for you, Nephew. It is too bad that one bad woman has ruined you for other women."

"She is not a bad woman, Uncle," Shadow Hawk said defensively.

Ataza shrugged. "But you have said you were deceived by her."

"I have thought much on it, and I am not sure she did anything wrong." Shadow Hawk shook his head after he uttered the words. "I feel like a fool, like a small boy." He picked up a stone and threw it, listening to it clatter down the slope.

"What did she do that was so bad?"

"I do not wish to speak of it. I will only say that she deceived me in a way that I could never forgive."

"How did you know she was lying, Shadow?"

"Because I am Apache and she is white."

"So, you conclude that she is a liar because she is white?" Ataza shook his head in obvious dismay. "This is not like

207

you, Nephew."

"It does not matter now, Uncle. It is over. I am back where I belong."

"If that is what you believe." Ataza stretched his legs out in front of him.

"It is what I believe."

Ataza sighed. "But you are not really with us, Shadow. You have not been with us since you returned. Perhaps you should spend some time alone and decide if you should return to this white woman."

"I would never do that, Uncle." Shadow Hawk stood up and began to climb down the rocks. Ataza grabbed one of Shadow Hawk's arms and he stopped.

"Why do you resist your white blood with such defiance, Nephew?"

"I do not know!" Shadow Hawk yelled, his voice echoing down the hill. "I do not know," he repeated softly, sitting back down next to his uncle.

"Perhaps because it scares you, Shadow. Was it not easy for you to be with this woman?"

Shadow Hawk nodded. "If she had not deceived me, I would probably still be there."

"I would say you have much thinking to do." Ataza started down the boulder stairway, but stopped. "Perhaps you should seek out this white woman, Shadow."

Shadow Hawk stared out over the valley, to the white expanse of sand that was the desert. Beyond that was Aissa. He could not forget Aissa, no matter how hard he tried. He kept remembering the look on her face when she had pleaded with him to stay.

Shadow Hawk stood up, never taking his eyes from the horizon. He knew why he had chosen to believe Grimes and not Aissa. As much as he had tried to lie to himself, even his uncle had guessed the reason. He was afraid of the white world, afraid that he would grow to like it, afraid that he would lose this part of himself.

He could never abandon his Indian ways—Comanche or Apache—for any woman. Nor could he abandon his Indian ways to live in the world of his enemy, the white man, and become one of them. He nodded. His future lay here, with his mother's people. No matter how much he felt the pull of the outside world, he would stay here where he belonged.

Chapter 10

Aissa had been married for only a month, but it felt like she had endured a lifetime of hell. The morning after her wedding day, she had managed to clean herself up and, with the help of one of Ray's servants, applied salve to her back.

She had made it a point not to upset Ray after that. A few days passed without him coming to her room. She pretended to be in more pain than she actually was and he left her alone, going out to the bunkhouse to drink and gamble with the hands. But he would be back, she knew. And he would beat her again, or worse. How could she keep him away from her?

The solution came less than a week later. Ray insisted that she accompany him to town, in spite of the fact that her back was still extremely painful. While she waited for him to finish his business in the bank, a tinker's wagon had come down the main street. To take her mind off her pain, Aissa got down from the carriage and joined the crowd around the wagon.

The driver was a tiny Chinese man, his English broken but clear enough to understand. He walked through the crowd, hawking bottles of remedies that promised relief from everything—carbuncles, thinning hair, shingles, colic, and fever. As people paid for the little blue glass bottles and left, Aissa lingered, waiting until she could talk to the man alone.

Glancing back nervously at the bank entrance, Aissa stammered out her question and the man nodded enthusiastically. He climbed into the back of the wagon and Aissa could hear the clinking of glass as he rummaged through his trunks. When he emerged, he carried a bottle of smoky brown glass.

He told her the liquid contained opium. A few drops would make anyone sleep soundly through the night. Then he shook a wrinkled brown finger in her face. If she took too much, he warned, she would soon not be able to do without it. Aissa gave him the money, wishing she had some way to conceal more than one bottle. But perhaps by the time this was gone, she wouldn't need it.

After that, Aissa made it a point always to put laudanum in Ray's whiskey before dinner. By the time he had eaten and had his brandy, he had usually passed out in his chair. As a result, Ray had shown no interest in Aissa and she intended to keep it that way.

Aissa saw her father twice a week; that was all that Ray would allow. But no matter how hard she tried, she couldn't convince her father that she was happy being married to Ray. She no longer discussed the marriage with him, but instead chatted endlessly about the ranch and how much she missed teaching. Ray would never let her teach again, she knew that, and she hated him for that as much as anything else.

It wasn't long before the cook, a Mexican woman named Moya, became her friend. Moya had helped her after her beating and since then, Moya was the one who had looked after her. Moya, too, hated Ray and wanted to be free of him, but she had nowhere else to go. Aissa and Moya helped each other. Aissa began teaching Moya English and helped her to read and write, while Moya gave Aissa the companionship she so desperately sought. Aissa learned from Moya how to avoid triggering Ray's temper; he was particular about every detail of how his house was run. As time passed, the two women became friends.

It was during one of these days that Ray came home unexpectedly. Aissa and Moya were in the kitchen, laughing as they baked bread, flour on their hands, arms, and faces. Ray became incensed.

"What the hell are you doing in here?" he demanded, knocking the dough from Aissa's hands onto the floor.

Aissa glanced furtively at Moya, and wiping her hands on her apron, backed away. "I was learning how to bake Moya's bread. I thought you would be pleased."

"That's what we have servants for. If I wanted you to bake bread, that's what you'd be doing." He grabbed her arm. "I want you to come with me." He glared at Moya. "I'll speak with you later!"

"Sí, señor," Moya muttered softly, lowering her eyes.

"Come on," Ray said angrily, pulling Aissa along behind him as he left the kitchen.

Aissa tried to free her arm, but Ray had a firm grasp on her. When Aissa saw that he was taking her upstairs, she resisted, holding onto the banister. "No." She said firmly, trying to sound brave.

"Do you remember what happened to you the last time you tried to fight me?"

Aissa stood her ground. "How could I forget?" She knew she should be more submissive, but it wasn't her nature. Still, she wasn't prepared for Ray's sudden blow across her face.

"You're just like a stubborn bronc that doesn't want to be broke." Ray pulled Aissa up and stared coldly into her eyes. "I've never seen a horse that couldn't be broke, Aissa. Same thing goes for a woman."

Her head throbbing from the blow, Aissa didn't resist as Ray dragged her up the stairs to her room and slammed the door shut. While she stood by the door, he rummaged through the room, throwing clothes from the closet, knocking bottles from the vanity, checking under the bed. It wasn't until he stuck his hand under the mattress that Aissa felt a stab of fear. She knew as soon as Ray glanced back at her that he had found the laudanum. When he stood up, she backed toward the door, her eyes large with fear. He came toward her, waving the bottle in front of her face.

"Did you honestly think I wouldn't find out?" He shook his head. "It took me a while. Couldn't figure out why I was so tired every night and so slow in the mornings. Thought I had some dread disease until I talked to Doc. He checked me out and said I was as healthy as could be. He said I sounded like some old biddie on laudanum. Got me thinking. So last night I didn't drink that brandy you brought me." He stepped even closer to Aissa. "I said I couldn't imagine who would do such a thing." He held the bottle in front of her face. "Where did you get it?"

Aissa refused to answer.

Ray shrugged his shoulders. "I suppose it doesn't much matter." He uncorked the bottle and held it to his nose. "Doesn't smell much. Doesn't taste much either. I suppose that's how you were able to get me to drink it." He reached out and placed his hand on her throat, forcing her head back against the wall. "Now it's your turn." He pressed the bottle to Aissa's mouth but she jerked her head to one side and the liquid dribbled down her neck and chest. Ray pinned her with his weight, sliding his hand to cup her jaw roughly. He slid his thumb into the side of her mouth, prying it open, then tipped the bottle and poured some of the liquid into her mouth. Aissa struggled, trying to wrench away but he held her fast, shifting his hand to her hair. He jerked her head backward with such force that Aissa had to swallow, choking.

Aissa tried to spit out the bitter liquid but she could not. She didn't know how much she had swallowed but she was frightened. What would Ray do to her once she was unconscious? He was smiling now. He stepped back, corked the bottle, and put it in his pocket. Aissa felt slightly dizzy.

But whether it was fear or the effect of the laudanum, she couldn't tell.

"How do you feel, Frenchy? Feel like being a wife to your husband tonight?"

Aissa turned, fumbling frantically with the door handle. She put her hand to her head, suddenly feeling faint. She felt Ray's hands on her, leading her back to the bed. Confused and weak, she tried to fight, but her body wouldn't obey her. Aissa couldn't fight Ray. She tried to push his hands away as he touched her breasts. "Don't," she said, but her voice drifted out her mouth too slowly, too quietly. When Ray pushed her back on the bed, she closed her eyes. She didn't even care. There was no fight left in her and her body wasn't her own anymore. All she wanted to do was sleep. Or maybe she was already asleep and this was a nightmare.

When Aissa awoke the next morning she was alone. She looked around her. Her room was a shambles and the bed was torn apart. She looked down at herself. She wore only her slip, which was pushed up to expose her thighs. She pulled it down to cover herself and struggled to sit up. She felt dizzy, tired, as if she had drunk too much wine. When she tried to stand up she realized how really sick she was. She went to the washbowl and vomited until she felt some relief. She wiped her face and mouth and sat back down on the bed. What had happened? She looked around the room again and it began to come back to her. It had all started when Ray had come home, when he had found the laudanum bottle. She quickly pulled on a dress over her slip and opened the door, listening to make sure Ray wasn't home. When she was sure she was alone, she went slowly down the stairs to the kitchen.

"Moya?" She called softly. But Moya was not there. The flour had been cleaned up and there was no smell of baking bread in the room. There was another woman working at the table.

"*Señora,* may I help you?"

"Who are you? Where is Moya?"

The woman shook her head. "I do not know Moya. My name is Lupe. The *Señor* told me you had been sick."

"I've never seen you before." Panic gripped her. "What day is it?"

"What day, *Señora?*"

"Yes, what day is it?"

"It is Friday, *Señora.*"

"Friday!" Frantic, Aissa ran her hands through her hair. No, that wasn't possible. The last time she was awake, the last time she spoke with Moya, it was Tuesday. How could three days have gone by? "He told you to lie to me, didn't he?"

"Who, *Señora?*"

"My husband!" She paced around the kitchen, trying to let her anger bring her body and mind back to life. She still felt heavy, slow. Her mouth felt dry and her hands began to shake. "I demand to know where Moya is. I want you to tell me right now!"

"I am sorry, *Señora,* I do not know this Moya. I know only that you are ill and the *señor* wants me to take care of you."

"I am not ill, and my husband doesn't care about me. I know he did something to Moya. I know it." Aissa leaned on the table.

"Why don't I make you some tea, *Señora?* It is a good herb. It will calm you down."

Aissa clenched her shaking hands. Maybe this woman knew about plants, as Moya did. "All right, I'll have some tea."

"Why don't you go back up to your room. I'll bring the tea and something for you to eat."

Aissa nodded and left the kitchen, frightened. Her hands would not stop shaking. Her legs felt heavy, and she steadied herself with the banister as she climbed the stairs to her room. She barely glanced at the mess on the floor before she lay down on the bed and covered her eyes with her arm. What day had the woman said it was? She couldn't remember. She dozed for a while until she felt a hand on her arm, shaking her.

"*Señora,* it is time to wake up. I have some tea for you."

Aissa let the woman prop some pillows behind her and then place a tray across her lap. Aissa picked up the cup and saucer, but her hands began to shake and she spilled tea into the saucer. The trembling had gotten worse. She put down the saucer and picked up the cup, holding it with both hands. She sipped at the hot liquid, the cup chattering against her teeth. Slowly, she began to feel better. This was what she needed—something nice and warm to make her relax.

"Why don't you eat your bisquits and eggs, *Señora?* You need to eat."

Aissa shook her head. "I'm fine. This is all I need."

"I will tidy up this room."

"No, let it be." Aissa said brusquely. "Just leave me alone."

"Yes, *Señora.*"

Aissa finished the tea and poured herself some more from the delicate porcelain pot. As she relaxed against the pillows, she suddenly felt much better. Her shaking had stopped and she didn't feel quite so nervous.

When she finished the tea, she moved the tray to the other side of the bed and turned on her side. She hadn't felt this peaceful in a long time. Nothing seemed to bother her. She closed her eyes. She didn't even care about Ray. All she wanted to do was sleep.

Ray stood next to Aissa's bed, a sly smile on his face. She had been so easy. He'd kept her so drugged that she never woke up and when she finally did, all she wanted was more of the laudanum. She was hooked already. Before long, she'd do anything he asked her to do. Her skin looked pale and her hair was a tangled mess. Still, she was one of the most beautiful women he'd ever seen. If only he could make love to her, he thought. He shook his head. It didn't really matter. Even if he couldn't make love to a woman, he could still find pleasure in other ways.

Aissa would do anything for him now that she craved the laudanum. It would be one of the finer pleasurer in his life to see this woman humiliate herself day after day for him. This fine young lady of the proper manners and the proper parentage would soon become one of the best whores in the territory. And she wouldn't even put up a fight doing it. She would make him money, all the while doing things she'd never dreamt of doing with any man. Ray loved the irony in it. Her father was the sheriff and his daughter would be a whore. He reached down and touched one of Aissa's breasts and smiled. This was going to be better than he had hoped. By the time he was finished with her, Aissa Gerard would wish she'd never crossed Ray Grimes.

Shadow Hawk sat on his horse, watching the Gerard ranch. He had told no one except his uncle and mother that he was leaving. He had tried to go on with his life, but he couldn't forget about Aissa. He especially couldn't forget about the way she had pleaded with him that day. He needed to see her one more time.

He waited until dark to approach the ranch. He walked his horse, keeping to soft ground, and tied it away from the house. He stepped onto the porch and looked through the window. Ben was sitting at the table, reading a newspaper, a plate of food in front of him. Shadow Hawk couldn't see Aissa. He knocked on the door. He could hear Ben's boots as they crossed the wooden floor.

"Who is it?" Ben's voice sounded gruff.

Shadow Hawk smiled in the darkness as he heard Ben sliding a cartridge into the shotgun. He wasn't as mild mannered as he seemed. "It is Shadow Hawk, Gerard. May I come inside?"

The door opened immediately, and before Shadow Hawk could say another word, Ben rushed him inside.

"What the hell are you doing here? I thought I'd never set eyes on you again."

"It is good to see you again, Gerard."

Ben smiled. "It's good to see you, too. You hungry?"

"I could eat."

"Sit yourself down. I'll serve you up some dinner."

Shadow Hawk watched Ben as he moved around the stove, filling a plate with food. There was something different about Ben. What was it? Were his movements a little slower? Shadow Hawk continued to watch him until Ben set the plate of food in front of him and sat down. "Thank you, Gerard."

Ben nodded slightly. "Good to have company. Been lonely around here since . . ." Ben stopped. He pointed to the plate. "Eat up before it gets cold."

"What were you going to say?"

"Nothing." Ben lifted a spoonful of food to his mouth but put it back down. He shoved the plate away from him.

"What is it, Gerard?" Shadow Hawk reached out and grasped Ben's forearm. "I am your friend. I came back here to see you."

"You also came back to see Aissa."

"Yes, I cannot deny that."

"Might as well tell you, you'll find out anyway."

"What?"

"Aissa's not here." Ben picked up the small glass that was filled with whiskey and raised it to his mouth. His hand was unsteady.

Shadow Hawk leaned forward and took the glass from Ben's hand. "You do not need this. You are not well."

218

"I'm just tired, that's all."

"I will make you tea." Shadow Hawk stood up and walked to the cupboard. He smiled. It was there. He took down the jar that Aissa had filled with his healing teas.

"I don't want any of that stuff. I hate it."

"I will make you drink it if I have to, Gerard."

Ben shook his head. "Why did you come back here?"

Shadow Hawk poured hot water from the kettle into a cup with some of the herbs. "You are not well. I will help you." Shadow Hawk put the cup in front of Ben. "Drink."

Ben wrapped his hands around the cup, pushing it back and forth on the table. "Aissa's gone, Shadow. She's not coming back."

Shadow Hawk sat down next to Ben. "Is Aissa all right?"

Ben stared into the cup. "I suppose so. I haven't seen her much of late."

"Where is she, Gerard?"

"She's married, Shadow." Ben looked up, his eyes filled with pain. "She's married to Grimes."

Shadow Hawk shook his head slowly, uncomprehendingly. "No, that is not possible."

"It's real possible."

"I did not think she would actually marry him."

Ben shrugged. "She told me she loved him, always had. Said it was time to make it legal. Hell, I still can't believe it."

Shadow Hawk leaned back in his chair. "When did they marry?"

"Three days after you left."

Shadow Hawk sat very still. So, it was true. She had been using him and planning to marry Grimes all along. How could he have been so foolish?

"You all right?"

"It does not surprise me that she did this," Shadow Hawk responded, carefully keeping his voice even.

"Well, it surprised the holy hell out of me! If you understand it, why don't you explain it to me? I'd been trying to push them two together for a long time and she'd have no part of it. She never did like him. Then, when you came here, I saw how much she was growing to care for you. That's what I don't understand. If Aissa cared for you so much, why did she marry him?"

"Perhaps she did not care for me at all, Gerard."

"Why? It doesn't make any sense. There was no reason for Aissa to pretend. She never stopped thinking about you from the time you saved her. Why, suddenly, would she deny her feelings for you and marry Grimes?"

"I do not know the answer. Drink your tea." Shadow Hawk got up and walked around the sparsely furnished room. He tried to keep his eyes from all the things that Aissa had made, but it was difficult. This room was filled with her.

"She doesn't love him, Shadow."

"How do you know? You did not even know she was going to marry him."

"I think Grimes forced her into it." Ben started to get up, but Shadow Hawk gently pushed him back into the chair. "Drink the tea, Gerard."

"Oh, all right." Ben sipped at the tea, making a face. "This stuff will kill me before it will help me."

"Do not complain. That is not like you."

"Listen to me, Shadow. The last time I saw Aissa, she wasn't well. There was something wrong."

"What do you mean?" Shadow Hawk sat down again.

Ben shook his head. "I can't put my finger on it, exactly, but she wasn't her usual self. She hardly laughed, and her eyes were dull. Hardly had any sparkle to them." Ben leaned toward Shadow Hawk, his eyes filled with tears. "You know better than anyone how her eyes sparkle, Shadow."

"Yes, I know. What else?"

"She never said anything about Ray. Even when I asked her how she liked being married, she changed the subject. She's not happy, I know it."

"The marriage was her choice, Gerard. If she is unhappy, she must live with it."

"I don't think the marriage was her choice. Ray forced her into this somehow."

"How is that possible?"

"He could've threatened her in some way. He's a powerful man, Shadow."

Shadow Hawk shook his head. "If he was not good to her, she would just come back to you."

"You don't know Grimes very well." Ben sipped at the tea and looked at Shadow Hawk. "What happened that day you took off, Shadow? I need to know."

"It does not matter now."

"It does matter, damn it!" Ben slammed the cup down on the table. "Tell me what happened."

Shadow Hawk chose his words carefully. "We knew that we could have no future together, so I left."

"You're lying. There's something more."

Shadow Hawk reached for Ben's glass of whiskey and took a sip. He let out a deep breath after the liquid went down. "That day I told Aissa that I cared for her and she admitted the same thing to me."

"So what happened?"

"Grimes rode up while we were . . ." Shadow Hawk hesitated, "while we were embracing."

"And?"

"He said that Aissa loved him."

"That's false. She doesn't love him."

"I think you are mistaken, Gerard. She would not have married him if she did not love him."

"No, you're wrong. I know my daughter, and I know she doesn't love Grimes. We have to do something, Shadow."

"I will do nothing. Your daughter has made her decision."

"Then why the hell did you come back here?"

"I wanted to make sure that you were both all right. You were good to me, Gerard. I will never forget that."

"And what about Aissa? She's the one who saved your life."

"I do not want to speak of Aissa." He stood up. "I will leave now, if you wish."

Ben shook his head, obviously weary. "No, you stay here with me. I'd like the company."

"Thank you. Have you finished the tea?"

"Yes, I finished it."

Shadow Hawk picked up the cup and set it on the cupboard. "You should eat something."

"I'm not hungry."

"I will stay here a few days just to make sure you take care of yourself."

Ben pointed to Shadow Hawk's plate. "You hardly ate anything yourself, I don't know why you're harping at me."

"There is no need for us to fight, Gerard. I am your friend."

"I know that, Shadow. I had a feeling you would come back."

"I did not know white men had such feelings."

"You think Indians are the only ones who have hunches?"

Shadow Hawk's eyebrows knitted together. "I do not understand."

"Any person has the ability to feel things in here, Shadow," Ben said, putting his hand over his heart. "And I feel that Aissa is in trouble."

"We will talk more tomorrow, Gerard," Shadow Hawk said, cutting Ben short. He cleared the plates from the table and put them on the cupboard. "It is time for you to rest."

"Guess you're right," Ben said, standing up. "I dread going into town these days. My mind's not on my work."

"Do not go. You have men to help you."

"I have to go. I'm the sheriff."

"You are not well, Gerard. You need to take care of yourself."

Ben walked to Shadow Hawk, placing his hands on the

man's shoulders. "If you are my friend, Shadow, you will help me."

Shadow Hawk watched Ben until he walked out of the room. He turned down the lamp on the table, then went to the door. The night was cold and Shadow Hawk ran to clear his mind. He untied the paint and swung up. He rode back, put his paint in one of the corrals, and carried his bedroll to the house. He wanted to sleep outside, but he didn't want to leave Ben alone. Ben was one of the steadiest men he'd ever known; it wasn't like him to worry for no reason.

Shadow Hawk unrolled his blanket and lay down on the floor. For the first time he allowed himself to picture Aissa's face in his mind. Was she really in trouble? He turned onto his side. It was probably only Ben's terrible loneliness that made him suspect something was wrong with Aissa. Ben just wanted his daughter back.

Shadow Hawk closed his eyes. He couldn't get Aissa's face out of his mind. He pictured her smiling, then envisioned the look of distaste that had tightened her features the day Ray Grimes bothered her in the garden. The image in his mind changed again. This time Aissa's face was full of fear and anger as Grimes had so calmly told Shadow Hawk about her past. Then he saw her look of pleading, her desperately sad eyes, and the tears on her face. "All right, Gerard, I will help you," he said to himself. He owed it to Ben to find out if his daughter was all right. It was the least he could do for him. And he needed to know if Aissa was well. He couldn't live with himself if he didn't at least find out.

Shadow Hawk refused to let Ben go into town the next day. Ben grumbled for a short while, then admitted that Joe could probably handle anything that came up. Shadow Hawk forced Ben to drink more tea and made sure that he ate. As Ben rested on the sofa, Shadow Hawk looked through the bookshelf. Marsh had taught him how to read at an early age, but he had forgotten many of the letters and sounds. Aissa had helped him to relearn many of the things he'd forgotten, and when he had been recovering from his wound, he had begun to read again.

He looked through the books and picked one of Aissa's favorites, a book she had read many times. It was *Robinson Crusoe,* and Aissa had wanted Shadow Hawk to read it. She had thought he would find it interesting. He smiled at something she had said. "Friday is treated like such a savage when really he is so much smarter than Crusoe."

Shadow Hawk thumbed through the book, flipping the pages. A piece of paper fell out and fluttered to the floor. He picked it up and unfolded it. He could hear Aissa's voice as he read the paper. "You have changed my life forever. I was close to death until you gave me life. You were never out of my thoughts, and I knew that someday we would meet. When I saw you again, it was as if my life began anew. I knew I loved you from the moment you took me from the Apache camp, now I know it more than ever. I don't want you to leave, Shadow Hawk. I want you to be a part of my life forever." Shadow Hawk reread the perfectly scripted handwriting. If these words were true, why would she marry another man? Why hadn't she told him how she felt? But he already knew the answer to that. She had never told him how she felt because he had not let her.

Shadow Hawk put the note back inside the book and replaced the book in the shelf. He looked at Ben sleeping. Shadow Hawk's heart began to beat quickly, much as it did before he went on a raid. Tonight he would ride to Grimes's ranch. It would be dangerous, but he had to find out. He had to know if Aissa was all right.

Shadow Hawk hid in an oak tree close to Grimes's house. Although Grimes had men all over his ranch, they were lazy, noisy, and easy to avoid, and the dogs slept close to the bunkhouse, hoping for scraps. Shadow Hawk had tethered his horse to a tree about a mile away from the ranchhouse and had run the rest of the way. He had climbed the tree and waited until the noise from the bunkhouse died down. When he was sure it was safe, he crept along the yard to the side of the house.

Grimes' house was two stories high. Light shone from two windows upstairs and one below. Carefully, Shadow Hawk stepped onto the porch, ducking down beneath the level of the window. He moved slowly until he was close enough, then lifted his head just enough to peer inside. He could see a large room filled with books, a desk, tables, and chairs. There was no one there. He worked his way around to the side of the house to where the two windows were lit. He looked around him to make sure no one was in the yard, then quietly scaled the side of the house, using the ornate trim as hand and footholds. Using a vine that grew up the side of the house, he maneuvered until he was next to one of the windows. The curtains were partially drawn, and he had to lean over to look inside. The room was dimly lit, and he couldn't see much except Grimes sitting on the edge of a bed. He was leaning over it, doing something with his hands. Shadow Hawk pressed himself against the side of the house when he heard voices below. He saw two ranch hands walk from the bunkhouse to the outhouse. He didn't know how much they could see, but he kept perfectly still until they walked back across the yard and into the bunkhouse. As soon as they were inside, Shadow Hawk shifted his position. His fingers and toes had begun to cramp.

He leaned over again and looked into the window. This time Grimes was standing up. Shadow Hawk saw Aissa. She was lying in the bed on her side, barely clothed, her hair spread out over the pillow. When Grimes walked back to the bed she held out her hand and took a glass from him. The strap from her slip fell down and he saw her bare shoulder. Grimes reached down and stroked Aissa's skin. She did not resist him. She leaned toward Grimes, reaching out her hand.

Shadow Hawk climbed down silently. He ran through the darkness, across the yard, back to his horse. Once mounted, he had the urge to ride back to his people, but he couldn't leave Ben. Not yet.

When he reached the ranch, Ben was waiting for him.

"Did you see her? Is she all right?" Ben's voice was filled with hope.

Shadow Hawk quickly prepared some tea for Ben before sitting down at the table. "You need to drink this. You'll never get well if you don't heal from the inside."

"Did you see her, Shadow?" Ben pushed the cup away.

Shadow Hawk looked at him. "I saw her, Gerard."

"Did you speak with her?"

"No." Shadow Hawk pushed the cup of tea back toward Ben.

"Is she all right, Shadow?"

"Yes."

"If you didn't speak with her, how do you know she's all right?"

"Aissa is fine, Gerard." He motioned toward the cup. "Drink."

"I'm sick of this damned tea!" Ben said angriily, swiping the cup off the table onto the floor. "I want to know about my daughter."

Shadow Hawk leaned forward, his dark eyes meeting Ben's. "There were no guards, Gerard. I had no trouble getting to the house."

"That's because he wasn't expecting you. When I ride out there, he doesn't let me onto the place. There's a reason for that, don't you think?"

Shadow Hawk shrugged his shoulders. "Maybe Aissa does not wish to see you. She knows that you do not approve of Grimes. Perhaps she thinks it will upset you."

"He's keeping me away from her for a reason. I don't

know what it is, but I'll find out if I have to shoot my way into the place."

"I saw her with him, Gerard."

"What do you mean?"

Shadow Hawk lowered his eyes. "They were in a room together. She had on few clothes." Shadow Hawk looked up. "She didn't look frightened of him."

"I will never accept that bastard being married to my daughter." Ben got up, slamming his hands on the table. "You told me you came back to see me and I say you're a liar, boy. You came back for Aissa."

"No, Gerard. You are wrong."

Ben pointed to the bookshelf. "There's a book over there. Bring it to me. There's something I want you to read."

"I have read it." Shadow Hawk looked away from Ben.

"You read that letter?" Ben was indignant at first and then softened. "I suppose we both invaded her private thoughts by reading that letter. But why would she write something like that, thinking that no one would read it, and then marry a man like Grimes? Why, Shadow?"

"I do not know the way your daughter thinks, Gerard." Shadow Hawk got up and walked to the cupboard that held the whiskey. He poured himself a small glass. "I have just seen her with her husband. She has made her choice." He downed the liquid, making a gasping sound, and poured himself some more.

"In all the time you were here, I never saw you drink liquor. Now suddenly you're drinking whiskey like a drover at the end of the trail. Why is that?"

Shadow Hawk finished his glass and slammed it down on the cupboard. "I drink so that I may think more clearly." He paced around the room.

"Do you trust me, Shadow Hawk?"

Shadow Hawk stopped. He looked at Ben. Ben's voice sounded strong and in control. "I trust you with my life, Gerard."

"Then why don't you trust my instincts about Aissa? No one knows her better than I. What she wrote on that piece of paper is true. All those years after you brought her back, I would see her look at your mountains with a yearning that I couldn't understand. Aissa knew even then that you two would meet again."

Shadow Hawk put his hand up. "Enough, Gerard—"

"Don't interrupt, boy." Ben walked to Shadow Hawk. "I first found that piece of paper while you were staying here. It frightened me. I didn't want my daughter falling in love with a savage, an Apache." His eyes were gentle as they looked at Shadow Hawk. "But as I grew to know you, I understood why Aissa loved you. You're a good man with a good heart, and no matter what you say, I know you love my daughter. I would much rather see her with you and be happy than see her with that bastard Grimes."

Shadow Hawk hesitated. "I thank you for your words, Gerard, but I saw her with Grimes. She was in his bed."

"What did you see, Shadow? Tell me."

"I will not tell you, Gerard. It is not right."

"Tell me what you saw."

Shadow Hawk paced around the room, clenching and unclenching his fists. "I saw her lying in bed. She had few clothes on. Grimes was touching her. She was not fighting him, Gerard."

"That's it?" Ben laughed loudly. "You damned fool! That's what convinced you that she loves Grimes?"

"That is enough. She put up no fight. If she did not wish to be with him, she would have fought him."

"Is that what captive women do in your camp, Shadow? Do they fight?"

Shadow Hawk hesitated. "Sometimes."

"And what happens to them if they do?" When Shadow Hawk didn't answer, Ben persisted. "What happens to them if they fight?"

"They are punished. But that is different."

"Why is it different? Aissa could be a captive of Grimes."

Shadow Hawk shook his head. "No, she is too strong for that. Aissa would fight."

"You don't understand how powerful Grimes really is, do you? He could arrange to have me killed and have it look like an accident. He could also get enough men, possibly even soldiers, to raid all Apache camps between here and the Sierra Blancas. And I can guarantee you, he wouldn't leave any of them alive after he'd been there." Ben grabbed Shadow Hawk's shoulders. "How does a woman like Aissa fight a man as powerful as Grimes, Shadow?" He shook his head. "She doesn't. She submits so that you and I will live."

"What is it you want me to do, Gerard?"

"I want you to talk to Aissa alone and make sure she's all right. He won't let me in there."

"And you think he will let *me* in?" Shadow Hawk laughed. "You must think I have great powers, Gerard."

"I think you can do anything you want to do, Shadow. Do this for me."

Shadow Hawk sighed, nodding his head. "All right, Gerard, I will do as you ask. But when it is done and she wants to stay with him, you must accept it."

"If I know she's well, I will accept it, Shadow. Just find a way to get into that house and talk to her." Ben got paper and a pen and began drawing the layout of Grimes's house. He looked up at Shadow Hawk. "I'll tell you something else, boy—you're not going in there without a gun."

Shadow Hawk waited silently in the darkness. He and Ben had already decided that the best way to enter the house was through the kitchen. The door was on the side next to the smoke and ice house, and he could hide there without being seen.

Armed with one of Ben's pistols and his own hunting knife, he waited until the cook was gone and the house was silent. He opened the door just enough to squeeze inside and then carefully felt his way forward, through the kitchen to the dining room. He crept through the dining room to the main entryway, and paused to listen before he climbed the staircase. Shadow Hawk moved easily up the stairs, heeding Ben's warning to keep his weight against the rail so the stairs would not creak.

When he reached the top, he went down the hall to the left. Several doors opened onto the hallway. A sliver of light shone from beneath the second door. He listened, but heard no sound. Slowly, carefully, he turned the handle, opening the door just enough to see inside. He saw Aissa lying on her side as he had seen her before, but this time she was asleep. He opened the door a little further to look around. Grimes wasn't in the room. He went inside and shut the door.

He crossed the room silently and looked down at Aissa. Her hair was tangled and her skin had a sickly pallor to it. He knelt down next to the bed, putting his hand over Aissa's mouth, expecting her to scream out the instant he touched her. But she did not stir.

"Aissa," he whispered softly, pushing the hair back from her face. "Aissa, wake up." She mumbled slightly but didn't open her eyes. He put his hand on her forehead. Her skin felt clammy. He shook her shoulder gently, trying to get her to wake up. Her eyelids fluttered then opened. Her face had no expression. "Aissa."

"I want my medicine," she mumbled, her words slurred. "Aissa."

"I want my medicine. Please," she pleaded. "I'll do what you want, Ray. I promise."

Shadow Hawk saw sweat bead on her forehead. What was wrong with her? "Aissa, can you hear me? It is Shadow Hawk," Aissa opened her eyes and grabbed his arm.

"I'll do what you want me to do, Ray. I'll do anything. Please." Her voice was louder now, more insistent.

Shadow Hawk put a hand over her mouth. "You must be

quiet, Aissa."

She tried to struggle against him for a moment but soon gave up, her arm falling limply to the bed. "I'm sick. I need my medicine."

Shadow Hawk covered her mouth again, but Aissa jerked her head away and screamed. Shadow Hawk looked around the room for a place to hide. Quickly he opened the armoire door and stepped inside, pushing aside the clothes. He had to crouch down in order to fit. If Ray discovered him, he would be better able to defend himself than if he was under the bed—and there was no other place to hide. He left the door slightly ajar so he could see.

Shadow Hawk listened to Aissa's repeated pleas. She didn't seem aware of his presence at all now as she called Ray's name over and over, begging him to bring her medicine. Shadow Hawk fought the urge to take Aissa away from this place now, to get her to Ben's, where she could overcome this terrible sickness. But he could not. If Grimes spotted them and called his men, there would be no way that Shadow Hawk could fight his way through them. Aissa's pathetic pleading went on and on. Finally, Shadow Hawk heard Grimes's footsteps and watched him as he entered the room. Grimes was smiling. He reached down and touched Aissa's face.

"You're losing your looks pretty fast, Frenchy. The men aren't going to want to be with you."

Shadow Hawk resisted the temptation to kill Grimes now. Ben had told him that the white man's law did not allow such a thing. Ben respected that law and he had made Shadow Hawk vow that he would not violate it. He calmed himself, knowing that one day he would meet Grimes alone.

Aissa struggled to sit up. "Can I have my medicine now, Ray?"

Shadow Hawk couldn't believe how different she looked— her skin was pale, her hair tangled and dull, her extraordinary blue eyes shadowed and lifeless.

"I have it right here." Ray reached into his back pocket and pulled out a bottle. "Here it is, Frenchy. Now what are you going to do for me?"

Shadow Hawk put his hand on his knife but forced himself not to draw it. Aissa lay back down on the bed. "The light hurts my eyes. Turn it off, please."

Shadow Hawk watched as Grimes leaned toward the lamp, deliberately turning it up. "Look at me, Aissa. *Now!*"

Aissa looked at Ray, her face a mask of fear. "What do you want from me?"

"You know what I want from you, Aissa. I want you to be a real wife to me."

Aissa tried to turn away from Grimes but he pressed her into the bed. "Don't turn away from me."

"Why are you doing this to me?" Aissa began to cry, putting up a weak struggle.

Grimes looked at Aissa. "You really don't know, do you?"

"No," she sobbed.

"You said no to me. *To me!* You wanted to sleep with that filthy Apache. Do you know what that makes you, Aissa?"

Aissa turned her face away. "Leave me alone."

Ray slapped Aissa. "Don't you ever turn away from me again. You disgust me. When was the last time you took a bath and washed your hair?"

"You won't let me—"

Ray reached down and grabbed a handful of Aissa's hair. "I don't want to hear it. Tomorrow I want you to clean yourself up and we're going to take a little ride. I have some men who are interested in you."

"Ray, please." Aissa clutched his arm. "Let me stay here. I'll change, I promise."

"It's too late." Ray headed toward the door.

"What about my medicine?"

Ray stopped and turned around. "You want your medicine?" Ray walked to the window, opened it, and poured the liquid out. He threw the empty bottle onto the bed. "There, see what you can get out of that. I mean it, girl, you clean yourself up tomorrow or you'll get the beating of your life."

Shadow Hawk heard the door close and waited until he couldn't hear Grimes's footsteps anymore. Then he went to Aissa.

Chapter 11

"Aissa, it is Shadow Hawk. Do not scream."

Aissa struggled to clear her mind. Had Ray come back? Was he trying to trick her? Or was she just imagining voices again? She reached out, opening her eyes. Shadow Hawk stood beside the bed, looking down at her. "Is it you?" She knew her voice sounded weak and hollow.

"Aissa, I am going to take you home."

She touched him tentatively, reassuring herself that he was actually there. "Is it really you?" She began to cry.

"You must listen to me, Aissa. You have to be strong. We will go out of this house and into the yard. Until we are far enough away, you must be silent."

"No, I can't do that," she said, terror in her voice. "Ray will find us and he'll kill us."

"He will not kill us, Aissa. I promise you that."

"I don't think I can walk."

"I will carry you. You will not stay in this house another night."

Aissa couldn't fight down her fear of Ray. "He'll find us."

"He will not hurt you again."

She felt his arm tighten around her, her relief fading into shame. She was filthy, soiled. She shook her head. "I can't go with you."

"I will not leave you here."

She tried to pull away from him. "No."

"You are coming with me tonight, Aissa."

"I can't." She turned away from him. "If I leave here, Ray will kill my father."

"He will not kill Gerard."

"You can't stop him, Shadow Hawk."

"You must trust me, Aissa."

She held onto him, desperate for his strength and goodness. "I do trust you. I do."

"Then believe what I say—this man will not harm your father."

"I don't know. I—"

"We do not have time. You will need clothes."

Aissa tried to think. "In the trunk at the bottom of the bed."

Shadow Hawk rummaged through the trunk and dropped some clothes on the bed. "I do not know what you need."

Beginning to hope, Aissa frantically slipped on a skirt and blouse and pulled on some boots. She stood up, unsteady. "I'm ready."

Aissa leaned on Shadow Hawk as she began her first tentative steps across the room. She stumbled, holding onto his arm, but she forced herself to walk to the door. While she stood against the wall, Shadow Hawk opened the door and checked the hallway to make sure Grimes was nowhere around. When he was sure it was clear, he picked Aissa up in his arms and carried her down the stairs. Aissa couldn't look, closing her eyes, praying that Ray wouldn't hear them. She only opened her eyes when she felt the cool air against her cheeks. They were outside. She wondered about Ray's men and the dogs, but Shadow Hawk didn't stop, seeming to move as if he carried no weight. Aissa hid her face against Shadow Hawk's chest, afraid to believe that she would be

235

free of Ray.

She heard the whicker of Shadow Hawk's horse, and a moment later Shadow Hawk lifted her up onto the stallion, swinging up behind her. Aissa closed her eyes. She leaned back against him as they rode, feeling the warmth from his body, the strength from his arms. She didn't care where they went, as long as she didn't ever have to go back to Ray.

Shadow Hawk reined in his horse and Aissa opened her eyes. They were at her ranch. She sat upright, shaking her head. "No, we can't go here. This is the first place he'll look."

"I promised Gerard."

"No!" she said, hysterical. "I don't want him to see me like this. Please."

"He loves you, Aissa."

"What about Ray?"

"I will take care of him."

Shadow Hawk dismounted and carried Aissa up to the porch. Aissa shook her head. "I can't face him."

"He is your father. You should feel no shame." Shadow Hawk kicked at the door. There was the sound of footsteps, and then Ben flung it open. His face brightened when he saw Aissa.

"Aissa," he said softly, holding his arms wide.

Shadow Hawk put Aissa down and she went to her father, tears streaming down her face. "I am so sorry, Father."

Ben held Aissa, stroking her hair. "You have nothing to be sorry for, my darling. Come, sit down."

Aissa shook her head. "I'm so dirty. I don't want you to see me like this."

"Would you like a bath?"

"Yes," she nodded, her head lowered.

"Go sit. Shadow Hawk and I will get it ready."

Shadow Hawk helped Ben bring in the big tin tub and fill it with pails of hot and cold water. Briefly, Shadow Hawk told Ben of what he had seen at Grimes's. Ben's eyes darkened, but he kept up his facade of calmness.

"Why don't you go sit with Aissa?"

"I cannot. I have something I must do."

"You can't leave now, Shadow. If you leave, you have to take her with you. She'll be in danger here."

Shadow Hawk's eyes narrowed, his hand going to the butt of his knife. "You trust me, Gerard?"

"We've been over this before."

"Do you trust me?"

"Of course I do."

"I will be back. I will make sure that he does nothing to harm Aissa or you again."

Ben grabbed Shadow Hawk's arm. "Shadow, you can't kill him. If you do that, every ranger and soldier will be looking for you."

"I did not say that I would kill him, Gerard."

"What are you going to do, then?"

"I will make sure that he understands he must not threaten either of you again."

"You'll come back?"

"I will be back."

Shadow Hawk looked at Aissa once more as he went out the door. He never wanted to forget what Grimes had done to her. He went to the barn and got some rope, then swung up onto his horse and rode back to the Grimes ranch, tying the paint in the same place. He went into Grimes's house just as he had done before. He shook his head and smiled grimly. This white man thought he was so protected.

Shadow Hawk went to Ray's room. He listened at the door and then quietly opened it and went inside. He stood for a moment in the darkness, acquainting himself with the room. Grimes's snores echoed off the walls. The smell of whiskey permeated the room.

He took the rope, made a loop, and slid it around Ray's neck. He jerked the rope. Ray grumbled, but didn't wake up.

Shadow Hawk slapped him hard on the face. When Ray opened his eyes, Shadow Hawk pulled tightly on the rope, pressing the point of his knife into Ray's neck.

"Do not move or you will die, white man."

"All right, all right. What do you want? Do you want money? I have some. Let me show you where it is." Ray couldn't disguise the panic in his voice.

"I do not want your money."

"Horses? Of course, you want horses. Take as many as you want, and cattle, too."

"A woman."

"A woman? All right. There's a woman in the room across the hall. You'll like her. She had light hair. You Apaches like light hair, don't you?"

"Is she your wife?"

"Yes, but she means nothing to me. Take her."

"You would give your wife to me without defending her?" Shadow Hawk pulled sideways on the rope and Ray made choking sounds.

"Please, I can't breathe."

Shadow Hawk pressed the blade into Ray's neck. "Can you feel this, white man?"

"Yes."

"Does it cause you pain?"

"Take what you came for and get out of here."

"Or what? What will you do?"

"That wasn't a threat, I just—"

"Put your hands above your head. Quickly!" Shadow Hawk held the knife between his teeth and adroitly tied Ray's wrists together, looping the end of the rope through the headboard and around one of the bedposts. If Ray moved too much in either direction, he would strangle himself.

"Come on. I can't be like this. If I so much as cough I could choke."

Again Shadow Hawk pressed the blade to Ray's throat. "Perhaps I should end your life now."

"No!" Ray pleaded, his false bravado crumbling. "Don't."

"You are a coward, white man. I should kill you right now."

"I'll give you anything you want."

"Yes, you will." Shadow Hawk walked to the window, making sure the curtains were pulled, then he turned up the lamp. When he walked back to the bed, the look of terror on Ray's face gave him great satisfaction. "I see you remember me."

"If you've come for Aissa, she's in the other room. I never touched her."

"I already have Aissa. She is with her father."

"What?"

"Yes, this is my second visit to your house. Do you see how easily I can get in. I could've slit your throat and you would've choked on your own blood."

"What do you want?" Ray asked, trying to raise his head, but coughing.

Shadow Hawk held his knife a few inches from Ray's face. Slowly, he moved it to one side, watching Ray's eyes follow the blade in helpless fear. "I want you to stay away from Ben and Aissa Gerard."

"She's my wife."

"She is nothing to you. You treat your animals better than you treat her." Shadow Hawk tossed the knife up into the air and caught it by the handle. Again Ray's eyes followed the blade. "Do not scream out, white man, or it will end for you right now." Shadow Hawk staightened, looking down at Ray. "Have you ever heard of the many ways the Apache torture their captives?" When Ray didn't answer, Shadow Hawk slammed the butt of the knife into Ray's belly. "Answer me."

"Yes, I've heard," Ray gasped, struggling to breathe.

"So you know that I could take you to my people. They would torture you in many ways." Shadow Hawk leaned down, his face close to Ray's. "It would take days for you to die. You would be in such pain you would beg someone to kill you." Shadow Hawk watched as Ray began to sweat. "Can you take pain, white man?"

"I never did anything to you. I even let you ride away that day."

Shadow Hawk was so close to Ray that he could smell the whiskey on his breath. "You did something far worse than hurt me, white man. You hurt someone I care for. You hurt her and you shamed her. You deserve to die for that."

"No, no. Wait!"

Shadow Hawk's hand went over Ray's mouth. "Yell again and I will slit your throat." Ray nodded furiously and Shadow Hawk removed his hand. "You will not go near Aissa or Ben Gerard again. Ever. If I find out that you have threatened them in any way, I will take this knife," Shadow Hawk drew the knife up between Ray's legs, "and I will cut you. But I will make sure that you live." Shadow Hawk straightened again, watching Ray as he involuntarily twisted to one side.

"I have money, lots of money. Enough to buy your people rifles and horses."

Shadow Hawk smiled. The man's fear was making him stupid.

"If you untie me, I'll show you where the money is."

Shadow Hawk leaned down close to Ray, bringing the knife up where he could see it again. "I want only one more thing. I want you to remind yourself at all times how easily I got in here tonight. If I find that you have broken your word, I will be back. You will not know when, you will not even see me, but I will come. And when I do, you will pray to your God that you had kept your word."

"I'll keep my word. I won't do anything to harm Aissa or Ben."

"That is good."

"I'll even check up on them from time to time."

"Do not go near their ranch.

"All right, whatever you say."

Shadow Hawk looked into Ray's eyes. The man was lying. He had no intention of keeping his word. Shadow Hawk stepped back from the bed. Without warning, he threw the knife, sinking it into the headboard a few inches from Ray's face. Ray's entire body jerked, and he tried to turn to the side again. Shadow Hawk worked the blade free from the headboard and stepped back without speaking. This time he waited until he saw Ray relax slightly. Then he threw. The blade sank into the headboard on the other side of Ray's head. Again, he jerked involuntarily.

"Please, could you stop that?" Ray stammered, the sweat dripping down his face.

"Did Aissa ask you to stop?" Shadow Hawk's voice was barely audible.

"What?"

"Did Aissa beg you to stop?"

"Look, I didn't know she meant so much to you—"

"Enough!" Shadow Hawk put the flat of the blade across Ray's mouth. "Even if she meant nothing to me, to treat a woman in such a manner . . ." Shadow Hawk shook his head, taking the blade away.

"I've heard about the things your people do to white woman," Ray said sharply.

"I have done many things," Shadow Hawk said slowly, measuring his words, "but I have never hurt a woman. She should have been able to trust you. You were her husband."

"I was never her husband, not really. She never wanted me." He nodded toward Shadow Hawk. "She's wanted you for as long as I can remember. She never said as much, but I knew it."

"So you forced her to marry you. You told her you would

harm her father or me."

"She deserved everthing she got, the little bitch," Ray snarled, his face suddenly changing from fear to rage. "With her fancy ways. She's no different than her mother."

"You will never hurt her again."

"Threaten me all you want, Apache, but I'm the law around here. When you leave, I can do whatever I want."

"You are suddenly very brave, white man. Why is that?"

Ray smiled. "Because I just figured something out, Apache. I know you won't kill me. If you kill me, it'll look like she did it. You wouldn't want anything to happen to her."

Shadow Hawk reached up and jerked the rope once more. Ray tried to scream but the sound was cut off. He began coughing, gasping for air. "I have changed my mind. I think I will take you back to my people."

"No!"

"Why not, white man? Is it because you know no one will come looking for you in the Apacheria? I can take you from here, burn down your ranch, and make it look as if Apaches raided it. No one would suspect Aissa. They would be happy that she escaped with her life."

"All right," Ray gasped. "I'll do what you want."

"You are not a man of your word. But I will show you that I am a man of my word." Shadow Hawk pulled up some of the sheet from the bed and stuffed it into Ray's mouth. Then he pinned Ray, pressing a knee into his chest. He grabbed a handful of Ray's hair and jerked his head forward. "This will remind you that I mean what I say, white man." Shadow Hawk held Ray's hair tightly, pulling it away from his scalp. "I would not struggle if I were you, white man. You might lose part of your head." Quickly, with a clean stroke, Shadow Hawk cut the small clump of hair from Ray's scalp. Blood ran down Ray's face and into his eyes. He writhed on the bed. Shadow Hawk smiled. As Ray screamed silently,

Shadow Hawk held the bloodied piece of hair in front of him. "Keep your word, white man, or the next time I will have all of your scalp."

Shadow Hawk turned down the lamp and quietly left the house. He rode back to Ben's, feeling better than he had felt in a long time. He didn't really trust that his threats would work with Grimes forever, but for a time, at least, Aissa and Ben would be safe.

When Shadow Hawk went into the house, Ben was at the stove, pouring water into a cup. "Heard you ride up. You all right?"

"I am well."

Ben glanced at Shadow Hawk's hands. "You have blood on you."

Shadow Hawk looked down. He went to the bucket and washed.

"You didn't do anything I'd have to arrest you for, did you?"

Shadow Hawk thought for a moment. He didn't really know about the white man's laws. Perhaps he could be put in jail again for what he had done. The only thing he had promised Ben was that he wouldn't kill Grimes. "I do not know."

"You didn't kill him, did you?"

"No, Gerard, I did not kill him. It would have been easy to kill him."

"I know, I feel the same way." Ben gave the cup to Shadow Hawk. "Take this in to Aissa. She's worried you're not coming back."

Shadow Hawk nodded. "You look better already, Gerard."

"I don't know how to thank you for what you did for us, Shadow."

"Do not thank me, Gerard. You and Aissa saved my life. I am only returning the favor." Shadow Hawk took

243

the cup. "Do you know he was giving her some medicine?"

Ben nodded. "She told me. It'll be hard on her. She'll crave it. She may even act crazy for a while until it's out of her. We'll have to be patient with her."

"I do not understand, Gerard. What is this medicine?"

"I don't know how to explain it except to say it's not a good medicine. Don't your people use plants that are dangerous, make you sick?"

Shadow Hawk nodded slowly, thinking of Ocha. Many of her herbs were gathered in secret because she was afraid of someone misusing them. Once, one of the young braves had fed locoweed to Teroz's horse. The animal had gone crazy, almost killing Teroz. "This medicine will make her act crazy?"

"Worse than that, it makes people dream and they learn to crave those dreams. When they stop taking it, they want it so badly that their bodies ache and they're confused."

"How long will it be before she is well?"

Ben shook his head. "I don't know, Shadow Hawk. But she's going to need both of us."

"You rest, Gerard. I will care for her tonight."

Ben nodded. "Shadow—"

Shadow Hawk put his hand on Ben's shoulder. "It is all right, Gerard. You have done the same for me." He walked back to Aissa's room. The room was dimly lit. Aissa was dressed in a clean white nightgown, and her long blonde hair, pulled to one side, hung down her chest. It was still damp from her bath. She was propped against some pillows, her eyes closed. He sat in the chair that Ben had put next to the bed. She opened her eyes when she heard him set the cup on the night table.

"You're back." Her voice sounded weak.

"Yes. How do you feel?"

"I'm scared. I already wish I had the medicine."

"You are strong, Aissa."

"This is different. I have no control over this. The drug had taken control of my body."

"I do not understand this, Aissa, but I know you are strong." Shadow Hawk took her hand, holding it tightly. He handed her the tea. "Drink this."

"I don't want anything."

"Drink it. It will help to cleanse your body."

Aissa took the cup and sipped at it. "I don't know how you can look at me."

"It is easy to look at you. You are very beautiful."

"I'm not beautiful." Aissa turned her head away.

Shadow Hawk sat on the bed. "Please, drink, Aissa." He pushed the cup to her lips and held it there gently until she drank. When she was finished, he set the cup on the night table. He reached for a piece of her hair, twisting it around one of his fingers. "When I first saw you, I thought you were a white angel."

"Don't, please."

Shadow Hawk pulled Aissa close until her head rested on his shoulder. He wrapped his arms around her, stroking her hair and holding her. "It is over now, Aissa."

"No, it's not over," she said tearfully, pulling away from him. "He did things to me. He used me. Do you know what he was going to do with me?"

"It does not matter," he said calmly.

"Do you know?" Her voice rose to a feverish pitch. "He was going to make me be with other men while he collected money from them. And I would've done it. I would've done anything for my medicine."

"It was not your fault."

"It *was* my fault. I should've been strong enough to fight it."

"Do not do this to yourself, Aissa."

"Don't you see, I'll never be free of Ray Grimes. He'll always have control over me. Even if I don't need the

245

medicine, I'll never forget what he did to me. Never," she sobbed.

Shadow Hawk drew her to him, holding her even as she tried to pull away. "I will make you forget, Aissa," he said gently. "I will make you forget."

She buried her face in his shoulder, shaking her head. "You can't. No one can make me forget."

Shadow Hawk held Aissa's frail body as she cried. He kissed the top of her head. Without realizing it, he had already made the decision to stay here. He was beginning to think that his uncle was right—maybe he had been looking too hard to find a place where he belonged, when in his heart he had always known.

Aissa's screams woke Shadow Hawk with a start and brought Ben running into the room. They sat on either side of the bed, trying to calm her.

"No! Let me go. I know where he keeps it."

"You're not going back there, Aissa," Ben said firmly.

"I hate you. I wish I'd never come back here."

"Hate me all you want, girl, but you're staying here."

"I need a little, just to help me sleep. Please." She turned her blue eyes to Shadow Hawk. She reached out and touched his face. "You'll help me, won't you?"

Shadow Hawk nodded. "Yes, I will help you, Aissa."

"I knew you would." She threw herself against him, hugging him fiercely. "Will you get the medicine now?"

"No."

"But you said you would help me." Aissa pulled away.

"I am helping you."

Aissa became enraged. "You're just like him," she spat, nodding toward her father.

"I cannot think of any man I would rather be like," Shadow Hawk replied, his voice firm. He went back to the chair. "I think you should make more tea, Gerard. Stronger this time, with the herbs I gave you."

Ben hesitated, unwilling to leave his daughter. "Don't worry, Aissa. We will help you."

"I don't want your help!" She threw herself back against the pillows, refusing to look at her father.

Shadow Hawk stood up and walked to Ben when he saw the pained expression on his face. "This is not Aissa. You have told me that many times. You must be strong, Gerard. Make the tea."

Ben nodded wearily and left the room. Shadow Hawk walked back to the chair and sat down. Aissa stubbornly refused to look at him.

"Why don't you leave? I don't want you here."

"Your father wants me here. This is his house."

"But I don't want you here," she snapped. She faced Shadow Hawk. "As soon as you leave here, I'll find some more."

"I will not be leaving for a while."

"I hate you." Her voice was cold and hard.

"I do not hate you, Aissa."

"You left me. It's your fault that this is happening to me."

It was not the first time she had said it, and Shadow Hawk knew that in a way she was right. "I am sorry."

"What good does that do me now? Look what he's done to me. I can never look at myself again. No man will ever want me after what he's done."

"I will want you," Shadow Hawk replied gently.

"You're a liar. You always lie. I can't trust you." Aissa started to get out of bed, but Shadow Hawk put his arm out to stop her.

"Where are you going?"

"This is my house. I can go where I want."

"No, Aissa, this time you will stay here."

"You can't tell me what to do." Aissa rolled to the other

side of the bed and got out, heading for the door. But Shadow Hawk was already there. He caught her around the waist and lifted her back to the bed.

"I hate you!"

"So you have said." They had been through this a dozen times, but Shadow Hawk still could not understand her need for the drug. She was quiet now, staring at him with large eyes. He knew she was going to ask him. He walked back to the chair and sat down, eyeing her warily. He noticed that she was beginning to sweat and her breathing was becoming labored. Her body needed the drug and her mind was trying to think of ways to get it.

She moved to the other side of the bed, her bare legs hanging over the edge. She stared at Shadow Hawk. "Do you want me?" Her voice was deep.

Shadow Hawk looked at her long legs. They were beautiful, and yes, he did want her. "I want you to get well, Aissa."

Aissa stood up. She walked to Shadow Hawk and sat down on his lap, wrapping her arms around his neck. "I know you want me, Shadow Hawk. I know it." She lowered her mouth to his.

Shadow Hawk felt her lips on his, and for a brief moment he wanted nothing more than to take her. He could feel the warmth of her body through the thin cloth of the nightgown, and her lips were soft as they moved against his. He pulled away, taking Aissa's hands from around his neck. "Get back in bed."

"But I—"

He held both her hands with one of his. "I will not give you the medicine." He stood up, pushing her away from him. He glanced sharply at Ben as he entered the room.

"Everything all right?" Ben carried a tray.

"Aissa and I were just talking."

"I want him out of here, Father. I hate him."

Ben placed the tray on the night table. "Yes, I'm sure you do hate him, Aissa. Before the night's over, I expect you'll hate us both."

Aissa slipped a hand through her father's arm and rested her head on his shoulder. "We don't need him here, father. Make him go."

Ben took Aissa's arm and guided her back to the bed. "Sit down, Aissa," he said gently.

Aissa responded to the gentle tone of her father's voice and did as she was told.

Ben sat down on the bed next to his daughter. "You must listen to me, Aissa. Can you do that?"

Aissa took a deep breath and pushed back her hair. "I'm trying."

"Good." He reached up and touched his daughter's face. "You must know what Ray has done to you. Yelling and screaming at Shadow Hawk won't change anything. Ray's the one who made you take it and now you have to stop."

"I don't know if I can," she responded. Her voice sounded small.

"Of course you can."

Aissa shook her head. "This scares me, Father. I want it so badly."

"We'll stay with you until you don't need it anymore."

"I don't want you to see me like this." She glanced back at Shadow Hawk. "I don't want either of you to see me like this."

Ben took Aissa's hand. "I'm just glad you're back. I couldn't go on knowing you were with Ray and knowing something was wrong. We'll get through this."

Aissa rested her head on her father's shoulder. "I'm so scared."

Ben put an arm around Aissa. "It's all right. I'm right here. I won't leave you."

Shadow Hawk watched Ben and Aissa, and he felt a

heaviness in his heart. Ray Grimes had taken away much more than Aissa's innocence. He had stripped her of her pride and honor. She would never again look at the world with trusting eyes.

Shadow Hawk was awakened from his sleep by a jolting scream. He jumped up from his bedroll and ran to Aissa's bedroom. Ben was trying to hold Aissa, but she was kicking and hitting. Shadow Hawk came from the other side of the bed, behind her, pinning her arms against her body.

"Let me go!" Her voice was shrill.

Shadow Hawk shifted his grip to her shoulders. "Be still, Aissa, and I will let you go." He tightened his hold, glancing at Ben. He looked tired and worried. "Get some sleep, Gerard. I will stay with her."

"I can't sleep." Ben took out a handkerchief and wiped the sweat from his forehead. "She seems worse."

"Did she drink any of the tea?"

"No. As you can see, it never made it to her mouth."

Shadow Hawk looked on the floor. The teapot and cup were broken, the tea in a puddle on the floor. "Make some more, Gerard, and make it strong. Put in two pinches of my medicine."

"She won't drink it."

"I will get her to drink it. Go."

"Don't go, Father. Don't leave me with him. Please!"

Shadow Hawk held Aissa as she kicked and screamed, trying to loosen herself from his hold. He was surprised by her strength. As soon as Ben had left the room, Shadow Hawk let Aissa go. He sat on the bed, glaring at her. "I am more stubborn than you, Aissa. Do not fight me, I will win."

"I hate you!" She turned away from him, burying her face in a pillow.

"Listen to me."

250

"I don't have to listen to anything you say."

"Yes, you do." Shadow Hawk pinned her against the mattress so she was forced to look at him. "You are making this hard for your father. When Gerard comes back with the tea, you will drink it."

"I won't drink it. You're trying to poison me."

"If you don't drink the tea," Shadow Hawk continued, "I will pour it down your throat. Do you understand?" He could tell by the look on her face that she believed him. He sat back down in the chair. Aissa was silent. He wondered what Grimes had done to her.

When Ben came back into the room and handed Aissa the tea, she drank it without argument. Ben glanced at Shadow Hawk, but Shadow Hawk shrugged his shoulders, as if he didn't know why she'd given in. When Aissa was done with the tea, she turned over on her side and closed her eyes. Ben waved Shadow Hawk out of the room. "What happened?"

"I convinced her to drink the tea."

Ben smiled. "I'm glad you're here. I could go for a drink. How about you?"

"Yes."

They walked to the living room. After Ben poured them each a glass of whiskey, they sat down. Ben twirled the glass around in his fingers. "As a sheriff, I'm sure I could think of a few things to arrest Ray Grimes for, I just can't prove he did any of them. As a father," he took a sip of the whiskey, "I could kill the bastard. Just what did you do to him, anyway?"

Shadow Hawk sipped from his glass. "I gave him a warning."

Ben smiled "I don't know how to thank you for what you did, Shadow. I would've never been able to get in there and get her."

"Do not thank me, Gerard."

"I'll always be grateful, and someday she will be, too."

251

"I am sorry I rode away that day, Gerard. I feel responsible."

"It's not your fault, Shadow. Ray would've found another way."

"Why does he hate Aissa so much? I do not understand."

"Ray's just like his father. He thinks he can buy respectability. Hell, he thinks he can buy anything. I think he's just plain crazy."

"I am sorry you and Aissa have suffered."

Ben looked at Shadow Hawk, wiping at the tears that filled his eyes. "You know, sometimes I forget that you're Apache. You have more kindness and understanding in you than most people I know."

Shadow Hawk lowered his eyes. "You know I have to leave, Gerard."

"I know."

"Do you understand why? I only came back to make sure that Aissa and you were well."

"Thanks to you, we will be fine." Ben's voice had a sharp tone to it, and he took another drink of whiskey.

"You are angry."

"No, only regretful."

"You know that I care for Aissa, but we could not be together. It would be impossible."

"I know. I see you looking at those mountains all the time. You're not comfortable being cooped up in a house. It's all right, Shadow Hawk. I understand why you have to go. It's just that . . ."

"What is it, Gerard?"

"It's not right you leaving like this. If you have to go now, go, but come back again. See Aissa when she's well. She wouldn't want you to remember her like this."

Shadow Hawk shook his head. "I do not know."

"Please, Shadow. Do this for her."

Slowly, Shadow Hawk nodded. "I will come back in two

moons. But if something should happen, give this to Aissa."
Shadow Hawk reached into his pouch and pulled out Aissa's
locket. He set it on the table in front of Ben. "Tell her it
belongs to her. I have no right to keep it."

"She wanted you to have it."

"No, it belongs to her."

Ben picked up the locket. "Two moons, Shadow. You'll
return in two moons."

Shadow Hawk didn't answer. He didn't know how to tell
Ben that he was confused, that he didn't understand what
Aissa was going through. Things were much too complicated
in the white world, the people too different. He would come
back in two moons, but he would not stay.

Chapter 12

Shadow Hawk smiled as he watched Brave Heart and Singing Bird together. Finally they had gotten married and they couldn't bear to be apart. Brave Heart had grown tall and strong and he had become a good hunter. Many of the braves made fun of him because he spent so much time with his wife, but Brave Heart was oblivious to their jokes because he was so in love.

Shadow Hawk walked along the stream that led to the pond. It was hot and he wanted to swim. He hadn't said good-bye to Aissa when he left. He had watched her as she slept, kissed her on the cheek, and gone. Two moons had almost passed and he would have to return. He loved Aissa, he knew that now. But he also knew that they had no chance of a life together.

He bent over and picked up a flat stone, skimming it over the water. He smiled at the circle of rings that formed as the stone bounced lightly and then sank. He bent to pick up another stone but stopped. There was a movement in the bushes upstream. It was not a small animal. Perhaps a deer? He had no weapon with him except his knife. Still, he decided to see what it was.

He drew his hunting knife and walked carefully but quickly. As he got closer he could hear something, an odd sound, almost a whimper. Cautiously he moved forward. The sound grew louder, now reminding him of a wounded animal. Shadow Hawk eased himself into a thicket of willows, following the sound. He was careful to move silently. He heard it again. Someone was crying. Shadow Hawk pushed his way through the willows and saw Paloma. She was lying on the ground, her forearms and cheeks slashed and bleeding. He knelt down next to her, pulling her into his arms.

"Paloma, what has happened?"

"Leave me alone, Shadow Hawk." She reached for her knife, but Shadow Hawk knocked it away.

"Why have you done this to yourself?"

"Do you not know?" She sobbed. "I thought everyone knew."

Shadow Hawk sat down behind Paloma, pulling her against him. "Tell me, Paloma. I am your friend."

"Yes, you are my friend." She lowered her head. "I am so ashamed."

Shadow Hawk loosened his hold on her, moving to face her. He ripped some of the cloth from her skirt and wiped the blood from her cheeks. He took off her sash, ripped it in half, and wrapped the pieces around her forearms. "What is wrong, Paloma?"

"Miho has married." Her voice was so full of pain. Shadow Hawk took her hand.

"How is this possible? He has always loved you. I know this to be true."

"Do you see him here with me? No, he is gone, with another band. Ocha told me that he found a girl there that he loved and wanted to take for his wife. He will remain with her and her family."

"I cannot believe this. It does not sound like Miho."

"I have loved him since I first saw him." She looked at Shadow Hawk, her large dark eyes filled with tears. "I thought he loved me, Shadow Hawk. He said he loved me."

"Perhaps there is a reason he married this girl."

"It does not matter what reason there is. He is married to her and not to me."

"I am sorry, Paloma." Shadow Hawk put his arms around her and held her as she cried. She felt like a fragile bird in his arms. She was so small. How could Miho have married someone else? He didn't understand.

"I am with child, Shadow Hawk."

Shadow Hawk stiffened as Paloma's words sank in. Shadow Hawk couldn't believe it. Miho had made a child with Paloma and then married another. How was this possible? "You are sure?"

"Yes," she said, trying to stifle her sobs.

"Miho does not know?"

"No."

"Why did you hurt yourself, Paloma? You could have hurt your child as well."

"I do not want to live if I cannot be with Miho. I will be disgraced, Shadow Hawk. I will be an outcast."

Shadow Hawk took Paloma's hands in his. "You will not be disgraced, Paloma."

"Do you know what Sotso and Teroz will do when they find out? They will drive me from the band because I have shamed them. I have nowhere else to go."

"Does your mother know?"

"No, I could not tell her. You are the only person I have told."

"Good."

"How can this be good? Shadow Hawk, I may as well end my life right now!"

"No, Paloma, you do not have to end your life. There is another answer."

"No, there is no answer. I am being punished." Paloma fell against him, sobbing uncontrollably.

"Paloma, listen to me." Shadow Hawk gently lifted her head and pushed her hair from her face. Her cuts were bloody but not deep. There would be no scars. Good. Paloma did not deserve scars. Or more pain. "I will marry you." Shadow Hawk heard himself say the words and realized that he had changed the course of his entire life. There would be no going back to the white world. There would be no going back to Aissa. Now he could stop dreaming, wondering. Now his path would be clear.

Paloma was shaking her head. "No, I cannot let you do that."

"You cannot stop me." Shadow Hawk looked at Paloma. He had always liked her, had always considered her a friend. Marrying her would not be such a hard thing to do.

"But the child—"

"I will say the child is mine."

"No one will believe you. Ocha will know the truth. She is a witch—she can see into people's souls."

"Ocha is my grandmother and has been like one to you. She will do nothing to hurt us."

"It is not right, Shadow Hawk. You would be punished for my mistake."

"I would not consider marrying you a punishment, Paloma." Shadow Hawk smiled and kissed her on the forehead. "We need to clean you up. If people see you like this, they will wonder why one so eager to marry would try to hurt herself."

"Everyone knows I have always loved Miho. No one will believe that I love you."

"Am I so hard to love?"

"No!" Paloma brought one of Shadow Hawk's hands to her cheek. "No, you are easy to love. You have always been my friend. That is why I will not let you marry me."

"You do not have a choice, Paloma. I will not let you become an outcast."

Paloma bent a piece of willow, pushing on it until it snapped. "People will talk. They will ask questions.

"Let them talk."

"But what of your woman?"

"What woman?"

Paloma lowered her head, embarrassed. "There has been talk."

"What kind of talk?"

"That when you leave us you visit a white woman."

Shadow Hawk looked at Paloma, forcing himself to show no emotion. "I desire no white woman. There are some white people who have befriended me, but that is all."

"You are being truthful? I could not live with myself if I knew you loved another yet still married me."

"There is no one else, Paloma." Shadow Hawk tried to believe the words as he spoke them. "Now, when will you marry me?"

She smiled shyly. "I do not know."

"Let it be as soon as possible. I will bring my horse to your lodge tonight."

"Tonight?"

"Yes, but you must not lead my horse back to my lodge until tomorrow night. We do not want people to think you are overly eager. We want them to think you are considering my offer."

Paloma squeezed Shadow Hawk's hand. "But there is no decision to be made. I will marry you now."

"It is better for you if you wait. Tommorrow night water and feed the horse, then tie him in front of my lodge."

"This is not good, Shadow Hawk. It will not go well with Teroz and Sotso."

"I am not marrying them, I am marrying you."

"But it is up to Sotso to accept you or deny you."

"No, Paloma, it is up to you. Sotso will not go against me in this. If he does, he will have to go against Ataza."

Paloma started to cry again, covering her face with her hands. "Why are you doing this, Shadow Hawk? Why?"

"Because it is the honorable thing to do, Paloma." He stood up and helped her to her feet. "Do not cry anymore.

There is no more need for tears. Come to the stream and let us wash your cuts. If anyone asks you what happened, you tell them you fell down a hill picking berries."

Paloma laughed for the first time. "No one will believe that. I am the one the women always send up the steepest hills because I have such good balance."

"So, this day you lost your balance because you are so much in love."

She put her hand lightly on his chest. "I do not know how I will repay you, Shadow Hawk. But I will someday, I promise you."

They walked to the stream, and as Paloma washed her cuts, Shadow Hawk felt an emptiness he hadn't felt since his father had died. It was as if a part of him was lost forever.

Shadow Hawk went to Ataza's lodge and asked for permission to enter.

"Come in, Nephew."

Shadow Hawk entered the lodge and sat next to him. "How are you today, Uncle?"

"I am well. Do you have news for me?"

Shadow Hawk was silent. Had Ataza guessed about him and Paloma? "Yes, I do. How did you know?"

"You have a look of anticipation on your face. You have made a decision?"

"Yes, Uncle." Shadow Hawk cleared his throat. "I am going to marry Paloma. I will tie my horse in front of her lodge tonight."

Ataza said nothing, but only stared at Shadow Hawk for some time. "That is what you have come to tell me?"

"Yes, Uncle."

"You have nothing else to say?"

"No, Uncle."

"What about the white woman, Nephew? What of her?"

"It is impossible for us to have a life together, Uncle."

"And when did you come to this decision, Nephew?"

Shadow Hawk hesitated. "I think I have always known that we could not be together."

"Yet you continue to think of this woman."

"Uncle—"

Ataza put up his hand to silence Shadow Hawk. "I have come to know you well, Shadow. You are like one of my own sons. Do you think I do not see you staring into the fire so deep in thought that you cannot hear what others say to you? Can you go on without this woman?"

"I have no choice."

Ataza was silent a moment, picking at some berries in a basket. He held them out to Shadow Hawk. "So, you wish to marry Paloma?"

"Yes, Uncle. It is best."

"Yes, I am sure it is the best thing for Paloma."

"Paloma is a good woman, Uncle. She will make me a fine wife."

"With that I will not argue."

"But you do not approve."

"I did not say that."

"I can hear it in your voice."

"What you hear in my voice is sadness, Shadow."

"Do not be sad for me, Uncle."

Ataza set down the basket. "We do not have the privilege of walking this earth for very long, Shadow. You have had sadness in your life. I would hope that you live the rest of it with some measure of happiness."

"I thank you for your concern, Uncle." Shadow Hawk met Ataza's eyes and nodded. "She cannot live in our world and I cannot live in hers. It is best this way."

"You are sure?"

Shadow Hawk nodded.

"What of Paloma?"

"I care very much for Paloma."

"I know that you do."

"I must ask you a favor, Uncle."

"Ask it, then."

"The words that I now speak must not leave this lodge."

"You may trust in that."

Shadow Hawk nodded. "It must not be common knowledge that I cared for the white woman. People in the camp must think that I am marrying Paloma because I love her." Shadow Hawk paused, reluctant to go on.

"What is it, Shadow?"

"Paloma is with child, Uncle. She is afraid that Teroz and Sotso will banish her if they find out. That is why we must marry as soon as possible and you must bless the marriage."

Ataza was silent. He frowned slightly. "You are not the father of this child?"

"It does not matter who the father is—"

"It matters very much to me." Ataza leaned forward. "I do not even have to ask who the father is."

"I say again that it does not matter, Uncle. All that matters is that you do not seem surprised by our marriage. You must act as if you have known all along."

"Does Miho know of the child?"

Shadow Hawk knew there was no point in trying to conceal anything from Ataza. "No, he knows nothing."

"Miho, my eldest, my best, that he would do such a thing . . ." Ataza shook his head.

"Do not judge him, Uncle. He did not mean for this to happen."

"He is a man, Shadow. He knew that it could happen."

"There is no need to tell him now that he is married."

"He disappoints me greatly."

"Listen to me, Uncle. Miho is a good man. When I came here, he defended me many times when others would not accept me. He allowed me to become close to you. He also helped Brave Heart many times when he was struggling to learn Apache ways. I know he did not mean to hurt Paloma in any way."

"You are a loyal friend and cousin, Shadow Hawk. You are an honorable man."

"I do only what Miho would do for me."

"So, it will not bother you to raise this child as your own?"

"No, I will be proud to raise this child of Miho and Paloma."

Ataza grasped Shadow Hawk's arm. "You make my heart full, Shadow Hawk. I am proud that you are my nephew. And I know that your father is looking down at you with the same pride in his heart."

"Thank you, Uncle."

"I will bless your marriage, and I hope that your life with Paloma is a good one."

Everyone had seen Shadow Hawk's horse tied in front of Paloma's lodge. People could talk of nothing else. Shadow Hawk couldn't help but smile when he walked past Paloma the next day and a charming blush spread over her cheeks. All the women in the camp giggled as he passed by and quickly gathered around Paloma to hear her tale of love. It made him feel good to see her so happy.

His next task, however, would not be so easy. Sotso had summoned him to his lodge. Shadow Hawk knew that Sotso would try to stop the marriage, but it would do no good. Shadow Hawk came from a good family, he had many horses to give for Paloma, and most important, he had Ataza's blessing.

When he reached the lodge, he asked permission to enter. Teroz appeared at the flap, looking as imposing as ever. Shadow Hawk had had very little contact with his cousin since he had returned, but their dislike for each other was still strong. Neither had spoken of the knife fight. It was as if it had never happened, except for the scar across Shadow Hawk's belly.

"Is your father here?"

Teroz said nothing, nodded, then stepped aside. Shadow Hawk walked into the lodge, greeted his uncle, and sat down.

"So, you wish to marry Paloma?"

"Yes, Uncle."

"Do you love her?"

"Yes, I love her."

"How will you provide for her?"

"I am a good hunter, I will raid if I must, and—"

"Yes, I have heard that you like to raid certain white ranches," Teroz interrupted.

Sotso frowned. "Quiet, Teroz."

"Yes, Father."

"Paloma is a good worker. We will miss her sorely. What do you intend to give us in return for her?"

"I have twenty horses that I will give you, Uncle."

Sotso could not contain his surprise. "Twenty? That is a large number."

"Paloma is worth it, is she not?"

"Yes, of course."

"He is lying. He does not have twenty horses. He has only the horse he has tied up in front of our lodge."

Shadow Hawk ignored Teroz. He was right. Two days ago he had had no horses. But Gitano had insisted he take twenty horses as a wedding gift. "I have the horses, Uncle. They are in a safe place."

"He is lying, Father!" Teroz stepped forward.

"Enough, Teroz. Do not interrupt again." Sotso appraised Shadow Hawk. "If Paloma accepts your offer of marriage, I will expect to see these horses soon after. If I do not, there will be no marriage."

"You will have them, Uncle."

"It is the custom of many of our people for the woman and her new husband to live with her family." Sotso looked from Shadow Hawk to Teroz. "But in this case, I think it would be wise for you two to live away from them."

"Yes, I agree."

"Does Ataza approve of this marriage?"

"Yes, Uncle."

"I will speak to him about it."

Shadow Hawk knew by Sotso's tone that he was being dismissed. He stood up. "Thank you, Uncle." He left the lodge, knowing that Teroz was behind him.

"Wait."

Shadow Hawk stopped. "What is it, Cousin?"

"Do not call me that. You are no cousin of mine." Teroz stepped close to Shadow Hawk. "Paloma does not love you."

"Paloma is going to marry me, and there is nothing you can do about it," Shadow Hawk replied coldly. "Do not interfere with this marriage in any way. Paloma deserves to be happy."

"You do not deserve Paloma."

"Neither do you." Shadow Hawk's eyes were cold as he stared at Teroz.

Teroz nodded his head. "It is not over between us."

Shadow Hawk watched Teroz as he went back inside the lodge. Teroz could have killed him when they had fought, but he had not. He had even offered to help him. Shadow Hawk smiled slightly and started walking. He didn't like Teroz, but he found that now, he didn't hate him, either.

As was expected, Paloma accepted Shadow Hawk's proposal of marriage. She fed and watered his horse and led it back to his lodge on the second night. The next day, Shadow Hawk went to the valley and rounded up the horses and drove them to the upper pasture where Sotso received them. Sotso formally gave Paloma to Shadow Hawk.

Shadow Hawk's gift of twenty horses caused a stir. No girl's family had ever received that many horses. The women and girls hovered around Paloma as they made plans.

Shadow Hawk and Paloma were no longer allowed to be alone and were constantly watched by aunts or uncles.

Ataza took Shadow Hawk to a place miles away from the camp to help him erect a lodge for his honeymoon. It was a peaceful place in a small valley. They erected the lodge under the shelter of some cottonwood trees, not far from a stream. Once the lodge was finished, Ataza filled it with food, enough to last Shadow Hawk and Paloma a week.

"This will be a good place for you and Paloma to get to know each other," Ataza had said thoughtfully, looking around him.

Shadow Hawk had nodded in agreement, wondering what it would be like to be alone with Paloma for that amount of time.

Shadow Hawk took Paloma for his wife seven days after he found out she was carrying Miho's child. Shadow Hawk was dressed in new buckskins that his mother had made for him and a blue shirt that he belted with a yellow sash given to him by Ataza. Paloma wore a beautiful deerskin dress covered with beads and fringe, her hair braided into one long plait that draped over a shoulder. Sotso gave Paloma to Shadow Hawk, making no pretense that he was going to miss the girl. Ataza, as leader of the band, spoke some words and blessed the marriage. Then the celebration began.

It would go on for at least three days, but Shadow Hawk and Paloma could leave whenever they wished. Paloma's friends had dug deep roasting pits and had baked deer, rabbit, corn, and yucca stems. There were also mescal stalks and hearts, wild onions, raspberries, and chokeberries. Ocha made steaming cups of coffee from chechil acorns and tea from cota and lip ferns. Then there was tulpai and tizwin.

Ataza supervised the making of tulpai. It was a potent corn beer, boiled and fermented for up to twenty-four hours. It had a pleasurable effect on the body. Tizwin, another drink, was made from the mescal plant. The women had cooked the mescal hearts until they had become sticky and then squeezed them to extract the liquid. The liquid was set aside to ferment. Both drinks spoiled quickly, so large quantities had to be consumed hurriedly. Ataza walked back and forth, refilling cups. It was not long before most of the people in the camp were wildly drunk and encouraging Shadow Hawk and Paloma to join them.

Shadow Hawk drank one cup of the potent tulpai and refused another. He looked around for Paloma. She was surrounded by a group of women and girls, all laughing and giggling. Shadow Hawk frowned slightly. He could imagine what advice they were giving her for her wedding night.

He saw his mother and walked to her. Her smile broadened when she saw him.

"You look handsome, my son. Are you happy this day?"

"Yes, Mother, I am happy."

"Paloma is a good name for her—she is like a little dove."

"Yes."

"You wear your happiness on the outside but not on the inside, where it is most important. Why is that, Shadow?"

Shadow Hawk looked at his mother. She was happy and he didn't want to upset her in any way. "Do not worry so, Mother. I am well."

"You could never lie to me, Shadow. Never."

"Mother—"

"Do you think your father was the clever one in this family, eh?" She poked him in the chest. "No, it was I. I am the one who knew whenever you did anything wrong. Your father never wanted to believe that you would do anything wrong."

"I fooled you many a time, Mother."

"When?"

"Do you remember the time the corral was broken and many of the good horses ran off?"

"Yes, I remember it well. Those were valuable horses."

"Yes, war horses. Father and the others were angry. They couldn't figure out how the horses got out."

Broken Moon nodded. "Yes, your father was upset for quite a few days. It was a good thing for you that I did not tell him you were the one who was responsible."

"You knew?"

"Yes, I knew. You were trying to climb into the corral to get a good look at the bay stallion that had been captured and the gate broke."

"How did you know?"

"When your father and the others asked the boys if they had been playing at the corral and none of you admitted to it, I looked into your eyes. You could not hide your guilt."

"But you did not tell Father."

"I felt there was no need. I knew that it was not your intention to break the corral and free the horses. Besides, when I saw how hard you worked to help recapture them, I felt you had been punished enough."

Shadow Hawk shook his head and smiled. "You knew."

"Yes, I knew, just as I know right now that your heart is not really here with Paloma. It is still with the white woman."

"You have talked to Ataza."

"No, my son, I have only to look into your eyes again. Since you have come back, you have not been the same. I will not ask what happened. I just hope that you and Paloma can make each other happy."

"We will, Mother."

Broken Moon smiled. "Here come Gitano and Brave Heart, each carrying a cup. Be careful of the tulpai."

"Mother." Shadow Hawk looked at his mother's gentle face. He took her hands in his. "I love you."

Broken Moon reached up and touched Shadow Hawk's face. "You are all that a mother could wish for in a son."

"Shadow Hawk!"

They both turned. Broken Moon laughed as they watched Gitano and Brave Heart approach. Neither of them was able to walk straight. "I will let you alone with these two brave warriors, my son. Let us pray that the enemy does not attack us on this night or we will all die."

Shadow Hawk smiled as he watched his mother walk away. His father would be proud to see how strong she had become. Or perhaps she had always been that strong and he had never noticed it before.

"What is the matter with you, Cousin? Have you already had too much tulpai?"

Shadow Hawk looked at Gitano. "No, I was just thinking."

Gitano held out a cup. "This is not a time for thinking, it is a time for drinking."

"No, I do not wish to have any more of that."

Brave Heart stumbled slightly as he put his hand on Shadow Hawk's shoulder. "It is a very interesting drink, Brother. I think you should have some. It will make it easier for you when you go to Paloma tonight." Brave Heart looked at Gitano and they both dissolved into laughter.

"Come, Cousin, just one drink." Gitano held the cup out again.

Shadow Hawk took the cup, quickly drank the bitter liquid, and handed it back to Gitano. "There, are you satisfied?"

"That is not enough, Brother," Brave Heart said, laughing hysterically.

Gitano clapped Shadow Hawk on the shoulder. "Are you sure you are ready for Paloma, Cousin?"

"What does that mean?" Shadow Hawk asked defensively.

"I have known Paloma a long time. She is very shy."

"That is no concern of yours, Gitano."

"But it is, Brother," Brave Heart said. "We want to make sure that your wedding night is a memorable one."

"I do not trust you two."

"Brave Heart has some advice for you, Cousin. I think you should listen to him."

"Brave Heart has advice for me?" Shadow Hawk couldn't

contain his smile.

"Yes. After all, he is a married man. I think you should listen to him."

Shadow Hawk thought for a moment. "All right. I will listen."

"Well, Brother," Brave Heart began, leaning toward Shadow Hawk. He lost his balance and stumbled forward, leaning against Shadow Hawk's chest.

"Yes, Brother?"

"You must be gentle with her. If you are not, you will frighten her."

Shadow Hawk stood Brave Heart back on his feet. "This is your advice? This is what I get from a married man?"

"I am not finished yet." Brave Heart handed him his cup. "Take a drink. It will be a long night."

Shadow Hawk drank from the cup and handed it back to Brave Heart. "Tell me, wise one, what else do you have to say to me?"

Brave Heart held up his hand as he walked away from the others. He looked around him, as if searching for something, and sat down when he found a rock that looked particularly comfortable. When Shadow Hawk and Gitano joined him, sitting on the ground, he continued. "You must be gentle, but you must appear to have knowledge. If you do not appear to be experienced, it could frighten her."

"So, how did you appear to be experienced when you were not?"

"I did not say that I was not experienced, Brother."

"Well, we both know that you were not. So, what did you do?" Shadow Hawk enjoyed the confused expression on his brother's face, laughing with Gitano as Brave Heart tried to arrange his thoughts.

Brave Heart finished the cup of tulpai. "I waited until she gave me a sign that she wanted to . . ." Brave Heart shrugged his shoulders. "You know . . ."

"What kind of sign should I look for, Brother?"

"Maybe you should look for smoke signals, Cousin!" Gitano laughed loudly.

Shadow Hawk looked at Gitano bent over, laughing so hard that tears streamed down his face, and he laughed with him.

"Laugh, then, but when Paloma leaves your lodge, do not come to me for advice."

Shadow Hawk forced himself to look serious. "I am sorry, Brother. It is Gitano's fault. He makes me laugh." Shadow Hawk cleared his throat. "I thank you for your advice, Brother. I will try to heed it."

"Good. Remember something else. You must tell her she is the most beautiful woman you have ever seen, even if you do not believe it."

"This is too complicated for me," Gitano said, drinking from his already empty cup. "I do not want a woman who will watch my every move and make me suffer if I do not do as she asks."

"Your sister does not do that."

"Singing Bird is different. She is sensible."

"What of Paloma?" Brave Heart asked. "Is she also sensible?"

Shadow Hawk shifted uncomfortably as the others looked at him. "I do not know. I know that she has a kind heart and a gentle soul. She will make a good wife."

Gitano stood up. "I think you have given enough advice for tonight, Brave Heart. I am thirsty for more drink. What about you, Cousin?" Gitano held out his empty cup.

Shadow Hawk shook his head. "No. I think I will look for Paloma."

"Good luck, Brother," Brave Heart said, standing up to embrace Shadow Hawk.

Shadow Hawk held Brave Heart tightly for a moment, then released him. "Thank you, Brother."

"Good-bye, Cousin. I am the only one who is free." Gitano staggered, then righted himself as he attempted to walk away.

Shadow Hawk smiled as he watched his brother and cousin, their arms around each other's shoulders, trying to walk in unison as they swayed. He was glad they had become such good friends.

He stared up at the clear night sky. He thought of Aissa and wondered if she was completely free of the medicine. He wondered if she still thought he was coming back. He heard footsteps and didn't turn, thinking it was Gitano or Brave Heart playing one of their foolish games.

"Are you thinking about the white woman, Comanche?"

It was Teroz. Shadow Hawk didn't turn at the sound of his voice. He stood still, continuing to stare up at the sky. "Are you watching me, Teroz?"

"I always watch you, Comanche. I do not trust you. Why is it you are here instead of with my sister?"

Shadow Hawk looked at Teroz. "She is not your sister, Teroz. You and your father have never treated her better than a slave."

"And you will treat her better, I suppose."

"I will treat her with respect."

"You will treat her with respect and then you will go to the white woman, yes?"

"There is no white woman, Teroz."

"We will see."

"What does that mean?"

"It means that I will never forget that you have come here and tried to act like one of us. I am the only one who is clear-headed enough to remember that you are the enemy. Someday I will make you pay for marrying Paloma."

"You are jealous," Shadow Hawk said, nodding his head. "She is not really your sister and you thought that someday you could take her for your wife. You thought that you could frighten away every other man who was interested in her. But you did not scare Miho and you do not scare me."

"Miho is a dog like you. Why else would he desert his own people?"

271

"I will not discuss Miho with you. It is time for me to find my wife." Shadow Hawk brushed by Teroz.

"Wait!"

Shadow Hawk stopped without turning.

"Remember this, Comanche. Someday I will have what is yours, just as you now have what is mine."

Shadow Hawk continued walking. As he neared the large fire and the throng of people who danced and sang, he saw Paloma. She walked toward him.

"Shadow Hawk."

Shadow Hawk smiled when he saw her pretty smiling face. "Hello."

"Would you like to eat?"

"No, I am not hungry."

"Would you like something to drink?"

"No."

"Are you all right, Shadow Hawk?"

Suddenly he wanted nothing more than to be away from the drunken shouts and laughter. He smiled at Paloma. "I am well. Perhaps it is time for us to leave."

"But all the people—"

"I do not think they will miss us, Paloma."

"If you think it is best."

"Yes, I am ready to be away from here."

"I would like to say good-bye to my mother and some of the others."

"Paloma," Shadow Hawk took her hands, "let us just go."

"I understand." She lowered her eyes, and he knew she was blushing. "I have to get my pack. It is in my lodge."

"Singing Bird got it for me earlier. Our things are ready. We can leave now."

Paloma looked with yearning back at the camp. "If you are ready."

"Yes." Shadow Hawk took his new wife's hand and led her down the path. He was about to start a new life, but he didn't feel any of the excitement or anticipation he knew he should have. As much as he liked Paloma, their marriage was not based on love, and they both knew it. It was not a good way to begin a life together. But he had done the honorable thing and he would make the best of it.

Shadow Hawk looked at the stars above. He wondered if his father could see through them to the earth below. He and Paloma had made their way to their camp and Paloma had cooked. They had eaten and then taken a walk. Now, as Paloma readied herself for sleep, Shadow Hawk hesitated, sitting outside the lodge.

What was he to do? Paloma was young and pretty, the kind of wife any man would want. But he did not desire her in the way that he desired Aissa, and he knew that Paloma still loved Miho. Yet he and Paloma were now married. He had a responsibility, especially if she expected him to be a real husband to her.

He sighed and stood up. It was time. He walked to the small lodge and pushed back the flap, closing it after he stepped inside. It was dark. The night was warm, there was no need for a fire. He waited until his eyes adjusted to the darkness. He could see the outlines of their robes where Paloma had placed them opposite the door. He walked quietly over, sat down on the robe, and removed his moccasins. He pulled off his shirt but hesitated before he took off his buckskins. Finally he stood and removed them, wearing only a breechcloth. He sat back down on the soft robe and lay back.

"Shadow Hawk?"

"Yes." He thought Paloma's voice sounded scared.

"I am your wife."

"I know that, Paloma. We were married just this day."

"Do not joke with me. Please."

"I am sorry."

"I am your wife in every way. I will not fight you. I will

273

gladly give myself to you."

Shadow Hawk closed his eyes. "Paloma—"

"Please, Shadow Hawk, you have done an honorable thing for me. I must be a good wife to you in return."

"Paloma," Shadow Hawk said gently, reaching out for her hand. "You do not love me in that way."

"But you are my husband."

"We must deceive the others, but there is no need to deceive ourselves." He squeezed her hand to soften his words and willed her to understand. She lay down on her robe and soon Shadow Hawk heard the slow, deep breathing that meant she was asleep. He lay still. So this was his wedding night. The moon rose and he could see the silhouettes of the lodgepoles above him. The moon was nearly full. He wondered if Aissa had gotten well. Had she regained her beauty and her stubbornness? How long would she wait for him to come back? And he knew the answer even as he thought it. She would have to wait forever.

Chapter 13

Ben brushed his pants off on the porch and opened the door. Aissa was lying on the sofa, a blanket over her legs, her head resting against the side. A book lay in her lap. Within easy reach, the Colt pistol he had given her lay on the floor. Ben still didn't trust Grimes. He had made Aissa practice with the pistol until he knew she was good enough with it to defend herself. Ben shut the door quietly, but she lifted her head and opened her eyes anyway.

"Hello, Father."

"Hello, honey. I'm sorry I woke you."

"You didn't. I was just resting. Aren't you home early?"

"Joe is on duty tonight. Not much doing, anyway. A couple of Jaminson's boys had a fistfight, but they're cooled off now. I had some shopping to do. I went over to the mercantile and found some things I think you'll like."

"Good," Aissa replied without much emotion.

"Since you're awake, I'll bring them in." Ben walked back out to the wagon and brought the packages into the house. It had taken some of his secret money, but it would be worth it to see her smile. He shut the door and pulled a chair out from the table and sat down. "Do you want to see what I bought?"

Aissa nodded without replying.

"Well, here's a bottle of some kind of cream that's

275

supposed to be real good for your skin. Flora said so, anyway. Came all the way from Paris, so I had to buy it." He handed it to Aissa. "Smells real good, too. Let's see, besides beans, flour, and sugar, I got us some canned goods. Got some peaches and pears. Brandied plums, too. And look at this little tin, it's full of tea. Came all the way from China. Imagine that."

Aissa smiled weakly. "I'm sure I will like it, Father."

"They had some new candy sticks in, and I got some of those. Got this, too." Ben handed Aissa a wrapped package. "Go ahead. Open it."

"Father, why are you buying all these things? You know we can't afford it."

"Yes we can. Now open it."

Aissa unwrapped the package. It was a blue dress she'd been looking at for a long time but couldn't afford. "You didn't buy this at the mercantile. You bought this at Bessie's shop. It's much too expensive, Father."

"Nonsense, nothing's too good for you."

Aissa laid the dress across her legs and looked at her father. "Where are you getting the money for all these things? You've been buying things for me ever since I got better. There's no need to do that."

"I like buying you things. You're my daughter."

"Did you borrow some money from the bank?"

"No, I didn't. We have money saved up."

"We don't have that much."

"We have enought to send you to Paris when you're well enough."

"I know exactly how much money we have in that account and it's not nearly enough."

"You haven't been around for a while, Aissa. There's more in there than you think." Ben saw the look in her eyes when he spoke. She had recoved physically, but emotionally she was still an invalid. It wasn't just because of what Ray had done. Why hadn't Shadow Hawk come back? Aissa blamed herself and there was no getting around it. Ben forced himself to smile. "I mean it, Aissa, I want you to take that trip to Paris."

"I don't want to go to Paris, Father. I want to stay here."

"You can't stay holed up in this house for the rest of your life."

"This is where I want to be for now."

"What about your students?"

"They'll be fine. Bradley Choate is very competent. They'll learn a lot from him."

"But he's not you. Those children need you."

Aissa sat up, folding the blue dress. "Don't, Father. Don't push me."

"I'm worried about you, Aissa."

Aissa rested her head against the side of the sofa. "I just need time."

"You've had time."

"Can't you leave me alone, Father?"

"No, I can't, not when I see you lying on this sofa day after day doing nothing. Is it Shadow Hawk?"

"No, it has nothing to do with him."

"Is it because he didn't come back?" Ben pulled the chair close to the sofa and took Aissa's hand. "Talk to me, girl. I love you." Ben saw the pain in her eyes when she looked at him. There were no tears, but the sadness was overwhelming.

"I miss him."

"I know."

"I don't blame him for not coming back. I was awful."

"It wasn't your fault, Aissa. He knew that."

"Why did he go without saying good-bye?"

"Aissa, he's an Apache. That's where his true ties are. I know he's fond of us in his own way. Lord knows, when we both needed him, he was here. But we can't blame him if he wanted to go back to his own kind."

"Why did he tell you he'd come back, then? Why?"

"Maybe he can't come back, honey. Hell, the kind of life

277

he lives, he might already be dead." Ben regretted the words as soon as he said them.

"You don't really believe that, do you, Father?" Her voice was sharp, frightened.

"Honey, I don't know. You know better than I the kind of life those people live. When Shadow Hawk can come back here, he will."

Aissa nodded absently, closing her eyes. "I'm tired, Father."

Ben stood up and took the chair back to the table. He shook his head in disgust. What could he do for her? Nothing, really. It was up to Aissa; she was the only one who could make herself well. He put the food away, poured himself a whiskey, and went out on the porch to sit in his rocking chair.

He couldn't believe how dramatically Aissa had changed in so short a time, and all because of Ray Grimes. Ben was still sheriff, and while he was, he was sworn to uphold the law. But as soon as he turned in his star, which he was considering, he'd go after Ray and make him pay for what he'd done to his little girl. He'd make Ray wish Shadow Hawk had killed him that night.

"Where are you, Shadow?" Ben said aloud. He had been sure the Apache would come back, and he was as surprised as Aissa that he hadn't. Probably he was dead. It was the most logical thing. Nothing else could have kept him from Aissa.

Ben stood up and went back inside. His mind was too preoccupied with Aissa to notice the lone rider in the distance.

Aissa lay awake in her bed. She had read until her eyes ached, and finally she put out the lamp. But still she couldn't sleep. She felt as if she was someone else, as if her thoughts had been taken over by another person. She couldn't even cry anymore.

She thought about Ray all the time, but she couldn't even stir up enough feeling to hate him. She blamed herself for letting him overpower her. She blamed herself for everything.

Eventually her thoughts drifted to Shadow Hawk. She had driven him away, she knew that. Why would he have wanted to come back? She winced, remembering how she had acted. What man would want to come back to a woman who had been more in love with a drug than with him? That had to be the reason he wasn't here. It had to be. He couldn't be dead.

She turned on her side and looked out the window. There was a moon out tonight, and the light shone into her room. She'd always wondered how something so far away could still shine so brightly. As her thoughts wandered, she closed her eyes. Moments later, she opened them, feeling as if someone was staring at her. She looked around the moonlit room, then at the window. There was no one. Still she felt uneasy, as if someone were close, watching her. Aissa kept her eyes open. This time she saw a movement outside the window. She lay still, barely breathing. Was her mind playing tricks again? No—there was someone. She could see a silhouette now. Someone was looking in her window. Fear gripped her, but she remained motionless. At first she thought it might be Ray, but she could see by the moonlight that it was an Indian, and it wasn't Shadow Hawk. She reached for her pistol, then hesitated. She might get a shot at him, but that would alert the others. The Indian remained by the window for a few seconds more and then moved.

Aissa quietly rolled out of her bed and opened the door of her armoire, pulling on pants, boots, and a shirt, and grabbing the Colt pistol from under her pillow. She stuck it into the waistband of her pants and ran to her father's room.

She opened the door and crawled across the floor, shaking his shoulder until he grumbled.

"What is it?"

"Father, be quiet. There's someone outside. An Indian."

Ben sat up and grabbed his pants from the bottom of the bed. "Get the shotgun."

Aissa brought him the gun from behind the door. She scooped up a box of shells from the top of her father's nightstand.

Ben took the rifle and shells from Aissa and opened the door. "You have your gun?" he whispered.

"Yes." She touched the butt of her pistol.

Ben gripped her shoulder. "Stay away from the windows. Come over by me."

They moved into the small space between the two bedrooms, a tiny hallway that separated their rooms from the front room. This was the only place in the house where they couldn't be seen.

"Did you see how many there were?"

"I saw only one."

"It wasn't Shadow Hawk?"

"He wouldn't be sneaking around if it was. Father, listen."

They could hear horses whinnying frantically. Then there was the smell of smoke.

"The haystack's on fire," Ben said, striding angrily across the front room to look out.

"Father, get away from the window," Aissa cried, but her words were too late. A shot shattered the window, spinning Ben around, knocking him to the floor. Aissa ran across the room, kneeling next to him. His shoulder and face were bloody. "Father, Father!"

"Aissa, get out," Ben said weakly.

"No, I won't leave you."

"Get the rifle. Do it."

Aissa looked around in the darkness for the rifle. As she laid her hand on it the door crashed open. She picked up the rifle and shot without aiming as the Indian fell to the floor. For an instant Aissa thought she'd hit him, but he had fallen too quickly, before she had pulled the trigger. She raised the rifle again but this time the Indian was on her, wrenching it from her hands. She reached for her pistol, but he slammed her hand back against the floor, knocking the gun away. She tried to crawl toward it, but he pulled her back.

He yanked her to her feet and pulled her out of the house. "No!" She screamed, clutching onto the door frame. She looked back into the house. She screamed over and over for Ben, but he didn't answer. Aissa kicked wildly, but the Indian wrapped one arm around her and forced her to walk. Aissa twisted and fought, but he kept her moving. The haystack was still burning, the smell of smoke filling the night air. A breeze blew sparks toward the house. "Let me get my father out of the house," Aissa pleaded in Spanish, praying that the Indian would understand her. "Please. The fire." She struggled against iron-strong arms that held her fast.

Without speaking, the Indian put her across his horse as though she were a doll and swung up behind her. Aissa tried to slip down, but he held her and kicked his horse into a gallop. She tried to scream, her stomach slamming against the horse's withers. She looked back through the curtain of her own hair and saw the amber light of the fire. She twisted, trying to see if it had spread to the house. The flames leapt into the night sky, sending a shower of glittering sparks upward. Aissa fought to breathe as the pounding rhythm of the horse's gallop jarred and bruised her ribs. She could feel the relentless grip of the Indian's hand on the back of her shirt. This time, she had lost everything—her father, her home, and her freedom.

A sharp pain forced Aissa to leave the comfort of her oblivion. Instinctively she rolled away from the pain, opening her eyes. The Indian sat astride his horse, his face turned away from her, drinking from his water bag. Aissa sat up, rubbing her hip. Her chest and stomach were bruised and aching. Slowly her thoughts began to make sense. She didn't know how far they had ridden or where she was, but it was obvious that the Indian didn't care how much he hurt her. He had pushed her off the horse. Was he going to make her walk? He was still looking off across the desert. His skin was very dark and his hair fell loosely past his shoulders. He wore buckskins and moccasins but no shirt, and his torso was heavily muscled. When he turned around she stifled a scream. Involuntarily she inched backward. This was the same man who had kidnapped her all those years ago. She would never forget his face or his cold eyes. He smiled as he dismounted, an incredibly menacing smile.

"So, you remember me." He spoke in Spanish.

Without realizing she was doing it, Aissa looked around.

"There is no one here to help you."

"Shadow Hawk—" was all she said before he laughed harshly.

"Shadow Hawk?" Teroz laughed again. "Who do you think gave you to me, woman?" He bent down next to Aissa. "He did not want you, so he gave you back to me."

Aissa took a quick breath. "No."

Teroz sat down. "He is now married."

Aissa understood his awkward Spanish. "Married?" She shook her head. "I don't believe you." Her voice trembled as she spoke.

"He is married to my sister."

Aissa sat on the hard ground in the early morning sun, stunned by what Teroz had just told her.

"You do not believe me?" Teroz shrugged. "You will see soon enough for yourself. I am taking you back with me. I have a use for you."

Aissa instinctively crossed her arms in front of herself as she felt Teroz look at her.

"You will do as you are told."

"Let me go. I've done nothing to you."

"You have done more to me than you know, woman." Teroz stood up, slinging the water bag over his shoulder without offering her a drink. "Get on the horse."

Aissa drew back. But with the quickness of a snake, Teroz grabbed her wrist and forced her to her feet. The crushing pressure of his grip was painful. She walked submissively to the horse.

He released her wrists, obviously confident that she wouldn't try to escape. And he was right, Aissa realized bitterly. The desert stretched as far as she could see in every direction. If he left her here, she would die. But maybe that would be better.

Teroz adjusted the blanket on the horse, calmly, not hurrying. He was powerful and he frightened her. But she refused to be shamed by any man again. Without thinking, Aissa bolted and ran. She ran as fast as she could, heading for a small stand of scrub oak in the distance. She kept running even after she heard the hoofbeats. Suddenly she was hit from behind and she went sprawling face forward onto the ground. She could taste the bits of grit and sand in her mouth.

"That was a very stupid thing to do, woman." His voice was cold. "I should kill you right now."

"Why don't you?" The steadiness of her voice surprised her. She turned over and sat up, brushing the sand from her face.

Teroz dismounted and sat with his arms resting on his knees, his eyes squinting into the rising sun. "You wish to die?"

"I have nothing left. If you're going to kill me, do it now." Aissa looked down at the sand, her hands clenched in her lap.

"What of Shadow Hawk, do you not wish to see him again?"

Aissa regarded Teroz. His face was less cold now, almost curious. "The only thing I want is to go home. I don't care

283

about Shadow Hawk."

Teroz nodded his head. "You lie well, woman, but not well enough. Your eyes betray you."

"Think what you want, I don't care about anything but going home."

"You will not go home. You will go with me. You will do as I say."

"I would rather die than go with you." She tried to hold his black eyes, but they frightened her and she had to look aside.

"I do not think you want to die."

"You know nothing about me."

"I think I do." Teroz picked up some sand, slowly letting it run through his fingers. "Shadow Hawk is going to have a child with his new wife."

Aissa felt a heaviness in her chest. She couldn't hide the pain she flet this time. She didn't want to hear any more. "Are you going to kill me or not?" she demanded.

"I am not going to kill you."

"What, then? Are you going to make me your slave?" Aissa looked at Teroz, her eyes challenging him.

"I will take you back to my people. We will share a lodge. You will work as the other women work, and you will not complain. When we walk through the camp together, you will act like you are grateful to me. If you do all these things, I will treat you well."

Aissa's cheeks flushed with anger. "No matter how you treat me, it won't be the same as being with my father."

"It appears you do not have much of a choice."

Aissa sighed, picking at the pebbles in the sand. "Why are you doing this?" When Teroz didn't answer, Aissa persisted. "It's Shadow Hawk, isn't it? You hate him."

"Yes," Teroz replied coldly, "I hate him. He took my woman, and now I will take his."

"No. I won't do it. I won't go with you."

Teroz reached out and grasped Aissa's forearm, his fingers digging into her skin. "Understand me, woman. I would kill

you and be done with it in seconds. You mean nothing to me.
You are merely a way for me to get to Shadow Hawk. Do
you understand?"

Aissa didn't move. This was not the time to defy Teroz.
Slowly she nodded and he released her arm.

"When you see Shadow Hawk in the camp, you will tell
him that I have treated you well. You will make him believe
it. In time, you will also make him believe that you bear some
affection for me."

"He won't care. You told me yourself he loves your sister."

"When he sees you with me, it will be different. Although
he gave you to me, he will want you back. He still thinks of
you as his property." Teroz nodded. "He will care."

Aissa looked at Teroz, gathering her courage. "If I do as
you say, is there a chance you will let me go back to my
father?"

Teroz's black eyes pierced Aissa. "Do not push me,
woman." He picked up another handful of sand. "Tell me,
why do you care so much for a man who cares nothing for
you?"

Aissa avoided Teroz's piercing black eyes. "I am alive
because of Shadow Hawk."

"And now you are alive because I wish it to be so. Go
against me and you will get your wish. You will die."

Aissa nodded without speaking. She could not fight this
man and win. She didn't want to die. Her words had been
hollow, empty. She would do whatever she had to do to live.
She would play Teroz's game until she gained his trust and
then she would find a way to go back to her father. Her
father? He had to be alive. When she got home, they would
take their money and they would leave. They would go to
Paris to be with their relatives, as far away as they could get
from this savage and brutal land.

When Shadow Hawk and Paloma returned from their

285

time away, they erected a lodge on the side of camp, close to the piñon trees, where it was most isolated. Shadow Hawk was content with Paloma; she was a good wife, she worked hard, and she cooked well. As for love, neither of them spoke of it, nor of Miho or Aissa.

It wasn't long before Paloma began to show that she was with child, and questions as to the paternity arose. But Shadow Hawk put an end to all gossip when he let everyone know that he had loved Paloma for a long while and the child was his. Certainly, to anyone who looked at the young couple, it appeared that they were in love. They walked together hand-in-hand and they always laughed. Indeed, there was a genuine affection between the two, but there was not the kind of love that people assumed there was.

When the men of the band weren't hunting or raiding, they spent some of their time making new weapons and tools, but mostly they gambled. They gambled anything and everything including their wives. While the men gambled, the women worked. They knew no other existence. Their days did not consist of games and gambling, but of gathering water and wood, tanning hides, digging for roots and vegetables, gathering berries, making clothes, moccasins, baskets, and water jars, cooking food, and raising children. Their day began at sunrise and did not end until after dark. It was into this kind of life that Teroz brought Aissa.

Unlike the last time she had been taken to the Apache camp, Aissa observed everything around her as she and Teroz rode. They crossed the hot desert that was dotted with saguaros and agaves, ocotillos and mescal plants. Lizards and snakes staked their claim to the hot sand, and jackrabbits hopped from one sparse patch of shade to the next. The desert seemed endless. Aissa's lips cracked and her fair skin turned pink in the hot sun.

As they rode up out of a dry wash, Teroz turned his horse toward a towering rock formation. Aissa could see that it was the entrance to a canyon. Teroz rode between the sheer walls and Aissa tried to memorize every detail. The barren desert gave way to darker, richer soil. There were fewer cactus and desert plants, and thickets of sumac and sage lined the trail. Sunflowers bloomed a brilliant yellow, and the red tassel-like flowers of the pigweed splashed the hillsides. The higher they rode, the more the terrain changed. Cedar, yellow pine, piñon pine, and juniper trees grew in abundance on the canyon rim. By late afternoon, the desert had given way entirely to mountains.

Aissa was silent and paid fierce attention to everything, praying that someday she would have an opportunity to escape. When Teroz swung off the horse to pick and eat berries, she memorized their color, the shape of their leaves. When she looked at the hills above them, she wondered how anyone could live there.

As they rode up a narrow, rocky path, Aissa could see a valley off to one side. It was lush and green, and she could see the glint of sunlight off of water. She recognized choke-cherry bushes among the pines. The air was sweet with the rich smell of pine and cedar. She had been here only once, at night, and that was five years ago. But was that here? Perhaps this was a different camp. She didn't know.

A shrill whistling sound echoed from the boulders above, and Aissa looked up. There were men standing on the rocks high above them. She hadn't seen them before. Where had they come from? The sound came again and suddenly, behind her, Teroz echoed the call. When she looked for the men on the rocks, they had disappeared.

Soon, Teroz reined in his horse. He dismounted, pulling Aissa with him. She watched as Teroz led his horse up the steep, curving path. For an instant, she fought the impulse to run. But the stinging scratches on her face and the weariness in all her muscles reminded her that it was useless. Teroz knew it. He continued upward on the steep path without even glancing back at her. Aissa followed, stumbling but not giving in to her fatigue. The path twisted and turned, skirting rough boulders and wind-bent piñon pines. Aissa struggled to keep up, gasping for breath as they gained altitude. Teroz did not look back at her, nor did he slow his easy, ground-covering stride. They rounded a curve in the path and Aissa was startled to see the rocky mountainside give way to a lush pasture where hundreds of horses grazed.

Teroz slipped his horse's bridle over its ears, uncinched his riding pad and dropped it on the ground. He slapped the animal on the flank to send it out with the others. Without waiting for him to order her, Aissa picked up the pad and supplies. Teroz glanced at her and then continued walking on a trail that led up from the pasture. Aissa could hear voices from the rocks above.

They continued up a steep, narrow trail and Aissa slipped numerous times but she kept up with Teroz. She couldn't remember the path or the village. She wasn't even sure if this was the same village. She had been here only once, at night, when she was a frightened young girl. Now she was grown and she wouldn't allow her fear to dull her senses.

Once they reached the top, the land flattened out into a large area where Aissa saw at least a hundred hide lodges and wickiups. Pine trees bordered the camp on one side, and a rocky hillside on the other. Children ran through the camp laughing and playing, and women worked in small groups around the camp performing various tasks.

"Stay behind me," Teroz commanded. He began walking again. "And lower your eyes."

Aissa followed Teroz as they walked through the village. Women and girls followed, laughing and giggling, pulling at Aissa's long blond hair, and touching her pants and shirt. The men, most of whom were sitting in small circles in the camp, stared at Aissa but didn't move. Aissa wanted to see if Shadow Hawk was there but she kept her head lowered, adhering to Teroz's command. Teroz stoped in front of a lodge. He spoke a few sharp and guttural words to the women who had followed them, then he told Aissa to wait while he went inside. She stood outside the lodge, her hands shoved inside her pockets, trying to ignore the stares and taunts of the women and children. One woman was so bold as to step forward and touch Aissa's breasts. Shocked out of her numbness, Aissa shoved the woman away and covered herself with her arms. She watched as a young man stepped forward and spoke to her in Spanish.

"They are confused."

Aissa looked at him. "Why?"

"You have a woman's face and body, yet you dress like a man. They do not understand."

"Oh." Aissa nodded.

"You are the white woman I have heard so much about, yes?"

Aissa remained silent.

"Yes, you must be. You are beautiful, just like he said."

"Who?"

"Get away, Gitano!" Teroz threw the lodge flap open and shoved Aissa to the side. He glowered at Gitano, stepping toward him. "Do you try to take my captive away from me?"

Gitano shrugged his shoulders, taking a bite from a piece of smoked meat. "I have no interest in your captive, Teroz."

"Why are you here, then?"

"I was out for a walk."

"I heard you speak to her."

"So?"

"So, I do not want you to speak to her, Gitano. She is my captive. I do not want you near her."

"Or what?"

"Or you may find your throat cut in the middle of the night, Cousin."

"That is your way, isn't it, Teroz? I say that is the mark of a coward."

Teroz lept forward and knocked Gitano to the ground. Teroz had his knife drawn before Gitano could move. Aissa drew back, frightened.

289

"Enough, Teroz? Stop!" An older man came out of the lodge and pulled Teroz from Gitano. "What is the matter with you? He is your cousin, your blood."

Teroz scraped the blade of the knife along his buckskins. "Gitano is sharp like a thorn in my side. If he were not my cousin, he would have died long ago." He went inside the lodge, pulling the flap shut after him.

The man looked at the woman and children who were standing around watching. "You have things to do. Go now." He waited until everyone was gone and then faced his nephew. "Leave, Gitano. You should not be here."

"I did nothing, Uncle. He came at me with his knife."

"You are in front of our lodge." He glanced at Aissa. "Were you fighting about the girl? If you were, I'll kill her myself and have it done!"

"We were not fighting about the girl, Uncle. We were just fighting as we have always done."

"Stay away from Teroz. You anger him."

"Forgive me, Sotso, but this is my camp also."

"You are insolent like your brother."

"My brother is a brave warrior. I will accept your compliment, Uncle."

Sotso muttered something, glared at Aissa, and went back into the lodge.

Gitano walked over to Aissa. "Are you hurt?"

"No."

"Teroz lives to frighten people." He took another bite of the meat. "When I was a small boy I was terrified of Teroz. If I was swimming, he would jump in and hold me under the water. If I was playing a game with the other boys, he would come from behind and push me down on the ground and not let me up."

Aissa looked toward the lodge nervously. "You don't seem to be frightened of him anymore."

"My brother told me that Teroz loves to see fear in people's eyes. He told me if I faced up to him I would not be so frightened of him anymore."

"You are braver than I," Aissa said softly, again glancing toward the lodge.

"It is different for you. You are a captive." Gitano stepped closer. "Listen to me, white woman. Do as Teroz tells you. If you do not, he will make you suffer."

Aissa looked at Gitano, not sure how to respond. He seemed kind, but she had to remember she couldn't trust anyone but herself. "I'll do what I must."

"What is your name, white woman?"

"It is Aissa. What is yours?"

"My name is Gitano." Gitano took the smoked meat from his belt pouch and handed it to her. "I am sure that Teroz did not feed you. Hide it from him or he will take it away. We will speak again, Aissa."

Aissa shoved Gitano's gift into her pocket. "Thank you, Gitano." She smiled only slightly. She had to be careful. She had trusted Shadow Hawk and it was because of him that she was here. She sat down next to the lodge, her arms wrapped around her knees. She could hear Sotso and Teroz speaking in angry tones inside the lodge. Although she couldn't understand a word of Apache, it was obvious from the sound of their voices that they were arguing.

She thought about Shadow Hawk and wondered where he was. He hadn't even come to see if she was all right. At least Teroz had been truthful about that much—Shadow Hawk cared nothing for her anymore. Teroz had said that Shadow Hawk thought of her as a piece of property. She felt betrayed. She wouldn't allow herself to be deceived by any man again.

Shadow Hawk carried the fresh meat to his lodge. Paloma was outside, kneeling close to the cook fire. A pot hung from the green wood frame. Paloma was heavy with child and she looked pretty. Shadow Hawk smiled when he saw her.

"Meat for you and the child."

"You have done well, my husband. But if you keep feeding me like this, soon I will be unable to walk, I will be so large."

Shadow Hawk hung the slabs of meat on the wooden rack outside the lodge and handed some to Paloma to put into the pot. "Do you want me to help you cut it up for drying?"

"No, I will do that. You sit. You must be hungry."

Shadow Hawk sat down by the fire. Paloma brought him a water jar. She had just finished making it. Her basketwork, like everything else she did, was careful and meticulous. The design formed by the yucca and juniper roots was intricate and lovely. The inside of the jar had been carefully smeared with pitch so that it wouldn't leak. Shadow Hawk extended his hands and she poured the water over them while he cleaned himself of dirt and blood. Then she handed the jar to him. He took a long drink and handed the jar back to her. "Thank you."

"There has been much excitement in the village today."

"Why?"

"Teroz has returned."

"I do not find that to be exciting news, Paloma."

"He has a captive. A white woman."

"Did you see her?"

"No, I do not wish to be anywhere near him. But Gitano was there. He spoke with her."

"Gitano spoke with the woman? I cannot believe Teroz would allow that."

"Teroz got very angry at Gitano. Sotso pulled Teroz away and told Gitano to leave."

"How do you know so much if you were not there, Paloma?"

Paloma lowered her eyes, blushing. "I have heard it from the women. You know how they talk."

Shadow Hawk smiled. "Yes, I know how they talk."

Paloma spooned some soup into a bowl and handed it to Shadow Hawk. "The woman say that she is strange looking."

Shadow Hawk held the clay bowl up to his mouth and drank. "What is so strange about her?"

"They say she is like this," Paloma said, reaching above her own head. "Larger than most of our own men."

"That does not mean she is strange, Paloma."

"They also say she is dressed in the clothing of a man. Brown Feather had to feel her to make sure she was a woman."

"What did the white woman do when Brown Feather touched her?"

"She pushed her away. She does not seem to be afraid."

"Well, Paloma, for never having seen this captive, you seem to know everything about her." Shadow Hawk finished the soup and handed the bowl to his wife. "Perhaps I will take a look at her myself."

"Teroz will never let you near her."

"I do not care about Teroz."

"Please, Shadow Hawk, stay away from him. He hates you."

"You worry too much, Paloma. More soup, please." Shadow Hawk drank his second bowl, ate the meat that was at the bottom, and handed the bowl back to Paloma. "You are feeling well?"

"Yes."

"Good." Shadow Hawk stood up. "I will seek out Gitano, since he knows so much about this white captive." He gently brushed Paloma's cheek and walked in the direction of Ataza's lodge. Ataza, Little Fox, and Gitano were sitting in front of the lodge eating. "Greetings, I have come to speak with Gitano."

"Your hunting went well, Nephew?"

"Yes, Uncle. Are you in need of meat?"

"I have no need. How is Paloma?"

"She is well."

Gitano stood up, chewing the meat off of a bone. "I hear you are always hunting, Cousin. You are making the rest of us look lazy."

"Paloma needs to eat well, now that she is with child."

"Paloma works too hard," Little Fox said. "She should get more rest."

"I tell her that, Aunt, but she will not listen."

"It is because of Sotso and Teroz. They made her work too hard. You take care of her," Little Fox admonished.

"Yes, Aunt, I will do that. I am going for a walk, Gitano. Do you want to come?"

Gitano gnawed on the bone for a moment longer, then tossed it to one of the camp dogs. The animal grabbed the bone and then ran. Gitano dragged his hand across his mouth. "Yes, a walk sounds good."

Ataza poked at the fire with a stick. "You two stay out of trouble. Stay away from Teroz."

"We are only going for a walk, Father."

Shadow Hawk bid his aunt and uncle good-bye, promising Little Fox again that he would look after Paloma.

They were only a short distance from the lodge when Gitano spoke. "I was wondering when you would come."

"What do you mean?"

"You are curious about Teroz's captive, are you not?"

"What is she like?"

"She is short and squat, with dirty brown hair. Very unattractive."

"You are lying, Gitano. Paloma told me all about her."

"What did Paloma tell you?"

"She said that the woman is strange looking."

Gitano grinned. "Leave it to a woman to say that."

"What does that mean?"

"The captive is beautiful, cousin. Her hair is the color of cornsilk, and her eyes are a color such as I have never seen, clear and blue. She stands tall and straight. She has no fear in her eyes."

"You spoke with her?"

"Yes. She is not at all like what I have heard white people

294

to be. I find her pleasant enough." Gitano stopped. "We are heading in the direction of Teroz's lodge. You appear to have an interest in this captive."

"No more than you."

"I do not believe you, Cousin. Look, there she is." Gitano pointed to the front of the lodge.

Shadow Hawk stopped and looked at the woman on the ground. She was lying on her side, facing away from him. He knew by the color of her hair that it was Aissa. He started forward, but Gitano gripped his arm.

"That would not be wise, Cousin. Teroz is looking for an excuse to fight you. Do not give him one."

"It's she, Gitano. It's Aissa."

"I know. I knew it the moment I saw her. I remembered her. She did not recognize me when I spoke to her."

"Of all the white women he could have captured, why would he take Aissa?"

"Why do you think? You married Paloma and you gave a wedding gift of twenty horses. You made him look like a fool and took the woman he cared about. Teroz does not forget."

"Aissa has done nothing to hurt him.

"But Teroz knows that her pain will hurt you, Cousin. And it is working, is it not?"

Shadow Hawk wanted to go to Aissa, to pick her up in his arms and carry her away, but he knew better. Things were different now. He was married. He had promised Paloma that he would care for her and her child. But what about Aissa? He had promised her and Ben that he would return, and he had not. Now, Aissa was paying for Teroz's hatred of him. "I must speak to her."

Gitano tightened his girp. "Not now. Wait until Teroz gives her some freedom. If you try to speak to her now, Teroz will know that you still care for her. You must act as if this woman means nothing to you, Cousin. Her life may depend on it."

Shadow Hawk nodded, turning around and walking back

through camp. Gitano followed. "I deceived her, Gitano. I told her father I would come back."

"It is obvious that you still care for her, Cousin. If that is so, why did you marry Paloma?"

"Paloma is a good woman." Shadow Hawk was silent as they walked between two lodges and headed toward the woods until they were away from the camp. "Paloma is a good wife."

"I know that Paloma is a good woman and a good wife, but you have not yet said that you love her."

Shadow Hawk picked a pinecone from the ground and began breaking the brittle cone apart. "I love her like a sister."

"Just as I thought."

"You thought nothing."

"I knew you did not love her. Miho has always loved her, just as Paloma has always loved him. So, I asked myself, why has my brother suddenly disappeared, and why is my cousin suddenly marrying Paloma? It did not take me long to figure out the answer."

"There is only one answer, and that is that I wanted to marry Paloma."

"You are not a good liar, Cousin. You married Paloma becasue she was carrying Miho's child, and that is the only reason."

"Keep your voice down."

"So, I am right. I knew it. Did Miho know of the child before he left?"

"No, he knew nothing. Paloma was desperate. She had already used the knife on herself. I had no choice but to marry her, Gitano. Sotso would have banished her from here."

"You would raise Miho's child?"

"I have promised Paloma that I would do that."

"And what of this white woman, Cousin? What about her? Will you let her suffer at Teroz's hands?"

"What do you want me to do, Gitano? If I help her, Paloma will be shamed."

"But you do not love Paloma."

"Stop, Gitano."

"You know what Teroz will do to her." Gitano grabbed Shadow Hawk's arm. "You care for this woman. You are the one who talked me into distracting the lookout while you helped her to escape. You do not have to shame Paloma, but you can help this woman again."

"You just told me to stay away from her."

"There will come a time when Teroz will not be so protective of his newfound property."

Shadow Hawk shook his head. "It is as if she and I are bound together somehow. I know you are right, Gitano. I must find a way to help her." He patted Gitano on the shoulder. "Thank you for the talk, cousin. As always, your wisdom has enlightened me."

Gitano grinned, but the grin faded as he watched Shadow Hawk walk away. He felt sorry for his cousin. Because of what Miho had done to Paloma, Shadow Hawk was not free to follow his heart.

Chapter 14

Aissa held her skirt out, using it to carry the roots she had just dug. The cloth was stained and torn, a cast-off from Sotso's wife. Her fingertips were blistered and a few bled, but she continued working without complaint, keeping her expression carefully bland, detached. She had kept count of the days she'd been held captive by carving marks into a tree by the stream—only twenty-three days, but it felt like an eternity. Teroz had kept his word and had not harmed her in any way and she had kept her word: She worked hard.

She looked around her. Most of the women were off in small groups chatting, ignoring her, so she sat back on her heels and rested for a moment, moving her head around to relax her shoulders. She'd never felt so tired or sore in her life, yet to her surprise, she'd never once felt as terrified as she'd felt with Ray. Here, at least, there were rules. If she followed them, no harm befell her.

She saw the girl Paloma working nearby, talking to the women around her. Aissa thought she was delicate and pretty. Even the size of her stomach didn't detract from her petite beauty. Aissa jammed her root digger into the ground, grimacing as the tool rubbed against her fingers. She'd seen Shadow Hawk only once. She had been sitting in front of

Teroz's lodge scraping a hide when laughter had made her look up. Shadow Hawk was walking with Paloma, a tender smile on his face, as if he adored the girl. When he glanced at Aissa, there was no affection or even recognition in his eyes. The longing that Aissa had felt for him had quickly been replaced with a rage she had never before felt. She had vowed not to waste even one more moment thinking about him but to concentrate all her efforts on learning Apache ways and eventually finding a way to escape.

"Ow," she muttered to herself, rocking back on her heels. She blew on her fingers, trying to ease the stinging pain.

"You are the white girl?"

Aissa flinched at the sound of the voice. She still was amazed by how quiet these people were and how they seemed to appear out of nowhere. She turned. An old woman with a walking stick was standing behind her. It was the old blind woman, Ocha, Teroz's grandmother. Aissa had asked him about her; Teroz had said she was strange and to ignore her. But she fascinated Aissa. Her Spanish was good and she had an intelligent face. The old woman repeated her question impatiently.

"Yes, I am the white girl."

"What is your name, girl?"

"My name is Aissa."

Ocha considered it for a moment. "Aissa," she repeated. "It sounds good on the tongue. It is a Spanish name?"

"No, it's French."

"I do not know of these people."

Aissa blew on her fingers for a moment. "It is a land far from here. My mother came from there."

"What noise is it that you are making?"

"I'm blowing on my fingers."

"They are blistered from the digging?"

"Yes, but they're fine." Aissa didn't want anyone to tell Teroz she had complained, especially the old woman he had

299

told her to ignore.

"Stand up here by me."

Aissa looked at the other women, hesitating. Some of them had turned to look at her.

"Why do you hesitate?"

"I haven't finished my work. I do not want to make Teroz or his family angry."

"Stand up here."

This time Aissa didn't hesitate. She let the roots roll from her skirt onto the ground and she dropped the root digger. She stood up next to Ocha. "I am standing."

"My name is Ocha."

"I know."

"Why do I not hear fear in your voice? Surely Teroz has told you not to talk to me."

"He did not say that exactly."

"You dance around the question, girl. Why do you not fear Teroz?"

"I fear him and I respect his power. But there was a time in my life when I was more frightened than this. I was so terrified that I almost lost myself. Do you understand?"

"Yes," Ocha nodded, "I understand very well. Give me your hands."

Aissa held out her hands in front of her. Ocha took them in her own. Her hands were small, dark, and calloused, but her touch was gentle as she deftly ran her fingers over Aissa's. "I have medicine that will help your hands heal quickly."

"Lota will see that I am gone. She will tell Teroz."

"She will say nothing. She hates Teroz more than anyone."

Lota had not said a word to Aissa, but she had given her food and shown her how to work. Aissa didn't want to make her angry. "But I am to stay with Lota."

"Your hands will get worse if you do not tend to them."

"I am fine. Thank you." Aissa slowly drew her hands away. "I must go back to work."

"Aissa." Ocha's voice was gentle but commanding.

"Yes."

"You will come with me. No harm will befall you."

"What of Lota? Sotso and Teroz might get angry with her if I am with you."

"Sotso and Teroz would not dare to speak against me, girl. One is my son, the other my grandson. Lota will be fine."

"Perhaps I should tell Lota?"

"There is no need. Come."

Aissa followed Ocha without looking back. Many times she felt the urge to take the old woman's arm to guide her over the rocky ground, but Ocha walked confidently, her stick in front of her, as if she could see perfectly. Ocha skirted the village and walked toward the woods. Aissa had seen the small lodge that rested among the pines, but she'd never dared to go near it. Teroz had warned her to stay away. Now Ocha was inviting her in.

"Why do you wait out there, girl? Come inside."

Aissa ducked past the flap and into the lodge. Immediately she was assaulted by many smells, some sweet, some pungent, all so strong that her senses were overwhelmed. There were baskets around half of the lodge; the other half was lined with clay bowls. A variety of dried plants hung by sinew from the lodgepoles above and in the middle of the lodge, there was a fire ring. A large pot hung over the fire, and the steam that arose from it filled the air. Aissa took a deep breath. The steam smelled sweet and it somehow made it easier for her to breathe.

"Sit down here, girl. Here."

Aissa walked over to Ocha, who was now squatting in front of one of the bowls.

"Put out your hands."

Aissa complied and watched as Ocha reached into the

bowl and applied a foul-smelling concoction to Aissa's hands. She turned her face away but said nothing, not wanting Ocha to know what she thought. "Thank you."

"You are determined."

"What?" Aissa asked.

"You are determined to keep your feelings inside." Ocha scraped the remaining salve on the edge of the pot and rubbed the rest into her own hands. "This is good for the skin, whether you have blisters or not. How do your hands feel now?"

Aissa smiled. It was as if she had dipped her hands in cool water. "They feel very good. Thank you."

"You will drink with me."

"No, please," Aissa started to demur, but Ocha had already moved to the pot that was hanging over the fire. Aissa watched as Ocha reached outside the fire ring and picked up a clay bowl. She dipped it into the steaming pot and held it out, reaching for another. Aissa took the bowl of steaming liquid. She could barely hold it in her hands, it was so hot, yet Ocha had reached into the bubbling pot without being able to see. Maybe she was a witch. Aissa looked down at the drink. She could pour it out and Ocha would never know.

"Drink it. It will keep harm from you."

Tentatively Aissa put the bowl to her mouth and sipped at the hot liquid. She was surprised to find that it had a sweet, minty taste and she took another drink.

"You like it." Ocha sat down on a robe and patted the place next to hers. "Sit here by me." She sipped from her own bowl as Aissa sat down. "There is no need to hurry, girl. They will not come for you here."

Aissa closed her eyes for a moment, pretending that she was far away and safe. She started to think of her father but quickly pushed the thought from her mind.

"What of your family, girl? Do you have any?"

Aissa looked at Ocha. Had the woman read her mind? "I have a father," she stammered.

"You do not sound so sure."

"I don't know if he is alive."

"Give me your hand."

Again Aissa stared at Ocha, but she obeyed. The old woman put Aissa's hand between her own and began to chant quietly. She closed her sightless eyes and her voice filled the lodge with an eerie sound. Aissa was not afraid. As Ocha continued to chant, Aissa finished the liquid in the bowl and set it down in front of her. She let her thoughts drift and looked again at the herbs and medicines stored in Ocha's lodge. This was a place that housed many secrets— life, death, spirits, love and hate—and Ocha was privy to it all.

"I feel very strongly that your father is still alive." Ocha's voice was low, but it seemed almost to echo in the lodge.

Aissa squeezed the woman's hand. "How do you know? How can you feel such a thing?"

"Do you feel it, girl? Look deep into yourself and see what you find. You have been afraid to do that, have you not?"

"Yes."

"Do it now. Close your eyes. Think of your father and see what you feel."

Aissa closed her eyes. She was still holding Ocha's hand. She felt fear rising inside her as she remembered her father lying hurt in the dark. Ocha squeezed her hand and Aissa found the strength to think about her father. She saw him sitting on the front porch, a cup of coffee in his hand. She recalled his love and concern the day she had married Ray, and the way he had helped her believe she would get well from the laudanum. Aissa didn't feel the overwhelming sense of loss she had expected. Instead, she felt peaceful. She opened her eyes. "I don't feel in my heart that he is dead, but perhaps it's because I don't wish it to be so."

"You would know the difference, girl."

"I'm afraid to hope."

"You should never be afraid to hope."

Aissa picked up her empty bowl and turned it slowly in her hands.

"You do not need to hold so much inside, girl. You even keep your fear hidden."

"I cannot show fear around Teroz."

"Why?"

Aissa thought for a moment. Could she trust this woman? Was this a trick? But she knew in her heart that it wasn't. Although Aissa had only been with the old woman a short while, Ocha was the closest thing to a friend she had found in this camp. "Teroz has no tolerance for cowards," Aissa said finally. "If I am to remain alive, I must be strong."

"You know Teroz well, it seems."

"He captured me when I was a young girl."

"Yes, I know, and Shadow Hawk helped you to escape."

Aissa shifted uncomfortably. She didn't want to talk about Shadow Hawk. "Thank you for your kindness, Ocha, but I should be getting back."

"It makes you uneasy to speak about Shadow Hawk?"

"No, but I have been gone for some time now. I don't wish to make Teroz angry."

"I understand. You will come back tomorrow. I will put more salve on your hands."

Aissa stood up. "No, it's all right, really."

"Nothing will happen to you, girl. Come back tomorrow."

"All right," Aissa replied, grateful for the old woman's kindness. She looked around. "Can I do anything for you before I leave? Can I get you anything?"

"No, I have all that I need."

Aissa nodded silently and ducked beneath the door flap. When she was outside, she looked around, making sure no one had followed her. But as usual, not even the children played near Ocha's lodge. Aissa walked back to the place where she had been working. The women were gone and she hurriedly gathered the roots she had dropped. Teroz would be angry when he found out she'd left Lota. She heard footsteps behind her and steeled herself. It was too late. Teroz had already come to look for her. Pretending she hadn't heard him, Aissa began to walk quickly toward the camp. She felt a hand on her shoulder and whirled around to face Teroz.

Instead she saw Shadow Hawk. Her hands fumbled and she dropped the hem of her skirt, the roots falling to the ground. She knelt down, frantically trying to pick them up.

"Let me help you," Shadow Hawk said, squatting next to her.

"No, I don't need your help." She looked around, praying that Teroz was nowhere near.

"I have been waiting for a chance to speak to you. Are you all right?"

Aissa looked at Shadow Hawk, trying to still any emotion. "Teroz treats me well enough." She stood up, clutching the hem of her skirt. She had to get back before Teroz came looking for her. "I have to go now."

"Aissa, wait."

"What do you want, Shadow Hawk?"

"I need to explain why I did not come back."

"You don't need to explain anything. I must go."

Shadow Hawk grabbed her arm. "I was going to come back, but something happened."

"I don't want to hear it. Please, let go of my arm."

"You and your father are very important to me, Aissa."

Aissa jerked her arm away from Shadow Hawk's grasp. "Don't lie to me. You cared nothing for us or you would've come back. Instead, you gave me to Teroz because you found a wife. I don't even know if my father is alive or dead. I blame you for that, Shadow Hawk."

"Is that what he told you? Aissa, I never gave you to Teroz." Shadow Hawk gripped Aissa's shoulders from behind and turned her to face him. She stepped backward, freeing herself from his grip.

"I don't believe you. I'll never believe anything you say again. I've seen you with your new wife."

"Paloma is a good woman."

"I'm sure she's like all the other women here. She probably doesn't dare to question you in any way."

"I see your tongue has grown even sharper since I last saw you."

"If it has, it is because of you."

"And what of you, Aissa? What of the way you acted when I took you away from Grimes? You said that you hated me. More times than I could count. Do you feel no shame?"

"Why do I need to feel shame for something that man did to me?" Aissa's voice was harsh. "Is it the custom of the women here to feel shame when a man has forced them to do something?"

"Lower your voice."

"Why? Why should I lower my voice? What can happen to me that hasn't already happened to me?" Aissa felt her cheeks burn with anger.

Shadow Hawk's face hardened. "Teroz can kill you, Aissa. Remember that. I shouldn't even be talking to you."

"Then go, leave me alone." Aissa dragged her hand through her hair. She was tired and she was scared. Why couldn't he just leave her alone? She had been able to pretend he didn't exist. She hadn't been thinking about him or hoping that he would help her.

"I will find a way to help you, Aissa," Shadow Hawk said, echoing her thoughts.

She stopped when he spoke. "Just stay away from me. Go back to your wife. That's where you belong." She turned to go but stumbled, dropping some of the roots. She knelt,

306

frantically picking them up and putting them in the hem of her skirt. For the first time since she'd been in the camp, she felt as if she might cry. She stood up, her resolve beginning to crumble. "Teroz has treated me decently, Shadow Hawk. The only way my life will be in danger is if he sees us together."

"You are right. I am sorry." He touched her arm and it held her still in a way that his harsh grip had not.

"I should go now."

"Aissa?"

"Yes."

"Do you want me to find out about your father?"

A myraid of emotions battled each other inside Aissa. "Couldn't you just help me escape?"

"I could, but things are not so simple now. Teroz could raid your ranch again and kill you and your father. He could hurt Paloma while I am gone, or even Gitano. He cares little about anyone. But I could find out about your father."

Aissa wanted desperately to know if her father was alive, but it would kill her to find out that he was dead. "No, I don't want to know. It's better this way."

"Aissa—"

"Please, Shadow Hawk, leave me alone." She hurried away from him and almost ran toward the camp and Teroz's lodge. She prayed silently that Teroz wouldn't beat her if he found out she'd been with Shadow Hawk. But if he did, she would keep her vow to run away, even if he caught and killed her. Or would she? For the first time since her capture, Aissa felt more than a wish to survive. She felt a rushing desire to live.

People stared disapprovingly at her as she walked through the camp alone, but she ignored them. She knew none of them would dare to harm her. She smiled bitterly. They would not risk damaging Teroz's property. As she got closer, she saw Teroz and his father sitting in front of the lodge.

Lota was handing them bowls of stew. Aissa took a deep breath and walked up to Teroz.

"I'm sorry I am late. I was with Ocha."

"Yes, I know." Teroz drank the contents of the bowl and set it down. He stared into the fire, leaving Aissa to stand anxiously, waiting for him to tell her what to do.

"Bring the roots inside, girl," Lota commanded.

Aissa nodded respectfully to Sotso and went inside the lodge, placing the roots in Lota's basket. When she turned around, Lota was standing behind her. Her face was not bruised. Thank God. Sotso had not beaten her for returning without Aissa.

Aissa moved close and whispered to her in Spanish. "I am sorry, Lota. I hope you are not in trouble because of me."

Lota glanced toward the door flap. "No one argues with Ocha. I am not in trouble."

Aissa smiled tentatively and nodded. She watched as Lota filled another bowl from the pot that hung over the fire. She took the bowl from Lota's hands. "I will take the bowl out. "You eat." She touched Lota's arm lightly before she went out of the lodge. The two women exchanged a smile.

Aissa ducked under the door flap, careful not to spill the stew. Sotso was gone and Teroz was sitting alone. She handed him the bowl of stew, then turned to go back into the lodge, but he reached up and firmly held her wrists. "Sit down."

Aissa sat on the ground next to him, covering her crossed legs with her ragged skirt. She watched him eat, wondering if he would punish her after all. Teroz was in no hurry. He ate his stew slowly and Aissa was forced to wait, imagining all the ways he could punish her. She stared down at the ground, trying her best not to betray her fear.

"So, what did the witch tell you?" Teroz asked when he had finally finished.

Aissa kept her eyes down. "Nothing. She took me to her

lodge and gave me medicine for my hands." She lifted her hands, palm up, so that he could see the blisters.

"What else?"

"There was nothing else. We spoke only of her medicines."

"You did not speak of Shadow Hawk?"

She thought of lying but decided against it. "She spoke of him once. I said very little."

"You spoke of nothing else with her?"

"No."

"Do you have anything else to tell me?"

So he knew. Lying would anger him further. Aissa tried to swallow, but her throat was dry. "I talked to Shadow Hawk."

"Did you seek him out?"

"No!" Aissa looked at Teroz for the first time. "I left Ocha's lodge and went back for the roots. He came up behind me. He said he wanted to talk to me."

"What did you talk about?"

Aissa considered lying again, but what was the point? "He said he could find out if my father was dead or not."

"I told him it didn't matter. I told him to go back to his wife." To Aissa's surprise, Teroz laughed.

"You continue to surprise me, woman."

"Why?"

"I was sure you would lie to me. I did not think you would admit you had talked to Shadow Hawk."

"I have nothing to hide, Teroz. I despise Shadow Hawk for what he did to me and my father."

"And did you tell him you despise me also?"

"No. I kept my word. I told him that you treat me well."

Teroz nodded. "That is good. You are doing well, woman. I have given you freedom in this camp because I know you are not stupid enough to try to escape. You know that I would hunt you down and kill you?" He brushed her cheeks with his fingers. "Yes, you know that." He handed his bowl to Aissa. "You may speak to Shadow Hawk as often as it pleases you."

Aissa met his eyes, startled. "But I don't want to talk to him. I don't even want to see him."

"But he will seek you out, I know him." He looked at her. "I want you to wash yourself. Lota will get you clean clothes." He reached out and wrapped a piece of Aissa's hair around his finger. "You are probably not a bad-looking woman when you are clean. I want to remind Shadow Hawk that he can no longer have you."

Aissa cringed at the thought of playing yet another part in Teroz's ugly game, but she knew she had no choice. If she was to survive, she had to make him believe that she was trustworthy. Eventually her time would come.

Aissa was excited. The woman were going down to the desert to harvest the mescal plants, and Teroz had surprised her by allowing her to go. She suspected that Ocha had had something to do with his decision. The old woman had sought her out several times, at first to insist on salving her hands, and then, once they were healed, to sit and talk. She asked many questions about the whites, about their towns, and about how they lived their lives. It seemed odd and dreamlike to Aissa, talking to the old woman about her own people. She had even described Bessie to Ocha, and Ocha had laughed loud and long.

"Yes, child. Every band has one such as this, with a life so empty that she lives other's lives instead."

Aissa stood a little apart from the other women, looking around. The women had dressed festively, wearing clean cotton skirts and blouses, the colors bright in the early morning sun. They would not wear their best—the work would be too hard and too dirty—but they wanted to begin the journey in high spirits, and many had braided flowers into their hair.

Aissa recognized many of the women. Teroz had begun talking to her more often, teaching her the ways of the Apache, and explaining the relationships of the people in the camp. Aissa envied the women laughing with their friends, and she wished that Ocha would be going. But of course her age and her blindness made it impossible. Paloma was not going to gather the mescal either—she was too close to her time. But most of the others were gathering, standing in groups of three and four, talking. Lota stood with her friends, her usually frowning face lit with contentment. Aissa smiled to herself. Lota's life, at least, had improved when Teroz had brought Aissa here. Sotso barely beat Lota now, and never as brutally as he had in the past. The work was always done. With two of them to do it all, Sotso had little reason to get angry. Aissa had noticed a change in Teroz, too. She could not imagine him being gentle with her, but he was less tense, less impatient. Aissa wasn't sure what was causing the change, but she was grateful for it.

The sun was filtering through the tops of the pine trees now. The women stirred. Aissa could only understand part of what they were saying in Apache, but many of them called to each other in Spanish, too.

"Let's go," one woman called out, and the others murmured in agreement. They began walking, adjusting their carrying bags. Aissa followed Lota, a few paces behind her and her friends. No one spoke to Aissa, although the hate-filled looks of her early days in the camp were gone.

Aissa saw Broken Moon, Shadow Hawk's mother, walking along easily, laughing. Teroz had said she was a good woman, and that her brothers cared for her very much. But he had also ordered Aissa to stay away from her. Aissa had never had to worry about it, though. Broken Moon had avoided her entirely.

As they topped a rise and started down into the foothills,

311

Aissa was pushed from behind. She stumbled and turned, recognizing the woman who had grabbed at her breasts that first terrible day in camp. Several of the woman's friends laughed, but a few sharp words in Apache from a sweet-looking girl stopped them. Aissa shot the girl a glance of thanks and the girl nodded slightly and smiled. Teroz had told Aissa the girl's name. She was Singing Bird, the wife of Shadow Hawk's brother, Brave Heart. Teroz had spoken of her in gentle, almost loving tones. It was obvious that the girl was special to him. Singing Bird and Brave Heart were almost always together, always touching hands, or always standing close.

The conversations ebbed and swelled, mixing with the early morning bird songs. Aissa walked easily, without tiring, and she realized how strong she had become. The constant downhill slope did not make her thighs ache nor did she have any trouble keeping up. The morning sun was bright, but it would not get too hot until they got closer to the desert.

As they descended the mountain, Aissa watched the other women. Broken Moon had dropped back to walk with Singing Bird and they talked quietly. Aissa stayed close to Lota but walked alone. The morning passed slowly, but no one stopped to eat. Aissa took some smoked meat from her carrying bag and ate as she walked. Aissa saw some of the women eating reddish prickly fruit from the cactus they passed. After a while, Aissa strayed from the group and reached up to pick one for herself.

"You will have to peel it," she heard someone say behind her. She turned, startled. Broken Moon was regarding her with curiosity. "Do you have a knife?"

Aissa shook her head, fighting a wild impulse to laugh. Teroz would hardly allow her a weapon. Lota called to her, but Broken Moon turned and waved her on, saying something in Apache. Lota nodded reluctantly, and began walking again, following the line of women.

"Here," Broken Moon said, holding out a small knife.

Aissa walked closer, took the knife, and set about peeling the prickly fruit. The skin was tough, and her fingers were soon pricked all over by the tiny spines. She cleaned the knife on her hem and gave the knife back to Broken Moon when she was finished.

"So, you are the one," Broken Moon said. She looked into Aissa's eyes. "I have wanted to speak to you in camp, but I thought it would only cause you more difficulty if Teroz found out. Or Shadow Hawk, for that matter." She shook her head and made a helpless gesture with her hands. "Nor did I wish to hurt Paloma." Her Spanish was halting but clear. She gestured to the line of women and began walking. Aissa walked beside her.

Aissa glanced sidelong at Broken Moon. She was a pretty woman, small and strong looking. Aissa tried to remember eyerything that Shadow Hawk had told her about his mother. Aissa raised the fruit to her mouth.

Broken Moon smiled. "You will like it."

Aissa bit into the fruit and was surprised by its pungent sweetness. She looked up to smile at Broken Moon, but the older woman was hurrying ahead to rejoin her friends. The women at the front of the line were shouting, and Aissa saw Broken Moon and her friends begin to run. Laughter and shouts rang out as the women ran downhill. Aissa followed them, going more slowly. The women split into small groups, carrying their hatchets and sharpened piñon sticks.

"Come," Broken Moon called back to Aissa. Aissa followed Broken Moon. "Here," Broken Moon pointed, "this is the mescal." It was a large plant with thick green leaves that had sharp spikes at the end. The plants grew in patches, and large red flower stalks pushed up between them. The women spread out. Some of them began digging. "We will need a pit," Broken Moon said gesturing, "to roast the bulbs." Aissa nodded. Ocha had already explained to her how the mescal was prepared.

Aissa watched silently as Broken Moon chopped off the spiked leaves with her hatchet, leaving only the heart of the plant. Then she took her piñon stick and began to chisel around the roots, hammering on the end of the stick with her hatchet. Finally, Broken Moon bent down and pulled out a large white bulb and handed it to Aissa. "Take it to the pit and come back. You will help me."

Aissa carried the large bulb and added it to the growing pile close to where the woman were taking turns digging the pit. Lota waved to Aissa. She and some other women were tearing up thick clumps of grass and piling them next to the pit. Aissa walked back and forth many times. Once the pit was dug, the women lined the bottom with stones and started a fire. They kept throwing wood onto the fire as the hours passed.

Broken Moon worked tirelessly, and after a while, Singing Bird joined her. Aissa wanted to take a turn with the hatchet, but knew that she would not be trusted with such a weapon. Singing Bird and Broken Moon talked as they worked, mostly in Spanish. Aissa smiled at some of their jokes but was careful not to join their conversation.

The smoke from the firepit changed from white to black as the sun crossed the sky. Finally the layer of coals was thick enough. Aissa helped fill the pit with the white bulbs. The women covered the pit with a thick layer of grass, then more stones were added and a layer of dirt. When the pit was sealed over, the women set about making a temporary camp. Finally, the sun setting, they sat around their fires, eating the food they had brought with them. Aissa sat near Broken Moon and Singing Bird. She was tired but strangely content. She had worked as hard as anyone else and had not felt faint in the sun. Perhaps she was growing strong enough to cross the desert on her own.

314

"You did well today," Broken Moon said, smiling at Aissa.

"Thank you," Aissa said politely.

Broken Moon had insisted that Aissa stay with her, and Singing Bird and Lota had not seemed to mind. Aissa noticed Singing Bird watching her. There was a look of obvious curiosity on the young girl's face, and Aissa finally had to smile. "Have you ever seen a white person before?"

Singing Bird lowered her eyes and shook her head. Then, smiling shyly, she looked up. "Your hair . . . the color is so strange to me." Singing Bird reached out and lightly stroked Aissa's hair. "It feels no different," she said wonderingly, and Aissa could not keep from laughing. Singing Bird pulled her hand away quickly, but when Broken Moon began to laugh, she joined in.

After a moment, Broken Moon touched Aissa's arm. "I remember what it was like to be a captive. I missed my people terribly. You must be patient. Your time will come."

Aissa wanted to ask her what she meant, but Broken Moon stood and busied herself with laying out their sleeping blankets. All the women were tired, and the campfire talk quickly died as one by one they fell asleep. Aissa watched the stars until her eyes grew heavy.

In the morning the pit was still steaming, and the women began pushing back the thick layer of dirt and stone. They took turns, standing back from the heat as they rested. Before long the women were using their sharpened digging sticks to pull the mescal bulbs from the pit. Laughing and jubilant, they peeled the bulbs, using flat rocks that had been cleaned off for this purpose. Their fingers and hands sticky, they ate as they worked. The fibrous pulp was spread in thin sheets on the rocks. Aissa ate with the others. The mescal was sweet and gooey, and extremely filling. She helped Lota pound the mescal. It was hard work, and as the day went on Aissa was again surprised at how her strength and stamina had grown. That night, they once again slept under the stars. All the next day, the women lifted and turned the drying mescal. By the next morning, they were ready to leave. Aissa thanked Broken Moon for showing her how to harvest the mescal—and for her kindness. As they rolled and packed the dried mescal, Broken Moon looked grave and serious and Aissa hoped that somehow she had not offended her.

"I know you look to me for friendship, but that cannot be. Even if I did not have my son to consider, it would be impossible. Singing Bird and Brave Heart have decided to leave this band. They will live with Little Fox's cousins for a time and have asked that I go with them. I think it is best that I go. Shadow Hawk is a man now and must find his own path." Broken Moon squeezed Aissa's hand, then stood quickly. "I wish you well and hope that by the time we return, you will not be here."

Aissa watched Broken Moon walk away, and she felt empty and sad. She had thought she had found a friend, and she realized now how lonely she had been. Aissa heard the rumble of thunder and looked up. Below her, dark clouds roiled along the horizon. The women began to hurry. Within an hour, the mescal had been packed and they were walking back up the path to the camp.

Aissa followed Lota, keeping her eyes on the ground. She did not want to look at Broken Moon or Singing Bird—or any of the others. For a brief time, she had almost forgotten that she was a captive, an outsider, a woman without a home. There would be a feast when Broken Moon, Brave Heart, and Singing Bird left camp. Teroz would not allow her to go, of course. It was just as well. She wasn't sure she could control her emotions. Broken Moon had been right— the hope of friendship was impossible.

Shadow Hawk handed the bowl to Paloma. Since his

mother and Brave Heart had gone, he had found himself almost resenting Paloma. Her pregnancy made it impossible for them even to consider such a journey. Already he missed his family.

"Do you want more?"

"No."

"But you always eat more than this. Did you see, I found wild potatoes and onions." Paloma quickly refilled the bowl and brought it back.

"I said no, Paloma. I am not hungry tonight." He shoved the bowl away.

"Ocha gave me checil and mesquite beans. I ground them and made bread." Paloma turned back toward the lodge.

Shadow Hawk stood up. Her eagerness to please him only irritated him even more. "I am going for a walk."

"All right."

Shadow Hawk could see that she was hurt, and he almost apologized. Instead, he chose to go find Gitano. He was tired of trying to please women. They were never happy. He found Gitano sitting outside the lodge with Ataza, throwing the bones. It was apparent that Gitano was winning by his smiles.

Shadow Hawk greeted Ataza first to show his respect. "Hello, Uncle."

"Greetings, Nephew. I hope you have come to take this coyote away. I do not trust his luck."

Gitano grimmed. "That is not a kind thing to say, Father. Is it my fault that you never learned how to gamble?"

Shadow Hawk smiled, amazed that Gitano was able to joke with his father. As much as Shadow Hawk had admired and loved his own father, he had never felt able to joke with him in such a way.

Ataza waved his hand as Gitano had another lucky throw. "Take him away. I grow tired of his face. You, Nephew, are always welcome here."

"Thank you, Uncle." Shadow Hawk shook his head as he

looked over at his cousin. Gitano stood up, stretching. Without speaking, they walked toward their favorite spot above the camp, where they could see the moon rise. "Why do you not let your father win once in a while, Gitano?" Shadow Hawk asked as they climbed.

Gitano laughed. "He never let me win when I was growing up. He said that it would make me work harder to learn the game."

"It is a game of luck, Gitano, not of skill."

"You wound me, Cousin," Gitano said, putting his hand over his heart as they rested on a ledge. "You have that look on your face."

"What look?"

"That look you used to wear all the time when you first came here. The one that tells me something is wrong." Gitano deftly pulled himself upward from the ledge like a mountain cat, jumping from rock to rock until he found one to his liking.

Shadow Hawk followed Gitano and sat down next to him. "I spoke to Aissa before the women left."

"And it did not go well."

"She hates me."

"Do you blame her? You told her you would go back for her. Instead, Teroz went for her." Gitano reached into his belt pouch and brought out a piece of dried mescal. He took a bite. "Apache and white do not mix, Cousin."

"Thank you for your words of wisdom, Gitano. How have I lived so long on this earth without your guidence?"

"No need to be bitter because Teroz has the woman you desire."

"One day I will push you from this rock and you will never be seen again."

"If you push me, I will fly."

"Your belly is always so full of food you would fall like a rock."

Gitano laughed, pointing. "Look, the moon." He threw back his head and howled like a coyote.

"What is the matter with you? You act as if you have been drinking tizwin."

"I am a young warrior in my prime. All I need now is a good woman to keep me warm at night and to give me children."

"It is not that easy with women, Gitano. It is never that easy."

"Is Teroz treating her well?" Gitano's grin faded.

"Well enough, I suppose. She would not say much."

"Give her time, Cousin. She is afraid for her life. If she shows her feelings for you, Teroz will make her suffer."

"He has already made her suffer."

"She was with grandmother today."

"Aissa spoke with Ocha?"

"Yes, and you know how Teroz feels about her. She is the only person Teroz is afraid of."

"Why was Aissa with Ocha?"

"My mother say that Ocha visits with Aissa often."

"Why would Ocha seek out Aissa?"

"Why does grandmother do anything?"

Shadow Hawk shrugged. "I do not understand."

"It is good, Cousin. Think about it. Teroz fears grandmother. He will not interfere if Ocha seeks Aissa's company."

"Do you not find it strange, Gitano? Why would grandmother seek to spend time with a white woman?"

"Perhaps she sees something of value in her that others do not see. Grandmother cannot use her eyes, but she can feel things that others do not."

"She likes to frighten people," Shadow Hawk said, smiling, thinking of the way the children in the camp ran past her, squealing in fear.

"She used to frighten me when I was a child. My mother

would send Miho and me to her lodge to take her meat. She would sit in the shadows of her lodge, and no matter how quietly we entered, she always knew we were there."

"How did she lose her sight?"

"You do not know this?" Gitano shook his head. "You have been with us for almost six summers and you do not know this?"

"I never asked. I knew that she had lost her sight long ago, but I do not know how she lost it."

"Did you mother not tell you what happened?"

"No, she said to repeat it would bring bad luck to Grandmother."

"I do not believe that, and Grandmother does not believe it, either."

"So tell me, how did Grandmother lose her sight?"

Gitano stared out into the night. "It is said that she was possessed of great beauty when she was a girl. Her face was one that many young braves fought over. Many wanted to marry her. But there were two young braves Ocha had loved since childhood. They were called Gray Fox and Wandering Man. Both sought Ocha's hand in marriage, but she was unable to decide.

"Soon the young braves went off to raid a fort in Mexico, and both returned with many horses and gifts to give to Ocha. Still she could not decide. Finally, she asked them both a question. The question was this: If you could give me anything in the world, what would it be? Wandering Man thought and then replied, 'I would give you horses. If I could give you a thousand horses, you would be rich and you could buy anything you desire." She then asked Gray Fox. He thought for a time before he answered. "I would give you nothing, only myself. For in that simple gift, I would give you love that would surround you all your days on this Earth.'

"Ocha did not have to think long. She chose Gray Fox and

they were soon married. But Wandering Man was angry. He could not believe that Ocha had chosen Gray Fox over him. So during the next raid, he feigned illness and went to Ocha's lodge in the night. He tried to force himself on her, but she fought him. She told him she loved Gray Fox. He began to hit her face with his fists, and he hit her so hard that he injured her eyes. Ocha could not see after that. When Gray Fox returned from the raid and found out what had happened to his wife, he went to find Wandering Man. But it was too late. Wandering Man had killed himself with is own lance."

"He killed himself?" Shadow Hawk asked, astonished. He, like all Indian children, had been taught that suicide was forbidden by the gods. "But his spirit will never rest."

"I hope it never does after what he did to Grandmother."

"What happened to Grandmother then? Did Gray Fox stay with her?"

"Yes, and they had my father and Sotso. But your mother was the 'special' one."

"What do you mean?"

"Grandmother said that when she held Broken Moon in her arms, she was able to see her face for a brief moment in the light of the moon. She said it was as if the moon had broken into little pieces and scattered its lights on your mother. That is how she got her name."

"My mother never told me the story. It is a good one."

"Yes, it is my favorite. Many of the old ones tell stories, but the people are only names to us. But in this story, the people are real."

"What of Gray Fox? Did you know him?"

"I was very young when he died, but I remember him. He was strong, like Teroz, but gentle, like my father. He laughed often and he was a great maker of weapons. He loved grandmother very much. When he died, everyone thought she would die of a broken heart. Instead, she seemed to be more filled with life, and that is when she began to study the plants. Many in this camp are frightened of her and many think she is a witch, but she is a good woman and she knows much about healing."

Shadow Hawk smiled. "I have much respect for Ocha, but she is mysterious to me."

"Grandmother is strange sometimes, even I admit this, but she is a great and good woman. Always treat her with respect, Shadow Hawk. There is much you can learn from her."

Shadow Hawk reached between the crevices of the boulders and found a small pebble. He threw it sidearm and it made a whirling sound as it fell downward. "Do you miss Miho?"

"You also are in a strange mood tonight, Cousin. You ask too many questions."

"Do you miss him?"

"Yes, I miss him. Miho is my brother. I still cannot understand why he left and never came back to see any of us. His wife must be very ugly."

"Why do you say that?"

"If she was not, he would have brought her to meet us."

Shadow Hawk laughed, then he became solemn. "Have you thought of going to see him?"

"No, I do not think he would want me to. He does not want to see any of us and I will respect his wishes."

"But how do you know he feels that way?"

"I feel it. That is all. I will not invade Miho's territory unless I am invited by him." Gitano's voice was uncharacteristically harsh. "I will say no more about it, Cousin."

Shadow Hawk climbed down the rock until he was on a level place. He waited for Gitano to join him. "I should go back to Paloma, but I do not want to. She will think I am angry at her."

"Are you?"

"No, I am angry at myself. I am going to walk awhile."

"Do you want company?"

"No, go back to your father. You might think about letting him win once in a while."

"You are too soft, Cousin, that is your problem."

Shadow Hawk wanted to smile at Gitano's words, but he didn't because he knew they were true. They climbed down the rocks and parted in silence. Shadow Hawk walked downhill through the pine trees until he reached the stream, then followed it, heading for the beaver pond. The night was warm and clear, and the moon was so bright it cast shadows. Shadow Hawk was tired, but he knew that he would not be able to sleep. Perhaps a swim would clear his mind. He stripped off his clothes, except for his breechcloth, and dropped them on the bank.

As Shadow Hawk approached the calm water of the pond, he could hear the sound of water lapping against the banks. Someone was already swimming. He stopped, standing very still. In the moonlight, he saw Aissa's golden hair. He ducked into the cover of the trees, but he could not keep himself from watching her. Her back was to him and her hair hung down to her waist. She dived under the water and a few seconds later came up standing. She pushed her hair back from her face and walked toward the shore. Shadow Hawk couldn't believe how beautiful she was—her body was strong and slim, her legs long and tapered, her breasts full but firm. When she stepped onto the bank, she quickly pulled on her skirt and blouse and sat down to pull on her moccasins. Shadow Hawk stepped out of the trees and walked up behind her.

"You think nothing of bathing alone when it is dark?"

Aissa jerked around. "Shadow Hawk." She quickly pulled her skirt down to cover her bare legs.

"It is dangerous here at night."

"Teroz told me it would be all right."

"Then Teroz should take care to watch over you."

Aissa pulled on her moccasins, picked up the bundle of her old clothes, and stood up. "I'm not your concern. You have a wife to worry about." She tried to walk past Shadow Hawk, but he stepped in front of her. "Move."

"No, I do not think so." Shadow Hawk reached up and touched Aissa's face with both hands. "You are so beautiful. I had forgotten just how beautiful."

"Don't."

"I hate to think of you being with Teroz." He gently ran his fingers along her jaw and down her neck.

"I don't have a choice." She turned her face away from his touch.

He lowered his hand. All he wanted to do was to love this woman, to take care of her, and to be with her. But he couldn't. Too many things came between them. He couldn't blame her for hating him. "I'm truly sorry about your father, Aissa. I blame myself for what happened to him."

Aissa reached out and tentatively took his hand. "I don't blame you. Not really. You told me your life was here, and you said you would come back only because my father talked you into it." She smiled, her eyes flooding with tears.

"No, I was going to come back, but then—"

"No, you weren't. I remember the way you looked at me. You never wanted to see me again, and you were right." She let go of his hand and looked out over the water. "You couldn't have known what Teroz was going to do. You were always the one who said we couldn't have a life together." She glanced back at him, forcing a smile. "It's impossible for us, Shadow Hawk. Please don't speak to me again."

"How can I not?" He lowered his mouth, brushing his lips against hers. "Your lips tremble, Aissa. Are you afraid?"

"Yes."

"You are afraid of me?"

"I have always been afraid of you, Shadow Hawk."

"What have I done to make you afraid?"

"It is the power you have over me that makes me afraid."

"Then I, too, should be afraid, for you have power over me, Aissa." He wrapped his arms around her and pulled her to him. He could feel the softness of her breasts through her blouse, and it excited him. He covered her mouth with his, tasting the sweetness, taking everything he could from her kiss.

Aissa put her hands on Shadow Hawk's chest and tried to push him away. "We can't do this. You have a wife. And Teroz—"

"I do not love my wife, Aissa."

"That's a terrible thing to say."

"And she does not love me."

"Then why did you marry?"

"She needed my help. If I had not married her, she would have been banished from the camp. But we do not love each other. The only love I have ever felt has been for you."

Aissa tried to find the strength to leave. Teroz had said that he wanted to talk to Shadow Hawk, but this was something else. "If Teroz finds out . . ."

"I do not fear Teroz."

"But I do. I do." She put her hands on his chest, pushing him away.

Shadow Hawk held her until she quit struggling. He kissed her softly. "I want to take you away from here. I want to find a place where we can be together."

"You know that's impossible. I will never escape Teroz." Aissa managed to free herself. "I must get back. He will be looking for me."

"I love you, Aissa. I never wanted to leave you."

Aissa stopped, not daring to face him but unable to walk away. "Shadow Hawk, please."

Shadow Hawk put his arms around Aissa, pushing aside her wet hair to kiss the back of her neck. "I should have listened to my heart, but I did not. I tried to be honorable and I lost you."

Aissa turned in his arms, reaching up to touch Shadow Hawk's face. "You did a good thing."

"And what of your father? If I had not left you and come back here, perhaps he would still be alive."

"I don't want to talk about him. I must go, Shadow Hawk. The only way I can survive is if I stay away from you. Please, let me go."

Shadow Hawk looked at her in the moonlight. He had never known a woman with such a face, a face that showed every emotion. Again he touched his mouth to hers, but this time it was with more urgency. He held her against him tightly. He felt the warmth of her body through her damp clothes. Without speaking, Shadow Hawk lifted her into his arms and carried her into the shelter of the trees.

"Aissa," he breathed, moving his mouth down the line of her neck, as he set her down. He ran his hands over her breasts, down the curve of her hips and over her buttocks. He fumbled, untying the thongs that held his breechcloth in place. He let it fall to the ground. Aissa moaned slightly as he slowly pulled up her skirt and ran his hands over her naked flesh. Her skin felt hot and smooth, and he brought his hand between her legs, pressing, stroking. She wrapped her arms around his neck, moving against his hand, her soft little cries exciting him even more. He dropped to his knees and kissed the soft skin of her inner thighs. Aissa bent to kiss him and he pulled her down until she was straddling his legs. He continued to touch her, biting gently at her neck and breasts, until she moaned continuously. He felt himself grow harder and gently pulled her forward, guiding himself into her. Aissa cried out. He covered her mouth with his, stifling her cry with his kisses. He lifted her slowly, up and down, moving her until Aissa began to match his rhythm willingly—eagerly. He put his hands on her buttocks, pushing her against him, hearing her moan, as he reached deeper inside her. Aissa's fingers dug into his back and she cried out his name. Suddenly, the movement was too intense, too overwhelming, and finally he lost control, losing himself inside her with a thunderous shudder. He relaxed slowly, and she fell against his chest.

Aissa opened her eyes, pressing her face into his shoulder. The pain had surprised her. Had Ray done something to hurt her so she could never be with a man without feeling pain?

"Aissa." She did not answer him. "Are you all right?"

She nodded, still hiding her face against his shoulder. "I think so . . ."

He gently pushed her back, searching her eyes. "What? What is it, Aissa?" She began to cry, tears rolling down her cheeks. He recalled the way she had cried out when he entered her. He suspected, for the first time, that she had never been with a man before, not even with Teroz.

"Aissa?"

"Yes."

"Teroz has not touched you?"

She shook her head.

"And neither did Grimes."

"But he touched me a lot when I was taking my medicine. After that . . ." she shivered. "I can't remember. He said he could have me whenever he wanted me."

"That is because he wanted you to believe you were with him."

"He was always there. He made me feel so dirty." She pressed her face against his bare chest.

"That is how he wanted you to feel. That was his power over you. That and the medicine."

"No, I must have—"

Shadow Hawk kissed her gently. "You have never been with a man before, Aissa, until now."

327

"Oh, God," she held onto him. "He was going to sell me to other men."

"But he did not."

"Only because you took me away from him." Aissa couldn't stop crying.

Shadow Hawk stroked her hair. "It will be all right. Grimes will never hurt you again."

"But Teroz . . ."

"I will find a way to help you. You must trust me."

"I do trust you. I do."

Shadow Hawk pulled Aissa to him, holding her tightly, unwilling to let her go. She had never been afraid to admit how she felt about him and she still wasn't. Now, he was no longer afraid to admit how much he cared for her. She was everything to him. He would find a way to get her away from Teroz. "I love you, Aissa." He said the words and he wasn't ashamed of them. He held her as she cried. Nothing could change the fact that they were now a part of each other, and no one could take that from them—not even Teroz.

———

Chapter 15

"Aissa!" The harsh voice echoed, jolting Aissa into sitting up. She tried to pull away from Shadow Hawk. "It's Teroz."

Shadow Hawk put his hand lightly over Aissa's mouth. "Keep quiet," he whispered. "He will not come into the trees to look for you."

Aissa pulled her skirt around her thighs, standing up. Shadow Hawk stood, close beside her, one arm around her shoulders. Aissa felt Shadow Hawk's strength but knew that he couldn't protect her unless they left tonight, together. And that was impossible.

"Aissa!" Teroz yelled her name again.

Aissa held her breath, waiting for Teroz to find them. But Shadow Hawk was right. Teroz left, muttering Apache curses.

"He is gone now."

"What will I do? Someone will say you came this way, too. He won't believe anything I tell him."

"He will believe only one thing." She started to cry, but he put his arms around her and held her close to his chest. "He will believe that I forced myself on you. I am sorry, Aissa. I am sorry you always have to be hurt."

"He'll come after you."

"He can do nothing to me. This is the only way to make sure you are safe. You will tell him that you came out of the pond and I was standing there. Then I forced myself on you and dragged you into the trees. Cry if you must."

"I've never cried in front of Teroz. Never."

"Perhaps now is the time. He might feel sorry for you."

"Are you sure he won't try to kill you?"

Shadow Hawk touched her cheek. "You must make him believe that you hate me, and I will continue to play the loving husband to Paloma."

"What about Paloma? What about your child?"

"It is not my child, Aissa. It is the child of my cousin. He left Paloma to marry another."

"Then you can't leave her."

"Paloma does not love me. She is still very much in love with Miho."

"What will you do?"

"I will find a way for us to be together. Go now, before Teroz comes back. No matter how I act toward you, remember what we shared this night and remember that I love you." Shadow Hawk kissed Aissa.

Aissa held onto Shadow Hawk's hand for a second and then left the woods and walked back toward camp. She took a deep breath and let it out. Facing Teroz was a frightening thought. If he ever found out that she'd willingly been with Shadow Hawk, he would make her suffer and he might try to kill Shadow Hawk. Suddenly decisive, she bent down and picked up some dirt, smearing it on her face and clothes, and ripped her blouse so that it hung off one shoulder. She tried to think clearly. She knew Teroz. He would notice every detail. She walked faster and a twig scratched her leg. Aissa stopped, realizing what she had to do. She lifted her skirt around her waist and forced her way into the brush. She turned, then even walked backward, until her legs and arms were scratched and bleeding. She had to make Teroz believe that Shadow Hawk had taken her by force. Before she started up the path, she closed her eyes for a moment and thought of what she'd just shared with Shadow Hawk. It gave her strength.

Teroz paced outside his lodge. He had searched the entire camp for Aissa, and she was nowhere to be found. Could she have tried to escape? No, it wasn't possible, unless she had done it with Shadow Hawk. He had walked past Shadow Hawk's lodge earlier and seen Paloma outside, a blanket wrapped around her shoulders. He had started to ask her where her husband was, but the look of worry and unhappiness on her face had stopped him. He had noticed that look on her face too often lately. At first it had pleased him, because it meant that Shadow Hawk was also unhappy. Now it bothered him. He had never meant to hurt Paloma. She had already suffered unfairly at his hands. Shadow Hawk was not with his wife, and Aissa was missing.

So, they were together. He had known it would happen, but he didn't think Aissa would give in so easily. He had trusted her, he realized, and that trust had been betrayed.

Teroz looked up, hearing footsteps from behind the lodge. He saw Aissa standing in the shadows alongside the lodge. "Come here, woman."

"I'm afraid."

"Come here." He waited impatiently. But when she stepped forward, her face was lowered, her hair tangled and dirty. "I told you to wash."

"I tried."

"What do you mean you tried?" Teroz forced her to look at him. He hid his surprise when he saw her face. "What happened to you?"

"I was running through the woods and I fell."

"You fell?" Teroz sat Aissa down by the fire in front of the lodge. "Do not lie to me, woman. You did not fall."

"You'll punish me."

"I will punish you more if I find out you have lied."

Aissa kept her eyes down. "I took my bath as you told me to, and when I got out Shadow Hawk was standing there."

"Shadow Hawk?" Teroz's anger was mixed with disbelief. "What did he do?"

Aissa spoke in a low, frightened voice. "He said he wanted to talk to me, and I told him to go away." Aissa crossed her arms in front of her chest in a protective posture. "I tried to reach for my clothes, but he threw them into the woods and laughed. When I ran after them he followed me."

"Go on."

"No, I don't want to say any more."

"Tell me, woman!"

Aissa looked up, tears running down her cheeks. "He dragged me into the woods and he . . ." Aissa hesitated.

"Tell me," Teroz urged, his voice softening slightly.

Aissa sighed deeply. "He forced himself on me. I begged him to stop but he wouldn't." Aissa covered her face with her hands.

Teroz watched the woman. Was she lying? He couldn't trust her or Shadow Hawk. If Shadow Hawk had taken her this roughly, there would be scratches. "Stand up."

"What?" Aissa asked in a dull voice.

"Stand up." He waited until she got to her feet and then turned her around. He lifted up her skirt and looked at the backs of her legs. There were deep scratches, some of them still bleeding. "Sit." He watched her carefully as she sat down, her head lowered. The woman's story seemed genuine, but still he couldn't bring himself to believe it. He had never heard anyone say that Shadow Hawk had been rough with a woman. A fleeting image of Paloma's unhappy face came into his mind. Was Shadow Hawk beating her?

Teroz turned away, stunned. One thing he had counted on

in this game of revenge with Shadow Hawk was his cousin's honor. From the day Shadow Hawk had ridden into this camp, he had been foolishly and proudly honorable. Teroz had despised him for it, but he had also, he now realized, envied him. "I will take care of Shadow Hawk." He watched her face for a reaction but there was none. She was shaking and her skin was pale. He thought she should sleep inside the lodge but he knew his father wouldn't allow it. Still, she was hurt. She shouldn't sleep on the ground. "You will stay with Ocha tonight."

"Why?"

Teroz stood and offered Aissa his hand, helping her up. "You need someone to care for you. She will know what to do."

"Will you walk me there? He might still be out there."

"Come." Teroz walked out of the camp toward Ocha's lodge. He was alert, taking in every sound and movement around them. When they reached Ocha's lodge, he bent down to the flap. "Greetings, Ocha, it is Teroz. May I enter?"

"You may enter, Teroz."

Teroz went into the lodge, leading Aissa. "I would like this woman to stay with you tonight. She needs your help."

"What has happened?"

"Your grandson, Shadow Hawk, has forced himself on her and hurt her. She needs care."

Ocha nodded. "She can stay, Teroz."

"I will come for her tomorrow."

"Thank you, Teroz," Aissa said.

Teroz nodded his head and left the lodge. Shadow Hawk. For the first time in years, Teroz felt unsure. He hated his cousin for what he had done to Aissa and for what he might be doing to Paloma. But how could he? How was it possible to hate a man for something he himself had done?

*　　*　　*

Shadow Hawk turned over on his robe, trying to sleep but unable to still his mind. He knew it wouldn't be long before Teroz would seek revenge for what he thought he had done to Aissa.

Aissa. Shadow Hawk closed his eyes and thought of what it had been like to make love to her. She had been so passionate, beyond anything he could have imagined. Now, her life was in danger. He had to convince Teroz that he had raped her and that he had no feelings for her. He felt Paloma's hand on his back. She had been affectionate lately, as if suddenly she wanted to be a real wife to him.

"You are restless, my husband."

"I cannot get comfortable."

Paloma ran her hand along his shoulders and down his bare back to his waist. "Perhaps I can make you comfortable. You have never let me try before."

Shadow Hawk turned over on his back. "What is this change in you, Paloma? Never before did you have an interest in me as a man."

"You are my husband, Shadow Hawk. I want to please you."

"You do please me, Paloma."

"I want to please you in every way."

"We did not marry for those reasons, Paloma."

"Would you not like a son of your own, Shadow Hawk?"

"Perhaps, someday," he replied, thinking of Aissa.

"Then we must share a robe."

"I do not think of you in that way, Paloma." Shadow Hawk turned on his side again. "I do not wish to talk anymore. I am tired." He closed his eyes, realizing what a mistake it had been to marry Paloma. He thought he had been doing the honorable thing when, in fact, he had been living a lie. He would never love Paloma as a husband should love a wife and Paloma deserved much more. And what of Aissa? What had he done to her? He sighed, trying

334

to ignore Paloma's soft crying. Honorable was not always right.

Shadow Hawk was leading his horse out of the pasture when he saw Teroz walking toward him. Shadow Hawk ignored Teroz as he picked up a brush made of yucca fiber and began grooming the paint. Shadow Hawk barely glanced at Teroz when he walked up to him.

"You look as if you had no sleep last night, Cousin," Shadow Hawk said lightly. "I myself slept like a baby."

"You are a still a Comanche dog."

"Why is that?"

"You know why. You take my woman and you force yourself on her. What kind of a man are you?"

"You should be able to answer that question, Cousin. You have taken many women in your time." Shadow Hawk stepped to the other side of the paint, expecting Teroz to come at him, but he did not.

"You surprise me, Shadow Hawk—either that, or you are a very good liar."

"You are surprised because I took what was mine to begin with?"

Teroz smiled. "Did she fight you?"

"Her pathetic little pleas meant nothing to me."

Teroz tilted his head slightly, staring at Shadow Hawk's face. "How did you acquire the cut on your chest?"

"She scratched me and I hit her." Shadow Hawk stopped brushing his horse, leaning across the animal's back. "She really is not that good, Teroz. She cries too much. It is too hard to take pleasure in a woman who cries."

"I should kill you for this, Comanche."

"Why, because you did not take her first? Do not be so sensitive, cousin." Shadow Hawk watched Teroz's face carefully. He seemed genuinely concerned about Aissa.

335

"Do not go near her again. If you do, I will—"

"You will what?"

"I will make sure that Paloma never has your child."

Shadow Hawk stood up straight, looking at Teroz over the horse. "You would threaten a woman with child? You would threaten your own sister?"

"She is not my sister. She means nothing to me and the child means nothing to me. But it is different for you, is it not? Stay away from the white woman."

"Do not threaten me, Teroz."

"Remember what I sad about Paloma, Comanche. If you go near the white woman again, Paloma will suffer."

Shadow Hawk watched Teroz as he walked away. He hadn't expected this. How could Teroz threaten Paloma? Shadow Hawk threw the brush down on the ground. He and Teroz had fought since the day they had met. They had never liked each other. Still, Shadow Hawk was sure he had seen a softening in Teroz's face when he spoke of Aissa. And Singing Bird had told him of the many times Teroz had been kind to her. It made no sense. How could a man who could show kindness also threaten someone like Paloma? Shadow Hawk knew he would have to be careful or Aissa and Paloma would both end up suffering because of him.

Teroz watched Paloma for a moment as she washed clothes in the stream. Her belly was larger now, but she still looked lovely and delicate. He had told Shadow Hawk that he would hurt Paloma's child, but how could Shadow Hawk know that it was an empty threat? He could not hurt Paloma, not anymore.

Teroz knew she was frightened of him. From the day she and her mother had come to the camp, he had treated her badly. At first bullying Paloma had given him the strength to stand up to Lota's beatings. Then he had begun to enjoy his power over Paloma. But he could gradually see her fear turn to strength as her friendships with Miho and Shadow Hawk grew stronger. Still, he had always thought of her as his own and had always thought that one day they might marry. If Miho hadn't fallen in love with her, things might have been different. And now there was the Comanche. He didn't even care for Paloma.

Teroz walked up behind Paloma. She sat back on her heels and closed her eyes. She pressed her hands against the small of her back and kneaded her muscles. Teroz thought she was the most beautiful thing he'd ever seen. "Are you all right?" He asked quietly, not wanting to frighten her. He could see the caution in her eyes as she looked at him. She was still scared of him.

"I am well." Paloma leaned forward, scrubbing a blouse on a rock.

"Your marriage goes well?" Teroz squatted next to Paloma.

Paloma stopped, her dark almond-shaped eyes narrowing as she looked at Teroz. "I do not wish to talk about my marriage with you."

Teroz smiled slightly. Paloma had always had spirit. Even when she was frightened of him, she had spirit. "Do you love the Comanche?"

"I told you, Teroz, I do not wish to talk to you about my marriage. I want you to go." Paloma leaned forward, put the blouse in the water, rinsed it out, and draped it on a nearby rock. She picked up a skirt and plunged it into the water, ignoring Teroz completely. He turned his face as the water splashed him.

Suddenly she clutched her stomach, bending over, crying out in pain.

Teroz reached for her, gently pulling her back against him. "What is wrong?"

"I have a pain." Paloma's breath were quick and shallow.

337

"Relax, Paloma, you will be all right."

"I have had these pains before. What if I lose the child?"

"You will not lose the child." Teroz took the skirt that was clenched in Paloma's fingers and threw it on the ground. "Have you spoken to Shadow Hawk of these pains?"

"No, I do not wish to worry him. Shadow Hawk has other things on his mind."

"Yes, I know."

"What does that mean?"

"Nothing. It means nothing."

"Tell me what you mean, Teroz!" Paloma's voice was almost shrill.

"It does not matter."

"Tell me!" Paloma demanded, her voice rising.

"Your husband has already been with the white woman, Paloma. Has he not told you that?"

"He would not do that to me." Her voice dropped almost to a whisper.

"Perhaps you should ask him."

Paloma pulled away from Teroz and sat up. "You are saying this to hurt me. You have always hated me." Her dark eyes widened in anger. "Ever since your father married my mother and brought us to this camp, you have hated me. You would do anything to hurt me."

"No, that is not true."

"Why do you lie, Teroz? Have you already forgotten that you used to hit me?"

"I have not forgotten. Nor have I forgotten how your mother treated me. I am sorry, Paloma."

"You are not sorry for anything you do. Go, and leave me alone." Paloma refused to look at Teroz.

"I am not lying about Shadow Hawk and the white woman. They were together. He forced himself on her. When she tried to get away, he hit her."

"No, Shadow Hawk would never hurt a woman."

338

"Talk to the white woman if you do not believe me." Teroz looked at Paloma. Her head was lowered, as if in defeat. "You should rest, Paloma. I will tell Ocha to go to your lodge."

"I do not need your help, Teroz. You never helped me before."

"You never let me. You always went to Miho."

Paloma raised her eyes. "Miho was my friend. I needed someone to defend me against you."

Teroz nodded. Paloma was right, of course. He had treated her badly and he hadn't tried very hard to be a good or honorable person. "I am trying to change, Paloma."

"You will never change." Paloma reached for the skirt that was on the ground and she slapped it against the rock, stubbornly refusing to look at him. When she bent over to rinse her hands in the water, she stiffened and her hand involuntarily went to her stomach. She struggled to stand but slipped in the mud and fell sideways. Teroz caught her, easing her onto the bank.

"Paloma." Teroz stared at her.

"Help me to my lodge, Teroz. Please."

Teroz picked Paloma up in his arms and carried her gently through the camp. He ignored the curious stares of the men and women as he passed. He entered her lodge and very gently put her down on a robe. She rolled to her side, pulling her knees up. Teroz touched her cheek. "It will be all right, Paloma." Paloma reached for his hand and held it tightly.

"I am frightened, Teroz."

"Do not be frightened. You will be all right. I will get Ocha."

"No, do not leave me alone." Paloma moaned slightly, and her body stiffened again.

"You need help, Paloma."

"I do not want to be alone, Teroz. Do not leave me."

Teroz took Paloma's hand. He stretched out beside her so

he could see her face. He brushed her cheek lightly. "I am sorry for any hurt I ever caused you when we were young, Paloma. You did nothing to me. I am truly sorry."

Paloma smiled slightly, squeezing Teroz's hand. "I must be dying. I never thought I would hear the great Teroz be so kind to a woman."

"I will never cause you harm again. I promise you that."

"Yet you caused me harm today, Teroz. You told me lies about Shadow Hawk."

"They were not lies, Paloma." Paloma tried to take her hand from Teroz's, but he held onto it. "I do not say this to hurt you, Paloma. I think you should know the truth."

"And what does the white woman mean to you, Teroz? Do you care for her?"

"I admire her strength and courage. That is all."

"Then why did you take her from her people? She has done nothing to harm you."

"You are right. She has caused me no harm."

"So tell me, Teroz, is it giving you the kind of pleasure you thought it would give you?"

Teroz shook his head. "No, the woman is strong and does not even complain. Sometimes I look at her and wonder why I did it."

"She is braver than I. I was never able to stand up to you."

"The white woman spoke of wanting to die when I captured her."

"She told you this?"

"Yes. She said she preferred death to having any man force himself on her."

"And still you took her from her people?"

"Yes."

"You have a heart of stone, Teroz. There is no hope for you."

"And what of Shadow Hawk? At least I have not hurt the white woman."

"Do not speak to me of Shadow Hawk." Paloma cried out suddenly. She tucked her knees up by her stomach.

"I will get Ocha," Teroz said, starting to stand.

"No, please—stay, Teroz."

Teroz felt Paloma's desperate grip on his hand and he sat down, gently pulling her into his lap, cradling her in his arms. "Am I hurting you?"

"No, you are gentle, Teroz. I did not think it was possible." Paloma closed her eyes.

Teroz brushed the hair from Paloma's forehead and gently touched her cheek. He did not want anything to happen to her or her child.

Paloma opened her eyes. "I think the pain has passed."

"Let me carry you to Ocha."

"No, I am frightened of Ocha. She is a witch."

"Ocha is no witch."

"I have heard you say the very words."

"Ocha is my grandmother. She knows me. She could see through my hatred even when I was a child. I never liked her because of it. But she is no witch. She knows more about healing than anyone in this camp."

"Is this true?"

"Yes, Paloma."

Paloma shook her head, her expression weary. "What has happened to you Teroz? Have I died and met someone who looks like you?"

Teroz smiled slightly. "Perhaps you have. Let us go now."

"No, let us wait a while longer. I feel safe here with you." Paloma closed her eyes again.

Teroz felt his hands begin to shake as he held Paloma. No one had ever spoken to him with such kindness except his mother and Singing Bird. It took him off guard, made him defenseless, but he didn't want to fight it. He rested his head on top of Paloma's and closed his eyes. He enjoyed holding her in his arms. For the first time, he was taking care of her.

He heard voices outside the lodge and opened his eyes. He could hear Shadow Hawk's voice before the flap was pushed aside. Shadow Hawk stepped inside, rushing forward, a look of rage on his face.

"What are you doing to her?"

"I am doing nothing." Teroz held onto Paloma as Shadow Hawk tried to pry her free of his grasp.

"Shadow Hawk, please. I am well." Shadow Hawk opened her eyes and spoke. Her voice sounded weak.

"Did he harm you?"

Paloma sat up, holding her stomach. "No, he helped me."

"What happened?"

"I was washing clothes and I had many pains. He carried me here."

Teroz saw the look of anger on Shadow Hawk's face and he stood up. No matter how he felt about Shadow Hawk, he didn't want to upset Paloma. "I will go now. Go to Ocha, Paloma. Let her help you."

"Thank you, Teroz."

Teroz nodded in Paloma's direction and left the lodge. He was barely outside when he stumbled forward, shoved from behind. Shadow Hawk grabbed his arm and yanked him around. "What did you do to her?"

"I did nothing." Teroz jerked his arm free.

"You said you would harm her and the child. I did not think even you would stoop so low, Teroz."

"I did nothing to her. It was as she said."

"Paloma is frightened of you. She will say anything you want her to say."

"I would never harm Paloma."

"Then why did you threaten her?"

"Because I knew it would upset you." Teroz started to walk away but Shadow Hawk went after him, again shoving him forward.

"You are a coward, Teroz. The only way you can feel like a

342

man is to hurt people."

Teroz could not defend himself this time. All his life he had done things to hurt people. Only now was he beginning to realize he did not have to live that way. "I have never hurt the white woman."

"You lie."

"Ask her. Ask her if I have ever touched her in anyway."

"She, too, is frightened of you. She will say what you have told her to say."

"And what of you, Cousin? What did you tell her to say after you forced yourself on her?"

Shadow Hawk dropped his hand. "I did not mean to harm her."

"But you did. I believe she is more frightened of you than she is of me."

"You are a sly one, Teroz. You twist things around to make yourself look brave and make me look like a coward."

"I have never harmed the white woman, nor did I harm Paloma today. These words I speak are true." Teroz didn't wait for a reply but instead, walked away. Strangely, he didn't feel like fighting. That, too, was something new for him.

Teroz released his arrow and watched as the bull elk bounded, crashing through a stand of pines. He lowered his bow in disbelief. The bull had been standing still in the center of a small clearing. How had he missed? Teroz held the bow out at arm's length, sighting along its curve, but he knew it was straight. He had missed because his mind would not focus. Images of Paloma's face disturbed his thoughts. He had seen her going about her work but her face had looked drawn, frightened. He had wanted to talk to her but knew that when Shadow Hawk found out if would only bring Paloma more trouble.

Teroz walked into the clearing to retrieve his arrow. He found it solidly embedded in a pine tree. He glanced back, then walked to find the elk's tracks. Again he shook his head. His shot had been more than ten paces to the side. "Teroz the great hunter, shooting like a child of ten summers." He smiled and almost laughed aloud.

Twigs snapped at the edge of the clearing and Teroz spun, notching an arrow. This time his aim was true and a cow elk fell where she stood. Teroz walked to the animal and saw the light of life leaving its eyes. He reached out and touched the animal's smooth flank. "Thank you. Your death will mean life for many of my people." Teroz pulled the arrow free then hesitated. He had never done that before, had never thanked the animal, and had always laughed when Ataza had admonished him. Suddenly, he knew what he wanted to do with this meat.

He butchered the animal quickly and carried it back to his horse. This time he would not ride through the center of camp, enjoying the envy of less skilled hunters. He would not boast of the difficult shot he had made. He swung onto his horse and rode. He did not use the main trail but rode in from above, heading toward the small lodge at the edge of the camp.

He dismounted and walked to the door flap. "May I come in, grandmother?" When Ocha answered, he went inside. Aissa was sitting next to Ocha. She was handing the old woman herbs and roots to put into a pot.

"Greetings, Grandmother."

"Teroz." Ocha tilted her head to the side. "You are different today."

Teroz felt the old fear at Ocha's words. Perhaps she was a witch. "Yes, Grandmother. May I speak to you?"

"You wish to speak to me alone?"

"Yes, Grandmother."

"Go, girl, gather more of the roots."

Teroz followed Aissa as she left and watched her walk into the woods. She was spending more and more time with Ocha now. He pulled the meat from his horse and took it into his grandmother's lodge.

The old woman smiled her thanks. "Aissa will help me cut it up later. I thank you, Grandson."

Teroz sat down next to his grandmother, studying her. Her face was small and covered with lines. It was as if her life and every event in it had been mapped out on her face for all to see. "You must wonder why I am here, Grandmother."

"It does take me by surprise, yes," Ocha replied, breaking up pieces of root and dropping them into a pot.

"I have not been a very good grandson."

Ocha shrugged. "You have been what you had to be."

"I have not been an honorable person."

"What brings you to this conclusion so suddenly, Teroz? Did you fall and hit your head today or has a spirit spoken to you?"

Teroz smiled, handing his grandmother a root as she felt on the ground for another. "I do not know."

"Did something happen to you?"

"Yes."

"Tell me."

"I was with Paloma. She was in pain and I carried her to her lodge. I stayed with her. I wanted only to protect her." Teroz hesitated. "It was a good feeling, Grandmother."

"Why do you think you felt this way, Teroz?"

"I do not know, Grandmother. I do not understand."

"I think you do."

Teroz thought about the first time he had seen Paloma. She was only ten summers old, small and shy. "Paloma is a gentle person. And I have always taken advantage of her. I have always hurt her in some way."

"Why did you do that, Teroz?"

"I do not know. Paloma never did anything to hurt me."

345

"You grew very angry when she and Miho became friends."

"Yes. I hated Miho."

"Why?"

"Because he was . . ."

"Tell me, Teroz."

"Miho was everything I was not. Miho was good. People liked him. Paloma loved him."

"But Miho is not here and you are."

"And so is Shadow Hawk."

"Ah, Shadow Hawk. You hate him too, do you not? Is that not why you took his woman?"

Teroz was silent, staring at the old woman in front of him. How could she know these things? "I wanted to pay him back for marrying Paloma. I regret that I brought the white woman here. I no longer wish to cause her pain."

"You like this woman."

"Yes, I do. She is strong and she is honest."

Ocha crumpled another root into the pot, brushing her hands together. She looked toward Teroz. "Take the white woman back. She does not deserve to be between you and Shadow Hawk."

Teroz nodded. "You like her also."

"Yes, I also admire her strength. She has a pure heart."

"But it will bring me nothing if I take the white woman back to her people."

"You should take the white woman back for one reason, Teroz, and that is because it is the right thing. Is that not what you want to do?"

Teroz looked into the fire and nodded. "And what of Shadow Hawk? He has deceived Paloma."

"It is between them, Teroz."

"He does not love her, Grandmother."

"And you do, do you not?"

Teroz looked at Ocha and nodded, as if she could see him.

"I feel as if I have been taken over by a spirit."

"Perhaps you have."

"Is it possible, Grandmother?" Teroz looked down at his body.

"Anything is possible, Teroz. I never thought you and I would sit before my fire and speak as we are now speaking. Perhaps the spirit of your mother has come back to guide you."

Strangely, Teroz did not feel frightened by the thought. Ocha often talked of good and evil spirits, and that was why most of the poeple in the camp were scared of her. They didn't like to speak of the dead; they considered it bad luck. But Ocha was different. "My mother was also gentle."

"Like Paloma."

"Yes."

"You have come to me today, my grandson, and for this I am thankful. In your heart, you know what you must do."

Teroz nodded in silent agreement. He had known for some time.

Aissa was walking toward Ocha's lodge when she saw Teroz coming in her direction. His face was clouded. He knows, she thought. He knows that I lied. He gestured and she stopped, waiting for him.

"Come with me," Teroz said, his voice giving her no sign.

"But I have roots for Ocha."

"They will wait." Teroz took the basket from her hand and set it down. Without saying more, he led Aissa along. They walked through the camp and over the ridge behind it. The stream, Aissa realized—he's taking me to the stream. Had he found something in the woods? She glanced into the trees where she and Shadow Hawk had made love. Did Teroz know?

"Sit down."

Aissa sat on the bank, her hands folded in her lap. She lowered her head, unable to meet Teroz's eyes.

"Look at me."

Aissa looked up, fighting her fear. Teroz betrayed nothing. Perhaps he was ready to torture and kill her. She forced herself to remain calm.

"I am sorry for what Shadow Hawk did to you. You did not deserve that."

Aissa lowered her eyes again. She didn't understand. What was he was doing? Was he trying to trap her?

"Look at me, Aissa."

Aissa forced herself to meet his gaze. This time she could see something different in Teroz's eyes. It wasn't anger and it wasn't hatred.

"You have done all that I asked you to do. I had no right to take you from your people. You were only a way for me to get back at Shadow Hawk. I have caused you much pain because I brought you here. For this I am sorry."

Aissa couldn't speak. She would have expected anything from Teroz but this. "Is this a trick?" Her voice trembled slightly.

"This is no trick, Aissa."

"I don't understand." Tears filled her eyes. She wanted to hope but she was afraid to.

"I have been filled with hatred most of my life. Only now am I beginning to understand that. I thought it made me strong to hurt people, to frighten them."

Aissa sat in silence.

Teroz reached for Aissa's arm. He ran his fingers along the scratches. "You loved Shadow Hawk and he hurt you. I blame myself for that."

"It wasn't your fault." Aissa couldn't look at Teroz. She was afraid he would see the lie in her eyes.

"I will take you back to your father."

"My father?" It was the first time she had let herself

think of her father since she and Ocha had talked about him.

"I only hope he is alive. If he is dead, I do not expect you to forgive me."

"You would take me back to my father?"

"Yes."

"Why? Why would you do this, Teroz? I thought you hated Shadow Hawk."

"I have had enough of hating, Aissa. You have taught me something of honor and courage."

Aissa shook her head, fighting back tears. "No, I am not an honorable person, Teroz. I'm not."

"Yes, you are. You have been honest with me. You have not lied. You have done all that I have asked you to do."

"No, I haven't," Aissa stammered, covering her face with her hands. His sudden kindness unnerved her, destroyed the defenses that had cost her so much to build. She felt his hands on hers, pulling them away from her face.

"What are you saying, Aissa?"

"I lied to you." Her voice was shaking. She was almost sobbing. "Shadow Hawk didn't force himself on me. We wanted to be together." She looked at him, wiping the tears from her face. "I wanted him to make love to me." Aissa waited for Teroz to explode in anger, for him to lash out at her in some way, but he did not. Instead, he nodded slightly, his voice low and even when he spoke.

"Yes, I should have known. Shadow Hawk is not a violent man. I know how he feels about you."

"Do what you must to me, Teroz. But do not hurt Shadow Hawk."

He ran his hand along her cheek. "You love Shadow Hawk very much. You were willing to risk your life to be with him."

Aissa nodded.

"What about Paloma?"

349

"Shadow Hawk cares for his wife. He would never hurt her." Aissa shrugged her shoulders. "He was not going to leave Paloma. He was only going to take me back to my father."

"Does it hurt you to see him with Paloma?"

"Yes."

"He does not love her."

"I know he cares for her and he will not leave her." She folded her hands together. "I have willingly given myself to another woman's husband. I am much less than honorable."

"Aissa—"

"Shadow Hawk will never leave his people to be with me. I've always known that. I even knew he would never leave Paloma. What I did was wrong."

"You love him."

"It was still wrong. I feel ashamed."

Teroz nodded his head. "Shame—I know this word well. I have shamed myself and my family many times."

"Why are you being so kind to me? Why?" Aissa began to sob again.

Teroz gripped Aissa's shoulders. "Listen to me, Aissa. Tomorrow I will take you back to your home."

Aissa looked at Teroz and suddenly she couldn't control her sobbing. Tomorrow she would be back to her old life but her life with Shadow Hawk would be over. She felt Teroz's arms go around her and she leaned against his bare shoulder. She couldn't believe that she was finding comfort in the arms of Shadow Hawk's enemy, in the arms of the man who had hurt her father. "I'm afraid," she whispered against his shoulder. "I will never see Shadow Hawk again."

"You are strong, Aissa. You will forget Shadow Hawk when you are with your own people."

Slowly, Aissa sat up, wiping her face. She willed herself to stop crying, breathing deeply until she was in control. She looked at Teroz. "You have been honorable with me, Teroz.

You have kept your word. I thank you for that."

"Do not, Aissa. If it were not for me, you would be home with your father."

"But I do thank you." Impulsively, Aissa hugged him, pulling away when she felt his body stiffen. "I told you the truth about me and Shadow Hawk, and you have treated me well. You are a good man, Teroz."

Teroz lifted a strand of Aissa's hair and let it fall through his fingers. "Perhaps we will meet again someday and you will remember that there was a time when I was kind to you." He lowered his lips to hers, barely brushing her mouth with his.

Aissa smiled at Teroz and again rested her head on his shoulder. She could still feel Teroz's kiss on her lips. It had been a sweet gesture, one of friendship. It was not the kind of kiss she had shared with Shadow Hawk. She closed her eyes and imagined what it would be like to be home, but all she could see was Shadow Hawk's face. She wondered if she could ever forget what it had been like with him.

Shadow Hawk hurried toward the stream. He had seen Teroz leading Aissa this way. Teroz's expression had been strange. He had not tried to talk to Paloma again, and Shadow Hawk was glad. But he knew that Teroz would be angry and he was afraid that he might take out his anger on Aissa.

He slowed down, taking care to move silently. There. They were below him. Aissa was crying and Teroz was holding her hands. He touched her cheek and Aissa looked up at him. Shadow Hawk strained to hear what they were saying.

"You have been honorable with me, Teroz. You have kept your word." The squawking of crows overhead distracted Shadow Hawk. He silently picked up a stone and flung it,

351

but it only frightened the birds and they wheeled, cawing raucously. Whatever Aissa was saying was lost in the noise overhead.

Teroz spoke next but Shadow Hawk still couldn't hear the words because of the noisy birds. He watched as Aissa wrapped her arms around Teroz's neck, resting her head on his shoulder. Shadow Hawk leaned toward them involuntarily. The crows quieted, settling back into the trees. "I told you the truth about me and Shadow Hawk and you have treated me well. You are a good man, Teroz."

Shadow Hawk stood rigidly, unable to believe what Aissa had said. The crows above him rose again, their shrill cries drowning Teroz's response. Shadow Hawk could hear nothing. But he could see. He dug his fingers into the bark of a cedar when he saw Teroz lift Aissa's face and kiss her. She did not struggle; she did not even try to pull away from him. She rested her head on Teroz's shoulder as if it was a familiar place to her. Shadow Hawk felt his heart beat thunderously in his chest. He had never felt such rage in his life, not even when his father had died. His father's death was natural; Aissa's treachery was not. He turned away and headed back toward camp. He had given his love to a white woman and she had betrayed him with one of his own kind.

Chapter 16

"Teroz!"

Teroz opened his eyes at the sound of his name. He forced himself out of his sleep. He recognized Shadow Hawk's voice. He got up and walked to the flap of his father's lodge and ducked outside. Shadow Hawk was standing with an obviously distraught Paloma. "What is it you want?"

"I have divorced Paloma. She is yours."

"Shadow Hawk, please!" Paloma implored.

"Go to him, Paloma. He cares for you more than I." Shadow Hawk let go of her arm.

"Why do you do this, Shadow Hawk?"

"It seems Paloma would rather be with you."

"No, that is not true, Shadow Hawk. Please," Paloma pleaded.

"It is all right, Paloma. I was not the best of husbands anyway."

"Paloma does not want to be with me—"

"Do not argue, Teroz. She is yours. You do not want her to be dishonored, do you?"

Teroz looked at Paloma's tear-streaked face. "Go into the lodge, Paloma. Rest. We will speak later." He walked up to Shadow Hawk. "You have dishonored her by doing this in public."

"It was the only way."

"She is your wife, Shadow Hawk. She is carrying your child."

Shadow Hawk lowered his voice for the first time. "She is carrying Miho's child. That is the only reason I married her."

"Miho," Teroz repeated, shaking his head. "I cannot believe it."

"Paloma deserves better than me and that is why I have divorced her. She is yours." Shadow Hawk's eyes grew dark. "But do not ever harm her. I will kill you if you do."

"I will not harm her."

"I want something in return, Teroz. You know what it is."

"You want Aissa."

"Yes, I want the white woman."

"I was to take her back to her people today. I have given her my word."

"I will take her back."

"Today?"

"Soon."

Teroz shook his head. "I told her it would be today."

"I am giving Paloma to you, Teroz. You owe me the white woman."

"Why are you angry, Shadow Hawk?"

"You and I are not friends, Teroz. How should I act?"

"Aissa is a good woman, an honorable woman. Treat her well."

"You give her to me, then?"

Teroz hesitated but nodded his head. "Yes."

"Where is she?"

"She is with Ocha, Shadow Hawk." Teroz waited for Shadow Hawk to turn. "I will give you the same warning. Do not harm Aissa or you will regret it."

Shadow Hawk ignored Teroz's words and went toward Ocha's lodge. The rage he felt would not subside. He went into Ocha's lodge without asking permission. Ocha was sitting quietly on her robe, chanting a song. Aissa was not

354

there. "Where is Aissa, Grandmother?"

Ocha kept chanting, ignoring Shadow Hawk's presence.

"Where is she, Grandmother?" Shadow Hawk demanded again.

Ocha chanted unhurriedly, purposefully making Shadow Hawk wait. When she was through, she took a deep breath. "Did you bid me good morning, or have I also lost my ability to hear?"

Shadow Hawk shook his head, feeling like a small child. "I am sorry, Grandmother. Greetings. Now, where is Aissa?"

"What is the matter with you, Shadow Hawk? There is a tone to your voice that I do not like."

"Never mind. I will look for her myself."

"Do not leave, Shadow Hawk," Ocha commanded.

He stopped. Ocha was his grandmother and he owed her his respect. No matter how angry he was at Aissa, he had no right to take it out on Ocha. "I am sorry, grandmother," he said, walking to her.

"What has happened to you, Shadow Hawk?"

"Nothing has happened to me."

"You are filled with anger. That is not like you."

"I must go now."

"Shadow Hawk, let this feeling go or it will consume you."

"It has already consumed me, Grandmother." Shadow Hawk left the lodge and skirted the camp, crossing the ridge and following the stream to the place where the women dug for roots. There was a group of women there and Aissa was off to herself. He walked up behind her. "I want you to come with me."

Aissa turned and smiled when she heard Shadow Hawk's voice. Her blue eyes sparkled. Her blond hair was braided into a thick plait that hung over one shoulder. "Shadow Hawk, have you heard the news? Teroz is taking me back home."

"Stand up."

"Did you hear what I—"

Shadow Hawk didn't want to hear anything she had to say. He reached down and grabbed her arm, pulling her to her feet. With one arm around her shoulders, he forced her to walk with him.

"Shadow Hawk, what are you doing?"

Shadow Hawk ignored the stares of the people in the camp. When he got to his lodge, he ducked into the flap and pulled Aissa after him. He closed the flap behind him.

"Please, tell me what I have done." Aissa looked at him, her eyes reflecting her hurt.

"You do not know?" Shadow Hawk glared at her.

"No, I don't."

Shadow Hawk crossed his arms. "How many men have you given yourself to?"

"I don't understand what you're asking me." Aissa sat on a robe, hugging her knees to her chest.

Shadow Hawk squatted down, his eyes hard and cold. "I was not the first, Aissa."

Aissa reached out, putting her hand on his arm, but he pushed her back. "Why are you doing this?"

"I do not have to explain myself to you. You are my woman. You will do as you are told."

"No." She sat straighter, her eyes defiant. "I belong to no man."

"You are wrong about that." Shadow Hawk saw how frightened Aissa was, but he didn't stop. He moved forward, shoving her backward onto the floor of the lodge. He straddled her, his hands on her chest, pinning her to the floor. "Tell me about Grimes."

"I hate Ray."

"But you would have done anything for him so that you could have your drug. Were there others?"

"There was no one."

"How do you know? You have said you do not remember."

"But you said that Ray hadn't . . . Shadow Hawk, what

have I done to make you hate me?"

"You still do not know?"

"No."

Shadow Hawk took Aissa's wrists and pinned them to the ground above her head. He leaned down, his face close to hers. "You are mine, and you will do as I say." Aissa started to speak, but Shadow Hawk covered her mouth with his, forcing his tongue between her lips, ignoring her cries and her struggles. He could feel her body underneath his, the warmth of it, the feel of it against his.

"Please don't do this, Shadow Hawk," Aissa whispered. "Please."

"You did not mind it before in the woods, or have you already forgotten?"

Aissa turned her face away. "I haven't forgotten." When she turned back, there were tears in her eyes. "When you loved me in the woods you were gentle. Something has happened. Please, tell me."

"I will tell you this: you are not going back to your people."

"But Teroz promised—"

"Teroz has given you to me. I divorced Paloma so that she could be with Teroz."

Aissa struggled against Shadow Hawk's hold. "You told me you loved me. You told me you would find a way for us to be together."

"I have found a way."

"No!" Aissa screamed out, but Shadow Hawk covered her mouth with his hand.

"Do not scream again or you will be punished."

"You don't think I've been punished enough? You and your people have taken my life from me."

"You wanted us to be together, Aissa. Now we will be, here in this camp."

"Let me go. I'll find my own way back."

"No."

"Why? You obviously don't care for me anymore. Just let me go back."

"You will stay here as long as I want you to stay. You will do what I tell you to do and you will stay away from Teroz."

"Teroz never lied to me."

Shadow Hawk tightened his hold on Aissa's wrists. "Do not speak to me of Teroz. Teroz is my enemy. If I see you with him, I will consider you my enemy."

"What's happened to you?"

"Better I should ask that question of you, Aissa." His voice was cold when he said her name. He let go of her hands and sat up, still straddling her. Aissa tried to twist away but Shadow Hawk's weight pinned her to the ground. He ran his hands along her thighs.

"Don't."

"Why do you suddenly resist me, Aissa, when you were so willing before?" He put his hands on her breasts. As he ran his fingers over them, he felt Aissa grow still. He moved between her legs, forcing her legs apart. He lifted up her skirt. "Is this what you want, Aissa?"

"No!" she cried out, trying to twist away. He ran his hands along her thighs. Her body went rigid. Shadow Hawk saw her fingers dig into the dirt. He felt no pity or love for her. He felt only rage. She had led him away from his people, his life, then she had betrayed him.

"You are my woman. I can take you whenever it pleases me."

"Take me then," she responded, her voice barely audible. "But know that every time you do, I will hate you even more than I do right now."

"It does not matter if you hate me. Your hatred means nothing." Shadow Hawk thought of Aissa in Teroz's arms, thought of the way Teroz had kissed her, and it angered him. He leaned forward, covering her body with his, and forced her to look at him. "You are mine, Aissa. You will never belong to any man but me." He kissed her fiercely and felt her struggle against him. She tried to turn her head, to free her mouth from his, but he held her, moving his tongue against her lips, softly, sensuously, until she began to respond. He traced her neck with his fingertips and opened her blouse, kissing her breasts, gently nuzzling them with his lips. He ran a hand along her inner thighs until he found her center. He gently touched her there, increasing the pressure until he felt her move against his hand. She was no longer struggling and he eased himself into her, putting his hands underneath her buttocks. Her eyes were closed, her cheeks were flushed, and her lips were full and trembling. She looked beautiful. He moved faster and faster, reveling in the feel of being inside her, overwhelmed by the softness, the sweet scent of this woman. His passion rose until he exploded inside her. His body moved feverishly until he was spent and he lay atop her, his face against her neck. He moved a hand to touch her perfect breast and he felt her flinch. Slowly he rolled away from her.

Immediately Aissa pulled down her blouse and skirt and rolled onto her side. She began to cry. He wanted to reach out to her, to take her into his arms, but he had nothing to say to her. He had forced himself on her, he had taken her, and now he would have to live with her hatred.

Aissa cut the meat skillfully, with quick strokes. She slammed the knife into the meat, thinking of Shadow Hawk. They had barely spoken and when he came to her at night, she fought him until she gave in. She hated him. Even more, she hated herself.

She looked up and saw Teroz approach the front of the lodge. She stood quickly, turning toward the lodge door. But Teroz yelled her name.

"Aissa, wait!"

Aissa turned, waiting for him. It wouldn't matter. Even if she didn't speak to Teroz, Shadow Hawk would hear that he had come to the lodge. "You shouldn't be here, Teroz."

"You must come. It is Paloma."

"What's the matter?"

"She is ready to have the child, but something is wrong. Ocha said she needs your help."

Aissa didn't hesitate. She dropped the chunk of meat into the pot, washed her hands in the bowl by the lodge, and quickly followed Teroz. She could hear Paloma's screams long before they reached the lodge and she could see that Teroz was scared. Aissa took his arm. "Do not worry, Teroz, Ocha will help her."

"I knew she was in trouble all those weeks ago by the river. It is because of me that Paloma is suffering such pain."

"You haven't done anything to her, Teroz."

"Yes, it is because I treated her so badly for so long. It is my fault. The spirits do not take kindly to such things."

Aissa saw the misery on his face. There was nothing she could say to comfort him. "We must think of Paloma now, Teroz."

Aissa entered first. The lodge was filled with a pungent-smelling smoke and Ocha was passing a bundle of plants over Paloma's body as she chanted. Aissa knelt next to the old woman.

"What do you want me to do, Ocha?"

"Find some of the yellow-flowered root. I have shown you what it looks like. Hurry."

Aissa took a root digger from one of Ocha's baskets and left the lodge. She ran down the path that led to camp. She slipped numerous times on the rocky ground but she never fell, running as if she had been born to this place. She stopped when she reached the place where the canyon rim started and she began to climb. She dug her feet and hands into the dark soil of the hillside until she got halfway up the bank. The plants were not so common this time of year, but Ocha had shown her where they could always be found. She searched the hillside, looking through different shrubs and bushes until she found what she wanted. She dropped to her knees and began to dig with her fingers, quickly pushing dirt away from the base of the plant. Then she stuck the digger into the ground and dug a deep circle around the base of the plant until the root was exposed. She kept digging, loosening the root from above, until she was able to dislodge it. She stood up and started down the bank, slipping most of the way. She ran along the rim until she found the path again and she ran hard, ignoring her own strained breathing. As she started up the path to camp she saw Shadow Hawk. She started past him but he grabbed her arm.

"What are you doing?"

"Ocha needs this."

"I did not say you could visit with Ocha."

"I'm not visiting her." Again Aissa tried to get past Shadow Hawk and again he held her back.

"You will do what I tell you to do."

"No, not this time." Aissa hit Shadow Hawk in the chest with the heel of her hand and started to run. She felt him behind her but she didn't stop until he grabbed her blouse, jerking her backward. "Let me go!"

"You still do not listen well, Aissa."

"Ocha needs this root. It's for Paloma. She's having trouble with the baby."

Shadow Hawk let Aissa go. "Paloma?"

"Yes, she's in great pain, Shadow Hawk. We don't have time to argue."

Shadow Hawk nodded. "Let us go, then."

Aissa ran to Ocha's lodge, hardly aware that Shadow Hawk was running next to her. Paloma's screams were louder now and when Aissa entered the lodge, she could see Paloma's dead child in Ocha's arms. Paloma was bleeding heavily. Ocha wrapped the child and handed it to Teroz.

"Bury it quickly," she said and turned to Aissa. "You found the root?"

"Yes, I have it here."

"Grind it up and add hot water to it." Aissa found a bowl and broke the root into it, grinding it up with a stone. She added water from one of the pots Ocha always kept on the fire. "I'm finished, Ocha," Aissa said as she handed it to the old woman, her hands steady although she felt like crying.

Ocha reached into the bag around her neck and sprinkled some of the mixture into the bowl, stirring it with her finger. "Hold her up."

Aissa got behind Paloma, trying to ignore her cries of pain. Paloma seemed so small, so fragile. Aissa propped her up and took the bowl from Ocha's hands. "You must drink this, Paloma."

Paloma turned her head away. "No! Leave me alone!"

"Force her to drink it," Ocha said firmly.

Aissa used her right arm to steady Paloma's head and put the bowl to her lips. But Paloma swatted it away, spilling some on herself.

"I will hold her."

Aissa looked up. Shadow Hawk had entered the lodge. She didn't argue with him. He could easily keep Paloma still. She waited until he held Paloma and then she forced Paloma's mouth open and made her drink. Paloma tried to spit it out, but Shadow Hawk forced her head backward so that she had to swallow. "She is done, Ocha."

"Good. Now get some of the cloth by my baskets. Put it between her legs. She will bleed for a while."

Aissa brought the soft cotton cloth, lifting Paloma to place some of it underneath her and the rest between her legs. "What now?" Aissa asked Ocha.

"There is nothing. I will chant and say some prayers for Paloma and the child. You did well, girl."

"Are you sure you don't need me for anything else? I can sit with Paloma."

"No, leave us now. Come later." She looked over at Shadow Hawk with her unseeing eyes. "It was good of you to be here, Grandson. Be good to Aissa. She does not de-

362

serve your hatred."

Aissa left the lodge, shaking. She looked down at herself. Her hands and skirt were covered with blood. She thought of the small bundle that Teroz had taken out of the lodge and she closed her eyes at the thought of it. She heard Shadow Hawk behind her.

"Are you all right?"

"I'm going to the stream to wash."

"Aissa."

Aissa turned around. "If you're going to tell me that I can't go, I won't listen. Punish me if you must, but give me some freedom. You have taken everything else away from me."

"I will walk with you to the stream."

Aissa wanted to tell Shadow Hawk to leave her alone, but she didn't. She just wanted to get clean. They walked in silence. Aissa wondered where Teroz had buried the child and her heart was full of sadness for Paloma and the child she would never come to know. When they reached the stream she knelt down, plunging her arms into the cold water, washing away Paloma's blood. She bent over, letting the front of her skirt fall into the water. She rinsed until the stains were gone, then she splashed her face. She sat back on her heels, feeling exhausted. She wished Shadow Hawk were somewhere else so she could cry. She stared ahead, unable to think of anything but Paloma and the child she'd lost.

"You did well. You were a help to Ocha."

"I wish I could've helped Paloma."

"There was nothing you could do."

"How do you know? You didn't even care enough about her to stay with her." Aissa covered her face with her hands. "My heart aches for Paloma."

"You should go to the lodge and rest."

Aissa faced Shadow Hawk, her eyes wild. "I don't want to rest in the lodge. I hate the lodge. I hate this camp."

"And you hate me."

"Yes," Aissa answered, her voice trembling. "I hate you."

"I told you once before that your hatred means nothing to me. If you expect me to take you home, I will not."

"Why? Why do you want a woman who doesn't want you?"

"You do want me, Aissa."

"Don't tell me what I feel." Aissa felt Shadow Hawk's hand gently brush across her cheek. She closed her eyes and imagined for a moment that he was still the same caring man she had known before.

"You want me as much as I want you."

"I don't have a choice, do I? You would force yourself on me anyway."

"I will give you the freedom you desire as long as you do not try to escape."

"Would you kill me if I did?" Aissa glared at Shadow Hawk.

Shadow Hawk stood up. "Come back to the lodge before dark."

Aissa didn't watch Shadow Hawk as he walked away. She didn't want to think about going back to the lodge. She knew what would happen when she did, she would wind up loathing herself again.

She stood up and waded across the stream. She walked through trees and climbed rocks until she was able to see the valley below. She wondered if it was possible for her to escape. Even if she managed to get down the side of the mountain and into the canyon, she would have to walk across the desert on foot, something that was impossible for her to do. She shook her head. It would still be a while before she could leave this place.

Aissa walked around the periphery of the camp until she came to the large boulders that overlooked the valley and desert. This was the place she had seen Shadow Hawk and Gitano go to many times. She started to climb but slipped, dragging her palms along the rock as she fell. She leaned against it, looking at the bloody scratches.

"You do not climb rocks very well, white woman."

Aissa smiled to herself. It was Gitano. They had seen very little of each other lately, but she liked him. He was always kind to her. She looked up. He was standing atop a boulder.

"I didn't see you up there."

"I did not wish to be seen. I had to see what made so much noise."

Aissa held up her red palms. "You're right, I'm not very good at climbing these rocks."

"Over there." Gitano pointed to a series of rocks that led upward to another boulder. "Go there and I will help you."

Aissa climbed the rocks, stepping carefully from one to the next. She looked up. Gitano was still high above her. She stuck her foot in a small crevice and pulled herself up until she found another foothold. When she was almost to the top, Gitano grabbed her hand and pulled her the rest of the way. Aissa sat down, smiling at him. "Thank you."

He sat down next to her. "Why did you come here?"

"I have seen you here many times. This looked like a good place to be alone." Aissa looked out at the white stretch of desert. She wondered about her father—if he was still alive, if he was able to run the ranch, if he was still sheriff. She wanted to see him so badly.

"You look unhappy."

"Have you heard about Paloma?"

Gitano shook his head. "What?"

"She has lost her child."

Gitano was quiet for a long while. "This is sad news."

"I don't know her well, but she seems kind. I feel sorry for her."

Gitano shrugged his shoulders. "Perhaps it is for the best. I do not know if Teroz could have been a father to my brother's child."

"And you think Shadow Hawk could?" she asked, unable to conceal her anger.

"I think Shadow Hawk wanted you more than he wanted

365

to be a father to Paloma's child."

"That doesn't make him very honorable, does it?"

"He saved Paloma's life. She would have killed herself and the child if he had not married her. She knew he did not love her. He was honest with her."

"What about Teroz?"

"Teroz cares for her." Gitano shrugged. "Perhaps he can learn to love her." Gitano squinted up at the sky above. "It will be winter soon. We will be moving down into the valley before the snow falls."

"Where will we move?" Aissa asked, trying to sound only casually interested. She might have a better chance of escaping then.

"We change camps every winter. My father and some of the elders will decide."

"Has anyone ever escaped from this camp, Gitano?"

"Only you, white woman, when my cousin took you away." Gitano looked at Aissa. "Are you thinking of trying to escape again?"

Aissa did not meet Gitano's eyes. "Maybe."

"It is dangerous for you to tell me this. Shadow Hawk is my cousin and my friend. I could tell him of your plans."

"I have no plans." Aissa blew on her palms.

"There has been a change in Shadow Hawk."

"You have noticed it?"

"Yes, it seems both my cousins are changing. Teroz grows more tolerable and Shadow Hawk grows more intolerable. I do not understand what has happened."

"I don't either."

"He will not take you back to your people?"

"No. Something happened and I don't know what it was. He's so angry at me."

"My cousin has been angry for a very long time, even when he came to us."

"He's not the same person, Gitano."

"We all change, Aissa. It is part of the way of things. Look

366

at the leaves on the trees." Gitano pointed down the hillside. "See how they change?"

"Yes, but they come back again in the spring, full of life. I see nothing of that in Shadow Hawk."

"It is not yet spring. There is time."

"Not for me."

"So, you will try to escape."

Aissa studied her hands. "Maybe."

"I would not advise it."

"Because you'll tell Shadow Hawk?" Aissa looked at Gitano.

"No, because you would die out there alone. You can't make it."

"I can't stay here. I need to be with my own people."

"I cannot help you, Aissa."

"I'm not asking you to help me. I will do what I have to do alone."

Gitano shook his head, rolling a small rock between his hands. "You will not make it."

"I won't make it here either." Aissa stood up. "I should go. I want to see how Paloma is doing."

"I have made you angry."

"No, you've been honest with me."

"I will help you down."

"No, I'll find my own way down." Aissa looked below, trying to figure out the best way down. She lay flat on the boulder and hung down, feeling her way until she dropped to the rock stairway. She stood up and carefully began to climb downward.

"White woman!"

Aissa turned around and looked up at Gitano, who was now standing on top of the boulder. "If this is something you are determined to do, talk to me again."

Aissa nodded slightly and waved to Gitano. Was he going to help her? She shrugged her shoulders. It didn't matter. She had to find a way to help herself.

She went back to Ocha's lodge and asked permission to enter.

"Come in, girl."

Aissa entered and knelt next to Ocha. Ocha was sitting silently, wiping the sweat from Paloma's face.

"How is she?"

"The bleeding has stopped, I think. She has been resting."

"Will she live?"

"If she wants to live, she will live."

"Do you think it was my fault, Ocha?"

"What are you saying, child?"

"If Shadow Hawk had not divorced Paloma, perhaps she wouldn't have been so upset. It's because of me that this terrible thing happened."

Ocha sat down on the ground, crossing her legs. She sighed deeply. "You give yourself too much power, girl. You are not responsible for this. Neither is Shadow Hawk. Neither is Teroz. It is just something that happened."

"I'm going to leave, Ocha."

Ocha turned her face toward Aissa. "Shadow Hawk is taking you back to your people?"

"No, I'm going to find a way to escape."

Ocha shook her head, her face wrinkling in disapproval. "Ah, girl, that is foolish. You would never make it out of here."

"That's what Gitano said."

"Why do you not tell the entire camp that you plan to escape? Maybe they can show you the way out."

Aissa smiled. "I must appear foolish to you."

"You appear desperate. I can understand that."

"I can't stay with Shadow Hawk. I know he's your grandson and you love him, but something has happened to him."

"He is confused by what he feels for you."

"He doesn't feel anything for me."

"You are wrong."

"Do you want me to stay here and accept the way he treats me? I'm not like your women, Ocha. My father treated me as more of an equal."

"You are a captive, girl. Do not forget that."

"I cannot forget it."

"Do not let your desperation overwhelm you."

"Why not? Am I supposed to let Teroz and Shadow Hawk toy with my life because it brings them pleasure? I will find a way to leave, Ocha."

"And you will die or be captured."

"I don't care anymore. You've taught me about plants and roots and I've learned something of using a bow and arrow from watching the men."

Ocha gently wiped Paloma's forehead. "You are determined then?"

"Yes." Aissa leaned closer to the old woman, gently touching her arm. "I am dying here, Ocha."

"You will die out there alone."

Aissa glanced at Paloma. "I don't care."

Ocha sighed, shaking her head. "I will help you then."

"No, I don't expect you to help me."

"Of course you did, or you would not have spoken of it to me."

Aissa lowered her voice, as if Paloma could hear her. "All I need is to find the best way out."

"I cannot be your eyes, but Gitano can help you with that. I can give you food, water, and medicine." Ocha shook her head. "It is much too dangerous. You are not an Apache. You are not strong enough to make this trip alone."

"But I am strong, Ocha. I've been through much and I've survived. I'll make it back to my father."

"We will be moving our camp soon. Perhaps you should wait until them."

"No," Aissa said decisively, "Shadow Hawk will assume that's when I'll try to escpe. I should do it here. He'll never suspect that I'm planning to escape from this mountain."

"Make it soon. The more you talk about it, the better the chance he will hear of it."

Aissa reached out and squeezed the old woman's hand. "Thank you, Ocha. You have been a friend to me. I will never forget what you've done."

"Do not thank me, girl. I may be sending you to your death."

"If I die, it is my choice."

"Tell Gitano to come to me tomorrow. He and I will talk."

"He hasn't said he'll help me."

"He will help you."

Aissa stared into the flames of the fire, thinking of the dangers she would face alone. She would have to find a way down the mountain, find her way through the canyon, and do it alone, at night. And if she made it that far, she would have to cross the desert. She shivered slightly as she imagined herself lost in the desert, unable to find her way. But she knew she couldn't stay here any longer. She had to go.

Aissa feigned illness that night so that Shadow Hawk wouldn't lie with her, but he didn't seem to be interested in her anyway. She slept fitfully. The next day, after giving Shadow Hawk his morning meal, she said she was going to see Paloma. Shadow Hawk didn't object.

Aissa walked through camp to Ataza's lodge. Ataza had always been kind to her, but he frightened her. She hoped he was nowhere around. As she approached the lodge with the buffalo and horses painted on it, she saw Ataza and Gitano sitting in front of it. She had to think of a reason to speak to Gitano, or Ataza would be suspicious. Ataza was working on a shield and barely looked up at Aissa.

"Greetings, Ataza," Aissa said in the proper respectful tone.

"Greetings, Aissa. What brings you to our lodge so early

in the morning?"

"I have a message for Gitano from Shadow Hawk."

Ataza nodded. "Speak to him, then."

Gitano quickly rose. "I will walk with Aissa, Father."

"Fine, fine." Ataza was barely paying attention as he worked on the painting of his new shield.

"It was dangerous for you to come here."

"Ocha wanted me to bring you to her lodge."

Gitano shook his head, looking around. "This is a stupid thing you do, white woman."

"Come with me a moment, Gitano." Aissa tugged at Gitano's arm and led him around the camp to the place by the boulders. They stood at the edge and Aissa pointed in the distance. "You see out there, Gitano? That is where I live. I long to be there again."

"I understand that, Aissa."

"What if you were down there, looking up at these mountains? Wouldn't you want to find a way to get back to your people? Would you let a white man keep you as his slave?"

Gitano looked at Aissa, a disgruntled expression on his face. "You are persuasive, white woman."

"I need your help, Gitano. If you can only show me the best way out of here."

"How do you expect to escape without a horse?"

Aissa lowered her head. "I hadn't even thought of a horse."

"Did you plan to walk back to your people? You are strong but not strong enough to outwalk an Apache on foot, and Shadow Hawk will be following on horseback."

"There isn't any way for me to get a horse."

"Come, let us go to Ocha's."

They walked in a companionable silence to Ocha's lodge. Aissa realized as they walked that she felt close to Gitano, that she trusted him. He was one of those rare poeple who had nothing to hide.

Gitano entered Ocha's lodge first and Aissa followed. Paloma was lying on a clean robe, in clean clothes. There was no sign of the blood from the day before. Aissa was amazed by Ocha and her ability to do things as if she could see.

"Is that you, Gitano?"

"How did you know, Grandmother?"

"I can always smell you." She lifted her nose. "You had roasted deer this morning, yes?" She patted her robe, "Come, sit next to me."

"Why do you always say that? I bathe in the river."

"It is not a dirty smell. It is a food smell or sometimes the smell of mint. You are always chewing on the mint leaves, are you not?"

Gitano smiled at Aissa. "Yes."

"Sit, girl, on the other side of me."

Aissa sat down next to Ocha. "How is Paloma?"

"She is resting. The bleeding has stopped. I think she will get well."

"And Teroz?"

"Teroz has surprised me. He stayed the night. I sent him away only a short while ago to rest. I believe he truly cares for Paloma."

"I am frightened, Grandmother," Gitano said, his voice low.

Ocha reached out and found Gitano's hand. "Why are you frightened, grandson?" Her voice was soft, caring.

"Teroz has a heart. Never in my life did I think I would live to see such a thing."

Ocha swatted Gitano's hand. "Do not be unkind, Gitano. It is not like you."

"I am not being unkind, Grandmother. I am being truthful."

"Yes, I must admit it comes as a surprise to me. But it pleases me greatly." Ocha was silent for a moment. "But I am troubled by Shadow Hawk. You know him well, Gitano.

What has happened to cause this change in him?"

Gitano glanced at Aissa. "I do not know, Grandmother, but I do not believe he has the right to keep Aissa as a captive. Even Teroz was going to let her go. She has suffered long enough."

"Yes, I agree. It is time to do something."

"If you help me, Shadow Hawk will be angry with you both."

"He will not be angry with me, girl," Ocha said gently. "Even if he is, it will not last long. I am his grandmother. He will not ignore me."

Aissa touched Gitano's arm. "But you are his friend, Gitano. I cannot put myself between you and him."

"I love my cousin, Aissa, and I would do anything for him. But something has made his heart grow cold."

"Shadow Hawk is a good man. I know that. He saved my life two times, but suddenly he has grown to hate me. I cannot live with his hate any longer."

"Do not make excuses for Shadow Hawk, Aissa. We will find a way to get you back home. Can you get her a horse, Gitano?"

"I will have to lead her out at night, but I can do it. I can take her down the mountain to the canyon, and from there she will have to cross the desert."

"Can she do that alone?"

Gitano looked at Aissa. "Aissa is strong, Grandmother."

"Many people are strong, Grandson, but they cannot cross a desert."

"I will tell her the way to go. She will make it."

Aissa reached for Ocha's hand. "Do not worry for me, Ocha. It is my decision. Whatever happens, I will always thank you two for helping me."

"All right, it is decided. You will find a way to lead her down the mountain, Gitano, and I will make sure she has supplies. You must also tell her of places to hide, if necessary."

"I will do that, Grandmother."

"Both of you go now."

"Thank you, Ocha." Aissa leaned over and kissed Ocha on the cheek. She followed Gitano out of the lodge, grabbing his arm before he could walk away. "Gitano, please think about this. I know how much you care for Shadow Hawk. You don't owe me anything."

"Do not worry about me, white woman. I will do it because it is something Shadow Hawk would do if he were thinking clearly. It is the right thing to do."

Aissa squeezed Gitano's hand. "I don't know how to thank you, Gitano."

"Do not thank me yet. We have to get you down this mountain first."

Ben winced as he shifted positions on the bed. His arms and legs were bandaged and his face was still blistered from the fire. The fire . . . he would never forget the feeling of being trapped inside his house as it went up in flames, as the heat seared and blistered his skin. Funny, he thought he was going to lose the house the night the Indian kidnapped Aissa. But the fire had never spread beyond the haystack. The Indian had only meant to scare him, unlike Grimes.

Ben thought about the strongbox that was hidden under the floor planks in his bedroom. He hadn't even told Flora or Joe about it. It contained everything he owned in this world—not to mention some very incriminating evidence on Grimes. But what worried him even more was the letter to Aissa. He had written it for her to have in case Grimes managed to kill him. If Aissa was alive and she went back to the house and found it, she'd assume he was dead. He had to get that box as soon as possible.

Ben thought back to the night of the fire, his rage growing. He had been sitting at his table, looking over maps of known Apache strongholds. He had decided to look for Aissa. He had nothing to live for otherwise. He had even found a scout who would translate for him and take him into the various camps. he had plenty of goods for trade but would promise the Apache more if he received news of Aissa. He was going to do anything it took to get his daughter back.

But as he sat scouring the maps, a lantern came crashing through the window, and before Ben could get out the door, a wall of flames shot up in front of him. Another burst through the window in his bedroom. He heard men outside, heard more lanterns crashing against the house. He fell to the floor and crawled toward his room, keeping low. He pulled his bandana up around his nose so he could breathe. The entire house was engulfed in flames, and he inched along the hot floor until he reached his bedroom and the half-broken window. He turned on his back and kicked at the window until it completely shattered, spilling glass over him. He pulled himself over the glass shards and fell outside, gasping for air. He got up and ran, back into the small stand of oak trees behind the house. He hid behind one of the large trees and watched as his house burned to the ground and as men rode through Aissa's garden, purposefully destroying it. Then he recognized Ray's gelding and he saw Ray, sitting on his horse, staring at the fire, a look of satisfaction on his face.

Ben groaned now as he thought about it. He tried to sit up. He heard the sound of heels on the wood floor and smiled when Flora came into the room, holding a tray.

"I told you I'd help you with that, Ben," she admonished softly, setting the tray on the table next to the bed. "You're never going to heal if you don't sit still." Flora plumped up the pillows behind him. "There, sit back." Flora placed the tray across Ben's lap. "Sausage, eggs, fresh muffins, and coffee with cream. I'm going to make you the best stew you've ever had for dinner."

"You spoil me, Flora." Ben cradled the cup of coffee in his bandaged hands and looked at Flora. She had saved his live not just once, but twice. After Celou had died, he was on his way to destroying himself. Aissa was just a young girl and already had taken on too many responsibilities. He couldn't face life without Celou. But he had talked to Flora, and she had helped him through the lonely times. Slowly their friendship had grown into something more, until one day, Ben realized he was in love again. It wasn't the passionate, fiery kind of love that he had had with Celou, but it was a comfortable, secure love. He could talk to Flora about anything. She was an ex-saloon girl, so nothing embarrassed her. Ben liked holding her in his arms at night. Ben just plain liked Flora Simms.

"Why're you staring at me like that?" Flora put her hand up to her red hair. "I took great pains to make sure I looked good when you woke up."

Ben sipped at the coffee. "You look real good. I wish I could move. If I could—"

"That's enough of that kind of talk, Ben Gerard. There'll be enough time for that later when you're well."

Ben set the cup down. "How's my face looking, Flora?"

"Still the handsomest face I ever saw," she said, smiling. She sat on the bed next to him. "Does that hurt you if I sit here?"

"No, I like it."

"I'm going to have to get back to Agua Prieta pretty soon. I want to see what's up with Grimes."

"You steer clear of him, Flora. He's proven just how dangerous he can be." Ben shook his head, halfheartedly picking at his food with a fork. "I can't believe I tried to push Aissa into marrying that son-of-a-bitch."

"You didn't know, Ben."

"You did. You even tried to warn me about him."

"That's cause I knew him from the saloon. I saw the way he treated the girls there. The kind of bastard that would beat them because he couldn't do anything else with them."

Ben laughed, rubbing a bandaged hand up and down Flora's back. "Not many men tried to hit you, did they Flora?"

"Last one who tried, almost got his . . ." Flora hesitated, narrowing her eyes at Ben. "Almost got his you-know-whats blown off."

Carefully, Ben leaned against Flora. "You smell good, woman."

"That's enough, Ben. You eat your breakfast. You need to heal so you can get on with your search."

"The search." Ben nodded. "She has to be all right, Flora. I keep getting this feeling that Shadow Hawk will find her if she's out there."

"I'm sure he will, darlin'."

"But if he doesn't, I will. I'll find my girl."

"I know you will, Ben."

"But there's something I want almost as much as I want to see Aissa again." Ben's eyes narrowed and his voice grew hard. "I want to see Grimes ruined. I want the sonofabitch run out of town. I want to kill him."

Flora wiped Ben's forehead. "You relax, now. There's no use getting yourself all worked up. Ray Grimes will get his due."

Ben nodded. Yes, he thought, Grimes will get his due. As soon as I'm able, I'm going after him. I'll ruin him, and after I do that, I'll kill the bastard.

Chapter 17

Shadow Hawk ran up the mountain, his heart beating so hard he felt it would burst inside his chest. He kept his mouth closed and breathed through his nose, as he had been taught to do years earlier. He liked to run. It cleared his mind and worked his muscles. The running helped, but he knew he needed something else. He knew he had to leave for a while.

When he reached the lodge, he found Aissa in front, working a hide. She had become quite adept at tanning, and there was a small pile of the soft, folded hides in the lodge. She worked hard and tirelessly, never complaining. But when she spoke to him, there was no meaning in her words. Even though she was here, he had driven her far away.

Shadow Hawk sat down, picking up a bowl and dipping it into the pot. "I am leaving today. We are in need of fresh meat."

"How long will you be gone?" Aissa asked, never raising her eyes from her task.

"Two, three days, maybe."

"Why're you going now when we'll soon be leaving the mountain?"

"I go now because I choose to go now," he answered abruptly. He stood up. "Come into the lodge with me." Shadow Hawk went to his robe and sat down. He saw the resentful expression on Aissa's face and ignored it. "Sit here by me."

Aissa sat down, staring stright ahead.

"I know you, Aissa."

"What does that mean?"

"I know how your mind works. I know you would escape from this place if you could. Do not try when I am gone."

Aissa glared at him. "What will you do to me if I try to escape, Shadow Hawk? Will you torture me or kill me, perhaps?"

Shadow Hawk hooked an arm around her shoulders and turned her toward him. "I could do many things to you, Aissa, many things to make you wish you had not deceived me."

"You have already done many things to me, Shadow Hawk."

Shadow Hawk ran his fingers up and down Aissa's neck. She squirmed and moved her shoulders. He ran his fingers around to the front of her blouse and traced her collarbone. He leaned forward and kissed the hollow of her neck. "Tell me that you do not desire me, Aissa." He looked into her blue eyes, forcing her to look at him.

"I do not desire you, Shadow Hawk." Aissa lowered her eyes.

Shadow Hawk held her face in his hands, forcing her to look at him. "Tell me again that you do not desire me." He touched his mouth to hers, gently kissing her. "Tell me, Aissa."

Aissa closed her eyes. "I cannot."

Shadow Hawk pulled her into his arms, holding her against him. "I will never let another man possess you, Aissa."

"Why is it you think of me as a possession and not as a woman?"

Shadow Hawk pulled away. "I know that you are a woman, Aissa."

"But you have no respect for my feelings. Sometimes you treat me the way Ray treated me."

"Is that true? Is that what I have done?" Shadow Hawk stiffened, sitting up straight. "And what about you, Aissa? How have you treated me?"

"What do you mean?"

"The last time I saw you before Teroz brought you here, you said you hated me."

"You know why I did that. My body needed the drug that Ray gave me. I would have said or done anything. I have told you this over and over."

"Yes, I know."

"How can you blame me for something that wasn't my fault?"

Shadow Hawk ignored her question. "Then you came here. I was worried for you because of Teroz."

"You weren't that worried. You were already married to Paloma," Aissa replied angrily.

"I had no choice, Aissa."

"Just as I had none with Ray." She looked at him, her eyes full of sadness. "You said you would come back."

"I wanted to come back to you," Shadow Hawk said gently. "I thought of you and your father."

"But neither of us mean enough to you. Paloma was more important."

"I had to make a choice. If Paloma had been banished or had died, I could not have lived with myself."

"But you could live with yourself knowing that you would never see me again."

"I knew that you were strong. I knew that you were with your father and your people. I knew that you would be fine."

"You were wrong. I wasn't fine. I missed you. I waited for you to come back every day."

In all their arguments, Aissa had never admitted that she was unhappy, that she had missed him. He put his arm around her, pulling her toward him, but she shoved him away.

"Don't! You've made it clear how you feel about me. You use my body for your pleasure, but that's all. You have no feeling for me anymore."

"You are very wrong, Aissa." In spite of her protests, Shadow Hawk held Aissa in his arms, his face close to hers. He covered her protests with his mouth, pressing his lips against hers. He felt her body stiffen, but he pulled her onto the robe, his arms still around her. "Lie with me, Aissa," he said softly, his mouth by her ear.

"No, not now. Not in the daytime."

"What does it matter if it is daytime or night?"

"People will know!"

"People already know the desire I have for you."

"I would rather you beat me," Aissa said, turning away.

"Why would you say such a thing?"

"Because I have no control over this. It's as if your body controls my body. It frightens me." Aissa turned onto her side.

"It frightens me also, Aissa. I have never felt this way about any woman." He moved behind her, his hand on her waist. "I will not force you, Aissa." He nuzzled the back of her neck.

Aissa turned on her back, looking up at Shadow Hawk. "Why are you doing this?"

"Doing what?"

"Why are you tormenting me like this?"

"I did not mean to torment you."

"It was easier when I was with Teroz. At least I knew what to expect."

Shadow Hawk pulled away from Aissa. "Why must you speak of Teroz? You know I hate him."

"Teroz treated me fairly. He never hurt me."

"Have I ever hurt you?"

"Yes, you've hurt me in the worst possible way." Aissa started to get up, but Shadow Hawk held her arm.

"No, you will not leave me. You are my woman, Aissa.

Remember that."

"How can I forget it?"

"Do you wish to be given back to Teroz? I am sure he would not refuse you."

Aissa looked at him, her blue eyes questioning. "At least Teroz was willing to take me back to my own people."

"That is what Teroz says, but he was also willing to give you to me, was he not?"

Aissa lowered her head. "All right, Shadow Hawk, you win. I am your captive. I understand that I must do as you say to stay alive." Aissa took off her moccasins and stood up. She took her blouse off and unbelted her skirt, letting them drop to the floor. She stood before Shadow Hawk completely naked. "Is this what you want?"

Shadow Hawk looked up at Aissa. She stood before him defiant and angry. Her body was long and slim, her breasts full, her stomach flat, and her legs tapered. Her hair hung around her shouders like a golden cape. Shadow Hawk got to his knees and put his hands on her waist. He pulled her to kneel before him and he pressed his face to her breasts, kissing them lightly, barely brushing his lips over her nipples. He traced a fiery path down her belly to her thighs and he felt her body quiver, her mouth seeking his. He felt her breasts press against his bare chest and it enflamed him. He untied the thongs of his breechcloth until he, too, was naked. He held her to him, moving his body against hers, feeling his desire grow.

He put his hands on her face. "I will not force you, Aissa." He saw the desire in her eyes and kissed her softly, parting her lips with his tongue. "Do you want me, Aissa?"

Aissa opened her eyes. "Yes."

"Are you sure?"

"Yes, yes," she sighed, her mouth opening to his, her hands touching his chest.

Shadow Hawk lay on his back, pulling Aissa on top of him. He pushed her up until she was straddling him, her legs apart. He pressed his hands to her breasts, then let them slide downward to her hard belly. He guided himself into her and she sat astride him, moving her hips against his. Aissa closed her eyes and arched her back as she met Shadow Hawk's every thrust. He watched as she bit her lower lip, her hands clenching his hips, her body moving with his. His excitement grew as he felt hers rise and he moved faster and faster inside her until he heard her cry out. She started to fall against him but he held her up, his hands on her waist, thrusting faster and faster inside of her until he couldn't stop. His sounds of pleasure mixed with hers as he spent himself inside her, moving until he felt he couldn't move anymore. He closed his eyes, trying to catch his breath, and he felt her warm, moist body on top of him. His arms went around her, holding her to him so tightly he never wanted to let her go.

They lay together without speaking, their bodies still as one. "I would do anything for you, Aissa," Shadow Hawk murmured, kissing her cheek. And he knew then what he must do. When he came back from the hunt, he would have to let her make her own choice. He would have to let her go.

Aissa rested her hands on her crossed legs, thinking about Shadow Hawk and what they had shared that morning. She could still see his face as she sat atop him, could still feel him inside her. Her cheeks burned at the thought, but still she couldn't push it from her mind. Shadow Hawk made her feel things she didn't know women were supposed to feel.

"Aissa, are you listening to me?"

"What?"

Gitano threw down his stick. "Do you want to do this or not? Where is your mind?"

Aissa sat up straight and attempted to concentrate. "Yes, I still want to do this, Gitano."

"Then we must plan now. Shadow Hawk is gone and it would be foolish to wait any longer."

Aissa nodded. "Yes," she replied, without much conviction. It would be so hard to leave him now. They had talked for the first time in weeks and he had spoken of his hurt. She felt they were getting closer.

"So, I think you should just jump off of the cliff and splatter your body all over the rocks below. What do you think?"

"Yes, if you think so."

"Aissa!" Gitano's tone was harsh. "Have you decided against this?"

"No, Gitano, I'm sorry." As much as Aissa wanted to believe that Shadow Hawk was changing, she couldn't stay. She couldn't live the rest of her days in an Apache camp. "I want to go. I'll pay attention."

"All right. Look at the map I've drawn." Gitano picked up the stick. "This is the mountain. I will lead you down it at night. This is the canyon below. It is narrow in parts and it turns a number of ways, but if you listen to me you will not get lost. And this," Gitano ran the stick over a large piece of dirt, "is the desert. Do you remember much of it from when you came in with Teroz?"

"I remember that it was hot and it all looked the same."

"That is why you must pay attention. When you come out of the mouth of the canyon, you must head west, in the direction of the setting sun."

"But the sun won't be setting when I come into the desert."

"Do you white people know nothing of direction?" Gitano shook his head in disgust. "By the time I get you down the mountain, the sun will be rising and it will be behind you. You ride into the desert. Midday the sun will be overhead, and in the later part of the day it will be in front of you. If you cannot figure that out, you deserve to get lost."

Aissa laughed. She leaned over and kissed Gitano on the cheek. "Thank you."

Gitano looked around him. "Why did you do that?"

"It is a sign of affection with my people."

"It is a strange custom." He cleared his throat, trying to compose himself. "Now, are you sure you know which way to go?"

"Yes, I keep the sun in front of me when I'm in the desert. I do know where the sun sets, Gitano."

"That is a start," Gitano said drily.

"How long will it take me to get through the desert?"

"It depends on you and the horse."

"And Shadow Hawk."

"Yes, and Shadow Hawk. Once you are in the desert, there are very few places to hide. And even if you do find a place, Shadow Hawk will probably track you down."

"So I must get down the mountain and through the canyon as quickly as possible."

"Yes, and there's a small chance that Shadow Hawk will see you as he returns from the hunt."

"I'll take the chance."

"Then we will do it tonight. We will wait until the camp is quiet and we will meet by Ocha's lodge." Gitano looked at Aissa, his dark brown eyes serious. "I hope I do not regret helping you. If something should happen to you . . ."

"Don't," Aissa said gently, taking Gitano's hand. "I told you before, this is my decision, not yours. If something happens to me, it's my fault. Promise me something, Gitano."

"What?"

"Don't tell Shadow Hawk that you helped me."

"I cannot lie if he asks me."

"Please, tell him you knew nothing about it."

"He will never believe that you were able to find your way down the mountain alone. He knows you and I are friends. I cannot lie to him, Aissa."

"And I couldn't stand it if your friendship was destroyed because of me."

"Do not worry so. Shadow Hawk has lost his way for a time, but he will find his way back to his true spirit. He will not stay angry at me for long." Gitano puffed out his chest and grinned. "No one can stay mad at me for long."

"Thank you."

"Go now. Remember to wear leggings under your skirt to protect your legs, and bring a blanket. The nights have been cold."

Aissa stood up. She nodded. She felt as if she were deceiving Shadow Hawk. But she knew she couldn't afford to think like that any longer. She had to be strong and think about the night and day ahead of her. It would be the longest day of her life.

She went to Ocha's lodge and entered. She noticed that Paloma was sitting up with Teroz at her side. The color was back in Paloma's cheeks and some of the sadness had left her eyes.

"Hello, Ocha," she greeted the old woman.

"Hello, girl. What brings you here?"

"I wanted to see how Paloma was doing." Aissa knelt next to Paloma. "I know you and I have never really spoken, but I am glad you are well. I am sorry about your baby."

Paloma's eyes filled with tears and she lowered her head. "Thank you."

"Paloma," Aissa said gently, "I am so sorry if I am the cause of this."

"You are not the cause." Paloma wiped the tears from her face. "Why would you say such a thing?"

"If Shadow Hawk had not divorced you . . ." Aissa stopped, unsure of what to say. "He cares for you, I know that. He was very sorry that you lost the child."

"I know. He came to see me."

Aissa glanced at Teroz, then back to Paloma. "I don't understand what has happened to Shadow Hawk and I'm sorry that you were hurt."

"I am fine. Do not worry about me. I do not blame Shadow Hawk for the loss of my child. He was good to me. You are the one who looks sad."

"Yes, Aissa, I fear we should be worrying about you," Teroz said.

"I'm fine." She squeezed Paloma's hand. "Be happy. I know Teroz will take good care of you." She looked at Teroz. "Thank you for your honesty."

"I am sorry, Aissa. I truly thought that he would take you back to your people. If I had thought that he would not—"

"It doesn't matter." She shook her head and went to Ocha. "When can we talk?" She whispered.

"Teroz," Ocha lifted her hand in the air. "I think it would be good for you to take Paloma for a short walk. She needs fresh air. Perhaps even a bath."

"I would love a bath," Paloma said enthusiastically.

Teroz helped Paloma to her feet and put his arm around her as he guided her across the lodge. He looked at Aissa sharply. "I would like to talk to you later." His voice was harsh.

When they left the lodge, Ocha spoke. "I think Teroz suspects something."

"Why?"

"The sound of his voice."

"Would he do something to stop me?"

"No. If anything, he would help you."

"I don't want to get him involved. Shadow Hawk hates him enough."

"I will keep him busy with Paloma today. Go behind my baskets. There is a leather pouch and a water bag. Bring them to me."

Aissa picked up the pouch and water bag and set them in front of Ocha. Ocha rested her hands on the pouch. "I have put many things in here. You may not need them, but it is better to be prepared."

"Ocha—"

"Do not interrupt me, girl. There is jerked meat, dried mescal, sunflower seeds, walnuts, and berries. Eat a heavy meal tonight before you leave; it will carry you through until

387

tomorrow. The food I have packed should last you three or four days. There is enough water to last you three days if you do not drink too much. Do you know how to get water from the cactus if you must?"

"Yes, cut into the stalk."

"Suck the liquid from it. It will sustain you." Ocha took a pouch from around her neck. "I want you to carry this. This is my special medicine. If you have a wound, mix this with mud or water and apply it. If you feel sick, mix this with water and drink it. This will help many ailments."

"I can't take your medicine, Ocha."

"I have much more of this, girl. Do not argue with me."

Aissa took the pouch and put it around her neck, tucking it under her blouse. "I don't know how to thank you, Ocha. You've been a good friend to me. But Shadow Hawk is your grandson."

"We have talked of this before, girl. I know my grandson. He is troubled right now, but he will see the truth in what Gitano and I are doing. Do not worry for us, worry for yourself."

Aissa hugged the old woman. "I'll never forget you, Ocha. Thank you."

"Let your spirit guide you, child. It is good and it is true. It will not fail you."

Aissa kissed Ocha and walked across the lodge, tears falling down her cheeks. She glanced back at the old woman before she left the lodge and hesitated. In the glow of the firelight, she saw tears glistening on Ocha's cheeks. In that moment, she realized how much she would miss Ocha and how much she owed her.

Aissa met Gitano behind Ocha's lodge. When the camp was silent, Gitano took Aissa's hand. He led her down the rocky mountainside, avoiding all the major paths. Twice he pressed his fingers to her lips and they waited in the darkness

388

until the voices of the lookouts assured them that no one was aware of their presence.

Aissa was amazed by Gitano. He seemed to be able to see in total darkness. While she hesitated with every step, afraid she would fall, Gitano moved as if it were daylight. He seemed to know where every rock and shrub was and he moved silently, squeezing her hand if she made too much noise. By the time they reached the pasture, Aissa was out of breath and Gitano pulled her down.

"Stay low and silence your breathing. You will frighten the horses."

Aissa squatted next to Gitano, taking deep breaths and letting them out slowly. The horses grazed quietly and Aissa was eager to be gone. But Gitano sat still, holding her hand. Aissa could hear the horses moving calmly, and after a moment she realized what Gitano was doing. Instead of taking the risk of startling any of the horses, he was going to wait until the animals moved close enough to be caught without creating a commotion. Several horses grazed closer and suddenly Gitano was in a half-crouch, freeing the ropes he'd carried around his shoulder. He disappeared into the darkness. A moment later he was beside Aissa again, pressing a bridle rope into her hand. He helped her onto the horse.

"Hold the horse still until I frighten the herd into covering the sound of our leaving."

The horse stood quietly, but its neck was arched and Aissa could feel the tension in its muscles. Gitano mounted and an instant later a high-pitched snarling sound shattered the silence. All around them the horses threw up their heads and began to mill uneasily. Gitano made the sound again and the herd began to run.

"Now," he ordered Aissa and she kicked her horse into a gallop, following him.

As they rode away from the sounds of the frightened herd, Aissa's eyes adjusted to the darkness. She could not see

Gitano in front of her but she could hear the hoofbeats of his galloping horse. After a few minutes Gitano slowed, then pulled his horse back to a walk.

"Shouldn't we keep going?" Aissa whispered.

Gitano dropped back until the horses were walking side by side. "They will have the herd quieted by now. Even at this distance they would be able to hear us."

Aissa nodded. Gitano had thought of everything. Still she fought the urge to kick her horse back into a gallop. As they rode, the moon rose and Aissa was grateful. There was not much light from the pale crescent but there was enough so that she could see Gitano riding in front of her. The shadow-shapes of rocks and trees were everywhere, providing eerie company for their ride. The hollow call of an owl persisted as they rode, and Aissa even heard the brush of its wings as it flew overhead. The air was cool and she began to shiver. She unfolded the blanket that had been tied around her waist and wrapped it around herself. She readjusted the hide straps that held her food and water bag across her shoulders. The constant rhythm of the horse's walk made her tired and she closed her eyes for a minute, wondering if it really was possible for her to make it home alone.

They made it down the mountain well before sunrise and Gitano led Aissa into the canyon. The sheer rock walls rose up around her, blocking even the dim moonlight. The darkness pressed in on her and she didn't want to be left here alone. She knew she couldn't have made it without Gitano.

"We will stop for a moment so you can drink."

Aissa lifted the water bag to her mouth and swallowed. She remembered Ocha's warning and stopped with one drink. "Will you be going back now, Gitano?" She tried to keep the fear from her voice, but she knew she hadn't succeeded.

"I think I will take you through the canyon. It can be very deceiving in the darkness."

Aissa didn't argue. "I'm frightened, Gitano."

"It is just the darkness, Aissa. Think of it as your friend."

Aissa pulled the blanket closer around her shoulders. 'That's hard to do. The light shows you what you are afraid of, but in the darkness you can only imagine."

"My people fear the dark. They think that the spirits of the dead walk after the sun sets."

"But you aren't afraid of the dark? Why not?"

"My father often told us that we should respect our fear but we should never let it rule us. He would take Miho and me out on hunts at night and he would purposefully take us through the woods. There are many sounds in the woods at night, many sounds to frighten young boys. But he taught us to listen and to become familiar with every sound. The darkness is not so frightening when you know what is there."

Aissa sighed loudly. "I am going to miss you, Gitano."

"Yes, I believe I will miss you also, white woman."

Aissa smiled to herself in the darkness. "I suppose we should go on now."

"Yes, the sun will soon be rising."

Aissa followed Gitano in the darkness of the canyon. She could not see the trail. Again she had to trust him completely. She hummed a French lullaby over and over until the first rays of sunlight struck the top of the canyon walls. She kicked her horse into a trot until she was next to Gitano.

"Good morning, white woman. What is the song you were singing?"

"It's a song my mother used to sing to me when I was a little girl, when I couldn't go to sleep."

"It is pleasant."

"Yes. *Her* mother used to sing it to her. It's an old song."

"You never speak of your mother."

"She died when I was a girl. I miss her terribly sometimes."

"I hope your father is well, Aissa," Gitano said abruptly, his voice serious.

"Thank you, Gitano."

"I wish you good fortune in your life."

Aissa tried to still her fear. Gitano was saying good-bye. The time had come to face the journey alone. "I don't know how I can ever thank you, Gitano. You have been a true friend and I'll never forget you."

"We are almost out of the canyon. If you ride hard and do not get lost, you should get to your home before the sun rises again.

Aissa sat up straight and nodded her head. "I will be all right, Gitano. Go back now. I don't want anyone to know you're gone." She looked up at the sunlight that was beginning to move its way down the canyon walls. "I guess your parents will already know you're gone. They'll know what you've done."

"I am always gone at night. My parents will not question me. Go now, friend. Let your spirit guide you."

Aissa fought back tears and kicked her horse into a gallop. She rode out of the canyon, not looking back, feeling as alone as she had ever felt in her life.

Shadow Hawk lay unmoving, even though the sun was already rising. He'd had no luck hunting the day before. There was a promising stream he had found at sunset the night before. The soft mud had been full of deer tracks. He knew he should already be up and on his way, but he didn't want to move. He liked looking up at the sky. He wondered if there really was a place where his people went after they died. He could not imagine such a place—where everyone was content, where there were many animals to be hunted, where berries and fruit grew in great abundance, where streams with fresh water were everywhere. He wondered if people loved in this place.

He knew he had veered greatly from the path his father had shown him and he had not followed his true spirit. When he was troubled, he had not sought out his own medicine, the hawk. Instead, he had done things that had made him ashamed, and he had let his anger control him. He had hurt many people because of this. But Aissa had wound up suffering the most. He had punished her because he had been jealous of her and Teroz. He had not trusted her.

He sat up, crossed his legs, and closed his eyes. "I am in need of your help, Father," he said quietly. He sat unmoving, his back straight, his mind attuned to times past. He recalled in vivid detail his first buffalo hunt and how it had made him feel. He could even smell the large beasts and hear them snort and paw the ground. He recalled how his hands shook the first time he pulled back on the bow his father had made for him and how it had taken many hours of practice before the arrow found its target. Most vividly, he could remember the warm pressure of his father's arm around his shoulders when he had done something well. It was a feeling of such great satisfaction that he would never forget it.

"What is troubling you, my son?"

"You are here, Father?" Shadow Hawk asked, his eyes still closed.

"Yes, my son, I am here."

"I have been troubled of late."

"Tell me."

"I am full of anger."

"Let the anger go, my son. It will do you no good."

"I have a decision to make and it seems I am unable to make it."

"You have strayed from the path for a time but you will find your way back. Your heart is true, your spirit pure. You will make the right decision."

"I am in need of your guidance, Father."

"You are your own guide, my son. Remember, I am always with you."

"Father!" Shadow Hawk opened his eyes and looked around him. The sun was well up in the sky and Shadow

Hawk lowered his eyes to escape its dazzling brightness. A quick movement on the ground caught his eye and he turned quickly, expecting to see a squirrel or rabbit that had been deceived by his stillness. Instead he saw a shadow. It was the shadow of a hawk. He looked up but saw no hawk in the sky. He knew then: he had found his medicine again.

"Thank you, Father," he murmured. He stood up. It was time to take Aissa home.

Aissa sat on her horse, sipping from the water bag. She dragged the back of her hand across her forehead. It was hot, hotter than she had imagined it would be. It was fall, and yet the desert felt no different from summer. She looked up into the sky. Dark clouds loomed above the mountains in the distance. For an instant she imagined how good a cool rain would feel. Then she realized there would be no place for her to find shelter if a storm came.

She put the blanket over her head for protection from the sun and slung the water and food bags around her shoulder. She kicked her horse into a trot. She tried to imagine what it would be like to see her father. Maybe the house hadn't burned down. She thought about sleeping in her own bed, what if would be like to take a bath with hot water, to drink a cup of coffee with sugar and milk.

She had no idea how long she'd been riding. The sun was well overhead, so it was at least midday. She felt sore and she had been fighting off sleep since early morning. There had been times she'd actually dozed for a few minutes and then her horse's footsteps had jolted her awake.

The clouds were moving faster and she knew the storm would soon overtake her. There were some rocks a mile or so ahead, and she rode for them. She could see flashes of brilliant light in the distance. Even the air seemed different. It felt heavy and moist.

As the flashes in the distance became brighter, Aissa's

horse grew more nervous. He pulled back and forth on the reins, his head tossing impatiently. The sudden crack of thunder caused the horse to rear suddenly, and Aissa did her best to hold him. She kicked him into a gallop when his forefeet hit the ground and she held the reins tight, trying to think only of the rocks. The desert seemed to turn into night and the crashing of thunder surrounded her.

Aissa felt the first spatter of rain as she reached the rocks. She fought her frightened horse to a stop and slid off. The thunder shook the ground as Aissa tried to lead the horse into the shelter of the rocks. The horse shied backward, dragging Aissa as she struggled to hold onto the reins. Lightning flashed and a second later the ground shook again. Her horse squealed and reared. Aissa lunged to escape the animal's hooves, trying to hang onto the slick reins. The horse twisted, rolling its eyes wildly, striking out at Aissa. Aissa felt a numbing pain in her shoulder and fell. Thunder crashed. Aissa sat up slowly, watching the horse gallop away. A moment later she couldn't even see the horse through the sheets of rain.

Lightning lit up the sky. Aissa scrambled into the shelter of the rocks, looking frantically for a crevice that would protect her. She found a place between two boulders and hunkered down between them. She gripped the edges of her blanket as the wind howled through the rocks. Thunder cracked all around her, and Aissa bent over, wrapping her arms around her knees. The rain came down even harder and she began to shiver.

She huddled against the rocks. They were still warm from the sun, but she could feel them cooling and knew that she could only hope that the storm wouldn't last too long. If it lasted through the night, she would have to stay among these rocks. And if it didn't, she'd have to start walking. She was afraid to start walking. She was afraid she would never make it on foot. Unconsciously she reached under her blouse for the leather pouch Ocha had given her. She wrapped her fingers around it, praying that it would give her the strength she needed.

Shadow Hawk walked the path from the pasture. As he climbed higher, he saw a bank of gray clouds on the horizon. He had hurried back, eager to see Aissa. He entered his lodge, dropping his bedroll and his weapons. He knew immediately that something was wrong. It wasn't just that Aissa wasn't there, it was that the lodge had a different feeling to it. He left and ran through camp to Ocha's. He entered without asking permission. Teroz and Paloma were sitting side by side on a robe and they were talking. They stopped and looked up when they saw him.

"What do you want?" Teroz asked, obviously annoyed by the intrusion.

Shadow Hawk ignored Teroz and walked to Paloma. He squatted down and looked at her. "How are you, Paloma?"

"I am well, Shadow Hawk."

"I am sorry if I caused you any pain. I am sorry—"

Paloma put her hand on his mouth. "You did nothing, Shadow Hawk. You helped me when no one else would. I will not soon forget what you did for me."

"But I fear I caused you to lose your child when I divorced you and took Aissa."

Paloma looked at Teroz and smiled shyly. "It was a good thing you did, Shadow Hawk. I knew that you loved the white woman."

"Thank you, Paloma, you have been generous in your forgiveness."

"No more generous than you when you gave up the woman you loved to help me."

Shadow Hawk smiled at Paloma and then looked across her at Teroz. "You and I have not agreed on much, cousin."

"You speak the truth."

"But I feel I must thank you for taking care of Paloma. It is obvious that your affection for her runs deep."

"Yes, it does," Teroz replied without hesitation.

"I must also thank you for treating Aissa with respect. She told me that you were fair with her."

"You have no reason to thank me, Cousin. It was because of my hatred for you that I took Aissa. It was wrong, I know that now."

Shadow Hawk extended his arm to Teroz. "We may never be friends, but let us try not to be enemies."

Shadow Hawk and Teroz grasped each other's forearms. The two locked eyes for a moment, then Shadow Hawk nodded and stood up.

"Do you know where Ocha is?"

"Probably across the stream. That is her favorite place to look for plants," Paloma said.

Shadow Hawk left the lodge and walked through the trees. He could see Ocha across the stream, hitting shrubs with her walking stick, feeling everything with her fingers. He waded the stream and went to her. "Greetings, Grandmother."

Ocha didn't turn from her task at hand, which was to tear off a leaf from a sumac bush, rub it between her fingers, and hold it up to her nose. Once she was satisfied what it was, she dropped the leaf into the bag that hung across her chest. "Hello, Shadow Hawk. How was your hunt?"

"It was not fruitful, Grandmother."

"I am sorry." Ocha pulled more leaves from the bush and deposited them into the bag.

"Have you seen Aissa?"

"Today?"

"Yes, today."

"No, I have not seen Aissa today."

"I feel there is something wrong, Grandmother."

Ocha stopped and turned to Shadow Hawk. "What do you feel?"

"I think she is gone."

397

"You think she is gone just because she is not in your lodge?"

"No, I have a bad feeling."

"Tell me."

"I do not know, I cannot explain it. When I entered the lodge, I felt strongly that there was something wrong with her."

"How are you, Shadow Hawk?"

"Grandmother?" Shadow Hawk looked at Ocha questioningly.

"I asked you how you are. Did anything happen to you on your hunt?"

"Yes, Grandmother, I found my medicine again."

"That is good. Tell me, how do you feel about Aissa?"

"I intend to take her back to her people."

"Take me back across the stream, Grandson."

Shadow Hawk helped Ocha cross the stream. "Do you want to go back to your lodge?"

"No, we will talk here." Ocha reached up and ran her fingers over Shadow Hawk's face. "You have a fine face, Grandson."

"Thank you, Grandmother." Shadow Hawk looked at Ocha. He was impatient, but he knew better than to interrupt her when she was talking.

"I had a feeling about you from the first. I knew you had a pure heart. I knew no matter what happened, you would always find your true path."

"Grandmother . . ." Shadow Hawk didn't understand what Ocha was trying to say to him.

"Your feeling is true, Shadow Hawk. Aissa is gone."

"She is gone?"

"Yes."

"How did this happen? She could not possibly leave here alone."

"Gitano and I helped her to leave."

Shadow Hawk took his hand from Ocha's arm. "You and

Gitano? Why? Why would you do that?"

"Do not insult me with such a question, Grandson. You already know the answer to that." Ocha reached out for Shadow Hawk, touching his arm. "You are angry."

"I feel betrayed."

"Why should you feel betrayed? We only did what you were going to do. It was time for her to go."

"I should have been the one to take her back to her people."

"Yes, you should have been the one, Shadow Hawk. But you were not willing to do it."

"I feel strange, Grandmother, as if I am not connected to anyone."

"Gitano and I love you, Grandson. We did not help Aissa to hurt you, we helped her because she needed help. You know that in your heart."

Shadow Hawk walked along the bank, staring down at the water. He turned around and looked into the trees, thinking of the first time he and Aissa had made love there. She was so beautiful and alive. And now she was gone.

"Are you all right, Grandson?"

"Yes, Grandmother—I was just thinking."

"Are you angry with us?"

"No, I am not angry. You listened to Aissa when I did not. Did Gitano take her all the way?"

"No, he took her down the mountain and returned this morning. We did not know how you would feel. We thought it best to let you believe Aissa had left on her own."

"Gitano did not take her all the way?" Shadow Hawk looked up at the quickly darkening sky. "There is a storm approaching. She will get caught in it."

"She is strong, Grandson. She will find a way through it."

"You know what the storms are like out there, Grandmother. She will be alone and frightened. There are few places to find shelter. It is very dangerous. I knew something was wrong."

"Go to Gitano. He can tell you where he left her." Ocha reached for Shadow Hawk's hand and squeezed it tightly. "You are a good man, Shadow Hawk. Go safely. Come back to us."

Shadow Hawk bent down and kissed Ocha on the cheek. "Do not worry, Grandmother. I will be fine." Shadow Hawk ducked as he ran throught the trees and came out into the camp. He ran to Ataza's lodge, barely stopping to great his uncle. "Where is Gitano?"

"It is good to see you, too, Nephew."

"I am sorry, Uncle, but this is important."

"He is inside the lodge, sleeping."

Shadow Hawk went inside the lodge. It was still warm from the night's fire. He walked to Gitano's robe and bent down, shaking his cousin. "Wake up, Gitano. Wake up!" Gitano tried to cover his head, but Shadow Hawk pulled his hands away. "Wake up or I will drag you outside."

Gitano turned over on his back, looked at Shadow Hawk, and sat up. "You are back."

"Where did you leave Aissa?"

"What are you talking about?"

"I know you helped Aissa escape. Where did you leave her?"

"She is probably just gathering berries."

"Stop it, Gitano! I know you took her down the mountain. Ocha told me. I am not angry with you. I just want to find Aissa. Have you seen the clouds? A storm is coming. I must find her."

"What will you do when you find her?"

"I will take her back to her father."

"I must have your word, Cousin. She said she would rather die than remain a captive here."

Shadow Hawk lowered his head, nodding. "You have my word that I will take Aissa back to her father. I swear by the name of my father, Black Hawk."

Gitano stood up. "I will go with you."

400

"No, Gitano, I must do this alone."

Gitano studied Shadow Hawk for a minute and nodded his head. "I took her down the mountain and through the canyon."

"You let her cross the desert alone?"

"We all decided it was best. You were not thinking too clearly, Cousin."

"I know, I am sorry. When did you leave her?"

"It was after sunrise. She could be halfway across the desert by now."

"Possibly," Shadow Hawk said, thinking of the approaching storm. "But she will have to stop somewhere. There are not many places for shelter."

"You have always boasted to me of the Comanche's prowess on a horse. Perhaps now is the time to show how good you really are."

"Thank you, cousin. You have been a true friend to Aissa and to me."

"I expected you to cut my heart out and throw it to the crows."

Shadow Hawk grinned. "Perhaps another time, Cousin." He left the lodge, stopping to speak to Ataza. "Good-bye, Uncle."

"Goodbye, Nephew. Where are you going?"

"I am going to do something I should have done long ago." Shadow Hawk had started toward his lodge when he heard Gitano calling his name. He turned and waited for his cousin to catch up with him. "Here, you will need these." Gitano thrust a water and food bag into Shadow Hawk's arms.

"Thank you, Gitano."

"I wish you a safe journey, Cousin."

Shadow Hawk waved and ran to his lodge. He quickly put on a shirt and grabbed his bedroll. He hung the bags that Gitano had given him over his neck and shoulder and rolled an extra blanket and tied it with a leather thong. He picked up his bridle rope and headed for the pasture. He went to the paint, slipping the bridle rope over its head, and swung up.

Shadow Hawk rode down the rocky mountain path, urging the paint into a gallop when possible. The air smelled heavy with rain and he felt the first drops. He saw the lightning in the distance and heard the rumble of thunder. As soon as he reached the canyon floor, he kicked his horse into a full gallop. Shadow Hawk let the horse have his head.

The thunder was louder and the lightning illuminated the sheer rock walls, giving them an unnatural shine for an instant. In spite of the thunder and lightning, the paint continued to gallop, surefooted, forced on by Shadow Hawk's will. By the time Shadow Hawk reached the mouth of the canyon, the sky was black with clouds from horizon to horizon. He slowed to look for Aissa's tracks, but the rain had alrady erased them. The lightning flashed over and over. It seemed as if the desert had come alive and all the plants and rocks were part of a bizarre dance.

Shadow Hawk could hear his paint's labored breathing and he pulled up, slowing the animal down. Shadow Hawk squinted into the rain. If Gitano had left Aissa at the canyon mouth at sunrise, she would have ridden hard at first, taking advantage of the coolness of the morning. Gitano would have made sure she set out in the right direction. The storm had come on suddenly, so for most of the day she had the sun to guide her. Shadow Hawk urged the paint back into a canter. If Aissa had made good time, she should have been able to see one of the rock outcroppings by the time the storm caught her.

Shadow Hawk rode as hard as he could, trusting the paint to pick his way through then heavy sand. He kept his eyes on the horizon. Every time the lightning flashed, he looked for the first spine of jagged rocks jutting up from the desert floor. When he got closer, he rode along the rocks, shouting into the wind. There was no answer. He had almost given up when the lightning lit the sky and he saw a flash of color among the gray rocks. He reined the paint in so abruptly that it reared, and Shadow Hawk urged him forward. When he could ride no farther, he slipped off and tied the paint's bridle rope to the tough weathered trunk of an old yucca. He picked up his gear, patted the horse's neck reassuringly, and ran.

The next flash of lightning showed him the way and he climbed over the rocks, relief and fear washing through him. Where was her horse? Had she been hurt? As he slid down the rocks to reach her, he cried out her name.

Chapter 18

Aissa's shoulder was aching. She was wet and cold, but she felt the warmth of Shadow Hawk's body behind her and felt comforted. She was so glad that he had found her. She didn't know if he would take her back to the camp, but right now she didn't care. Night had come quickly and with it the chilling cold of the desert now that the storm had passed.

She sat up, her teeth chattering, moving away from the welcome warmth of Shadow Hawk's body. "Will you be taking me back to camp?" she asked without even turning.

"We can talk about that later. Now we should think about a fire."

"How can we build a fire? Everything is wet."

Shadow Hawk stood up and climbed down the rocks in the darkness. Shadow Hawk heard his horse nicker at his approach, then Shadow Hawk's footsteps, moving away from her. She stood up and rubbed her hands together and then rubbed her legs. She stretched and tried to move around to get her body warm, but her wet clothes clung to her and the chill air made her shiver. She listened for Shadow Hawk and finally heard him coming back up the rocks. His arms were full of twisted branches. He dropped the wood and took out his knife. He began to dig a shallow hole and pushed the wet topsoil to the side. Then he reached into one of the bags around his neck.

Aissa watched intently as Shadow Hawk placed a flattened piece of wood in the firepit he had dug and then positioned a long, thin stick perpendicular to the bottom piece. He then reached into his bag again and sprinkled something that looked like dried leaves onto the bottom piece of wood. Shadow Hawk put the palms of his hands around the upright stick and began quickly rolling it back and forth between his palms. Aissa crouched down to watch. Soon a thin trail of smoke rose from the dried leaves, and then, as Shadow Hawk gently blew at it, a small flame. Shadow Hawk put in more leaves and broken twigs, until a small fire began to burn. He took out the fire sticks and laid them aside, then added pieces of wood to the growing blaze. Before long, a warm fire was burning.

Aissa looked across at Shadow Hawk and smiled. "I've never seen your people do that. The lodge fires are always kept burning."

Shadow Hawk held the sticks in his hand. "I was taught this by my father. These are the fire sticks that he made for me. This one," he held the bottom stick, "is made of cottonwood and this one," he held out the twirling stick, "is made of greasewood. Many of the Apache use the soapweed for the twirling stick, but I do not wish to give up the sticks my father made for me." He packed them away in his bag and held his hands over the fire.

"What was that you sprinkled over the sticks?"

"They are white sage leaves. They hold the spark." He added more wood to the fire. "You are shivering. You should take off your clothes."

"I don't have anything else to put on."

"Wrap this around yourself." He handed Aissa the rolled blanket. "It isn't too wet."

"What about you?"

"I will take off my shirt and leggings." Shadow Hawk stood up and pulled his shirt up over his head and laid it on one of the rocks. Aissa stared at him, transfixed by his body in the glow of the fire. He was incredible. His body was long and lean and his color was a beautiful brown. She continued to watch as he took off his leggings and stood only in his breechcloth, the muscles in his thighs flexing as he squatted down next to the fire. "You should get your clothes off soon. Your body is already cold."

"Yes," Aissa responded, quickly looking away from him. With her back to him, she began taking off her clothes.

"There is no need. I will look away."

Aissa turned around. Shadow Hawk had already moved away from the fire, his back to her. Quickly she stripped and wrapped the dry blanket around her, leaving her arms free. She draped her clothes over the rocks and walked over to Shadow Hawk. "I'm finished."

He turned around. "Come get warm." He gently took her arm and led her to a spot by the fire. "Wait, the ground is still wet." He picked up a rock and moved it close. "Sit." Aissa sat down and watched as Shadow Hawk brought another rock and placed it next to hers. He stretched his hands out toward the flames. "It feels good."

"Yes, it does. Thank you."

"You could have died out here alone."

Aissa tensed up, knowing where the conversation was going to lead. "I know."

"Why did you do it?"

"I had to go home." Aissa couldn't bear to look at him. His voice was not full of anger, as she had expected. He sounded almost sad.

"You would have perferred death to staying with me?"

"I didn't want to die, I just wanted to go home and find out about my father."

"And what of Gitano and Ocha?"

"I'm sorry, I didn't mean to involve them. But I knew I couldn't get down the mountain without their help."

"They are my people, Aissa."

"I know that." Aissa looked at Shadow Hawk. "They have not turned against you, Shadow Hawk. They love you. They only wanted to help me."

"But they did so behind my back."

"Yes, and I will always be grateful to them that they did," she replied angrily, pulling the blanket up around her shoulders.

"You could be punished severely for this, you know. I could even trade you to another tribe."

"Do what you will, I don't care anymore."

"If you had gotten back to your home, what would you have done?"

"Done?" I would've been with my father, if he's alive. I would've worked around the ranch and maybe tried to teach again."

"That is all?"

"Yes, that's all."

"What about love?"

"What about love?" Her voice was indignant.

"Would there not be room in your life for love?"

"I don't believe in love anymore. It doesn't exist between men and women, not really. Men use women as possessions to make them feel better, and they use their bodies for whatever purpose serves them."

"And what of women? Do they not use men for the same purposes?"

"No, I don't think so."

"Are there not women who marry rich men to make them feel important? Are there not women who use men to fulfill the needs and desires of their bodies?"

Aissa refused to look at Shadow Hawk. "I don't know."

"I think you do."

"I don't want to talk about this. It doesn't matter anyway. You won't take me back."

"What should I do with you, Aissa?" Shadow Hawk reached out and lifted a strand of Aissa's hair.

Aissa shrugged away. "I don't care."

"What do you want me to do?"

Aissa looked at Shadow Hawk, her eyes guarded. "I want you to take me home."

"That is what you truly want?"

"Yes."

"Then that is what I will do. Tomorrow, after the sun rises, I will take you home."

Aissa couldn't believe it. "You mean it? You'll really take me home?"

"Yes, Aissa, I am going to take you home. You should rest now. You are tired."

"What about you? You can't sleep like that. You'll freeze to death."

"I will not freeze to death. I will sit by the fire."

"You can share the blanket with me."

"No." Shadow Hawk continued to stare into the fire. "I do not think it is a good idea for us to share a blanket."

Aissa nodded. She stood up and looked around her. The ground was still wet and there was no place for her to lay down. Finally, she walked back to the rock by the fire and sat. "I'm not that tired."

Shadow Hawk smiled slightly. He stood up, took the blanket that he had hung close to the fire, and put it on the ground. "Sit here. The blanket is not too wet and you are close enough to the fire to stay warm."

"Thank you." Aissa sat down on the blanket and leaned against the rock behind her, stretching her bare legs out toward the fire. She closed her eyes and tried to sleep, but she couldn't. She looked at Shadow Hawk. He was still sitting by the fire, his body reflecting the flames. "Shadow Hawk."

He turned toward her. "Yes."

"Please, sit with me."

"Aissa . . ."

"Please."

Shadow Hawk walked to Aissa, sitting next to her. He took one side of the dry blanket and pulled it around himself. "This will not work, Aissa. We cannot both fit."

"Yes we can." Aissa sat on Shadow Hawk's lap and eased herself between his legs. She leaned back against his chest. "Now the blanket will fit."

Shadow Hawk wrapped the blanket around them both, trying to avoid touching her. He felt Aissa's bare skin against his chest and he felt her warmth. Her hands brought his arms around her waist and she snuggled back against him. He would be taking her back to her father tomorrow and he would never see her again. After hating and resisting him for so long, now she seemed to want him again. Why had it taken him so long to realize that she hated him because of the way he treated her and that forcing her would only increase that hatred? He didn't want to be this close to her again only to let her go. But he had no choice. He had promised her he would take her home, and this time he wouldn't break his promise.

Aissa couldn't contain her excitement as they neared the ranch. She held onto Shadow Hawk's waist and leaned around him, trying to see the ranchhouse. But as they topped the rise, her excitement quickly turned to fear. She couldn't see the house at all.

"Hurry, please," she implored Shadow Hawk.

Shadow Hawk kicked the horse into a gallop. But as they got closer, she could see that the house was gone. There was nothing left but charred beams and the ruins of the fireplace.

"No," Aissa said sadly, slipping from the horse when

Shadow Hawk reined in. She stared, tears in her eyes. Nothing was left, it was all gone. "I can't believe it."

"Did Teroz do this?" Shadow Hawk asked from behind her.

"I don't know." She looked around. "What about my father?" Aissa started forward, but Shadow Hawk pulled her back.

"I will search."

Aissa watched as Shadow Hawk walked carefully among the rubble. He bent down, running his fingers through the remains. He took his time, examining each room, moving things around with a stick, picking up different items and looking at them closely. When Aissa could no longer bear to watch him, she turned away and looked out toward the mountains, trying to still the hammering of her heart. Finally, she heard Shadow Hawk's footsteps behind her.

"Your father is not here."

"What do you mean?"

"Your father did not die here, Aissa. There are no bones in any of the rooms."

"You mean he might still be alive?"

"It is possible. We should look around the ranch."

"The barn." Hope flared in Aissa's heart. Maybe he was living in the barn and had just left for the day. Aissa ran to open the big double doors. The smell of rotting hay and the dank, airless smell told her even before she looked inside that her father was not there. Even so, she went inside, calling his name, searching. Shadow Hawk climbed the ladder to the loft and came back down shaking his head. He pulled her back outside. Aissa turned in a slow circle, desperate to find some sign of her father. Then she saw her garden, and started running.

"Shadow Hawk!"

"What is it?"

"Look." Aissa pointed to the hoofprints that crisscrossed

her now dead garden. The trellis had been completely destroyed and plants had been pulled out by the roots and thrown on the ground to die. Her primrose lay in a brittle tangle of brown leaves.

Shadow Hawk squatted down, examining each blurred print. He stood up and went out of the garden, walking around the remains of the house. When he came back he was carrying two broken lanterns. "I think I know what happened."

"What?"

"Many riders came from that direction," he pointed to the east. "They broke these against the back of the house and set it on fire." Shadow Hawk looked up at her. "They were not Indians, Aissa. Once the fire was started, they rode through the garden to the front of the house and threw more lanterns. One rider rode back and forth through here many times."

"Grimes," Aissa said the name quickly. "What about my father? Do you see any footprints that lead away from here?"

"There are many footprints. It is impossible to tell which are your father's unless I know his boots."

"But if there were solitary prints leading away from the house, those would probably be his, wouldn't they?"

Shadow Hawk nodded solemnly. "I will look."

Aissa walked back to the garden and pulled the broken trellis away. She stood in the now barren place that had been her mother's garden and a sadness welled up inside her. "Where are you, Father?" She said softly, beginning to cry.

"Aissa."

Aissa turned around and looked at Shadow Hawk. "What if he's dead? What if my father's dead?"

Shadow Hawk took Aissa into his arms, stroking her hair. "Gerard is a strong man. Perhaps he is with friends somewhere."

"But where? Aissa buried her face in Shadow Hawk's chest, crying uncontrollably.

Shadow Hawk picked Aissa up and carried her to the shade of the barn. He set her down on the soft grass. "You should sleep."

"I don't want to sleep." Aissa tried to get up, but Shadow Hawk held onto her arm.

"Stay here, Aissa. Rest your body and your mind. You have had a shock." Shadow Hawk lay down on his back next to her, pulling her close to him.

Aissa didn't fight anymore. She rested her head on Shadow Hawk's chest, feeling more tired than she realized. She couldn't believe that she was home. Home. But there was no home, and her father was nowhere to be found. She started to move, but Shadow Hawk held her close, stroking her hair. She closed her eyes. It felt good to be here, on her own land, and it felt good be in Shadow Hawk's arms. He gave her strength and comfort, and she wondered what she would do when Shadow Hawk was gone. What would she do without him?

Aissa woke up suddenly. She was alone. Shadow Hawk wasn't beside her. She got up and ran outside. Shadow Hawk and the paint were gone. Why had he gone without saying good-bye? She tried to calm herself.

She walked back to the house, or what was left of the house, and began to sift through the rubble. In what had been the kitchen there wasn't much left but burnt wood, melted tin cans, and some of the pots and pans. The fireplace stood with the iron soup caldron still hanging from the pot-hook. She waded through the burnt beams to her room and tears filled her eyes. The brass bed frame that her father had bought for her, sent all the way from Missouri, was darkened but still standing, a reminder of how much he had loved her. She wiped her face and stepped through the windblown ashes to her father's room. There was nothing left. His dresser was gone except for the blackened brass door pulls. The barrel of her father's shotgun lay in the corner where he had kept it next to the window. Aissa felt almost sick for a moment. If Ben had gotten out of the house, he would have taken his gun. She shook her head, letting herself cry. He was probably dead, and she was just going to have to accept it.

Aissa turned, wanting more than anything to be away from the ruins that had been her home. Then a sudden thought stopped her. She kicked away the ashes of what had been her father's bed, and searching with her fingers, looked for the seam in the charred floor planks. When she found it, she ran her fingers along it until she felt the hinges of a small trapdoor. She stood quickly and went into the kitchen. She sifted ashes with her fingers until she found the broken blade of a burnt knife. She used the blade to force the trapdoor open, reached inside, and took out a small metal box. She carried it to the barn and sat down on the grass.

For a few moments, she stared at the box, holding it tightly in her hands. From the time she was a little girl, her father had told her if anything happened to him, she was to open it. It had been years since he had said it and a long time since she had even thought about it. Her fingers trembling, Aissa worked the metal catch and opened the box. On top there was an envelope. She laid it aside carefully and looked through the rest of the box. There was a small leather pouch. It felt heavy. She turned the pouch upside down and emptied the contents into her palm, staring at five large gold nuggets. "My God," she murmured, quickly putting the nuggets back into the bag. Where had her father gotten gold, she wondered? She picked up a smaller box and opened it. Inside was her mother's locket, the one she had given to Shadow Hawk. She slipped it over her neck and pressed it against her chest, closing her eyes for a moment. She smiled slightly, looking down at the box on her lap. It was just like her father to make this like a treasure hunt. She picked up a rectangular cloth packet at the bottom of the box and unwrapped it. She gasped as she held a large stack of bills in her hands. Her father had managed to put away this much money? The deed to the land was also there. She put everything back into the box and picked up the envelope. Holding her breath, she opened it and unfolded the pieces of paper that were inside.

Dear Aissa,
First of all, the money I have left you wasn't stolen. I've saved it over the years for you. Why do you think I never wanted to fix up this place? There's ten thousand dollars, enough to give you a new start anywhere. The gold nuggets should be worth quite a bit, but don't have them appraised here. Go to a large city where you'll get the best price.

If you need help, which you probably will if I'm gone, go to Flora Simms. You know Flora. She's a good woman. She'll help you with anything. Even though she and I haven't been together in years, we still keep in touch. She knows you're to go to her if you need help. And you can always trust Joe.

Another important matter: Ray Grimes. When he married you, I should've killed the son-of-a-bitch, but I was afraid for you. Now that you're alone, he'll come after you. If I'm dead, chances are, he's the one who did it. There's only one way to get Grimes, and it's not through killing. I mean it, Aissa. Don't you dare try to avenge my death, or I'll come back to haunt you."

Aissa smiled in spite of her tears. She continued reading.

You're going to rob a bank.

"What?" Aissa said loudly. "Are you crazy, Father?"

Now, I know you think I'm crazy but hear me out.

Ray has over $100,000 in that bank—all his savings. Leave a note on the counter. Say that Ray was planning to take over the bank. In fact, he wanted title to every bit of property around here. Next, get a message to the newspaper, telling of the things Ray Grimes had done. Eathan is an honest man, and I think he'll print it. Then spread the rumor that Ray killed me and sold you to the Apache. You have to make sure people get so angry they don't listen to Ray Grimes anymore.

Grimes can't know you're alive, at least not yet, so make sure you're not seen. Have Flora help you. She can spread a rumor faster than flies go to honey. Then you go for Grimes's heart. Now this part will be hard, but you have to do it, Aissa. I know for a fact that Ray wasn't capable of making love to women, so he'd beat them up. He hurt quite a few of them in his time and then bought their silence. He also forced a few of them to become prostitutes down in Mexico. It's true, Aissa. It was never talked about because Ray bought their families off. I'm leaving a list of the names if you need proof.

Aissa stopped reading. "You bastard," she seethed, thinking of Ray. It didn't surprise her at all that Ray had done something like that—he had almost done it to her.

If you think I'm lying, Aissa I'm not. You know me better than that. And if you're having second thoughts, don't. Remember what Grimes did to you. Remember what you were like when Shadow Hawk brought you back here. Grimes would've killed you, Aissa. Think of all the people he's either forced out or burned out. He doesn't deserve what he had. He deserves to suffer in the only places he can, his pride and his pocketbook. Now, when he comes to you, and he will eventually figure out that you're the person who's doing all this, you be prepared. You make sure you meet him in a safe place. Bring Joe if you have to. Make sure you're armed. If you have to use a gun, don't hesitate. He won't. Tell him you want him gone or you'll take him to the Apache. In fact, tell him the Apache are watching him. Tell him if he doesn't leave, you'll make sure they burn down his ranch, steal all his livestock, and torture him to death. Tell him to leave with the clothes he has on his back and nothing more. Then divide up his land. Give back the ranches that were stolen if you can, and give the others money.

I wish I was there to see it happen, but at least I know if you're reading this you're well. Remember this, Aissa: I love you. You are a wonderful daughter. Your mother and I were very proud of you. Live your life. Do what makes you happy. Find love. Good-bye, chérie.

Your father, Ben Gerard

Aissa pressed the letter to her bosom, crying softly. She would miss him more than she thought possible, especially now that she was back here, at the ranch. She folded the letter and put it back into the envelope. She took out some money, stuck it in her moccasin, put the letter back, and closed the box. She went back to the house, replaced the box under the trapdoor, and covered it with ashes.

She heard hoofbeats. Whoever it was was riding fast. Shadow Hawk was coming back—or maybe it was Grimes. She ran to the barn and climbed up into the loft. She stepped quietly backward when she heard someone enter.

"Aissa?"

Aissa let out a sigh of relief at the sound of Shadow Hawk's voice. She walked to the edge of the loft. "I'm here." She climbed down the ladder. "I thought you'd gone."

"I would not leave unless I was sure you were safe. We

needed water. I went to the pond to refill our bags." He handed Aissa a water bag. "I searched the area and could find no bootprints leading from the house. But there are many different sets of hoofprints coming from the east, from Grimes's ranch."

"He's been here since the fire?"

"Yes, some of the prints are four, maybe five days old."

"Why would he come back here?"

"To see if you have come back."

"He probably thinks I'm dead. There must be another reason."

"Maybe he is looking for something. Perhaps that is the reason he burnt down the house."

Aissa walked out of the barn and into the daylight. She wondered if Ray knew of her father's list and whether that was why he had burned down the house. A sly smile came to her lips. Suddenly she relished what she had to do.

"What is it?"

"Nothing." She looked at Shadow Hawk. "I have many things to do. I have to go into town."

"I will go with you."

"No, you've done your duty, Shadow Hawk. Now you can finally be free of me." She hesitated, looking into his dark blue eyes, wondering how she would ever find a love like his. "It's time for you to go back to your own people. I don't fit in your world and you would never fit in mine."

"You want me to go?"

"Yes, I think it's best. We have no future together."

"And what will you do about this?" He pointed to the ruins of the house.

"I have something in mind."

"That is what worries me. I want to help you if I can."

"I have to do this alone."

"How do you know you can do it alone?"

"I have faced worse things and survived them." Her eyes softened. "You can't help me, Shadow Hawk. I have to ride

417

into town. Don't you think someone would notice you? You're different from my people just as I'm different from yours. Do you know how hard I tried to fit into the Apache camp? But I never did, that's the way it is with you. Even though you have white blood in you, you could never pass for a white man. Thank you for wanting to help me, but you have to go. Please." Aissa didn't realize how desperate she sounded until she stopped. She didn't understand why until she realized she would probably never see Shadow Hawk again. In spite of her resolve, she began to cry. Shadow Hawk put his arms around her.

"Are you sure this is what you want?"

"Yes, this is the way it has to be." She nuzzled her face in his chest.

"I will always be with you, Aissa. Remember that." He lifted her chin and gently touched his mouth to hers, caressing it for a moment.

Aissa held onto Shadow Hawk for as long as she could and then she let go. She watched him as he took the water and food bags from the horses and handed them to her. She shook her head. "I can't take these. You'll need them."

"I will be fine. Be safe, Aissa." He touched his hand to his heart and then to hers.

Aissa couldn't stem the flow of tears. She watched Shadow Hawk as he swung up onto his horse and rode off, stopping only once to turn and look back at her. She put her hand over her trembling lips. "Good-bye, my love."

Aissa waited until sundown and began walking the two miles into town. She would have to get a horse, some men's clothes, guns and ammunition, and supplies. Most important, she would have to sneak into Flora Simms's house without anyone seeing her.

She was surprised by how easy the walk was. She'd worked hard in the Apache camp for months, tanning hides, digging roots, lugging water up and down hills. The work had served her well. She didn't feel at all tired.

Flora lived in a neat white house on the edge of town. Lights were on; Flora was home. The front of the house faced the road that led into town, the back was bordered by a grove of cottonwoods. It would be easy to make her way through the grove and up to the house, but she didn't want to frighten Flora. Flora was renowned for her markmanship and Aissa didn't dare do anything that might scare her, but if she went to the front of the house, she risked being seen by someone who was going into or leaving town. She sat down in the trees closest to the house and waited. A loud growl from her stomach reminded her she hadn't eaten a full meal in a day.

"I want a hot bath, some food, and a cup of tea," she said to herself, watching the road and Flora's house. She decided not to wait. She walked up to the back of the house and slowly inched her way to the front. The lamps in front were lit and were glowing brightly. Anyone from the road could easily see her and recognize her. Aissa quickly pulled her hair back, twirled it around in a coil, and tucked it underneath for a makeshift bun. She reached down and ripped part of the hem of her skirt and put it over her head, tying it underneath her chin. then she stepped over the small picket fence and walked up the stairs to the porch. She knocked on the door.

"Come on, Flora," she muttered, nervously looking around. She knocked on the door again. Finally, she heard footsteps.

"Who is it?" Flora asked loudly through the closed door.

"Ben Gerard sent me," Aissa said in a deep voice. "Please, Flora, open the door." Aissa crouched down slightly and the door opened. Flora grasped Aissa's arm firmly and pulled her inside the house, slamming the door behind them.

"Is that you, Aissa?"

Aissa stood up tall, taking the scarf from her head. "Hello, Flora."

"It is you. Good Lord, child, I thought I'd never see you again." Flora hugged Aissa, patting her back. "Come away from those windows and into the kitchen. You look as if you haven't had a good meal in months."

"I haven't."

"Come on, then."

Aissa followed Flora into the kitchen. It was a separate room, unlike the one at the ranch, and it was filled with Flora's own touches. There was a large black stove to one side, and opposite it was a large cupboard, floor to ceiling, with a wide shelf for cutting and preparing food. The shelves of the cupboard were generously stocked with jars of food and the bottom was filled with pans and bowls. A square wood table with four chairs was in the middle of the room, and on the table was a china sugar and creamer set. Different sayings in needlepoint hung on the walls, and Aissa was particularly taken with one of them: *You kin wash your hands but not your conscience.*

"Tea?" Flora asked.

"I'd love some. This is a nice room, Flora."

"Yes, I like it myself. I suppose someday I'll have to put a door on it. It's rather dangerous, you know, in case of a fire." Flora sliced some ham and put it on a plate along with some bread and cheese. "It's not great, but it's filling."

"This is wonderful," Aissa replied, piling meat and cheese on a slice of bread.

"Don't suppose you'd like a bath?"

"Lord, I'd love one."

"Well, I have a tub right over here." Flora pulled the round tin tub from the side of the cupboard. "I can start filling it up with hot water right now."

"Thank you. I've been dreaming of a warm bath for a long time." Aissa took a second piece of bread and began piling meat on it. By the time she was done, Flora had brought her a cup of tea and a slice of pie.

"I couldn't possibly, Flora," Aissa protested.

"Of course you could. It's apple. Now eat it."

Aissa sipped at the tea and took a bite of the pie. "This is wonderful. I never thought I'd eat pie again."

Flora poured water into the tub, refilling the pot from the pump next to the cupboard. Then she put the pot on to boil. "Apple is your father's favorite."

Aissa stopped, setting down the fork. She looked up at Flora. She was probably in her mid-thirties, well dressed, trim, with a beautiful head of red hair. She had soft blue eyes and a kind smile. When Aissa had first heard years ago that her father was seeing Flora, she had gotten angry and resentful. But as she grew older and realized that her father needed someone, she came to accept it. Even when her father told her he had broken it off with Flora, Aissa never believed him. She knew the two of them were still close. "You loved my father, didn't you, Flora?"

Flora looked up from the stove. She wiped her hands on the apron of her skirt and walked over to the table and sat down. "Yes, I loved him. Still do."

"It must be hard for you."

"Listen to me, Aissa."

"No, you don't have to explain anything to me. I understand that my father needed someone after my mother died. I don't blame you, Flora."

"Aissa, listen to me." Flora's voice was stern. "Ben is still alive," she said in barely a whisper.

"What?" Aissa stared at Flora, waiting for the woman to say it was some kind of cruel joke, but her face never changed. "You're not kidding."

"No, I'm not. Your father is alive."

"Where is he?"

"He's on my ranch in Oak Creek. It's about a hundred

421

miles northeast of here. No one knows about it."

"What's he doing there?"

Flora kept her voice low. "After the fire, he managed to make it here. He was pretty badly burned on his arms and legs. I did the best I could for him, but I didn't want to have Doc look at him. He's in Grimes's pocket, just like everyone else in this town. So Joe and I took him to my ranch." She reached out and clutched Aissa's hand.

Aissa smiled, tears filling her eyes. "Thank you, Flora. You did a wonderful thing."

"I love your father, Aissa. I figured he'd be in too much danger around here. We communicate through my foreman so no one knows your father is writing me. And Joe loves your father. He'd die before he'd say anything."

"What about the fire? Did father see who did it?"

"Of course he did. It was Grimes and his men. They actually sat on their horses waiting for him to stumble out of the house so they could shoot him. Instead, he went out the bedroom window and crawled into the trees. I guess Grimes thought he was dead. Ben stayed there until they rode away, then came to me."

"Why would Ray do it? He didn't have anything to gain by burning out my father."

"He had everything to gain, Aissa. He's always hated your father for one reason—Ben is honest. He could never be bought. That frightened Ray, that and the fact that people were starting to listen to Ben. And your father did a lot more talking once he figured you were dead. He didn't have anyone's safety to worry about but his own. With Ben gone, Ray could do anything he wanted."

"I can't believe it. I can't believe he'd do such a low-down thing."

"Nothing surprises me when it comes to Ray Grimes. There's something else, too. Ben thinks Ray will try to gain title of your land if he can convince the claim office that you

422

and your father are both dead."

Aissa shook her head. "What about Joe? Did he hurt Joe?"

"No, Joe played it real stupid. He just turned in his badge and started helping out at the stables. Ray put one of his own men in as sheriff. The town's gone half-crazy. But it won't last long."

"No, it won't, Aissa mused. "I need your help. Flora."

"Anything."

"First, get word to my father that I'm back and I'm well. Tell him that I read his letter and I'm going to follow his directions. He'll understand. Next, I need clothes, men's clothes—boots, pants, jacket, hat, gun and holster, and a rifle. And don't forget ammunition. And I'm going to need to talk to Joe."

"That shouldn't be a problem. I have him to dinner sometimes. I'll invite him for tomorrow night."

"Good. Does Walter Dickson still work late at the bank one night a week?"

"Yes, on Thursdays."

"You know him, don't you?"

"Walter?" Flora smiled. "He's been sweet on me ever since we were children."

"Good, that'll help. Listen to me, Flora." Aissa leaned forward, her eyes serious. "I'm going to rob the bank. I may need you to get me in there. Walter will trust you. Can you do that?"

"Is your plan going to ruin Ray Grimes?"

"I hope so. It's Father's plan."

"I'll do it. I said Walter was sweet on me, I didn't say I was sweet on him." Flora got up and dumped one more pot of hot water into the tub. Then she added several pots of cold water. "Why don't you take your bath now? We can talk more later. Go ahead and take your clothes off. I'll get some soap and a towel."

Aissa stood up, stripping off her buckskin skirt, her blue blouse and sash, and her leggings and moccasins. She took off her locket and put it on the table. She stepped gingerly into the hot water and then eased herself down into it. She barely fit in the small tub, but still it felt good. She leaned her head against the rim and closed her eyes.

"Here you go." Flora handed Aissa a bar of soap and set the towel on the floor. "You just take your time and enjoy your bath." She gathered up Aissa's clothes.

Aissa sat up. "My father and I owe you a lot, Flora."

"Nonsense. Your father has given me a lot of happiness over the years, and now you're bringing excitement to my life." She shook her head in disbelief. "Robbing the bank— have you thought how you're going to do it?"

"If you can get me in there, I'll have to threaten poor Walter Dickson until he opens the safe."

"He's a very dedicated man, Aissa. He might not do it. Besides, how are you going to sound like a man?"

"I don't know. I haven't figured it all out yet. I'm hoping Joe will help me. If we can get in there and get the money, we'll make sure old Walter understands that all we want is Ray Grimes's savings and no one else's."

"And what if I can't get you in?"

"Then we break in and blow the safe."

"Just like that?"

"No, Flora, not just like that. I'll have to learn how to use dynamite." Aissa leaned forward in the tub, resting her chin on the edge. "I suppose I could talk to Myron Salsbury. He worked on the railroad back east laying track. He'd know how to use it."

"You're not talking to anyone, young lady. No one is supposed to know you're here, remember?"

"Then you or Joe can talk to him. Somehow I have to get into that safe, Flora."

"Don't worry. I'll get you in there. I'll just bake one of my apple pies, put on one of my prettiest dresses, and put on lots of that French perfume, and old Walter won't know what to do with himself."

Aissa laughed. "Is that how you won over my father? With your apple pies?"

The smile quickly faded from Flora's face and she sat down. "Your father and I have been friends for years, even when he was married to your mother. And it's not what you might be thinking, Aissa, we were just friends. He helped me after my husband died, and when I still owned the saloon, he always threw out the drunks for me. I suppose after your mother died we just naturally sought each other out because we were both so lonely. Ben Gerard is one of the finest men I've ever known."

"Yes, he is," Aissa agreed. "Why don't you two get married, Flora?"

"Aissa!" Flora said in a shocked tone. "I'm an ex-saloon owner. Men like your father don't marry women like me."

"Why not?"

"Because they just don't that's all."

"Do you love my father, Flora?"

"Aissa . . ."

"Do you?"

"Yes, I love your father."

"And does he love you?"

"Oh, I don't know."

"I'm not a little girl, Flora, My father still seems to think I'm ten years old. I'm a grown woman, in case you haven't noticed, and I know about men and women. Does my father love you?"

Flora smiled slightly and a light blush came over her face. "Yes, I do believe he does."

"Good. When this mess is all over, I think you two should get married." Aissa put up her hands. "I don't want to hear any more about it."

Flora stood up and went to the tub, leaning over to kiss Aissa on the cheek. "You are a dear thing, you know that?" She stood up, straightening her skirt. "You'll stay here, of course."

"I don't think that's a good idea. I can't move around freely here."

"But where will you stay?"

"I'll stay in our barn. It's perfectly safe."

"You can't stay out there at night by yourself. It's dangerous."

Aissa laughed loudly. "After living with the Apache, my barn will seem like the finest hotel in Europe. I'll make sure I have some weapons. Besides, I'll keep in touch with you everyday. Can you get me a horse?"

"I'm sure Joe can. Where do you want him to put it?"

"He can tie it out in the woods behind your house. That way I can come and go without anyone seeing me. And if someone does see me, I'll be dressed as a man."

"You'll have to stay here tonight. I won't be able to get the clothes until tomorrow."

"A bed sounds awfully good. I'll stay the night."

"Good. I'll go upstairs and make up a bed for you and get you something to wear."

"Thank you, Flora." Aissa leaned back again, resting her head and closing her eyes. She couldn't wait until it was all over, until Ray Grimes was gone out of her life and everyone's life for good.

Chapter 19

Shadow Hawk hunched behind the woodpile, watching the men who walked back and forth. He'd seen Ray Grimes only once, when he rode in and got off his horse. He heard him yelling at a couple of men and then he stomped into the house. Shadow Hawk waited patiently, watching, observing, taking in every aspect of life on Grimes's ranch.

After sunset, Shadow Hawk could hear the rowdy voices of the cowboys in the bunkhouse. From what he had seen and from what Aissa had told him, it wouldn't be long until most of the men were drunk.

Shadow Hawk waited until there was no movement in the yard. As the moon rose higher in the sky, Shadow Hawk looked up at its bright light. He could hear the yipping of a pack of coyotes and the hunting call of an owl from a nearby tree. He waited until he didn't hear the cowboys' voices anymore. Then he stood up and carefully approached the back of the bunkhouse, slowly working his way around to the front. He pressed himself against the building and leaned around far enough to see around the corner. The dogs were asleep in the yard. Shadow Hawk lifted himself over the side railing onto the porch. The door to the bunkhouse was open and he could hear a variety of loud snores. When he entered the room, the smell of alcohol and stale breath assaulted his senses. He waited for a few minutes until his eyes adjusted to the darkness. Moving silently, he walked to the first bunk and picked up a boot and looked at it. It was half his foot size. He checked the man's clothes, holding them up, and they were too small. He went to the next bunk and picked up a boot—still too small. Same with the clothes. He went from bunk to bunk, looking for a boot that might fit his foot or clothes that might fit him. He was convinced that every white man in the room was no bigger than a child. When he got to the last bunk he picked up a boot and saw that it was bigger than the others and so were the clothes. He held the boots and clothes against him and started for the door when he stopped. He still needed a gun and holster. He went back and lifted the man's holster from the foot of the bed. He took another gun and holster from the next bunk and headed for the door. He stepped out and stood motionless on the porch until he was sure the dogs were still asleep. He stepped over the side railing and ran back to the woodpile. He sat for a minute, thinking. He needed a saddle, but his horse was not saddle broken and it would take too long to break him in. He could take one of Grimes's horses, but he knew that the white man's horses carried brands. What other choice did he have?

He decided it was an unnecessary risk to try to steal a horse. He put everything in the shirt, tied it in a bundle, and put the holster over his shoulder. He looked around, making sure none of Grimes's men were anywhere in sight, and he made his way back through the pasture until he came to the tree where his paint was tied. He swung on the horse and headed in the direction of Aissa's ranch. He had already found a place where he could hide. Aissa wouldn't see him, but he would be close enough if it looked like she needed his help. He would never let Grimes hurt her again.

*   *   *

Aissa crouched down in the back of the stable as Joe talked to a man and then led his horse into an empty stall.

"It's all right. You can come out now."

Aissa walked over to Joe as he removed the tack from the horse and put a feedbag on it. She reached out and rubbed the animal's nose. "I'm nervous."

Joe patted the horse on the flank and closed the stall door. He looked Aissa up and down. "You should be nervous."

"What does that mean?"

"I'm sorry to tell you, Aissa, but you don't look anything like a man."

"Shhh." Aissa looked around her.

"Don't worry, there's no one here. I think you should let me do the bank alone."

"No, it's my responsibility."

"Why?"

"Because—"

"Because you want to get Ray Grimes all by yourself, don't you?"

"I hate him, Joe. I really hate him for what he did to me and my father."

"So do I, but you have to be calm. If you get all emotional, this will never work." Joe reached for a pitchfork and started pitching hay.

"All right, I'll be calm."

Joe stopped. "First, you have to hide that hair of yours. If anyone sees it, they'll know it's you. Here." Joe removed the bandana from around his neck and tied it around Aissa's head, covering her hair. "Now put the hat on. Pull it down low over your eyes."

Aissa put on the hat. She stood up straight and hooked her thumbs through her belt loops. "Now?"

"That's better, can't see any hair now." Joe shook his head. "But we have a big problem."

"What?"

"It's your . . ." Joe put his hands out in front of his chest.

429

Aissa looked down at herself. "Oh, you mean my breasts," she replied nonchalantly, ignoring Joe as his face turned red. She pulled out her shirt so that it was baggy. "Is that any better?"

"Not much. Wait a minute." Joe went to the tack room and returned with a blanket. "Try stuffing this in your shirt. If we can't hide what you have, maybe we can just make you look fat."

Aissa took the blanket and shook it out as Joe turned his back. She pulled out her shirt, unbuckled her belt, and stuffed the blanket into her pants. She rebuttoned her shirt, pushing at he blanket until it resembled a cowpoke's belly. "What do you think?"

Joe turned around, narrowing his eyes. "It's not great, but it's better. Hell, it'll be dark outside anyway."

"I just have to make sure Walter Dickson doesn't get a good look at me."

"If all goes well, Flora will unlock the door and I'll go in first. You stay behind me."

"Do you think it'll work, Joe?"

"If it doesn't, you and I will be growing old in a territorial prison."

"The way my luck has been going this past year, that's always a possibility."

"Listen, Aissa, when we go in there tonight, you don't talk, not even a word. Let me do all the talking. After Walter opens the safe, we'll tie him and Flora up, we'll leave the note explaining why we stole the money, then we'll hightail it over to the newspaper and leave our other letter. Then you'll get the hell back to the ranch."

"All right." Aissa put her arm through Joe's, squeezing it slightly. "I don't know how to thank you for what you've done for me and my father, Joe."

"Your pa has treated me real good over the years, Aissa. It's the least I could do. 'Sides, I want a front row seat when I

430

see Ray Grimes take a fall."

"So do I."

"Why don't you go get some rest. We have a few hours. I'll go get us something to eat."

"All right." Aissa wandered back to an empty stall and closed the door after her. She sat down in the corner, crossing her arms in front of her, smiling slightly as she looked down at her new belly. She thought of her father and hoped he was well—she couldn't wait to see him again. She thought of Shadow Hawk. Already she missed him. She loved him and she felt that he loved her, but she knew it was best that they finally live in their own worlds, with their own people. But most of all, she thought of Ray Grimes. She couldn't wait until he found out that his money had been stolen and that there was a list containing the names of all the young women he had compromised because he was less than a man. Mostly, she couldn't wait to meet him face-to-face. She couldn't wait to make Ray Grimes pay for what he had done.

Aissa and Joe waited across the street from the bank, between the boot shop and the barber. Aissa held a bottle of whiskey in her hand to make it look like she and Ray were drinking, in case anyone walked by.

"There she is," Joe whispered.

Aissa stepped toward the front of the dark alley. Flora stood on the porch of the bank, basket in hand. Aissa saw Walter lift up the shade to the bank door and then open it. They talked for a few minutes and Walter looked up and down the street and let Flora in. He made sure to adjust the shade after Flora was inside.

"How long do we wait?"

"We'll have to wait for a while. If we go in too soon after Flora, Walter will know that we're with her."

"I hate this, Joe. I want it to be over."

"It won't be long now, Aissa. Be patient."

"What if it doesn't work?"

"It'll work."

"Ray never seems to pay for anything he does, Joe. It's not right."

"Aissa, relax. Look." Joe pointed across the street to the bank. There was a man walking in front of the building. He stopped, knocked on the door, and waited until Walter opened it. They spoke for a moment and then the man left.

"Who was that?"

"That's the new sheriff."

"Who is it?"

"Calvin Woodward," Joe said with obvious distaste.

"He's one of Gimes's men, isn't he?"

"Yep. Just checking to make sure his boss's money is safe, I guess." Joe chuckled slightly. "Won't be safe for long." Joe looked down the street. "A little while longer and we can go. Calvin will be done and he'll be hitting the saloon."

Aissa tapped her foot impatiently. She was afraid, but she was also exicted. She felt Joe's hand on her arm.

"All right, let's go."

Aissa put the bottle on the ground, pulled her hat low across her eyes, and followed Joe across the street. They both stepped carefully onto the plank sidewalk and stood to one side of the bank door. Joe nodded to Aissa. They pulled up the bandanas around their faces and Joe slowly turned the handle. He opened the door a crack and Aissa peered over his shoulder. They could easily hear Flora's laugh. Quickly, Joe opened the door and Aissa followed him in, locking the door behind them. Joe pulled out his gun and walked up to the small table.

"Don't say a word," he said in a deeply disguised voice. He walked to Walter, placing the barrel of the pistol at his forehead. "I'm going to make this real simple for you, mister.

We want you to open that safe, and we want you to open it now."

"But I can't do that. I'll get fired from my job."

"You'll be dead before you get fired, I can promise you that." He waved the butt of the gun toward Flora. "Tie her up, Will, and gag her."

"Don't you dare gag me!" Flora protested loudly, but Joe aimed the gun at her. "I could just as soon shoot you first, lady."

"No, no, don't do that," Walter protested. "I'll open the safe."

"Don't you dare help them, Walter," Flora protested.

Aissa walked up behind Flora and yanked her arms behind her, quickly tying them together. Then she tied a scarf around Flora's mouth. Aissa walked back and stood behind Joe.

"Now, do you want me to shoot your lady friend, or are you going to open that safe for us?"

"I'll open it." Walter stood up, unable to control his shaking. "Do you suppose you could move the gun away from my head?" he asked meekly.

"No tricks, mister, or I'll make sure you don't see tomorrow." Joe lowered the gun.

"There won't be any tricks."

Joe and Aissa followed Walter behind the counter and into a small room. The safe stood at the back of the room. It was imposing. It had been painted black with the name of the bank in fancy gold lettering. With his back to them, Walter turned the knob. Aissa heard a clicking sound, then a pause, then a clicking sound again. Walter cleared his throat. Aissa moved so that she could see what he was doing. He turned the knob once more to the right and it stopped on ten. He pulled the straight handle of the door and it opened.

Aissa stared at the shelves of the safe—they were covered with stacks of bills and bags with rawhide drawstrings. She had never seen so much money in her lifte. This was the money that ran the town, the money that so many people had worked so long and so hard for.

"How much money is in here? And don't you even think of lying to me," Joe asked, his voice hard.

"There's a little over $220,000," Walter replied nervously.

"I want $100,000."

"I don't understand."

"I said, I want $100,000 That is how much Ray Grimes has in his account, isn't it?"

"I'm not allowed to give out that imformation, sir."

"If you want to live to see the sunrise, you better give out that information."

Walter scratched his head. "Yes, sir, Mr. Grimes has a little over that much in his account."

"Then that's how much we want."

"Yes, sir." Walter started shoving bundles of bills into a large leather saddlebag.

"And when your sheriff comes in here tomorrow and wants to know what happened, you tell him it's Ray Grimes's fault that this bank was robbed. You tell him that everyone else's money better not be touched or we'll hit the bank again and then we'll hit Grimes's ranch."

"Yes, sir."

"You can also tell him that we never forgot what he did to our families. Now it's his turn to pay up."

"Yes, sir," Walter replied anxiously, trying to keep count of the money he'd put into the pouch. When he was finished, he handed it to Joe. "Here you go."

Aissa took the bag from Walter and left the safe. Joe took some rope from his belt. "Turn around."

"Please don't shoot me, mister. I'll do whatever you want," Walter pleaded.

Joe felt sorry for him and almost reached out to pat his shoulder, but quickly stopped himself. "I'm not going to shoot you, I'm just going to tie you up and gag you. If I'd wanted to shoot you, I could've done that as soon as you opened the safe."

"Thank you, sir. Here," Walter reached into his pocket and handed Joe a handkerchief. "Use this."

Joe smiled slightly under his bandana. "Thanks." He tied the handkerchief around Walter's mouth and then tied his hands behind him. "Now get down on the floor, on your belly."

Walter got to his knees but hesitated. "Could you help?"

Joe eased Walter forward, removing his spectacles. He pulled one leg up behind him and tied it to his hands. "I was going to tie both your legs, but that seems a mite too cruel. Don't worry, someone will be here early in the morning." Joe went out, leaving the door slightly ajar. When he got to the front, he pulled down his bandana and kissed Flora on the cheek. "Thank you," he whispered.

Flora nodded to Joe and looked up at Aissa, motioning toward the door. Aissa pulled down her bandana. "I'll be in touch. Thank you," she whispered. She grabbed Joe's arm. "Shouldn't we take Flora with us? The sheriff might think she was in on it."

"It'll look even worse if we take her."

"What if you tell Walter we're taking her with us as insurance that he won't tell anyone? Tell him he's to say he was alone, that someone was crying out for help at the door."

"What about the basket?"

"Let's take it. No one has to know that Flora was here except Walter. Flora will just have to stay hidden for at least a day."

Joe nodded, pulled up his bandana, and walked back to the room that held the safe, in spite of Flora shaking her head. He squatted next to Walter. "Listen. My friend and I decided we're going to take the woman with us. We figure she's a friend of yours and you won't send anyone to follow us if you want her to stay alive. Now, you know I'm a man of my word. I won't kill her if you don't send anyone after us for at least twenty-four hours." He pulled down Walter's handkerchief.

"How do I do that? The sheriff will want to know what happened."

"Well, I'm afraid I'm going to have to rough you up a bit, make it look like you were hurt. Just play real sick for a day. Can you do that?"

"Yes, I can do that."

"Good. If we don't see a posse, your lady friend will be on her way back here in a day. Agreed?"

"Yes."

"Good." Joe lifted Walter up. "I'm sorry, I don't want to do this. It'll be over quick-like." Before Walter could even blink, Joe punched the thin man in the face. As Walter was trying to regain his composure, Joe hit him two more times, knocking him out. Gently he laid Walter on the floor. He untied his leg and tied his ankles together. He walked out. "It's done."

Flora was standing, her wrists untied. "This is foolish, you two. You should just leave me here," she whispered.

"No, Flora, I'm sure Ray knows that you and my father were very close. He might suspect something and I don't trust him. He might hurt you."

"I agree," Joe said. "Let's go." He blew out the lamp and opened the door a crack to peek out. The street was empty both ways. "Come on." he whispered.

Aissa and Flora followed Joe out of the bank. They went behind the building and waited until they were sure no one was around. When it was clear, they hurried along the sidewalk to Flora's house and went inside.

"Don't turn on a lamp, Flora," Aissa cautioned.

"I'm going back to the paper," Joe said, standing by the door.

"No, Joe, I'll do that." Aissa handed the leather pouch to Flora. "Will you hold onto this for us, Flora?"

"Aissa, that's downright stupid. If someone sees you, it's all over."

"Don't argue with me, Joe. Flora, I'll need some rouge, if you have some."

Flora looked at Aissa. "What do you need rouge for?"

"Please, Flora, just hurry."

"All right." Flora left the room.

"What are you planning to do?" Joe looked at Aissa, a disapproving look on his face.

"I'm going to leave my letter on the window of the newspaper office. Then everybody in town will see it."

"Aissa—"

"Please, Joe, I'm not an idiot. I'll take my gun and I'll be careful."

"I wish I could talk you out of it."

"Well, you can't."

"Here you go," Flora said, coming back into the room and handing Aissa a pot of rouge.

"Thanks, Flora. Just stay out of sight tomorrow. I think Walter will be so afraid he won't say anything to anyone. No one will suspect you."

"Where are you going, girl?" Flora asked, stepping between Aissa and the door.

"I have something to do, Flora. After that, I'm heading back to the ranch."

"Why don't you stay here, Aissa? It's much safer." Flora voiced softly. "If something happened to you now, I'd never forgive myself."

"I'll be fine." Aissa hugged Flora. "Joe is certain to check up on me." Aissa kissed Joe on the cheek. "Get on back to the stables after I leave. I don't want you getting into trouble either. Thank you both." Aissa opened the door and stepped out onto the front walk, stooping down until she was sure no one was around. It was late now. Not many people would be out except the drinkers, gamblers, and womanizers. She plumped up her blanket to disguise her breasts and made sure her hat was low. She walked into town slowly, looking around as she did so. The newspaper office was across the street and two buildings down from the sheriff's office. She knew it well. From the time she was fourteen she had written letters to the editor and Eathan had always printed them.

She stepped as lightly as possible on the wooden planked sidewalk, trying not to draw attention to herself. She passed one man, tugged on the front of her hat, and passed on by. If she made any kind of impression on him, he didn't seem to show it. When she got to the sheriff's office she stopped, looked around, and slowly walked up the stairs. She peered into the small window. Calvin was asleep in her father's chair, his feet on the desk, his head on his chest, a whiskey bottle standing open in front of him. Good, she thought, he's already drunk.

Aissa tiptoed back down the stairs of the sheriff's office and ran across the street. The newspaper office had one big window. Eathan had set the printing press just inside, so that everyone could watch the paper being printed as they walked by. He had also set his worktable close to the window too. Everyone could see him setting letters on the big machine.

Aissa looked around her and pulled out the rouge. She dipped her finger into the rouge and wrote on the window: "Ray Grimes is a liar, cheat, thief and murderer. Before he is through, none of you will have a place to live. None of your daughters will be safe. Ask Grimes about his whorehouse in Mexico and the girls he takes there. Ray Grimes must leave Agua Prieta."

Aissa dropped the rouge in her pocket and looked around her. Still no one. It was hard to see in the feeble light, but the lettering was clear. She smiled. Everyone would read it when they came into town in the morning. She looked around her once more, stepped off the sidewalk, and ran through the dirt street, heading for the grove behind Flora's house where her horse was tethered. She smiled to herself as she ran. She felt good. In fact, she felt smug. It was almost over. All she needed to do now was see Ray face-to-face.

What she didn't notice as she ran down the street to Flora's was the cowboy who was hidden in the shadows watching her as she wrote on the window. He watched her for a moment longer and then left his spot by the sheriff's office. He followed Aissa, a certain urgency to his step.

Aissa lay in the hayloft, trying to blot out the sunshine that filtered through the cracks in the old wood. She was tired. It had been two days since the robbery. Joe had been out once. He said he heard that Grimes was going to make every family in town pay. Joe said he went crazy.

Aissa smiled. When all this was over, she was going to visit her father, and then take a trip to Paris. She'd even go shopping in St. Louis or New York and buy some beautiful clothes for the trip. She'd had enough of this place. There were too many memories here.

She was too deep in her reverie by the time she heard the bootsteps of the person in the barn below. How had she been taken off guard like that? She laid perfectly still, unmoving.

"I know you're in here somewhere, Aissa. You might as well come out."

It was Ray.

"Listen, Aissa, I've about had it with you and your father. Either you come out, or I'll burn this damn thing to the ground with you in it. I've done it before."

Aissa closed her eyes. She knew there was no way out. If Ray set fire to the barn, it would go up in minutes and she'd have no chance of escaping. She heard him walking around down below and she sat up, unbuckling her holster. She stuck her pistol in the waistband of her pants and pulled on her jacket, making sure it covered the pistol.

She started down the ladder of the loft without saying anything to Ray. She climbed halfway down and jumped to the floor before Ray finally saw her. She made sure to turn quickly, to keep her back away from him, and to keep the pistol hidden.

"Hello, Ray," she said calmly.

Ray walked up to Aissa, a nasty grin on his face. "I knew it was you. I knew it. I knew you'd find a way to get back at me."

"I only gave you what you deserve, Ray."

"Where's the money?"

"What money?" Aissa replied lightly. Ray lifted his hand to strike her, but Aissa put up her arm, deflecting the blow. "I wouldn't do that if I were you. I'm not the same person I was before."

"What do you plan to do? Use some Apache hocus-pocus on me?" Ray laughed when he said it.

"Maybe," Aissa replied, her voice serious. "Haven't you even wondered why I'm here, Ray?"

"What do you mean?"

"No one escapes from the Apache, Ray. You know that."

"So?"

"So, don't you think it's kind of strange that I'm here?" Before Ray could answer, Aissa glanced toward the door. "They let me go, Ray. But they watch me, you know. They take care of me."

"What do you mean, they watch you?"

"They watch me all the time. They're always around somewhere. You go outside, you won't see a thing, but I bet there's at least three or four of them real close by to make sure nothing happens to me."

"Why would they do that for a white woman?"

"I told you why, they trust me and they believe in me."

"You don't scare me none."

"I think I do."

Ray pulled out his gun. "They're not going to do anything if I kill you."

"Maybe not, but what about your money? You'll never find out where it is if you kill me."

"You are a little bitch, you know that?"

"There's something else I think you ought to know, Ray."

"What?"

"Just in case I don't come back, I've written a letter that might interest you."

"What're you talking about?"

"I've written a list containing the names of all the young girls you've turned into whores. If something happens to me, that list will be published in our newspaper and every paper in the territory."

"You're lying!" Ray said desperately.

"Am I? How would I even know about such a list, Ray, and why do you seem so guilty?" Aissa laughed. "I should've known when you beat me that you're incapable of making love to a woman. You're worthless, Ray."

"Damn you!" Without warning, Ray rushed forward, knocking Aissa backward. She lost her footing and fell to the ground. Quickly, she reached behind her and pulled out the pistol, aiming it at Ray's face before he had a chance to raise his again.

"I wouldn't," she said calmly. "Get off me!" She twisted, moving away from Ray, kicking him as she stood up. "Put down the gun. Easy. I'd love to shoot you, Ray. Just give me an excuse." Aissa walked over to Ray's gun and kicked it across the barn. "Now, take off your boots and don't get up. You stay on the ground."

"What?"

"Take off your boots. Your jacket, too." When Ray was finished, Aissa searched his belt for any hidden weapons and shook out his boots. There was nothing but a small bump in the side of one of his socks. "What do you have in there, Ray?"

"In where?"

Aissa kicked at his leg. "Get it out. Now!" Aissa pointed the gun at Ray as he took out the small derringer and dropped it on the ground. Aissa kicked it across the barn. "Now, Ray, what should I do with you?"

"Go to hell!"

"No, I think that place is already reserved for you." Aissa circled around Ray, holding the gun out in front of her with both hands. "Let's just recount everything you've done to my family. Well, it started long ago when my grandfather bought all this land, including yours, when he was here from France. He intended to bring his family over here, but instead your father stole the land from him and you perpetuated the lie. Then there was the fact that your father tried to get my mother to run off with him."

"How did you know about that?" Ray was genuinely surprised.

"You're as stupid as your father was, Ray," Aissa said with relish, watching as Ray's face turned red. "My mother was so in love with my father. She wouldn't have gone away with your father if he had given her all the money in the world, not to mention the land that was rightfully hers. Then there was the fact that you forced me to marry you. You kept me captive in your house, got me addicted to laudanum, and beat me unmercifully. You know, Ray, I could've lived with all that, but there's something I can't live with." Aissa stopped behind Ray, placing the barrel of the gun at the base of Ray's skull. "I just can't live with the fact that you set my father's house on fire and left him in there to die."

"Come on, Aissa—" Ray pleaded, his voice shaking.

"You're the worst kind of man, Ray. You're a coward and a liar. You're pathetic." She pressed the barrel of the pistol into Ray's skull, her finger slowly pulling the trigger. Her hand began to shake, but it didn't matter—she wanted it to be over. She couldn't wait to see Ray dead.

"Aissa!"

She froze at the sound of the voice. She looked up. She squinted at the silhouette of the man who stood by the doors of the barn. "Shadow Hawk?"

"He is not worth it, Aissa. This man has no soul."

"He deserves to die." She stared at the back of Ray's head and again she squeezed the trigger.

"He will suffer and he will die, but he will bring it upon himself."

"Do you remember what he did to me, to my father?" Her voice was angry, shrill.

"I remember, and so does he. He will remember forever, even after he has died."

Aissa looked up, tears filling her eyes. She pulled the gun away from Ray's head and walked around so she could see his face. He was white and visibly shaking. "What's wrong, Ray? Were you just a bit scared?"

"I swear, someday I'll —"

"You'll what? You'll burn me out? You'll beat me up? You'll take my land? You've done all that, Ray, and I'm still here and I'm much stronger than you are. No, I think you better listen to me." Aissa held the gun to his head again. "Look at me, damn it! The people of this town aren't going to listen to you anymore. If you value your pathetic skin at all, you'd better get the hell out of here today. Now."

"Now? But I'll need time to pack."

"You don't need time for anything. You ride out of here with what you have on your back, just like you made so many other people do." Aissa pulled a piece of paper and a fountain pen out of her jacket pocket. She'd been carrying them for over a week. "And I want you to sign this."

"What is it?"

"Just sign it, Ray, or I'll keep you here and invite the whole town out here for a hanging."

Ray glanced at the piece of paper. "It's giving you title to

443

my land."

"No, it's giving me back the land that belonged to my family in the first place. Sign it."

Ray threw the piece of paper on the dirt. "I won't sign anything."

Aissa picked up the paper. "Well, I thought I could handle this myself, but I guess I can't. Do you think you can help me out, Shadow Hawk?"

"I would like very much to see Grimes again," Shadow Hawk replied, his voice deep.

Aissa turned when Shadow Hawk drew near. She raised her eyebrows and tried to stifle a grin. Shadow Hawk was dressed like a cowboy, and it was obvious from the way he walked that he was having a terrible time with his boots. She looked back at Ray. "He won't listen to me. Maybe you could get him to sign this." She handed Shadow Hawk the paper.

Shadow Hawk took off his hat and threw it down. He reached down on his left hip and drew out his large hunting knife, squatting in front of Ray. "Do you remember what I told you the last time we spoke? I believe I warned you to stay away from Aissa and her father. You did not listen very well, did you?" With lightning quickness Shadow Hawk reached out and grabbed Ray's hair, yanking his head backward. He pressed the point of the knife to his forehead and into the scar that remained from the last time he had been with Ray. "I think it is time to finish what I started." He pressed the point of the knife into Ray's forehead. Ray was already screaming.

"All right, all right! I'll sign it."

"Good." Shadow Hawk held onto Ray's hair, his knife close to Ray's face, as Ray signed the paper.

Aissa blew on the paper to dry the ink, folded it, and put it into her jacket pocket. "Thank you, Ray. It's all right, Shadow Hawk. You can let him go now."

444

Shadow Hawk glared at Ray, his blue-gray eyes penetrating Ray's "Pity." Shadow Hawk stood up next to Aissa.

"All right, are you ready to listen?"

Ray dabbed at the blood on his forehead with his handkerchief. "Yes, yes. I'll do what you ask."

"Good. I want you to ride out of here right now. Don't go back to your ranch, don't go into town, just ride out. I don't care where you go, just stay away from Agua Prieta." Aissa squatted in front of Ray, forcing him to look at her. "Look at my eyes, Ray, and remember what you see there. I hate you more than anyone in this world. If you ever come back here again, I won't hesitate to kill you. Do you understand?"

Ray nodded. "What about my things, the things that are in my house that belonged to my father?"

"You won't have to worry about any of those things because the house won't be there."

"What?"

"I'm going to burn it to the ground, just like you burned ours. There won't be anything left, and that's the way it should be. When my grandfather bought this land, there was nothing there. It'll be like starting over."

"But there are valuable things in there—"

"I don't care."

"I'll need money."

"I'm sure you'll find a way to get by. Now get up and get out of here."

Ray stood up. "What about my boots?"

Aissa thought about the boots for a minute, then shook her head. "No, no boots. You get your horse and your life. That's more than you've ever given me."

Ray looked at Aissa and started out of the barn, but Shadow Hawk stopped him, a hand on his shoulder. "I have men out there, Grimes. They will make sure you do not come back here or go to your ranch. If you do, they will take you into the hills with them. You will wish Aissa had killed you here."

Ray hurried out of the barn and got on his horse. Aissa went to the barn doors and watched as Ray rode away. She shook her head. "I can't believe it. I can't believe it's over."

"I do not trust him. He will be back."

"Maybe." Aissa walked outside. But I don't want to think about Ray Grimes anymore. It's a beautiful day."

"It is good to see you smile again."

Aissa turned to Shadow Hawk. "Thank you for your help. You never left, did you?"

"I could not. I was even in town the night you wrote on the window. I followed you."

Aissa looked Shadow Hawk up and down. He looked like any other cowboy, except he looked uncomfortable. There was something else different. "You cut your hair!"

Shadow Hawk shrugged. "Yes, my people would say I am no longer a man because I have done such a thing."

"I think you're very much a man. You look handsome."

"I am in great pain."

Aissa laughed. "The boots. Why don't you take them off?"

They walked over to the shade of the old oak that had sheltered Aissa's garden and they sat down. Shadow Hawk pulled off the boots, wincing, and began rubbing his feet. "I can now understand why the white man is so hostile. His feet always hurt."

Aissa laughed loudly. "I've missed you."

"I was never gone."

"Why did you stay? Did you think you owed me?"

"No, that is not why I stayed, Aissa." Shadow Hawk took one of Aissa's hands in his and brought it to his mouth, kissing it softly. "I stayed because I knew I could not have a life without you."

"But you'll miss your people."

"I would miss you more."

"You'd be unhappy in this world."

"I was not unhappy here before."

Aissa snatched her hand away. "Why are you doing this? It was all decided."

"You decided, not I." Shadow Hawk put his hands on Aissa's face, gently forcing her to look at him. "I love you, Aissa. I do not want to live without you."

"Shadow Hawk—"

"There will be many problems, I know. We must overcome them."

Aissa closed her eyes. "I'm afraid."

"I am sorry for hurting you. The fault lay within me, not you."

"I don't know." She shook her head.

"Do you love me, Aissa?"

"I don't know. I'm not sure I even know what love is."

"Do you love me, Aissa?" Shadow Hawk's voice was deep and persuasive.

Aissa opened her eyes. "Yes, I love you. I don't want you to leave."

"Then I will not leave." Shadow Hawk touched his mouth to hers. "My life is with you, Aissa."

Aissa wrapped her arms around Shadow Hawk's neck. "I'm so scared."

"I am also scared, but we will be together."

"There's something else I didn't tell you."

"What is it?" he asked seriously.

"My father is still alive."

"Gerard is alive," Shadow Hawk said nodding, a smile on his face. "I knew he would be too stubborn to die."

"I want to see him. He's not here. Will you go with me?"

"Yes, I would like to see him."

"We need to get to know each other, Shadow Hawk. We are so different."

"We do know each other in many ways, Aissa. I want to be

with you and I want to love you." He kissed her deeply, his hand on her face. "I will do many things for you, Aissa. I will dress like a white man, I will live on a white man's ranch, but I will not wear these boots again."

Aissa laughed. "You don't have to wear boots."

She leaned her head agains his shoulder. "I love you, Shadow Hawk."

Shadow Hawk reached into the leather pouch that hung on the side of his gunbelt. He pulled out the shiny silver comb that his grandfather had given him. He handed it to Aissa. "I want you to have this."

Aissa looked at Shadow Hawk and then down at the comb. "It's beautiful. Where did you get it?"

"My grandfather gave it to me before I left. He told me to give it to the woman I would someday marry."

"Marry?" Aissa grasped the comb tightly, her eyes filling with tears. "I don't know what to say."

"Do not say anything, Aissa. Just know that I love you."

Aissa and Shadow Hawk sat in the shade of the old oak, content in their love for each other. There was the screech of a hawk above them and his shadow embraced them as he flew overhead. It was Shadow Hawk's medicine. At last he had found his home.